THE STRAWSTACK
MURDER CASE

THE STRAWSTACK MURDER CASE

KIRKE MECHEM

COACHWHIP PUBLICATIONS

Greenville, Ohio

CONTENTS

INTRODUCTION

PHILO ON THE PLAINS: KIRKE FIELD MECHEM AND *THE STRAWSTACK MURDER CASE* (1936)

CURTIS EVANS

The Original Dust Jacket
for *A Frame for Murder* (1936)

KIRKE FIELD MECHEM
(approx. 1930s)
Courtesy Kirke Lewis Mechem

PHILO ON THE PLAINS
Curtis Evans

By 1936, the year that Kirke Field Mechem's *The Strawstack Murder Case* appeared in print (under the publisher-mandated title *A Frame for Murder*), the American detective novelist S. S. Van Dine (the pseudonym of art critic Willard Huntington Wright) had written ten Philo Vance mysteries, the most recent of which, *The Kidnap Murder Case*, also was published that year. Back in the 1920s Van Dine had been the most popular mystery writer in the United States, scoring a string of best-selling detective novels, all of them with the words "Murder Case" in their titles (the most celebrated of these were *The Greene Murder Case*, 1928, and *The Bishop Murder Case*, 1929). Philo Vance, Van Dine's know-all, "g"-droppin' gentleman amateur detective—a literary descendant of Arthur Conan Doyle's Sherlock Holmes and an American cousin, if you will, of such contemporary British sleuths as Dorothy L. Sayers' Lord Peter Wimsey and H. C. Bailey's Reggie Fortune—became one of the truly iconic investigators in American mystery fiction. In addition to his great success in print, Vance was memorably portrayed in four successful film adaptations by noted actor William Powell.[1]

Success can be a transient thing, however. In the 1930s the popularity of the Philo Vance novels and films began to diminish

---

[1] These films are *The Canary Murder Case* (1929), *The Green Murder Case* (1929), *The Benson Murder Case* (1930), and *The Kennel Murder Case* (1933). Basil Rathbone portrayed Vance in the film *The Bishop Murder Case* (1929).

and critics who once had been nearly unanimously euphoric in their praise for Van Dine began entertaining doubts in their reviews about the author's pedantic sleuth. The poet Ogden Nash drolly declared that "Philo Vance/Needs a kick in the pance," while the hard-boiled crime writer Dashiell Hammett, who resolutely agreed with Nash about Vance's physical needs, created his own professional detectives, Sam Spade and the Continental Op, as more realistic alternatives to the Philo Vances of fiction. Symbolic of this shift in popularity, William Powell ceased portraying Philo Vance in 1933 and the very next year began appearing in the *Thin Man* series of films, which for more than a dozen years chronicled the adventures of Nick Charles, the last of Hammett's detectives, and his wife Nora, portrayed on screen by Myrna Loy. In 1939, an embittered Willard Huntingdon Wright, the man behind S. S. Van Dine, died prematurely at the age of fifty, his best creative days long behind him.[2]

In the 1930s Dashiell Hammett's novels proved hugely popular and hard-boiled crime tales by him and other "tough" writers such as Raymond Chandler (who published his first detective novel, *The Big Sleep*, in the year of Van Dine's demise) became the mainstay of widely read American pulp fiction magazines; yet the classical detective novel as epitomized by Philo Vance, with its bafflingly intricate murder puzzles and its impossibly erudite amateur sleuths, maintained a devoted following among mystery genre readers. At the height of the Philo Vance craze in 1929, the cousins Frederic Dannay and Manfred Bennington Lee with *The Roman Hat Mystery* launched their own popular Ellery Queen mystery series, clearly modeled after Van Dine's books; and a myriad of additional, lesser-known writers—most of whom are now forgotten—followed suit. With the publication of *The Strawstack Murder Case* in 1936, Kirke Mechem joined this goodly company of traditionalist mystery authors (though the fact that Mechem's publisher, Doubleday, Doran, insisted that the title of the novel be

---

[2] On the life of Willard Huntingdon Wright, see John Loughery, *Alias S. S. Van Dine: The Man Who Created Philo Vance* (New York: Scribners, 1992).

changed from the pleasingly Van Dineish *The Strawstack Murder Case* to the bland and meaningless *A Frame for Murder* suggests the diminishment of Van Dine's influence within the mystery genre).[3]

Kansan Steven Steele, Kirke Mechem's detective in *The Strawstack Murder Case*, is indubitably the Philo Vance of the Great Plains. The essential kinship of the two men is made amusingly apparent in the opening pages of the novel. Mechem wryly takes note of the displacement of the classical eccentric genius amateur detective, epitomized by Vance, by the professional tough guy shamus popular in the pulps by showing Steven Steele at the Wichita Town Club reacting with revulsion to a tarted-up account in a "true crime" magazine of his investigation in the Wade Packinghouse murder case, gorily entitled, on behalf of an intellectually flaccid, sensation-hungry readership, *The Slaughterhouse Mystery*. To such readers Steele disgustedly advises: "Go out and get some gangster's reminiscences." He observes with contempt that "readers nowadays don't want reasoning mixed with their detection. Action and gore—that's what they crave."[4]

To be sure, Steven Steele, as befits a son of the American Plains, is vastly less pretentious and affected than New York City's Philo

---

[3] Kirke Field Mechem's son Kirke Lewis Mechem has also noted to me in correspondence that "Doubleday didn't think strawstacks would sell books." Kirke Lewis Mechem to Curtis Evans, 5 June 2012 (email). Ironically, just three years after *The Strawstack Murder Case* was published by Doubleday, Doran's Crime Club under the title *A Frame for Murder*, the Oklahoma crime writer Dorothy Cameron Disney published a very well-received mystery entitled *Strawstack* (reissued in paperback as *The Strawstack Murders*). Disney's publisher, Random House, seems to have had greater perspicacity than Doubleday, Doran when it came to naming novels.

[4] Exemplifying this phenomenon of which Steven Steele complains, in his 1936 detective novel, *The Kidnap Murder Case*, S. S. Van Dine, aping the hard-boiled mystery, greatly ratcheted up the action level of the narrative by involving Philo Vance in automotive pursuit and gunplay. The *Kirkus* review of Mechem's mystery alludes to the novel's kinship with classical, puzzle-oriented detective fiction, noting that it is told "in the English manner, though the setting is in Kansas." *Kirkus Reviews*, 10 July 1936, at https://www.kirkusreviews.com/book-reviews/kirke-mechem/a-frame-for-murder/.

Vance (Mechem also omits the baroque footnoted esoterica that
gilds Van Dine's books, particularly the earlier ones). Yet Steele
is, like Vance, very much one of fortune's favorites. Steele's fer-
vently admiring sidekick, Bill, seems to exist in life to chronicle—
at considerable length—his hero's myriad fine qualities (in this Bill
resembles no one more than Philo Vance's similarly self-abnegat-
ing and fawning chronicler, Van). For example, when correcting
what he feels is an erroneous print description of Steele's physical
appearance, Bill protests: "Now it is true that Steele's most distin-
guishing feature is his red hair, but it is not fiery; it is really a very
attractive bright auburn."[5] Bill goes on to analyze the appeal of
Steele's outward form:

> His forehead is high rather than wide, and his cheeks,
> far from being emaciated, are not even hollow.
> Rather they are furrowed; but with the "jutting chin,"
> which, however, is round, not square, they perhaps
> do lend a semblance of leanness to his face. His skin
> is just a shade darker than the average "dark blond,"
> and this effect is heightened by the remarkably dark
> and piercing deep-set blue eyes. The ensemble of
> these features is a face that is often termed hand-
> some, certainly must be called forceful, yet which
> after all is only an unexpressive mask for the subtle
> and complex spirit that is the man himself.

From Bill we learn that Steele is thirty-five years old and that
he and Steele have been friends for fifteen years, since they were
roommates at the state university. Steele was but an indifferent
student, but only because in the classes of professors who bored
him—and most of them did—"he seldom attempted to conceal his
ennui." Nevertheless, Steele did distinguish himself in college as

[5] In connection with Steele's hair of a "very attractive bright auburn" shade,
it is interesting to note that Kirke Field Mechem's wife had auburn hair.
Kirke Lewis Mechem to Curtis Evans, 17 August 2013 (email).

an athlete—an All-American quarterback, no less. When the United States entered the Great War, he and Bill both left college to join the infantry. Steele was transferred in a matter of months to the Intelligence Section, where, it should not surprise us to learn, "he served with marked distinction." After the war, Steele, like Philo Vance, attended an English university for a time, before launching out independently on "an unorthodox but passionately intense pursuit of the subjects that interested him most," including, of course, criminology. "This apparently haphazard course," declares the worshipful Bill, "by virtue of [Steele's] extraordinary memory and powers of mental correlation, gave him the most amazing education I have known."[6]

In the 1920s Bill settled into a career as a Wichita newspaperman (he edits the Sunday magazine section of the *Wichita Times*), while Steele, still blessed by the gods, inherited an "independent fortune," allowing him to knock about the world, returning periodically to Kansas when there just happens to be a nice, juicy murder problem into which he can sink his teeth. Besides the slayings detailed in *The Strawstack Murder Case*, we learn as well that it was Steele who solved the devilish murder in Wichita of "old John Grayland." However, Bill weightily informs us that "consideration for the family still forbids a detailed study of the Grayland affair," so let us not tarry any further—on to *Strawstack!*[7]

---

[6] Numerous additional examples of Bill's awestruck admiration for Steele can be found throughout *The Strawstack Murder Case*. On a sweltering August day Bill contrasts the sodden appearance of the county attorney ("His seersucker suit was damp and wrinkled, and his bushy eyebrows seemed to drip perspiration") with Steele's immaculateness in a "fresh white suit" and "gleaming panama" (Steele's "crisp auburn curls no intensity of heat, apparently, could wilt"). And on an occasion when Steele smiles, we learn that he does so "in the peculiarly charming way he has with women." And so on. Of course the original models for both Philo Vance and Van and Steven Steele and Bill can be found in Arthur Conan Doyle's Sherlock Holmes and Watson.

[7] By my estimation the events in *The Strawstack Murder Case* actually occurred in 1930. The Grayland Murder Case, which likely took place the previous year, sounds strongly reminiscent of S. S. Van Dine's *The Greene Murder Case*, a tale of pathological dysfunction in an old money New York family.

The strawstack affair begins with the report of the discovery by two young boys of the body of Wichita entrepreneur Ralph "Lucky" Loundon buried at the top of—yes, you guessed it—a huge stack of straw. Now not only luckless but lifeless, the late Loundon has been fatally bludgeoned by the classic blunt instrument. Re-calling Steele's coruscating ratiocination in the Grayland matter, Sheriff Andy Burke is happy to allow Steven Steele, with the faith-ful Bill in tow, to horn in on the investigation. And a good thing Steele does too! "Burke was no man's fool, and in some ways above the average in natural shrewdness," concedes Bill, bluntly adding, however, that the sheriff is hobbled by "many of the disqualifica-tions of the half-educated politician." Nor is Jim Warren, the admittedly more sophisticated country attorney ("in his way as interesting and as stubborn a character as Steele himself," allows Bill judiciously, "if not so colorful"), really any more up to solving complex Kansas murder cases than Sheriff Burke.[8]

Independently wealthy and something of a genius, Steven Steele is hampered with no such limitations. Soon he and Bill are hot on the trails of the numerous possible suspects in Loundon's murder: Fielding Stone Garnett, partner in Loundon's oil operations, a "born speculator" and the "best poker player in town"; lovely Dora Monest, Loundon's desirable fiancée ("that girl could crash Holly-wood in a flannel nightgown!"); Juan Monest, Dora's idle uncle and an investor in Loundon's businesses; leading surgeon Dr. Herbert Vernon (a "stiff-necked domineering devil" married to "the most popular matron in Wichita"); Charles Ward Ripley, vice presi-dent, general manager and chief engineer of Loundon's Dragonfly Aircraft Company; the Reverend Raymond Dwight Van Roth, a portly and pompous radio pastor ("Two hundred and sixty-five pounds on the hoof," declares Steele derisively of the rotund man of the cloth); and the Reverend's problematic children, the way-ward Lola and the disgraceful scapegrace Jack, Wichita's go-to man

[8] County Attorney Jim Warren and Sheriff Burke recall S. S. Van Dine's New York District Attorney John Markham and Police Sergeant Heath. Mechem's father, James Harlan Mechem, served in the 1880s as county attorney for Jewell County, Kansas, where Kirke Field Mechem was born.

for illicit bottles of Jamaica Ginger.[9] And what exactly does Boloney the monkey have to do with the crime? "Did you ever read Poe's *Murders in the Rue Morgue*?" Steele smilingly asks the clueless Sheriff Burke.

[9] The novel's references to Jamaica Ginger may not be familiar today, but certainly would have been so in the United States in 1936, particularly to Kansans. Jamaica Ginger, or "Jake" as it was popularly known, was a highly intoxicating preparation (160 proof) of the fluid extract of ginger. It had long been marketed to Americans as a patent medicine said to relieve headaches, chronic coughing, flatulence and other maladies (and not incidentally making quite a potent tipple). As Cecil Munsey has noted, Jake "was readily available in local drugstores, groceries, and even dime stores; and anyone, including preachers and schoolmarms, could slip the little flat aqua or clear glass bottle into a pocket for a discreet nip at home or away." As a putative "medicine," Jake initially was exempted from the 1919 National Prohibition Act (popularly known as the Volstead Act). However, in 1925 the Treasury Department ruled that Jamaica Ginger could be sold over the counter only if the level of ginger root extractives in it was doubled, making the concoction extremely unpalatable. Not surprisingly, enterprising bootleggers immediately began selling illicitly adulterated Jake. Unfortunately, two Boston brothers-in-law chose to adulterate their Jamaica Ginger with a neurotoxic substance, tri-ortho-cresyl phosphate. TOCP was "a plasticizer used to keep synthetic materials from becoming brittle." Imbibers of Jake adulterated with TOCP became afflicted with paralysis of the hands and feet. This condition was dubbed Jake Paralysis or Jake Leg/Jake Walk, for the lurching gait of victims. In 1930, the year the events in *The Strawstack Murder Case* likely take place, Wichita recorded some of the earliest instances of Jake Leg sufferers, including "nine women, members of a bridge club in the fashionable College Hill district," who drank punch their hostess had spiked with Jamaica Ginger. By March, five hundred cases (about one percent of the adult population) had been reported in the city. Wichita's poorhouse was soon overrun with indigent victims of Jake Leg. In Memphis on May 5, 1930, the Allen Brothers recorded *The Jake Walk Blues* ("I can't eat, I can't talk/Been drinkin' mean Jake, Lord, now I can't walk"); the song sold over 20,000 copies. John Kobler, *Arden Spirits: The Rise and Fall of Prohibition* (1973; rpnt, New York: Da Capo, 1993), 301-302; Cecil Munsey, "Paralysis in a Bottle: the 'Jake Walk' Story," in *Bottles and Extras* 17 (Winter 2006): 7-12; "'Jake' Paralysis New Dry Era Malady," *The Delmarva Star*, 11 May 1930, 10; "Jake Paralysis Hits One in 100 in Wichita, Kan.," *Berkeley Daily Gazette*, 18 July 1930, 20.

Besides offering mystery fans an interesting, fair play murder puzzle, *The Strawstack Murder Case* also provides a rare glimpse, in a Golden Age detective novel, of a Great Plains city in the 1930s. Wichita, Kansas, which in the thirties had a population of not much over one hundred thousand, is not the typical American mystery genre novel setting. Golden Age crime writers favored locales in the Northeast, Chicago and California. Even when authors ventured outside these regions they tended to visit the "colorful" Old South, not the Great Plains. Oklahoma detective novelist Todd Downing once explained that he eschewed setting his crime tales in his home state because mystery publishers and readers would not accept such a locale for a modern murder mystery. Probably this same popular attitude prevailed—or was perceived to prevail—about neighboring Kansas.[10]

Yet for the modern reader, possibly surfeited with such fixtures of American Golden Age crime fiction as swanky Manhattan cocktail parties and gritty California mean streets, a 1930s crime tale set in the quintessentially Middle American city of Wichita, Kansas, may well seem something refreshingly different. And, to be sure, in *The Strawstack Murder Case* Kirke Mechem did not stint readers local color. Among other Wichita locales, Riverside Park, Union Station (complete with its Fred Harvey Dining Room) and even a humble White Castle hamburger stand all serve as unusual backdrops as Steven Steele and Bill vigorously pursue case leads. While it is difficult to imagine the hoity-toity Philo and Van sitting down at a cheap burger joint to feast on fast food (or comestibles, as Philo Vance no doubt would put it), during their investigation Steele and

---

[10] According to the United States Census Bureau, between 1930 and 1940 the population of Wichita increased by fewer than 4000 people, from 111,110 to 114,966. On Todd Downing's comment about Oklahoma as a setting for crime fiction, see Curtis Evans, *Clues and Corpses: The Detective Fiction and Mystery Criticism of Todd Downing* (Greenville, OH: Coachwhip Publications, 2013), 72. An exception to this rule of geography can be found in the critically acclaimed and commercially successful crime novels of Mabel Seeley, four of which were published between 1938 and 1941, at the tail-end of the Golden Age. Seeley's novels were mostly set in small-town Minnesota.

his sidekick pause after dark to discuss the tangled strawstack affair at the "tiny all-night stand" of a White Castle, as "the odor of frying beef" wafts over them. The White Castle hamburgers chain was, in fact, founded in Wichita in 1921.[11]

The local color centerpiece of *The Strawstack Murder Case*, praised by contemporary reviewers, is a massive oil rig fire, during which a second murder takes place.[12] Reading this section of *Strawstack*, I was reminded of *There Will Be Blood*, the vividly shot 2007 film about a maniacal, murderous American oilman:

"It's the oil well! They've had an explosion; it's on fire!"
I ran to the window and looked out. Through the treetops a gigantic orange flame was leaping and whirling into the sky. Clouds of black smoke shot with red boiled upward. The roar had become a blast that shook the earth like continuous thunder.

The Strawstack Murder Case also gives readers a glimpse of racism in Wichita in the 1930s. During this decade African-Americans made up only 5% of Wichita's population (indeed, in Wichita members of the Ku Klux Klan actually outnumbered the black population).[13] Despite their small percentage of the city's populace, African-Americans appear throughout *The Strawstack Murder Case*, though solely as waiters, porters and maids. In the novel these individuals are referred to as "colored," except on one occasion when a Wichita Town Club porter named John (we learn only

---

[11] On the White Castle hamburgers chain, see David Gerard Hogan, *Selling 'em By the Sack: White Castle and the Creation of American Food* (New York and London: New York University Press, 1997). On another occasion Steele and Bob also discuss with a third character the Coronado Sword (later proved spurious), housed in the Kansas Museum of History.

[12] In the *Saturday Review* mystery reviewer Judge Lynch noted that *A Frame for Murder* included "a swell description of the blowing out of a burning gusher." See *The Saturday Review*, 18 July 1936, 18.

[13] Gretchen Cassel Eick, *Dissent in Wichita: The Civil Rights Movement in the Midwest, 1954-1972* (Urbana and Chicago: University of Illinois Press, 2001), 18.

his first name) recollects that an inebriated Ralph Loundon "called me a lazy n——r" when he had difficulty understanding Loundon's drink-slurred speech. "He was from the South," John matter-of-factly explains, "and he always was that way to all the colored folks when he was drinking." Though enlightening about social conditions in the 1930s, this incident certainly will not endear Ralph Loundon to modern readers.

Intriguingly, Kirke Field Mechem's second Steven Steele detective novel, entitled *Mind on Murder*, dealt with miscegenation in Kansas. According to Kirke Field Mechem's son, the composer Kirke Lewis Mechem, his father "had a sharp sense of humor, but also a deep hatred of injustice." This latter quality probably was evident in *Mind on Murder*. Unfortunately, Doubleday, Doran timorously turned down his father's manuscript on account of this "sensitive" subject matter. "Doubleday (and I guess others, too) would not publish [the novel] because it dealt with 'miscegenation',," recalled the younger Mechem dryly. "This was evidently unthinkable in a backwoods region like New York."[14] Could this rejected manuscript have been Bill's account of the scandalous Grayland murder case, about which he makes so many portentous references in *The Strawstack Murder Case*? Unfortunately, we do not know, because the manuscript appears to have been lost since its rejection by Doubleday, Doran.

Just who was Kirke Field Mechem (1889-1985), the author *The Strawstack Murder Case*? Like many mystery authors of the Golden Age, Mechem was an accomplished person for whom mystery writing served as only a very minor sideline. Although today his son Kirke Lewis Mechem is much better known, the elder Mechem was a distinguished individual in his own right.

If there was one common thread that connected Kirke Field Mechem's varied creative endeavors, it was surely the state of Kansas. The easily jaded S. S. Van Dine tended with each new mystery to rhapsodize, through the pronouncements of his alter ego, Philo Vance, and a series of often quite lengthy footnotes, his latest divers

---

[14] Mechem to Evans, 5 June, 29 June 2012, 17 August 2013 (emails).

enthusiasms, be they Egyptian art, Chinese ceramics, Scottish Terriers, tropical fish, etc. The steadfast Kirke Mechem, however, remained constant to Kansas. It is the state of Kansas, not some esoteric piece of ancient bric-a-brac, about which Steven Steele waxes poetic in *The Strawstack Murder Case*:

> As the sheriff disappeared around the bend the sun was just sinking into an ocean of purple clouds above a clump of evergreen trees west of the lodge. Steele lifted his eyes from the road to the great orange ball and for a full minute silently watched it splashing lavender waves and pink-tipped surf against the blue beach of the sky. His hat was in his hand, and the deep hues from the clouds brightened the dark-red curls of his hair to a coppery gold.
>
> "I've seen a good many sunsets in a good many places"—he turned at last—"but there's something about these Kansas prairies that squeezes the tubes dry. Look at that salmon cloud over there with the lilac tail; I'll bet it's three miles long and a mile high!"

As a historian, poet and playwright Kirke Field Mechem was fascinated, like his creation Steven Steele, with the state of Kansas. Born in Mankato, Jewell County, Kansas in 1889, Kirke Mechem was the son of James Harlan Mechem (1859-1898) and Lura Allen Mechem (1868-1942). Originally from Iowa, where his father was a physician and state legislator, James Harlan Mechem was a popular lawyer who in the 1880s served two terms as Jewell County attorney. In 1888, the same year as his marriage to Mary Lavinia ("Lura") Allen, a schoolteacher and minister's daughter, James Mechem became the youngest man up to that time elected to serve in the Kansas state senate.[15]

---

[15] "Kirke Field Mechem" *Kansas Trails*, http://genealogytrails.com/kan/shawnee/bios6.html; *Lawrence Daily Journal-World*, 2 October 1930, 12; W. W. Admire, *Admire's Political and Legislative Hand-Book for Kansas* (Topeka: Crane, 1891), 404-405.

During what was to prove his single term in the senate Mechem immediately emerged as an energetic and ambitious legislator. A member of the anti-monopolist wing of the Kansas Republican Party, Mechem sought to advance legislation on behalf of the economically downtrodden. For example, Mechem introduced bills to make usury a misdemeanor and to regulate stockyards. "It is a very strange thing," Mechem pronounced in a senate speech about his anti-usury bill, "if a law cannot be devised . . . to prevent men from squeezing 36, 50, or 75 per cent out of the unfortunate with their bony fingers."[16]

Although James Mechem was a rising man in Kansas, only three years after his election to the state senate he and his family left the Sunflower State for Pueblo, Colorado. In May 1891, at the end of the impeachment trial of a state judge, the Kansas State Senate body resolved "That in Senator Mechem we recognize a gentleman of sterling worth and a lawyer of great ability, and it is with sincere regret that the Senators of Kansas learn of his intended removal; and, while doing so, we unhesitatingly recommend him to the favorable consideration of the whole people of Colorado." A railroad hub and the center of Colorado's steel and smelting industries, Pueblo in the 1890s was ambitiously bidding to displace Denver as Colorado's metropolis. The year before the Mechems arrived in the city, Pueblo had completed a splendid Romanesque-style Grand Opera House (the premiere performance was of Gilbert and Sullivan's *Iolanthe*). Clearly at home in this urban environment of ambition and self-advancement, Mechem quickly became

---

[16] Jeffrey Ostler, *Prairie Populism: The Fate of Agrarian Radicalism in Kansas, Nebraska, and Iowa, 1880-1892* (Lawrence: University Press of Kansas, 1992), 86; *Wichita Daily Eagle*, 16 January 1891, 1. A stockyard regulation bill eventually would be passed, by the Populist-dominated legislature elected in 1897, and signed into law, although it later was ruled unconstitutional, on equal protection grounds, by the United States Supreme Court (the law applied only to the Kansas City Stockyards Company). See Michael J. Brodhead, *David Brewer: The Life of a Supreme Court Justice, 1837-1910* (Carbondale: Southern Illinois University Press, 1994), 143.

a "very prominent member of the Pueblo bar . . . known over the entire state."[17]

In the 1890s James Mechem was a defense attorney in some notable criminal cases, including the 1897 murder trial of L. Carrie Johnson, a fifty-five-year-old physician with a large practice in Pueblo. Johnson, a doctor's daughter and a graduate of the Woman's Medical College of Chicago who had practiced medicine in Colorado for more than two decades, stood accused of having performed a "criminal operation" (i.e., an abortion) upon a woman, which resulted in the woman's death. Alongside Dr. Johnson's brother, county attorney (later judge) Charles Wesley Bramel of Wyoming, Mechem provided the defense at Johnson's second trial, which, like her first, attracted a tremendous amount of popular attention within Colorado. At the first trial Johnson had been convicted of second-degree murder and sentenced to a minimum of fifteen years in prison. However, a new trial was ordered and at this second trial Mechem and Bramel secured Johnson's acquittal.[18]

In Colorado James Mechem's brother George headed the Mechem Investment Company, which had purchased the Chicago and Cripple Creek Tunnel (CCCT), a gold mine started in the early 1890s in the boomtown of Cripple Creek. As the attorney for CCCT, James Mechem in late November 1898 was traveling on legal business to Cripple Creek on the Florence and Cripple Creek Railroad, when he was thrown from the train, breaking his neck and dying

---

17 *Cripple Creek Morning Times*, 27 November 1898, at http://files.usgwarchives. net/co/teller/newspapers/deathnot21gnw.txt/; *Trial of Theodosius Botkin, Judge of the 32nd Judicial District before the Senate of the State of Kansas* (Topeka: Kansas Publishing House, 1891), 1402. On the history of Pueblo, Colorado, see pueblo.org/history.

18 *The Woman's Medical Journal: A Monthly Journal of Medicine and Surgery* 6 (1897): 99; *Progressive Men of the State of Wyoming* (Chicago: Bowen, 1901), 162; *Portrait and Biographical Record of the State of Colorado, Part Two* (Chicago: Chapman, 1899), 952-953. "Much interest has been manifested in the [Johnson] trial by the public," the trial account in *The Women's Medical Journal* explained, "and the courtroom has been crowded every day since the trial began."

instantly. At the time of his father's fatal accident, Kirke Mechem was not yet nine years old.[19]

The tragic demise of James Harlan Mechem marked an epochal transition for his family, who with the attorney's passing went from enjoying the blessings of cultured affluence to suffering the pangs of straitened circumstances. Years later, in a bleak little poem entitled "The Casket," Kirke Mechem recalled in stark imagery and plain but penetrating words the cruel loss of a father taken much too soon:

> Nothing I remember of watching
> Fearful as the glimpses half-forgotten,
> Hushed, of my father shoved down to the snow
> In the iced wind round a water tower.[20]

Kirke Field Mechem grew to adulthood with what his son Kirke Lewis Mechem calls "the Charles Dickens syndrome: a boy suddenly thrown into a lower social class develops a compulsion to make something of himself." Having been "swindled out of her considerable inheritance" after her husband's death, Lura Allen Mechem was compelled to seek shelter for herself and her children in the Topeka, Kansas, household of her father, Edward Wesley Allen, a "very strict" Methodist minister. Although to help support his family Kirke Mechem worked six days a week, his insistently Sabbath-honoring grandfather refused to allow games or sports to be played on the one day, Sunday, that the young Mechem had free, a restriction the adolescent very much resented. When

---

[19] *Cripple Creek Morning Times*, 27 November 1898. Dr. Carrie Johnson's defense team at her second trial seems to have been ill-fated indeed. Ten years after Johnson's second trial, her brother Charles Bramel was shot and killed by an unsuccessful litigant in a case over which Bramel had presided as a judge. See Daniel Sandoval, "A Look Back in Time: Purpose Outpaces Distance," *Caspar Star-Tribune*, 29 October 2007, at http://trib.com/news/article_c367d5cf-0928-53e9-a73c-7e8a36ee70db.html.

[20] Mechem to Evans, 21 April 2013 (email).

asked later in life why he was not religious, Mechem remarked bluntly that "he had had 'too much religion' when he was a boy."[21]

Although a hard-pressed Kirke Mechem never finished high school, he attended business classes in Topeka and worked several years as a stenographer and clerk before accepting the editorship of the *Southwestern Grain and Flour Journal*, the first of the numerous editing positions he would hold over his life. Jobs at additional Kansas trade journals followed. Enlisting in the army when the United States entered the Great War, Mechem served as a corporal in Company M, 137th Infantry, 35th Division (the all-Kansas regiment) and saw action in France. After the signing of the armistice ending hostilities, Mechem edited the *Jayhawker in France*, a regimental newspaper, and published his first book, *Cooty Bill* (1919), a memoir of his war service. The same year he married Katharine Celia Lewis, a concert pianist and daughter of Hiram Wheeler Lewis, a Wichita banker. The couple had four children.[22]

Like his fictional Bill of the *Wichita Times*, Mechem in the 1920s found employment as a Wichita newspaperman, working for several years as a reporter for the *Eagle*. He also edited the *Kansas Legionnaire*, the American Legion state organ. In 1923 Mechem

---

[21] Mechem to Evans, 5 June 2012, 17, 20 April 2013 (emails). Around 1940 Kirke Field Mechem gave Kirke Lewis Mechem a copy of Moliere's play *Tartuffe* (1664), which famously satirizes a scheming religious hypocrite ("Forty years later, [*Tartuffe*] became my first opera," the younger Mechem has noted). Mechem to Evans, 20 April 2013 (email). Kirke Field Mechem's attitude about ministers and religion is evident in his mocking portrayal of the character Reverend Raymond Dwight Van Roth in *The Strawstack Murder Case*.

[22] *Lawrence Daily Journal-World*, 2 October 1930, 12; Mechem to Evans, 5 June 2012, 17 April 2013 (emails). Originally from Ohio, Hiram Wheeler Lewis was a Civil War veteran who after the cessation of the conflict settled in Mississippi for about a decade, where he owned a plantation, published a newspaper and served as a county sheriff and state legislator. He left Mississippi in 1876, after Democrats "redeemed" the state, and settled the next year in Wichita. "Hiram Wheeler Lewis" *Kansas Trails*, http://genealogytrails.com/kan/sedgwick/bios5.html. Kirke Lewis Mechem notes that Hiram Lewis was a "very religious man" whose mission in Mississippi "was to make sure that blacks actually were free." Mechem to Evans, 17 April 2012 (email).

co-founded the Wichita Publishing Company, which specialized in trade publications. Four years later, with the backing of William Allen White, the famed Progressive Kansas journalist (White was popularly known as the "Sage of Emporia," where he owned and edited the *Emporia Gazette*), Mechem founded *Current Contents*, which previewed articles that were to appear in future issues of leading national magazines. *Current Contents* became a casualty of the Great Depression, but in 1930 Mechem sold his interest in the Wichita Publishing Company in order to devote himself fulltime to what he had discovered was his great creative passion, writing. This same year Mechem was elected Secretary of the Kansas State Historical Society (he would serve for many years as the Society's Secretary, or Executive Director in modern parlance).[23]

Over the 1930s Kirke Mechem published pieces in *Harper's*, *North American Review*, *Saturday Evening Post*, *New Republic* and *Life*. He was a mainstay of the *Kansas Historical Quarterly*, contributing notable essays to the journal, such as "The Story of 'Home on the Range'" (1949) and "The Mythical Jayhawk" (1944). Many of Mechem's pieces in national magazines were poems and a collection of his poetry, *I Could Hear the Least Bird Sing*, was published on the occasion of his ninetieth birthday in 1979. In the late 1930s and early 1940s Mechem also wrote the texts for fifty-six Kansas historical markers. According to his son Kirke Lewis Mechem, the elder Mechem did all his writing (including that for his two detective novels) at the building which housed the Kansas State Historical Society—"not at his official office, but in a little hideaway on the third floor, where his secretary wouldn't disturb him for anything that wasn't important."[24]

Kirke Field Mechem also enjoyed artistic success as a playwright. The best-known of Mechem's more than a dozen plays was

---

[23] *Lawrence Daily Journal-World*, 2 October 1930, 12, 22 October 1930, 2; Mechem to Evans, 5 June 2012, 17 April 2013 (emails).

[24] *Lawrence Daily Journal-World*, 2 October 1930, 2; "Kansas Historical Markers (Texts by Kirke Mechem)," *Kansas Historical Quarterly* 10 (November 1941): 339-368, at *Kansas Collection: Kansas Historical Quarterlies* (http://www.kancoll. org/khq/1941/41_4_mechem.htm); Mechem to Evans, 20 April 2013 (email).

John Brown (1938), a three-act work based on the life of the con-
troversial radical abolitionist and insurrectionist, both apothe-
osized and abominated for his violent deeds on behalf of the anti-
slavery cause at Kansas and Harpers Ferry. *John Brown* won
Stanford University's Maxwell Anderson Award for verse drama
and was broadcast on radio by NBC. Kirke Lewis Mechem, who
composed an opera, *John Brown*, partly based on his father's play,
has recalled that the presentation of *John Brown* "on a national
radio broadcast was a thrilling event in my young life."[25]

Lilac Lake, a 1942 Kirke Field Mechem play about Russian
resistance to the German invasion of the Soviet Union, was a co-
winner of the Dubose Heyward memorial award for playwriting. It
was performed at Charleston's historic Dock Street Theater in 1943.
The leading character in the play, it was reported in a Charleston
newspaper, was a "Russian woman Captain" in the North Caucasus
charged with the responsibility for "holding a dam and preserving
an oil field as long as possible before an almost certain German
attack." Before he wrote *Lilac Lake*, Mechem "consulted experts
on the psychology of shell-shock, military tactics used by the Rus-
sians on this front, and Russian terms and pronunciation," lend-
ing the play a distinct air of authenticity.[26]

Mechem's life was not devoted exclusively to creative writing,
however. Suggesting his affinity for ratiocinative detective fiction,
Mechem once was the chess champion of Kansas. Additionally,
Mechem enjoyed physical as well as cerebral activity and distinguished himself as "the handball champion of Topeka" and "the
second-best tennis player in Wichita." Like his mother, two sis-
ters and his wife, Mechem also loved music and as a young man
had sung baritone in a barbershop quartet (the quartet's most notable moment was singing at an event held in Topeka for President William Howard Taft when the President was visiting the city

---

[25] "Why John Brown? Composer/Librettist Kirke Mechem Discusses His Opera," *Lyric Opera Kansas City*, at http://www.kcopera.org/pdf/John_Brown_
Afterword.pdf; *New York Times*, 10 February 1943.
[26] *New York Times*, 10 February 1943; *Charleston News and Courier*, 7 May 1943, 3.

in 1911). Kirke Lewis Mechem recalls that concerning music, his father "had the ear on the connoisseur."[27]

Kirke Field Mechem did many notable things over his long and interesting life. Some might not rank the publication of a single detective novel in the 1930s high on a list of Mechem's accomplishments, yet *The Strawstack Murder Case* merits reprinting today, nearly eighty years after its first appearance, as a fine formal example of a classical Golden Age detective novel that takes modern mystery readers down a road traveled but infrequently in crime genre tales, one that evocatively unwinds through Wichita and the wide open spaces of the great American plains, as the brilliant Great Detective Steven Steele and his faithful follower Bill pursue a clever and ruthless killer. Happy sleuthing!

[27] Mechem to Evans, 17 April 2013 (email). On President Taft's visit to Topeka, see the Kansas Historical Society website, at http://www.kshs.org/kansapedia/kansas-historical-society/12118. For a detailed piece on Kirke Field Mechem, see Neil Byer, "That a State Might Sing," *Kansas Historical Quarterly* 3 (May 1958): 3-6, at https://esirc.emporia.edu/bitstream/handle/123456789/1254/Byer%20Vol%202%20Num%202.pdf?sequence=1. A photograph of Mechem umpiring a Topeka tennis match is included in the article.

The Author would like to thank Kirke Lewis Mechem for sharing memories of his father and excerpts from his manuscript *Believe Your Ears: Memoirs of an American Composer*.

THE STRAWSTACK
MURDER CASE

1

RALPH LOUNDON MURDERED
PROMINENT WICHITA OIL OPERATOR
BRUTALLY KILLED NEAR HIS HUNTING
LODGE NORTH OF CITY; BODY
HIDDEN IN STRAWSTACK

NEXT TO THE Grayland murder case, which in official circles established my friend Steven Steele as one of the country's leading criminal investigators, the best example of his unique talents is unquestionably provided by his solution of the mystery surrounding the
crime first brought to public attention in the above headlines. Since
consideration for the family still forbids a detailed study of the
Grayland affair, this account of his analysis of the clues found in
the neighborhood of the strawstack where Ralph Loundon's body
was discovered must serve as the most representative evidence of
his abilities.

These pages, rewritten from day-by-day notes made at the time,
not only constitute the only authorized record of this case, but the
first Steele has permitted of any of his investigations. So long as
his fame was confined to the semiprivate recognition accorded by
police bureaus and criminologists he stubbornly refused publication of his exploits, colorful and exciting as many have been. But
when newspapers, magazines and even a book or two began bootlegging lurid accounts of his more spectacular cases, Steele at last

became convinced that only by printing the facts could he protect himself from the growing popularity of these pirated versions.

Steele's chief aversion to these fabricated stories, aside from their more glaring inaccuracies, lay in their grotesque description of his own person. I recall an amusing instance of this dislike, which is worth telling because it throws an interesting sidelight on Steele's personality, and also because it introduces a man who became an important figure in the subsequent investigation of the Loundon case.

Late one afternoon Steele and I happened to be sitting in the lounge room of the Wichita Town Club, two floors below the apartment where Ralph Loundon then lived, little suspecting the fate which was so soon to befall him. With one exception we had the room to ourselves. Our lone neighbor was the Reverend Raymond Dwight Van Roth, known throughout southern Kansas as the "radio pastor," who sat snoring a gentle broadcast from an armchair a dozen feet away.

"Here's the kind of tabloid authorship I mean," Steele sputtered, recovering a book from the wastebasket where he had thrown it in his exasperation, and fanning the pages with an angry thumb. "Listen to this nonsense!

"'Vincent Veale' (that's what they've made of Steven Steele!) 'Vincent Veale entered the refrigerating room gun in hand.' (Veale in the refrigerator! This particular travesty, apparently, is based on the Wade Packing House case. Naturally it is called the Slaughterhouse Mystery.) '. . . gun in hand. His fiery red mane shone like a torch in the icy atmosphere. The lofty brow and emaciated cheeks, denoting the scholar and the dreamer, were belied by the jutting chin and long sinewy fingers which clutched the handle of the heavy army automatic.'"

Steele sputtered again and came to a stop. Once more he threw the book into the wastebasket, this time adding a kick as a further expression of his indignation. The fact that it was the club wastebasket in the club lounge room meant nothing to him. But the fact that the spinning basket brought up against the legs of the Reverend Raymond Dwight Van Roth was an unexpected divertisement.

It was a heavy metal basket, and the solid rim sharply contacted the Reverend Raymond's unprotected shin. There was a hollow, painful bong, and Dr. Van Roth instantaneously arose, only to step into the overturned basket. As the rim flew up and bit again into his shinbone an agonized expression surged over his fat countenance. Involuntarily he lashed out with his foot. The basket sailed through the air and dropped on the davenport where we were sitting. The exertion of repulsing his unseen assailant unbalanced the Reverend Van Roth's corpulent figure, and he went down with a crash, grasping, at the last instant, at a floor lamp for support. The lamp swayed and then fell, delivering a vicious blow on the pastor's unguarded neck. He was threshing wildly about among its entangling remnants, uttering some of his most pious sentiments, when Steele went to his rescue, first replacing the wastebasket at the end of the davenport.

He helped the disheveled minister to his feet and solicitously asked if he was hurt. Dr. Van Roth did not answer. For a moment he looked about at his feet, unable to account for the fiendish blow which had aroused him to such a sudden frenzy of action. Seeing nothing, his wrath slowly changed to bewilderment; then he apparently began to doubt the evidences of his senses. To this view Steele characteristically gave a word of encouragement.

"Very strange, Dr. Van Roth," he commented with a frown. "All at once you lashed out with your leg as if you were defending yourself. Then you attacked the floor lamp. . . . Used to see soldiers do that in their sleep. Thought they were fighting, you know." He chuckled reassuringly. "Perhaps you were having a little tussle with the devil, eh?" He regarded the perspiring clergyman gravely, then added, as with a touch of suspicion, "You—ah—you aren't subject to attacks of this kind?"

"Not at all, not at all!" Dr. Van Roth denied with a crimson face, plumping himself down in the chair. "I had a very vivid sensation of a blow on the leg. Very vivid."

Steele received this assertion with a disbelieving lift of the eyebrows, then without further comment he returned to the davenport and stared down at me with an irresponsible eye. Chuckling

softly, he seated himself beside me. "One of life's little retribu-
tions," he murmured. "But perhaps you have never heard the doctor preach?"

I nodded.

"Ha!" Steele commented expressively. "How often, as I have
dialed past that voice on the radio, have I thought what a pleasure
it would be to give it a kick on the shins!"

I grinned at his metaphor, little realizing that at their next
meeting Steele would be interviewing Dr. Van Roth on a matter of
much graver moment than a dented shin. At the time, however, I
was not so much interested in Van Roth as I was in the book which
had been the cause of the disturbance. It had fallen to the floor,
and I picked it up with the idea of citing some of its extravagances
to reinforce my oft-repeated pleas for permission to write an account of one of Steele's cases for publication. But Dr. Van Roth's
Quixote-like assault upon the floor lamp had purged Steele of all
animus. He refused to listen.

"No, no! Not now!" He got up. "Some other time. . . . I'm not
what the public wants to read about—a trick detective with a pair
of blue glasses rounding up gunmen in an armored car. Go out and
get some gangster's reminiscences. Readers nowadays don't want
reasoning mixed with their detection. Action and gore—that's what
they crave."

So saying, Steele walked off and left me. As I had not seen this
book, I sat down and skimmed through the story. I smiled again as
I reread the paragraph which had so aroused his ire. I can hardly
give a better picture of Steele's appearance than by commenting
on two of the more amusing exaggerations of this highly colored
portrait.

The author seemed pleased with his phrase, "fiery red mane,"
for he used it several times. Now it is true that Steele's most dis-
tinguishing feature is his red hair, but it is not fiery: it is really a
very attractive bright auburn. And as for the "mane," that was
wholly imaginary, since Steele's hair is thick and curly, and he usually wears it cropped short. The second phrase, however, was more
typical of the kind of writing that aroused Steele's animosity: "The

lofty brow and emaciated cheeks, denoting the scholar and the dreamer, were belied by the jutting chin and long sinewy fingers which clutched the handle of the heavy army automatic."

How the chin and fingers clutched the automatic, and why the lofty brow and emaciated cheeks denoted the scholar and dreamer, it is probably not necessary to understand, but in any case they do not describe Steele. His forehead is wide rather than high, and his cheeks, far from being emaciated, are not even hollow. Rather they are furrowed; but with the "jutting chin," which, however, is round, not square, they perhaps do lend a semblance of leanness to his face. His skin is just a shade darker than the average "dark blond," and this effect is heightened by his remarkably dark and piercing deep-set blue eyes. The ensemble of these features is a face that is often termed handsome, certainly must be called forceful, yet which after all is only an unexpressive mask for the subtle and complex spirit that is the man himself.

I shall make no attempt here to describe the bizarre aspects of Steele's personality. It was his strikingly unique spirit that first attracted me and still often antagonizes and repels me. Scholar and dreamer he is undoubtedly, but chained to so restless an energy of body and to a mind of such unaccountable humor that to fix on one of the many facets of his character and say, "This is Steele," is an impossibility. To me—and I have often thought, to himself—he has always been a far more interesting mystery than any of the criminal problems which have engaged his attention.

I use the word mystery because, while I believe I am Steele's closest friend, I know very little of his family or his antecedents, and he is the last man in the world one would choose to question about his private affairs. What I do know may be summarized in a word. On the twelfth of August, just four days before Ralph Loundon's dead body came to light in the strawstack, Steele and I celebrated his thirty-fifth birthday and the fifteenth year of our friendship. Our acquaintance began at the state university, where later we became roommates. In college Steele was never a good student; if a subject or a professor bored him he seldom attempted to conceal his ennui. In fact it was only his wily elusiveness as

All-American quarterback that for two years kept him on several classroom eligibility lists. When war broke out Steele and I both left school to enlist in an infantry regiment, from which he was transferred within a few months to the Intelligence Section, where, I have learned, he served with marked distinction. After the war he attended an English university for a year, and subsequently followed his college studies with an unorthodox but passionately intense pursuit of the subjects that interested him most. Among these was criminology, to which Steele devoted himself spasmodically for several years, both in this country and abroad. This apparently haphazard course, by virtue of his extraordinary memory and powers of mental correlation, gave him the most amazing education I have ever known.

As for myself, it is enough to say that the post-war years during which Steele, thanks to an independent fortune, knocked about the world, settled me more deeply into the humdrum routine of newspaper work. Occasionally, however, he unexpectedly drifted in and spent a few weeks with me, then as unceremoniously took his departure. It was during one of these happy reunions that Wichita society and the oil fraternity of the Southwest were shocked by the brutal murder which led to the investigations here recounted. That was more than five years ago, yet it was only this month that Steele at last agreed to permit me to relate in detail how he penetrated the mystery which the murderer so carefully and cunningly wove about the crime.

2

AT THE TIME the Loundon story broke I was editing the Sunday magazine section of the Wichita *Times*. It was five-thirty of the hot afternoon of August 16. I had just decided to call it a day and was putting on my coat when the city editor hurried into the office.

"'Lucky' Loundon's been murdered!" His voice was tense with the suppressed excitement of a newspaperman facing a big story.

"Murdered!" I turned with my coat half on. "Where? Who did it?"

"Out at Loundon's lodge. Don't know who did it—Bob Pierson's on the phone now at the sheriff's office, where they just got the word. The sheriff's on his way out. Pierson's going—he's got a car—but this is too big for him to handle alone. You knew Loundon, and I thought maybe you'd like to go along and see that Bob doesn't muff it."

I jammed on my hat and grabbed the telephone. "Tell Bob to pick me up here," I told the city editor as I dialed. "I've got a dinner engagement with Steven Steele I'll have to call off. Maybe he'd like a murder to take its place."

I was correct in thinking Steele would forgo a meal any time for a murder. Ten minutes later he and I were vicariously slamming on brakes and dodging traffic as Bob Pierson burned the road north along the Meridian highway in an effort to catch the sheriff before he arrived at the scene of the murder. Bob was our courthouse reporter, a young fellow just out of college, and this was his first real excitement since coming to the paper. It would have pleased us more if he had confined his efforts to the wheel, but he insisted on adding to our trepidation by also talking at seventy miles an hour.

"It's at Loundon's hunting lodge," he stated as he cut between an oil truck and an oncoming bus. "He was found dead. Buried in a strawstack near the lodge. A couple of boys saw his feet sticking out and discovered the body at eleven-thirty this morning but were too scared to report it until their fathers came home from work."

I turned to Steele. "You met Loundon," I reminded him. "It was at Fielding Garnett's party. He was the big heavy-faced fellow with the Southern accent who told the story on Garnett—the one about the old woman who wouldn't sell him the oil lease unless he'd buy her pigs. Lucky Loundon. He cleaned up in the El Dorado pool before the war. Since then he'd made and lost two or three fortunes."

"I remember," said Steele. "He's the one who got drunk and tried to climb the piano."

I laughed. "Loundon never could hold liquor. He was really nothing but an overgrown boy. You got the wrong impression of him that night. I've never known anyone with more nerve or swifter judgment—or a bigger heart. He's helped half the oil men in the territory at one time or another. . . . I'd have said he didn't have an enemy in the world. . . . I understand he'd been drinking a lot lately. They say he usually came up here to his lodge, when he'd been on a tear, to sober up. Here, Bob, the next turn—to the left. And for God's sake use all four wheels. After all, the man's already dead."

I was well acquainted with Loundon's lodge. I had attended several of the stag parties for which he had made it famous. Situated on the west side of a wide wooded bend in the river north of the city, more than a mile from any public highway, it lay in one of the most isolated spots imaginable. That is, it had been isolated until by an ironical turn of fortune the Meridian oil field, which Loundon helped pioneer, had raised a forest of greasy derricks immediately across the river from the lodge building and had turned what was a quiet wheat field into a miniature Broadway.

The left turn brought us into the Hutchinson highway, ten miles north of Wichita. We crossed the Little Arkansas River bridge and continued west two miles until we came to the road to the lodge.

This was a narrow, sanded private lane that ran two miles due north between wheat fields, now nearly two months in the stubble and already beginning to lose their bright golden hue. The road then turned, angling east and a little north for nearly two miles more, and ended at the lodge on the bank of the river. From the lodge the stream flowed south in a crooked and well-timbered course to the bridge on the Hutchinson highway which we had just crossed. The farmland thus enclosed between the private road and the narrow fringe of trees along the river comprised the south half of Loundon's property. It had been sown to wheat for several years, and the fatal strawstack, I guessed, was somewhere here.

When we drove into the driveway before the lodge we saw one of the sheriff's deputies beckoning to us from a gate which opened into the south wheat field. As we went through he jumped on the running board and pointed out a huge strawstack that stood on the riverbank about two hundred yards south of the lodge building. We pulled up behind the sheriff's car, a few yards from the stack. Inside the car was another deputy and two scared-looking boys. Apparently Bob had succeeded in his race with the sheriff, for he had just got out of his car and stood waiting for us.

"There's a compliment for you, Steve," I said. "When our estimable sheriff shows consideration for anybody it means he has his reasons."

Steele smiled. He knew I referred to the manner in which Sheriff Andy Burke's hostility had changed to deference during the course of Steele's investigations in the Grayland affair. While Burke was no man's fool, and in some respects was above the average in natural shrewdness, he had many of the disqualifications of the half-educated politician. As we came up, however, his red face was wreathed in a smile and he shook Steele's hand with a respect that was almost effusive.

"Hello, Mr. Steele. Mighty glad to see you! When did you get back to town? Didn't know but what you'd left us for good."

"How are you, Sheriff?" Steele asked, shaking hands with the easy cordiality that was one of his most delightful characteristics. "Have you got another mystery on the stocks here?"

"Don't know. Not like that other one, I hope," Burke answered. "But from what I can get out of these boys it don't look too good. The body's up there on the stack just like it was when they found it—or anyway that's what they say—so maybe we can look it over without having everything all messed up to begin with." He turned to the two boys, who had got out of the car and now stood nearby with frightened faces. "That's right, ain't it, boys? The body's up on the stack just exactly the way you found it . . . covered up in the straw?"

The boys shook their heads in the affirmative, too terrified to speak. Having received this confirmation, Burke assumed a more official manner and glanced about at the rest of us. "Before we pull him down Mr. Steele and me will want to take a careful look around."

"Thank you, Sheriff," said Steele, with the faintest flicker of an eyelid in my direction. "I appreciate the opportunity. If you think there's a chance of anything unusual it will be interesting to be in on the ground floor."

Sheriff Burke's pudgy hand waved Steele's acknowledgment aside with the air of a man who can always be depended on to do the handsome thing by his collaborators, and he turned to begin his examination of the strawstack. It was by far the largest pile of straw I had ever seen, and from the size of the field I estimated that it had taken several harvests to build it to its extraordinary dimensions. One end hung over the river, and measuring from the bank to the outer edge it extended nearly fifty feet from east to west. With the exception of a fairly easy slope at the west end, the sides were steep and, I should have judged, impossible to climb. From where we stood the pile appeared flat on top, sloping up from the west end toward the river, with the highest point just over the bank. Over this high point a single strong wire binder was stretched. At the top it was imbedded in the straw by the pull from two heavy stones suspended from each side of the stack about fifteen feet above the ground.

Sheriff Burke, instead of climbing the stack to make an immediate examination of the body, as I expected, gave it one appraising glance; then, with what seemed unnatural restraint, he began making a minute inspection of the stubble-covered ground surrounding it. With the eye and the bearing of a Sherlock Holmes he circled from the bank of the river on one side of the stack to the bank on the other. Behind him strolled Steele, in a manner so casual as apparently to denote a complete lack of interest, but which, I was aware, disguised an attention alert to the smallest detail. The ground was soft from a rain two nights before, and the sheriff soon established the fact that there were no footprints leading to or from the stack except those of the two boys who had discovered the body, and the fact that the stack had not been climbed or descended at any other point. When Burke had reached this conclusion he glanced at Steele a little uneasily.

But Steele was not watching the sheriff. A large elm tree stood near the water twenty feet downstream from the stack. One of the limbs extended part way over the river end of the stack, and Steele was gazing curiously up at it. Our eyes followed his, and after squinting through the dark foliage a moment Burke, as he perceived what had attracted Steele's attention, uttered an exclamation. An iron gymnasium ring was caught among the branches, and the rope to which it was attached was tied to the limb so that the ring, when free, would hang directly over the stack.

"This tree has been climbed today by a large bare-foot man," Steele said, "and he didn't come back down!"

The sheriff opened his mouth. Steele did not often indulge in this sort of thing, but Burke was such a perfect foil for a little simple mystification that I suppose he couldn't resist the temptation. We followed Burke, as he rushed to the river's edge, and saw two footprints almost out of sight under the muddy sloping bank, apparently leading from the water to the gnarled roots of the tree. The first crotch of the tree was low and the trunk easy to climb.

"They're probably Loundon's," Steele said, as Burke turned away from the tree, obviously disconcerted by his oversight. "Nevertheless, Sheriff, it might be a good idea to tell the boys not to disturb them in case you should want a record made."

"Yeah, you're right," Burke agreed emphatically. "But if that is Loundon's own footstep, what the hell was he doing climbing up there barefoot? Well, maybe the answer's up on the stack. Let's get him down off of there, boys."

We followed the sheriff as he plunged up the dusty slope of the strawstack, and came upon the body where it lay completely buried in the straw at the end farthest from the river. The top of the stack at the other end, near the water's edge, looked as if a furious struggle had taken place. It was obvious that the weather-beaten top straw had been newly kicked off, for the fresher-appearing straw underneath had been turned up in a dozen places. Strangely, however, there were no signs of struggle on the surface of the stack where the body lay, almost thirty feet from the point where the straw had been disturbed.

When the sheriff uncovered the body it was at once apparent that Loundon had been killed by a blow on the back of the head, evidently delivered with some heavy blunt instrument. There were no other superficial marks except several severe bruises and a number of small lacerations where straws had been thrust into the skin of the right cheek. The hat was missing, but the body was otherwise fully dressed. A watch, pocketbook, keys, and other objects usually found in a man's pockets had been undisturbed. A thorough search failed to bring to light a weapon of any kind.

"He sure put up a battle," said the sheriff, "until he got that one back of the ear. Take him down, boys; the coroner will want him on the ground. . . . But on the other hand"—he paused and shook his head—"if this other guy had the pipe or whatever it was, why didn't he lay him out right at the start?"

"That's a fair question, Sheriff," Steele said soberly, again eying the ring on the limb over his head. "But I'm afraid it's only one of a number you're going to have to ask yourself. . . . If the struggle took place at the end of the stack overlooking the river, why was the body dragged to the other end? If it was dragged there, why doesn't the straw show it? If an attempt was made to hide the body, why weren't the feet hidden? Or were they hidden while Loundon was still alive and able to kick? Even if the feet were in sight from the ground, as the boys claim, still the body must undoubtedly have been hidden from anyone standing on the end of the stack over the river."

As Burke considered these questions his worried frown deepened into furrows of unwonted concentration. "Yeah, and there's this one," he finally said: "how the hell were there two people on the stack when so far as we can tell only one barefoot man went up?"

"That's one I'm going to try to answer right now," said Steele, sliding down the stack—"up in that elm."

Without waiting for a reply from Burke, Steele went to the tree and climbed nimbly to the limb from which the rope was suspended. As he reached it I saw him look up, and then I heard him utter a sharp exclamation. He climbed swiftly nearly to the top of the tree, went far out on a small limb and looked down. He remained there several minutes, peering about among the branches and intently surveying the lower branches and the top of the stack. Then he returned to the limb which held the ring and worked himself out to where the rope was tied. He examined the heavy iron ring carefully, then let it down and descended by the rope to the stack. The ring hung at about the level of his neck. He backed up, holding the ring in both hands, and ran swiftly toward the river's edge, swinging out over the water and back. Then he took out his knife, cut the ring from the rope and slid with it down the stack.

Loundon's body was lying face up in the shade of the sheriff's car. Steele turned it over and for several moments carefully examined the skull fracture in an effort to determine whether the ring could have caused the wounds. In the end he rose, shaking his head doubtfully.

"I don't know," he said slowly, in answer to our unspoken questions. "He was hit more than once in the same place; perhaps three times. But I don't believe this ring was used."

"Yeah," said Burke, with blunt sarcasm. "And neither do I! How would they hit him with a ring tied onto the end of a rope?"

Steele glanced at Burke as if he had only half heard his question. Without answering, he returned to the tree and stood for some seconds looking speculatively out to where one of its large limbs dipped almost into the water, then he returned, wearing a puzzled frown on his face.

"If I were an ape, now—" he faced the sheriff with a smile that was belied by his grave manner—"it would be very easy to demonstrate how the ring might have been used!"

Sheriff Burke's jaw dropped.

"If you were an ape!" he ejaculated, becoming red in the face. "What kind of damn foolishness is this, anyway, that you've been up to for the last five minutes? You wouldn't try to kid me, would you, Mr. Steele?"

Steele shook his head slowly, and the frown on his face deepened. When he answered, his voice was sober:

"No, I wouldn't, Sheriff. When I went up that tree I only wanted to examine the ring, to find out if I could why the barefoot man climbed up to it, and to assure myself that it had been hung, as I guessed, to dive from. But when I got there I saw something up above that startled me."

Steele turned and pointed.

"From the top of that tree branches are broken or bent all the way down," he said, turning to us again. "Either some large object was violently hurled through those branches, or somebody—or *something*—made a most devilish and inhuman jump down upon that strawstack!"

Steele's voice indicated he could not credit what he seemed to suggest, and his incredulity was reflected in Burke's staring eyes.

"Well, what *do* you think, Mr. Steele?" the sheriff demanded.

"Did you ever read Poe's *Murders in the Rue Morgue*?" Steele smiled.

"No," the sheriff answered; "and if it's going to make me go chattering around among the treetops, I'm not going to."

Steele looked at Burke thoughtfully, then began fishing in his shirt pocket with his thumb and forefinger.

"Well, if you should find yourself in a treetop," he said, "and discovered these sticking to a limb, what sort of language would you use?"

Steele held out his hand. On it was a matted bunch of coarse light-brown hairs nearly two inches long!

Whenever the sheriff's thoughts began to make the pull a little heavy for his brain he became red in the face. As he stared down at the palm of Steele's outstretched hand it was plain that his mind was having difficulty making the grade even in low gear. He breathed apoplectically.

"There ain't no such animal, is there, Sheriff?" Steele asked as he took an envelope from his coat pocket and laid the hairs carefully in it. "I don't think there is either—but there they are!"

"Well then, what the hell—" Burke at last found his voice. "You're not trying to tell me those belong to an ape, are you?"

"No," Steele replied slowly, "I don't think so. If I'd found them on the ground I'd say they belonged to a dog."

"Maybe it was a bear!" Bob Pierson suggested.

The sheriff wheeled on Bob with an indignant snort. "Yeah, or a lion!—A sea lion that swims in creeks and climbs trees! . . . Well, you birds can start in lookin' for him. I'm going back to town and get the coroner out here!"

Sheriff Burke turned on his heel and started for the car.

"Just a minute, Sheriff," Steele called, and as Burke turned, he smiled placatingly. "Before you go I'd like to ask these boys who found the body a few questions, if you don't mind."

"Sure, sure," Burke acquiesced gruffly, wheeling on the boys, who had remained by the sheriff's car as if rooted to the spot. "Come over here," he commanded; "and remember, anything Mr. Steele asks, you speak up and answer without any funny business."

As the two boys awkwardly stood before us it was obvious that they were far too intimidated by their predicament to attempt any "funny business." The younger, who proved to be the spokesman, was a chunky, swarthy youth of thirteen with quick black eyes and a neglected mat of curly black hair. His name, he said, was Joe Capello; that of his companion, a gangling boy of fifteen, whose chief concern at the moment was to swallow his Adam's apple, was Harry Todd.

Steele asked Joe to explain how they happened to find the body and to describe exactly everything they had done afterwards. The boy began nervously, but on the whole his account was intelligent and positive. They had been fishing in the river, he said, and were detouring around the stack when they saw a man's feet sticking out of the straw. At first they thought it was somebody asleep, then they climbed up and discovered it was Loundon's body. That was at half-past eleven. They immediately returned home, but had been afraid to say anything about it until their fathers came home from work. It was Capello's father who had called the sheriff's office.

"Joe"—Steele interrupted the boy's recital in a kindly voice—"how do you know it was exactly eleven-thirty when you found the body?"

"By my watch," said Joe, proudly producing a nickel-plated timepiece.

"Does it keep good time?" Steele asked, taking out his watch. "What time do you have now?"

"Twenty-five minutes to seven," Joe answered.

"Right," said Steele. "Now, Joe—" and suddenly his voice became stern—"why did you tell us that you saw the feet in the stack from the ground?"

"Because they was!" the boy declared.

"Then why did you tell us that you and Harry left the body exactly as you found it? When we came it was completely buried in the straw. Either you forgot, when you buried the body, to leave the feet out, as you claim they were at first, or you didn't realize when you covered it that you would want to say you saw them first, from the ground, 'sticking out.'"

Joe's face fell, and it was half a minute before he answered. "The feet was sticking out," he insisted finally, turning to the other boy, "wasn't they, Hen?"

Hen swallowed hard, then said, "Yes, they was; we seen 'em when we was going by. I guess we just covered him up because—because we was scairt."

When the sheriff realized that here was a flaw in the story which he had overlooked, he planted himself in front of the boys in righteous wrath. "Ah ha!" he began. "So you was up on the stack before you found his body, was you? Well, now, we'll just see if—"

"Never mind that now, Sheriff," Steele interposed, dropping a hand on Burke's shoulder and smiling at the now thoroughly terrified boys. "It's an important point, but not because it might implicate the boys. If they're lying it's probably only to try to keep out of trouble. Now the reason we want to know, Joe, whether the body was covered, is to find out whether someone tried to hide it or not. You see, that may make a big difference. In fact it might easily be the most important clue we have. . . . So you see we need your help. Now just try to remember exactly how it was."

Steele paused, and there was silence for a moment. Then Burke burst out:

"You mean, Mr. Steele, that if he wasn't hid something else might have killed him? This here a-ape, maybe?" He hesitated, then his imagination spurred him on. "Why, one of those apes could even have grabbed him up with one arm and bashed him over the head with the ring with the other, couldn't it?"

Steele smiled at the sheriff's earnestness, but as he answered his voice was grave.

"Exactly; although that isn't just what I had in mind. Nevertheless it is vital to know whether the body was concealed." He turned again to the boy. "How about it, Joe; can you remember?"

"Yes sir." Joe cast a quick glance of apprehension at the sheriff and then looked up at Steele's reassuring face. "It was just like I said: the first thing we saw of him was his feet sticking out."

Steele looked down at the boy sharply for a long moment. Then he nodded and gave him a pat on the back.

"O.K., Joe. I guess that's about all for this time. The sheriff will drop you at home when he goes back to town."

Steele smiled, and in answer Joe's white teeth flashed in his brown face. From the scowl on the sheriff's countenance I was aware that he did not approve, but a straight look from Steele nipped any objections he may have wanted to make, and he motioned the boys back into the car.

"You stay here with the body, Dodge," Burke instructed one of the deputies as he climbed behind the wheel. "I'll send the coroner right out. And if you see anybody, or anything, hold 'em here till we get back. We'll take a look around the house before we go."

We got into our car and followed the sheriff back to the lodge, which we had only glimpsed on our way to the stack.

The building stood on a slight elevation in an attractive, well-landscaped setting of grass and trees. Altogether there were not more than four or five acres in the formal grounds. The rest of the estate consisted of the wheat fields to the south, and back of the house to the north and along the river to the east, of a thick natural growth of trees. The lodge itself was an unpretentious building of two stories, constructed of plain boards stained a dark brown. A deep porch extended the full length and height on the south side. The white-barked trunks of four large sycamores, two stories high, made columns for the porch and gave the building a hospitable frontier-colonial appearance. Just east of the house, on the bank of the river, was a combination garage and boathouse. About twenty feet upstream from the boathouse a narrow rustic footbridge disappeared among the overhanging trees on the opposite bank. The doors and windows of all the buildings were closed, and there was no sign of life about the place.

We got out of the cars and tried the doors. As we anticipated, they were locked.

"Didn't Loundon keep a caretaker or anybody on the premises?" Steele inquired.

"No one who lived here," I told him. "He usually sent out servants from town when he had guests. . . . He used it mostly during the duck season, and occasionally for fishing or swimming during the summer; and about once a month, I understand, he staged a big poker party."

Steele nodded, then followed the sheriff down the sanded driveway toward the boathouse. When he came to the softer dirt parking area near the garage his keen face took on an expression of sudden interest. He leaned over and dropped to his knees. Then he whistled in startled amazement.

We hurried to him, and he pointed at the still moist ground. There we saw newly made imprints of heavy balloon tires, a number of footprints, and all about them what looked like the tracks of a large dog. When I said as much, however, Steele called our attention to a peculiar padded impression which, I instantly perceived, everywhere accompanied the doglike imprints.

"A dog, and *something else!*" I exclaimed.

"No," said Steele, still examining the strange depression, "the hind feet are like those of a dog, but the front feet—they are like nothing I ever saw before!"

He got up and turned to Burke, who was staring at the ground.

"And look here at what else I found, Sheriff."

As Burke looked up Steele held out another tuft of coarse golden-brown hair!

The sheriff's face became a study in scarlet. His voice, for once, failed him. Steele took out his envelope and dropped in the second bunch of hair. Then he pointed to the tire tracks.

"He—or it—or whatever it was, was brought out in this car—today—and presumably was taken away in the car."

"How do you figure that?" Burke found his voice suddenly. "How do you know he wasn't here before, or after—maybe now, running wild?"

"You can see the tracks everywhere except underneath where the car stood," Steele explained. "No, I'm quite sure he isn't running around loose."

"Well, what *do* you make of it, Mr. Steele?" asked the sheriff with an impatience in which I thought there was just a touch of alarm. "I've got to go back to town and get the coroner on the job. . . . Besides, I don't suppose we can get anywheres looking for the murderer out here in this Godforsaken place now."

"What are you going to look for, Sheriff?" asked Steele quizzically.

"A furry tree-climbing alligator, I suppose, if I was to listen to you long," Burke retorted. "I'll be back later. Have you got any tips at all that just one of my ordinary boys might get to work on?"

"Well," Steele answered with a mollifying smile, "I wouldn't worry them with the fur-bearing crocodile. I've no doubt that part is simple enough. Nevertheless something mysterious and sinister *has* happened here—and you know you can't scorn your imagination altogether." The smile left his face. "Unless I'm mistaken, you've got a dirty problem on your hands, Burke, and, frankly, I haven't a suggestion that would be worth offering."

Sheriff Burke looked at Steele for a long moment without a word, then he started for his car with a snort. From the way he turned the corner out of the driveway it was easy to guess at the strain he was again putting on his chameleon-like complexion.

3

As THE SHERIFF disappeared around the bend the sun was just sinking into an ocean of purple clouds above a clump of evergreen trees west of the lodge. Steele lifted his eyes from the road to the great orange ball and for a full minute silently watched it splashing lavender waves and pink-tipped surf against the blue beach of the sky. His hat was in his hand, and the deep hues from the clouds brightened the dark-red curls of his hair to a coppery gold.

"I've seen a good many sunsets in a good many places—" he turned at last—"but there's something about these Kansas prairies that squeezes the tubes dry. Look at that salmon cloud over there with the lilac tail; I'll bet it's three miles long and a mile high!"

For a moment we watched the vast canvas fade and glow; then Steele suddenly broke our contemplative intermission.

"No more sunsets for Loundon! No more clouds; no more rain; no more crimson or gold or grass, or cool rivers to swim in!" He turned to me. "By God, Sergeant, I'll never get used to death; I'll be damned if I will!"

(Steele had a peculiar habit of calling me by some army title, usually Sergeant or Sarge, although to everyone else I was Bill. On occasions when I irritated him I became Lieutenant or Captain, and there were times when I achieved the rank of Major or Colonel. Only by the most witless comment or the most remarkable act of stupidity, however, did I ever become General!)

Steele turned and walked toward the car, and I thought he had decided to go back to town. But instead he continued on down the driveway to the boathouse and garage. He shook the padlocked doors, then went around the north corner of the building and down a short flight of steps to the boat landing at the river's edge. Following him, we heard a delighted exclamation as he spied a small rowboat tied to the landing.

"Well, well, well! For once the Argus-eyed gods of detection are with us! What do you say we cut this rope in the name of the law and go on a cruise of exploration!"

"What do you mean, exploration?" I demanded. "If you want to go across the river there's a footbridge about twenty yards upstream."

"Listen, Sarge," Steele said as he took his knife from his pocket and opened it, "did you ever see a strawstack on the bank of a river before?"

"Why no, I don't think so."

"Neither did I. Ninety-nine times out of a hundred a strawstack is in the middle of the field, or in some place convenient to the threshers. There is no gate or road or any other good reason for its being there; as a matter of fact it's about the most inconvenient spot in the field, and the longest haul. One thought continues to bedevil me: If that stack were not just where it is Ralph Loundon's dead body would never have been found buried in it!—And so we're going to see just what it looks like from the river side."

There were no oars in the boat, and by the time Steele had found a piece of board and had propelled us into the shadow of the strawstack a cloudy twilight was settling over the quiet stream: The huge black bulk of the stack loomed above us like a cliff.

"Why, why, *why* is that strawstack there?" Steele mused as he gazed at the steep precipice of straw above us. "No one could climb that—no one *has* climbed it!"

As we sat in the silence of the river craning our necks upward we were startled by the crashing of branches on the bank south of the stack. Then a harsh voice challenged us:

"What do you want out there? Pull up here to the bank!"

We turned and saw Deputy Dodge, gun in hand, standing by the stack. As we swung about he recognized us.

"Oh, it's you!" he apologized. He put away his revolver and motioned to us excitedly. "Say! I ran into something! Loundon's car! It's in the woods on an old road just this side of the Hutchinson bridge."

We pulled up to the bank, and while Steele tied the boat to a limb Dodge eagerly told his story. He was a tall rosy young man with tallow hair roached back from his brow, much excited by the importance of his position and by his discovery. "I decided I'd look around a little and see if there wasn't something I could find while Burke was gone," he explained delightedly. "And so I just mosied along the bank here, wondering maybe if those tracks or something wouldn't show up again. And I kept on going until pretty soon I saw something bright shining on ahead of me, and then I—"

"Fine!" Steele interrupted him, turning away from the boat. "You lead on, and we'll follow. It's going to get dark on us here before we know it."

As Dodge had reported, the car was in the woods, about a hundred yards north of the bridge and out of sight of the highway. The road had been closed for years and apparently was unused except by occasional picnickers and fishing parties. It ended in an irregular loop under the trees where cars could turn, and it was here that we came to Loundon's big Packard coupé, jammed between two small cottonwoods. The windshield and the window next to the driver's seat were smashed. Broken glass lay on the floor of the car, on the seat, on the running board, and on the ground outside.

When I had taken in these details I looked at Steele.

"Why would anybody have had the driver's window up in weather like this?" I heard him mutter. "And how did that windshield get smashed? Certainly he didn't run into these trees. The bumper isn't even scratched."

"Yeah!" put in Dodge, who had been watching Steele in the manner of one who has still more wonders to show. "And let's see what you think of this, Mr. Steele!" He stepped a few feet off the road and lifted up a board. "This is what it was smashed with! And it's got hair on it!"

In the coarse grass lay a heavy wrench, which Dodge with professional pride assured us he had covered with the board to protect it from disturbance. Steele picked it up, taking care not to touch the handle, and examined it carefully. The top was bloodstained, and a few dark-brown hairs stuck to the sharp edge. A frown deepened on Steele's face as he turned it over in his hand.

"No, I don't believe the glass was smashed with this," he at last said slowly; "and if Loundon was killed with it—" he paused, and his face grew stern—"if Loundon was killed with this wrench I'm afraid there's been a deliberate attempt to manipulate our clues for us." He laid the wrench on the car seat. "If we find any finger-prints on this wrench or any footprints in the neighborhood of the car, I'll be much surprised."

A hasty examination in the growing darkness indicated that Steele's surmise was correct, although the grass and weeds were so thick that it would have been difficult to trace footprints had any been found. An inspection of the automobile disclosed that it was undamaged except for the broken glass. After Steele had sat-isfied himself that he could learn nothing more from the car he turned to the deputy.

"Dodge, I believe you'd better go on down to the bridge and flag the sheriff when he comes back. He'll want to see this car. We'll go back to the stack and wait for the sheriff at the lodge?"

We returned to the stack and embarked again in the rowboat. Deep shadows lay on the slowly swirling pool at the base of the huge mound of straw. Steele paddled the boat toward the pile until the prow bumped into the straw. The perpendicular face of the stack extended nearly twenty-five feet up from the surface of the water. Steele shook his head and lifted his makeshift oar to push away. At the touch a startled look came over his face. He prodded again. Then he jammed the board into the straw with all his strength. We nearly capsized, but the hollow wooden sound we heard drove the fear of shipwreck from our minds.

"A door—or something—covered with straw!" Steele exclaimed, and we hove to.

A few minutes excited straw-pulling revealed that it was a door. In the name of the law we broke the lock, which was cleverly con-cealed behind a guard of twisted straw, and entered.

For a few moments we could make out nothing in the black interior. Then our eyes slowly became accustomed to the dim light, and rows of bottles gradually took shape in the darkness. Finally we perceived shelf after shelf and a number of barrels, comprising what must have been one of the finest private stocks of liquor in the state!

"Ah ha! So this is why the stack is on the riverbank," exclaimed Steele with satisfaction as he looked about. "Apparently this was an old stable or hunting shack, and Loundon just had the threshers bury it in the interest of Prohibition! . . . And here, hanging on this peg, is the route to the top of the stack!"

As he spoke, Steele returned to the doorway with what, in the faint light, looked like a coil of rope.

"A rope ladder!" He shook it out. "These hooks at the end must fasten on the wire binder stretched across the top of the stack. You know, I wondered why anyone went to so much trouble to protect this pile of old straw, and why he thought one binder would do any good anyway. . . . I shouldn't be surprised if there are some more questions that will answer themselves in here!"

It was a large room, nearly eighteen by twenty-five feet, and accounted for the extraordinary size of the strawstack. There was a rack down the center on which several barrels and ten or fifteen cases stood. Around the walls, on inclined shelves, were individual bottles; wines, whiskies and brandies, for the most part.

After his first survey of this straw-thatched wine cellar, Steele began a methodical examination of its contents, going from shelf to shelf and lifting out an occasional bottle for closer inspection. When at last he returned to the slowly fading rectangle of the doorway I saw a puzzled look on his face.

"There's something odd about this collection," he said, bringing a bottle of gin to the light and peering down at its label. "From a casual inspection I should say that part of it, mostly what is against the back wall, is fairly old and good stuff. But here—" he indicated the north and south walls—"is what looks like a bootlegger's warehouse: fake labels, clean bottles, and all comparatively new." He looked up at me. "Sarge, you don't suppose Loundon was carrying on a little river traffic on the side, do you?"

I shook my head. "It doesn't sound reasonable to me. I understand he'd been pretty hard hit financially lately, but I don't believe he'd have bothered with anything as petty as this."

Steele nodded agreement. He put the bottle of gin in its place and began to examine the floor and walls back of the shelving more carefully. A moment later he dropped suddenly to his hands and knees with a startled expletive. He thumbed his cigarette lighter into a flame and peered down at the thick dust of the dirt floor.

"Well, well, and see what we find here!"

There on the floor, plainly outlined in the dust, were tracks of a barefoot man similar to those we had seen in the mud by the tree!

"And here he was with his shoes on," Steele said, pointing again. "Looks as if he changed under here. And if I'm not mistaken the same shoes made the prints we saw around the car at the lodge. I think while we're here I'll just make some tracings. . . . Let's have some of those newspapers over there in the corner."

When I brought the papers, Steele laid aside a fresh sheet and with the others started a small fire near the tracks. By its light he painstakingly cut the outlines of the footprints into the earth with his knife. Then, while I kept the fire going, he deftly cut outlines from the fresh sheet of paper to fit the four imprints he had marked in the ground. When he had finished he straightened up, put the slips of paper in his pocket and went to the door.

"I wish the sheriff could see what else I found on the floor there!"

I followed him to the light. There, in the palm of his outstretched hand, I beheld another small tuft of coarse golden-brown hair!

Steele laughed as he took out his envelope and placed the hair with his previous finds. I laughed too, a little hollowly, while Bob Pierson, now silhouetted faintly in the doorway, echoed with a sepulchral chuckle and put one foot in the boat.

"Any—any more tracks of the—ah—animal?" Bob decided to ask before embarking.

"No, none," Steele answered. "We'll be ready to go in a minute. I just want to take one more look at this window."

Behind the shelves, opposite the door, Steele had found what was once a window, now boarded up. By the dim flicker of his lighter he scrutinized it for a moment. Then he handed me the light and set to work to move the bottles and remove the shelving which had been built in front of it. After much prying with an old piece of iron, he loosened the boarding and tore it off. As he stumbled back with the boards in his hands there was disclosed, beyond the opening, a black tunnel leading out and up through the straw!

When I saw that black cavelike hole yawning just beyond Steele's shoulder I instinctively jumped to one side. What I expected might come plunging out of it, I don't know, but Steele only laughed.

"What's the matter, Lieutenant? You're not becoming gorilla-minded, along with the sheriff, are you?" He picked up the board which he had used for an oar, and before I could protest stuck it in the tunnel as far as it would go. Then he threw down the board and took off his hat and coat. "Here," he said, handing them to me, "hold these and give me a boost."

Knowing that it would be useless to attempt to dissuade him, I did as he requested. In a few seconds he had disappeared into the straw. Despite all the reassurances common sense so glibly provided, I experienced an uncomfortable two or three minutes before he reappeared.

"It leads to the far edge of the stack, all right," he reported, as we helped brush him off. "About ten feet north of and below where Loundon's body was found, I should judge. The outside entrance is covered with straw."

Immediately and almost in unison, Pierson and I asked if he thought Loundon could have crawled or have been pulled that way.

"Yes, it's possible—barely possible; not at all likely," Steele answered, picking up his oar. "My explanation for that tunnel is that it was dug by someone who knew Loundon's liquor was kept here. Probably it hasn't been used since the thief was boarded out. . . . And then again . . ."

Silently we got in the boat, and Steele closed the door, carefully pulling straw over the broken lock. He swung the boat about and began paddling back to the lodge. Only a faint glow from the distant horizon lingered between the tree trunks on the bank; the still waters of the stream were black in the shadows of the over-hanging trees. I knew Steele well enough not to attempt to ask questions; but Pierson, excited by the unexpected disclosures in the stack, endeavored to interrogate him as to the importance of our discoveries. When, however, he received a couple of grunted monosyllables in reply, and then nothing but silence, he resigned himself to listen to the quiet lapping of the water against the sides of the boat. When we reached the lodge landing, Steele tied up the boat and we returned to our car, more mystified, so far as I could see, than ever.

In front of us the white-trunked columns of the lodge glim-mered through the dim light like pillars of some uninhabited for-est temple. The heavy night smell of grass and leaves mingled with a drifting odor from the river. On the air, permeating it like an electric current, pulsated the constant metallic rasping of locusts, shrill in the heat of the August twilight. Steele stood wiping his face with his handkerchief, regarding the lodge with an air of per-plexed speculation.

"I'd give something to see the inside of that place." He at last broke his silence. "We can't leave without reporting to the sheriff; I wonder, Sarge, why we shouldn't fill in the time with a little more investigation? What's to prevent us from breaking in?"

With Steele, to suggest was to act, and without waiting for our acquiescence he walked rapidly up the graveled path, crossed the wide porch, and again tried the doors and windows which opened on it from the lodge. They were all securely fastened. He next went to the door at the east end of the building, which was sheltered by a small porch covered with vines. We had tried this door before, but he gave the handle of the door a perfunctory twist. To his as-tonishment it opened at his touch!

Startled, Steele backed swiftly out of the entrance. After a mo-ment of indecision he whispered to ask if we had a flashlight in the car. Bob nodded and ran to get it. When he returned, Steele took the light and led the way into the black interior. The first room we entered proved to be the kitchen. Steele found the light switch, and to our relief the lights in the room flashed on. We waited in silence for nearly a minute, then, leaving the lights burning, we proceeded to the main room of the lodge.

Here Steele played the light about the walls until he found the switch at the left of the main entrance. When he pressed the button a dim glow from a great iron-ring chandelier, suspended from the roof timbers on chains, threw back the shadows in a vast and curious room. It was two stories high and extended the width of the building. With the exception, as I remembered, of some rooms upstairs and downstairs at the east end, it also ran the full length of the lodge. A wide stairway at the west end of the room led up to a narrow balcony which encircled it and gave access to the upper east rooms and to the screened-in upper porch on the south. In the north wall downstairs was a large rough-stone fireplace. Hung against the balcony railings in lieu of pictures were brightly colored French scenic posters. Navajo rugs, bookshelves on each side of the fireplace, a long split-log dining table, and numerous card tables and easy chairs somewhat relieved the somber aspect of the high, dark-stained walls. But as we paused at the threshold in the uncertain light the oppressive heat filled me with a sense of gloom and an apprehensive feeling of suffocation.

For what seemed fully three minutes Steele held us there without a word. Then he flashed on his light, motioning us to silence, and led the way to the door of the downstairs bedroom. This was a simply furnished room with an adjoining bathroom, bearing no indications of recent occupancy. From this room we went up the stairway and around the north balcony to the upstairs bedrooms. The first two were counterparts of the one below, and in similar order. But in the third, which from the furnishings we guessed was Loundon's own room, we met with as confused a jumble of bedroom accessories as I have ever seen. The contents of all the drawers in the room had been dumped on the bed. The pictures on the walls had been pulled down, or were askew. Except for the closet, where several boxes apparently remained untouched, the havoc was complete. When Steele's swift glance encountered these undisturbed boxes a look of disquietude came over his face. He whirled to the door with a sudden signal to silence.

"Whoever did this found what he wanted," he said in a low voice, "or he was interrupted. . . . I wonder—"

Even as he spoke a shrill and horrifying scream shivered through the hot air of the dim room. Immediately the lights in the large room went out. The shriek had seemed to come from the upper porch. An instant later I was following Steele's flashlight where it moved swiftly along the balcony toward the porch entrance. When he reached the door I was less than fifteen feet behind. Yet I was too far to catch more than a glimpse of what happened. I saw him push open the door and saw his light flash inside. Then he was suddenly and violently hurled aside. As he fell, his flashlight was knocked to the floor. A black form darted out of the darkness, climbed over the balcony railing, swung a moment from the floor edge and dropped. There was a momentary clatter of chairs and tables below, the sound of a shuffling step toward the kitchen, and the room was silent.

Before I could reach him Steele had recovered the flashlight and was again on his feet.

"Are you hurt?" I demanded breathlessly. "Did you see it? What was it?"

"I'm all right." He dashed along the balcony toward the stairs. "Come on!"

Downstairs, Steele turned on the lights, gave one glance at the empty room, then rushed out through the brightly lighted kitchen into the darkness. I followed and caught up with him on the driveway. He stood, flashlight playing idly on the ground, staring down the driveway. Ahead of us the red taillight of our car was disappearing around the bend of the road!

"My God!" I exclaimed aghast. "Did it take our car?"

"It!" Steele turned on me testily. "I don't know what you mean, 'it.' There were two in that car, and the one who was driving was a woman!"

4

WE RETURNED TO TOWN in the sheriff's car. It was nearly nine o'clock, and after a hasty sandwich and a cup of coffee with Steele, Bob Pierson and I went to the *Times* to write our stories for the morning editions. At Steele's suggestion nothing was said of his participation or of the secret room under the strawstack, but I told Bob to turn himself loose on the other features. While he was only a youngster, he had a flair for words, and what he achieved was a gorgeous combination of an African gorilla hunt, a haunted-house thriller and a big-town gangster killing. I confined myself to bringing Loundon's "morgue" sketch down to date and preparing the picture layout. Between us we put the eye out of the opposition paper for twenty-four hours. The evening *Herald*, in its noon edition the next day, bannered the story across the front page, featuring the mystery element and Lucky Loundon's spectacular career, but it was practically a rewrite from our stories in the *Times*. By that time the case had become the "Strawstack Mystery," and Sheriff Burke's activities, theories, clues and misclues were being shouted from every downtown corner.

It was just past noon, and I was sitting at my desk doing a little private gloating over the *Herald* when Steele came in the office. I glanced up at his cool, immaculately white-clad figure, motioned him to a chair, flipped him a copy of the *Herald* and went on with my reading. He turned to the sport page, glanced over it a few seconds and threw the paper in the wastebasket. When I looked up again a moment or two later I caught him regarding me with an amused smile.

"Well . . . and what?" I challenged, knowing some comment was on the tip of his tongue.

He lit a cigarette and chuckled. "For high-hat disdain commend me to a newspaperman looking over the opposition's latest. No woman ever smiled such a sneer at a dowdy acquaintance. My boy, lorgnettes were made for faces like yours!"

"My boy—" I crumpled up the *Herald* and crammed it in the wastebasket—"faces like mine were made by reading papers like these! Now if you'll give me a cigarette I'll listen to your apologies for intruding among us Workers. . . . And what, by the way, is the great detective smoking today? Regiecides, or are you playing the violin and eating opium?"

Steel reached me his cigarette case. It was wrought of silver, beautifully filigreed with his initials in gold. It had a peculiar interest for me because it had been presented to him by the members of the Grayland family, whom he had saved from the toils of circumstantial evidence following the murder of old John Grayland.

"Neither," he answered my question. "Three hard sets of tennis on these damned white courts you have in this town will do more on an August morning to undermine the constitution than narcotics. . . . And, by the way, I see this youngster, Vines, is still hitting them on the nose. There's the way tennis ought to be played—shoot for the points and let the devil take the pat-ball artists!"

Steele was a "nut on tennis," as, indeed, he was on every competitive sport, while my interest was purely academic and non-argumentative.

"That's right," I said; "and where are we going to eat today?"

Steele grinned. "That's what I came in for. Jim Warren has invited you and me to take lunch with him at the club." He gave me a straight look. "Was that your idea or his?"

"Both," I told him, weighting down the loose papers on my desk; "I knew he'd be up a tree in this Loundon case, and I was afraid he'd be too stiff-necked to ask your advice, so I suggested lunch."

I was studiously avoiding Steele's eye. In a moment he laughed, and I knew my little strategy was forgiven; although I had not doubted that his interest in the affair was already strong enough to induce him to let bygones remain bygones.

Jim Warren (James Dourogette Warren) was our county attorney, and in his way as interesting and stubborn a character as Steele himself, if not so colorful. At the time of the Grayland case Warren had been running for re-election, and it was largely Steele's masterly unraveling of that gruesome tangle, for which he asked no public credit, that gave Warren his second term. Unfortunately, however, the *Herald*, which had never been a strong supporter of Warren, got wind of Steele's part in the investigation and, without his knowledge or consent, printed a lurid feature story in which the county attorney played a not too tuneful second fiddle. Although this was subsequent to the election, Warren became furious and, thinking Steele responsible, wrote a sharp note, which Steele showed to me and then destroyed. Warren afterwards regretted his hasty action and tried to make amends, but Steele had coolly ignored him during the rest of his stay in town.

Warren was a serious-minded, hard-working fellow, well liked and respected by the members of the local Bar. Physically, he was big and lumbering, slightly stooped, heavy-jawed, with small gray eyes which contrasted oddly with his dark bushy eyebrows. Between his practical mind, however, fixed in its orderly processes by the habit of the law, and Steele's swift and often seemingly intuitive judgments, there existed a gulf as wide as it was deep. While with the one exception their relations had always been amicable, there was a self-conscious restraint in Warren's personal contacts, a certain punctiliousness of manner, that always aroused a sort of puckish reaction in Steele. He disliked any semblance of pomp, and Warren's habitual and somewhat magisterial dignity seemed to tempt him as a top hat does a small boy. Steele appreciated the uses of formality, but I knew he felt that most personal dignity is either a mask for ignorance or a hiding place for inhibitions.

When we reached the club Warren was waiting for us in the lobby. He shook hands cordially, and it was typical of him that instead of tacitly assuming that the past was forgotten, he mentioned it immediately and apologized in his most honest and painful way. Having thus satisfied his sense of the strict proprieties he led the way to the dining room, where he had secured a secluded table in a corner.

During lunch he outlined what had been done by his office in the case, charted all his blind alleys and ended by confessing he hadn't a clue to go on.

"There's something mysterious about this thing," he concluded. "I'm afraid there's more behind it than the surface indications account for."

Steele leaned back in his chair and lit a cigarette.

"You mean, Loundon wasn't robbed, and there aren't any other motives in sight. I see you're old-fashioned enough to like motives in your crimes." He smiled and ran a hand through his thick red curls in a characteristic gesture. "Hadn't you heard that one doesn't go about searching for motives any more? . . . The methods of the modern Sherlocks are psychopathic and—" he hesitated—"osteopathic."

Warren shifted impatiently. But I had caught a mischievous gleam in Steele's eye that made me curious.

"I'll be your straight man," I grinned. "Why osteopathic?"

He gave me an infinitesimal wink. "The psychopathic consists in the inductive, the deductive and the reductio ad absurdum." He counted them off on his fingers professorially. "But when you come to grips with your murderer, then you slap on the osteopathic! This is all modern stuff; you've got to quit thinking of motives!"

Warren laughed, but his mind wasn't on it. His appreciation of the facetious had always been subnormal.

"This is pretty serious to me, Steele," he said apologetically. "If you've got any theories that might furnish a lead or two I'd appreciate having them."

"I'm sorry," said Steele, with his sudden disarming smile. "Tell me, now, just where you stand. . . . What has Sheriff Burke done so far?"

Warren looked at him suspiciously. "As nearly as I can discover he and his men propose to spend a good share of the time going about the country looking for some kind of strange beast—one that can swim and climb trees!"

Steele laughed. "From the way you exaggerate, I gather you don't approve!" He looked at the county attorney speculatively a moment, and then his face became grave. "But really, Warren, there is something extraordinarily strange about Ralph Loundon's death—something bizarre. I won't say with the *Herald* that it's demoniac: I don't think there's anything superhuman about it, and certainly I don't believe with some others that the act was maniacal, because there's been a logical mind at work—too logical, in fact. . . . I have been thinking about it ever since I saw Loundon dead in that strawstack, and I must confess I was never more puzzled in my life."

Steele hitched his chair up to the table and looked across at Warren earnestly. "Now if you want me to we'll go over it together and see what we can make of it."

This was just what Warren and I had hoped for, and we drew up our chairs eagerly.

Steele first carefully studied the results of the sheriff's and the county attorney's investigations. Very little additional information had been forthcoming. The facts, as they had been established up to that noon, August 17, may be set down briefly as follows:

The coroner had been out of town until a late hour the night of the 16th, and it was past eleven when he viewed the body. As a result of his belated examination he could not be certain as to the hour of Loundon's death, but he stated that in his opinion it could not have been later than eleven o'clock on the morning of August 16. Death unquestionably had been caused by blows on the back of the head from the wrench or some similar weapon. Severe bruises and several broken bones indicated extreme violence.

With the exception of the mysterious tracks of the animal and the man about the tire marks at the lodge, the footprints of the barefoot man near the tree and in the secret room, and the tracks made by the boys at the stack, there was no evidence that anyone else had been about the premises following the rainfall of the second night preceding the discovery of the body. Some incomplete fingerprints had been secured in Loundon's bedroom at the lodge, but there was no other trace of the intruders we had surprised there. All attempts to discover the owner of the car which had been parked in the lodge driveway and the makers of the tracks had failed. Exact patterns of the tracks of the strange animal and the footprints of the man had been made. The footprints in the mud near the tree coincided with those under the stack, as did the shoe prints about the car at the lodge. It had been proved they were not Loundon's.

The lodge, boathouse, garage and all outbuildings, with the exception of the kitchen door of the lodge, had been securely locked. This kitchen door, apparently, had been entered while we were in the boat. Loundon's regular cleaners and caterers stated that they had last opened the lodge for him on the night of August 10, when he gave a party to a few friends. They were positive all doors had been left locked when they cleaned the next day.

A careful examination of Loundon's car, the wrench, and the old road had disclosed nothing that would give a clue to the identity of the murderer. The hair on the wrench was Loundon's, and the wrench presumably was the fatal weapon.

That morning Warren and Sheriff Burke had again questioned the two boys who discovered the body. Despite Burke's insistent hazing they had not diverged materially from their first stories.

A porter at the Town Club, where Loundon lived, was believed to be the last person who saw him alive. The club steward stated Loundon had called the office for ice water at seven-thirty on the morning of the 16th. The colored boy who had delivered it said Loundon was then under the influence of liquor. He did not have breakfast at the club, and it was not known when he left the building. The attendants at the garage where he kept his car said it had not been left there that night. They explained, however, that when Loundon was drinking he sometimes parked it in the street near the club. This was verified by the police, although the patrolman on duty declared the car had not been on his beat the night of the fifteenth.

A telephone conversation with Loundon about nine o'clock in the morning had been reported by Charles Ripley, a business associate, who said Loundon had called from a pay station to say he would not be at the office. He knew it was a pay-station call, he stated, because Loundon was cursing drunkenly about having to pay an extra nickel. Since there were no pay telephones nearer the hunting lodge than the city limits, it was concluded that Loundon had been in town about nine o'clock. After this call at nine he was not seen or heard from until his dead body was found at eleven-thirty o'clock. Allowing thirty to forty-five minutes for the drive out, Warren had estimated that Loundon must have been killed between nine-thirty or nine forty-five and eleven o'clock.

Robbery could not have been the motive. Loundon's watch, pocketbook and other valuables were found on his body.

The *Times's* car, which was stolen from us at the lodge, had been found only an hour ago on the property of the Emsberg Lumber Company, dealers in rig timbers, at their Meridian field yards just off the Meridian highway. To go there by car from the lodge it was necessary to cross the Hutchinson bridge south of Loundon's estate, making the distance approximately eight miles.

This last item, with which Warren closed his resumé, seemed to have assumed a peculiar significance in his mind. He had already questioned Bob Pierson about every detail of our entry into the lodge the night before and had concluded that the prowlers were the murderers. Bob's hazy description of the mysterious figure which had dropped from the balcony to the floor, after turning out the lights and knocking Steele down, had not served to lessen this suspicion. But when he turned to Steele for corroboration of these views he was confronted with some disturbing observations.

"No doubt there is some connection between the prowlers and the murder," Steele agreed, tilting back his chair and blowing a couple of slow rings of cigarette smoke into the air. "But to conclude that one of them was the murderer, in my opinion, is contrary to reason. For all the *Times's* references to bestial 'its' and 'things,' I think they were both human, a man and a woman, surprised in a search or some clandestine enterprise. We must allow for the possibility that they did not know a murder had been committed. When they heard us enter the lodge they left the bedroom and went to the upper porch. When we went upstairs to the bedrooms, foolishly leaving our car unguarded, the man attempted to lower the woman to the ground from the porch. For some reason

she screamed; perhaps from fright, perhaps because he dropped
her too soon. He then showed his resourcefulness by turning off
the lights and waiting for us in order to gain time for his companion to get the car started. Then he rushed out and made his
escape. It isn't logical to suppose that the murderer would have
remained on the premises for over eight hours, or that he would
have returned to the scene of the crime."

Warren was disappointed and obviously unconvinced by this
simple explanation.

"Then you don't think it possible that the murderer might still
have been seeking something? If he was willing to kill for what he
wanted, wouldn't he have been willing to run any additional risk?"

"Of course, I don't mean to imply that any supposition which
will fit the facts is impossible or even illogical," Steele concurred.
"As a matter of fact there's a good deal to your idea, and it may
turn out that you're right. But what I do maintain is that the simplest explanation is the most logical until it has been disproved."

"Yes; but, Steele," I put in, "couldn't one of those great apes be
trained—even by a woman?"

"Perhaps; but again I say, it's not in the least likely." Steele
ground his cigarette butt impatiently in the ash tray. "If you want
something enigmatical to puzzle your brains about—something that
is either inhuman or irrationally clever—you can spend your time
pondering why Loundon left his car where it was found, there by
the river; why the wrench was found so far from the stack, or why
the body was so far from the wrench; why there were no signs of
struggle around the car; why, if there was no struggle there, the
windshield and window glass were broken and the glass was scat-
tered on the ground; why there were signs of struggle on the river
side of the top of the stack and none where the body was found;
why the feet were unburied. There, in my estimation, are points
that want more solving and in addition are vastly more pertinent
than the incident in the lodge."

As he spoke, Steel accompanied each of his queries with such a
solid rap of a table knife on the top of the table as to draw wondering glances from all the colored waiters in the now empty room.

"Those are questions, however, that we can't possibly answer from the data at hand. . . . Therefore," and he gave the table a double rap, "let's go to what is always the most fertile field—the victim's past. What do you know about Loundon's social and business friends and associates? Who would profit from his death? Who would want to kill him? . . . You know, Warren, the Chinese have a saying that one picture is worth ten thousand words. To paraphrase that aphorism in the field of crime, one good motive is worth ten thousand unrelatable clues."

5

WARREN RECEIVED STEELE'S rather vigorous outburst with a shrug of his heavy shoulders and a gesture of resignation. Apparently he had resolved that if it was necessary to pay for Steele's criminological experience and ability with patience he would do it at whatever cost to his own domineering nature. The wrought-iron smile with which he accepted Steele's suggestion amused me no less than it would have delighted many an associate who had suffered in the past from the county attorney's own high-handed methods.

"To be honest," he began, "we haven't a real suspect. But there are four or five persons who were intimate with Loundon in a social or business way whose knowledge of him or whose possible interest in his death will bear investigation." He managed another smile. "As a matter of fact I've arranged to see several of them this afternoon—and I'd like to have you come along."

Warren included me in the invitation with a glance and drew a small notebook from his pocket.

"I've engagements with four," he said, looking up from his book. "Fielding Garnett at his office at two; Dora Monest at home at three; her uncle, Juan Monest, at the club at four-thirty; and Charles Ripley at his office at five or five-thirty."

Steele received this schedule with a quizzical lift of the eyebrows. "The methodical procedures of the law," he observed, "are the envy of my life. If the villain gets away from you it will be only because he doesn't follow the rules." He looked at his watch. "We've got half an hour before we're due at Garnett's. Suppose you start with him."

Almost apologetically Warren referred to his notebook again. "I suppose the law *is* responsible for my methods," he confessed, "but I've jotted down here the principal facts I've been able to gather about each of these people."

Steele nodded. "Good," he said. "Let's hear Garnett's scenario."

"Fielding Stone Garnett," Warren read. "Age, thirty-nine; unmarried. Oil operator—reputed to be worth two or three million dollars. A born speculator; said to be the best poker player in town. At times a heavy drinker but never to intoxication. Rumored to have been interested in several women within the past three years, but keeps his relations with them strictly to himself. Went in for polo when he became wealthy; noted as a hard-riding player who never gives ground when in the saddle. Formerly a tool-dresser and lease broker in the El Dorado oil field. Given start as operator by Loundon, with whom he later became a partner. A captain of infantry in the war. After the war he wildcatted independently in Oklahoma and was reported to have staked Loundon twice, following the latter's bad luck in the Kansas fields. Interested with Loundon in the Oil River Machine Company, the Town Club Building Company, the Dragonfly Airplane Corporation and the Spang Refinery. He was Loundon's closest friend. Both lived here at the Town Club. Gossip that Loundon had been in financial difficulties and had been refused aid by Garnett apparently wholly without foundation. Their friendship was of long standing and had weathered every kind of financial storm."

Warren closed his notebook. "I believe that about covers Garnett."

"Very interesting," Steele acknowledged. Then he turned to me. "Sarge, as a newspaperman don't you have any gossip or scandal to add to this rather immaculate report?"

I laughed. Steele enjoyed harpooning me about my job.

"Yeah, I have—plenty!" I told him. "But none of it has been printed because the *Times*, quote, Kansas' Greatest Newspaper, unquote, hasn't wanted to hurt the feelings of the Oil River Machine Company and the Spang Refinery."

"Good and sufficient reasons," Steele admitted, "and such consideration should be reflected in the advertising columns!"

"It should and will," I declared. "But before I spill it, I'd like to hear what Jim's morgue has to say about Dora Monest."

Warren complied, getting out his notebook again.

"I have her and her uncle listed here together." He found the place and began: "Dora Monest. Age, about twenty-three. Single. Moved here a few years ago from New Orleans. Lives with uncle, Juan Monest, in the old Goodhugh mansion on Riverbank Drive. She is unusually beautiful and seems popular in the social set. Is very athletic; holds state swimming and diving championships. Reported engaged to Ralph Loundon, although there has been no public announcement.

"Juan Monest is about fifty and unmarried. Interested in oil properties. Said to have invested heavily in some of Loundon's wildcat activities."

"Is that all?" I asked, as Warren closed his book. He nodded.

I shook my head sorrowfully. "Well, Jim," I told him, "that would do very well for the social register, but it seems to me the county attorney should have a little more of the personal dirt that has been blowing around. You ought to get married or something so you'll have access to the scandal dope sheet."

"Or work on a paper," suggested Steele.

"Right!" I agreed. "And here's what any wife or society reporter would tell you: that Dora Monest is as shrewd as she is beautiful—which is shrewd enough. That she was engaged to Loundon until about three months after Garnett came back to Wichita. That when she saw Garnett play polo a few times, riding his ponies like the hard bronze devil he is, and saw him dive and swim like a brown Hawaiian native, and observed that he remained practically oblivious to her existence whenever they met, and realized that he had ten dollars to Loundon's one, with a brain capacity in the same proportions, she fell in love with him, intentionally and unintentionally, and fell hard.

"'And where did this leave Loundon' you naturally ask. It left him facing the loss of his fiancée and his finances at the same time, although it is possible he wasn't aware of it. I don't believe he ever knew Dora loved Garnett. The low-down is that when he began to drink to forget his oil losses and began showing up drunk at her house, she used that as a pretext to break their engagement.

"All this, of course, put Garnett in a pretty tough spot. He advanced money to cover Loundon's deficits, as he had before and as Loundon had done in the past for him, and they say he tried to stay away from the girl. But from all accounts he's no more than human, and along toward the last they were seeing quite a lot of each other—on the q.t. What their relationship was—or is—depends on the imagination and inhibitions of the person who tells it to you."

"And the uncle, Juan Monest?" asked Steele. "Do you have anything sub rosa about him?"

"No, not much," I admitted. "I've heard that he lost a lot in Loundon's wildcat ventures, and there was some talk of a row with Loundon about it. He's like his niece; he knows how to keep his mouth shut when he wants to. . . . Some of the local mesdames have tried pretty hard to make him romantic and mysterious because he is dark and Spanish, and has something of a reputation as a big-game hunter. He has a few trophies in the house, and he is clever and secretive; but if you ask me, he is a damn sight more interested in the smell of oil fields than in the scent of wild animals—or of cosmetics, either. He is suave, all right, but it's the suavity of crude oil, not romance."

Warren nodded. "He's got the oil fever, and he got it from Loundon." He pulled out his watch. "If we're going to see Garnett at two we'll have to get on."

Fielding Garnett's suite of offices was on the fourteenth floor of the *Times* Building. When we arrived his secretary showed us at once into his private office. It was a spacious room finished in dark walnut and furnished with handsome dark chairs, a large desk and a warm-hued green carpet, the general effect being one of richness and good taste. On the walls were several large framed

photographs of oil gushers, and there was one interesting paint-
ing depicting two polo players in a skirmish over the ball.

We had all met Garnett, and he greeted us pleasantly, shoving
a box of cigarettes toward us across his desk and motioning us to
chairs. He took one of the cigarettes himself and stood lighting it,
waiting for us to be seated. His figure was tall and lean, and his
face was handsome in a long, furrow-checked sort of way. His early
years of outdoor toil and his polo playing had given a deep tone to
a naturally bronze complexion. A faint suggestion of dissipation
about his eyes and mouth was subordinated to the predominating
expression of quiet but ready power. I noticed that Steele, who had
taken a chair near one of the windows, was regarding him with
uncommon interest.

Warren led up to his subject in his usual serious and slightly
awkward way.

"I presume you know why we're here, Mr. Garnett," he began—
"I mean, we are still completely in the dark about Ralph Loundon's
death. Since you said you wanted to help in any way you could, I
came over to see if you could give us any information that might
throw some light on his murder."

"What kind of information are you after?" Garnett's voice was
low-pitched in tone but crisp in diction.

"Well, financial or personal—anything. Do you know of any
reason why anyone should have killed him? Had there been anything unusual about his actions? When did you see him last?"

Garnett's dark eyes surveyed the county attorney steadily for a
moment.

"As you know, Ralph Loundon was my friend. I would give a
great deal to know who killed him." He spoke simply, in a steady
voice. "There have been a lot of lies told about him." He paused to
straighten the fountain-pen stand in front of him. "Financially, I
tell you in confidence, he was in bad shape. He had drilled a number of dry holes and was pushed for money. But we had arranged
to take care of all that. Personally, he had been drinking too much,
and he wouldn't take anybody's advice. The only change I noticed
in him was that he had allowed his affairs to worry him more in

the past six months than ever before. But he was a square shooter, and half the oil men in Kansas were indebted to him in one way or another. . . . So far as motives are concerned, I don't know of any reason why anybody would want to kill him."

Garnett threw his cigarette away. "The last time I saw him was at the Dragonfly plant the afternoon before he was killed. He was pretty well teed up, and I told him he ought to go to bed and cut out the booze for a while. . . . I didn't hear about his death until the *Times* office called me the next night. I'd been up at the Meridian field most of the morning bringing in a well, and at noon I watched them spud in on the Switzer farm north of Maize. I came back to town and spent the rest of the day here at the office."

There was a moment of silence when he finished. Then Steele leaned forward in his chair.

"You didn't know Loundon was going to the lodge then?" he asked.

Garnett took particular notice of Steele for the first time, giving him a slow appraising glance before answering.

"No. If I had, I would have dropped in on my way from the Meridian field to the Switzer farm to see how he was."

"You had to go past the lower end of his place to get to the Switzer farm, I believe? Along the Hutchinson highway?"

"Yes."

"Can you see the strawstack from the highway?"

"No."

"Are you sure?"

"Yes. Loundon located the stack there under the tree and hung the ring that the papers have been talking about to dive from."

"You know, of course, that he had a cache for his liquor under that stack?"

I thought a shadow of surprise and displeasure passed over Garnett's face. At Steele's request no mention had been made in the papers of the secret room, and I surmised that Garnett was unaware it had been discovered. But he answered easily and without hesitation:

"Yes. As a matter of fact, some of it was mine."

He offered no explanation and looked calmly at Steele, waiting for him to continue. But Steele seemed satisfied, and as Warren had no further questions he thanked Garnett, and we started to leave. When we were at the door, however, Steele turned, as if struck by an afterthought.

"Oh, Mr. Garnett," he said. "You told us a moment ago you couldn't imagine why anyone should want to kill Loundon. . . . I wonder if you happen to know anyone *he might have wanted to kill?*"

I seemed to sense a sudden tension in Garnett's attitude. Despite the careless manner of his question, I observed that Steele was watching Garnett narrowly. But if he expected to catch anything from the other's reaction he was disappointed.

"No," Garnett replied readily, "I can't imagine anyone."

"He may have been killed in self-defense, you know."

"Yes, I know. I'm sorry I can't offer any suggestions."

Steele received this reiteration with an expressionless countenance. "I suppose you don't happen to know who had keys to Loundon's lodge besides himself?" he asked.

Again I thought there was an almost imperceptible stiffening in the muscles about Garnett's mouth. But his answer was straightforward.

"I have one," he said. "I don't doubt there were others. Anything Loundon had belonged to his friends. . . . But I can't say positively that there were others."

Steele accepted this statement without comment and offered no further questions. As we left, Warren shook Garnett's hand cordially and thanked him. But as soon as we were alone in the hall he began complaining at the meagerness of the information we had secured. Steele turned to him in astonishment.

"What did you expect to learn?" he demanded. "You'll never find out any more from him than he wants you to. There's a man who can *think* while the average man is batting his eyes!"

6

THE COUNTY ATTORNEY accepted Steele's comment with a shrug of his shoulders.

"Well, maybe Garnett's lady friend isn't so close-mouthed," he said. "We'll go out and see Miss Monest. She said she'd be at home all afternoon."

"Let me off at the fourth floor," I told the elevator operator when we got in. And to Warren I explained, "I've got an Exhibit A I want to show to Steele before we go on to Miss Monest's. I'll be with you in a couple of minutes."

When I rejoined them outside I pulled a glossy-finished photograph from my pocket and handed it to Steele.

"Dora Monest," I announced: "state aquatic champion, and, so far as I'm concerned, Miss Bathing Beauty of the Universe."

Steele looked at a perfectly proportioned young woman poised on a diving board. When he saw her full half-parted lips, the delicate dusky cheeks and the bright black eyes his red hair seemed to curl a little tighter.

"Spanish vendetta!" he ejaculated. "So that's what brought Columbus to America!"

He handed the photograph back, and I gave it to Warren.

"You are badly in need of a few motives, Mr. County Attorney," I told him. "Let me respectfully suggest that any single man who ever saw this lady had a motive for putting her fiancé away!"

But Warren merely glanced at the picture and handed it back. He was always uncomfortable in the presence of women and sometimes found it difficult to unbend even when discussing them.

"It seems to me this is too serious a matter to be joked about so much," he said stiffly.

I apologized, glancing at the photograph again before putting it in my pocket. I had had my fun and felt repaid by the amused glance which Steele slyly directed at the grave face of our digni-fied collaborator.

The old Goodhugh mansion was a great sprawling pile of brown stone which had been erected during Wichita's boom days over forty years before. It was situated on the east side of the river in the center of three or four acres of blue-grass lawn and wide-spreading elm trees. At the rear the grass sloped gently to the river-bank, where there was an elaborate and attractive boathouse. In front, on the street, a wide veranda encircled the south and east sides of the house, and at the corner a large porte-cochère with a slate-colored cupola bearing the word SALVE chiseled above the entrance added an ornate touch. The only reason anyone had ever been able to advance for the Monests' occupancy of this rambling, out-dated structure was the fact that the house stood on the bank of the river. Dora Monest, in addition to being the town's finest swimmer, possessed the fastest speedboat on the river and also owned the largest pleasure motorboat. During the summer months she spent much of her time on the water, and the Goodhugh place, with its wide lawn sloping down to the water's edge, was ideally adapted to her hobby.

We were admitted by a colored maid through a double-doored vestibule into a large old-fashioned reception hall. On the right was a wide winding oak staircase; on the left, sliding doors opened on the drawing room. Opposite the outside entrance was a high stone-faced fireplace. While no effort had been made to modern-ize the room, it was tastefully decorated with hangings of a cool blue and furnished with comfortable chairs upholstered in a touch of the same color. What caught the eye immediately upon entering the room, however, were five masterpieces of the hunter's skill and the taxidermist's art grouped about the fireplace. This incongru-ous collection consisted of heads of male and female African lions, a water buffalo, a rhinoceros, and in the center the hairy bust of a

huge snarling-faced gorilla. So fascinating did we find this display
that we did not hear Miss Monest come down the stairway; she
spoke to us from the bottom landing. We turned from the hideous
gorilla to a vision of dark beauty.

"I'm sorry to keep you waiting," she said, coming to us. "But
thanks to Uncle's menagerie most visitors don't mind if I do take
time to get the powder on straight."

I realized, as I glanced from her trimly bobbed black head and
heavily lashed black eyes to the soft, delicate April blue of her gown
with its dash of butter yellow, and to the graceful curve of her sheer-
stockinged legs, that she didn't need to depend on a bathing suit
at all, and I pushed the photograph a little deeper in my pocket
and pulled the flap out over it.

Steele smiled in the peculiarly charming way he has with
women. His response was as unceremonious as her greeting. It was
one of Steele's pleasant gifts to be able to adapt himself instantly
and without effort to any personality.

"They are very interesting," he said in his slow drawl, "and it's
obvious that they aren't required for a foil."

Her eyes widened naïvely, and she turned and patted the snout
of the rhinoceros. "Oh, you surely didn't expect me to need *so much*
contrast, did you?" She gave him a swift glance, her eyes lingering
appreciatively for just a fraction of a second on his curly red hair.

"You are Mr. Steven Steele, aren't you? I recognize you from
the picture that was in the paper at the time Mr. Grayland was
murdered."

She turned to Warren, whom she knew. He introduced me, then
explained, almost apologetically, what he wanted. Apparently there
was no hesitancy in her quickly expressed desire to be of service.
She asked us to be seated and took a straight-backed chair in front
of the fireplace, looking at Warren expectantly.

Warren interrogated her as he had Garnett, but after ten minutes of his questioning her answers had apparently revealed nothing of consequence. Anything in the nature of a leading question
was parried so deftly that it is doubtful if he perceived the evasion. By this I do not mean to imply that the county attorney was

not a skillful cross-examiner. He was; but he was never at his best
except when he had the authority of a court of law at his back. He
seemed ill at ease in the semilegal atmosphere of our visit and was
at a loss in not having concrete accusations to work with. The only
point of particular interest he elicited was when he asked Miss
Monest about her last visit from Loundon.

The girl answered without hesitation:

"It was the night of August fifteenth—the night before he was
killed—a little after eight o'clock. He drove up to the curb and
stopped, and then honked until I waved. Then he went on. I
couldn't go out at the time, and he didn't come in."

"Was he driving his Packard coupé?"

"Yes."

"And he was alone in the car?"

"Yes."

Warren did not pursue this line of inquiry further, and after
two or three more questions tacitly turned her over to Steele.

When Steele began I thought Miss Monest sat up a little
straighter in her chair, and her black eyes regarded him with an
expression that seemed faintly suggestive of wary defiance.

"You haven't chosen to say anything out of your personal knowledge of Mr. Loundon, Miss Monest," he said in his quiet voice, "and
if you have no wish to, I have no desire—" he paused—"unless it
should later become necessary . . . to inquire further." Her eyes
narrowed almost imperceptibly, but he seemed not to notice. "I
wonder if you would mind showing me what window you went to
when he drove up and honked the night before his death?"

For some reason Miss Monest seemed relieved at the question.
She went through the double doors to one of the drawing-room
windows and pulled aside the curtain for Steele to look out.

"I believe you said he pulled up to the curb at the sidewalk a
little past eight and honked until you appeared at the window?" he
asked.

She nodded.

"And after you waved, he drove on?"

She nodded again.

"He didn't get out of the car, and you didn't go out?"

Steele loosed the curtains.

"I'm sorry, Miss Monest, but that seems a little unusual. . . . Would you mind explaining?" She hesitated, and he added, "I know that may seem an odd request, but in a case so unusual anything that may lead to a revelation of Mr. Loundon's subsequent actions may have a vital bearing on our understanding of what happened to him. . . . He drove up here a little after eight and honked until you waved. Why didn't he come in, and why did you only wave at him?" She hesitated, then answered bluntly:

"He was drunk, and he knew that I knew it. He sometimes did that when he had been drinking. I knew he wouldn't go away until I answered."

"I believe you said he was alone in the car?" Steele asked.

"Yes."

"You say he had acted this way before. Was he always alone?"

"No. Once or twice he had others with him."

"But you are positive he was alone this time?"

"Yes. He had to lean across the empty seat to wave."

"And you say that was the last time you saw him alive?" He watched her sharply, but her answer seemed frank enough.

"Yes, that was the last time I saw him."

Steele seemed to be considering her reply. But his next question entirely changed the subject.

"You told Mr. Warren a moment ago that on the sixteenth you were in your boat alone most of the morning. Did you happen to go up the river as far as Mr. Loundon's lodge?"

Miss Monest suddenly seemed on guard again.

"No." Her black eyes looked directly into his.

"You do go up that far in your boat sometimes?"

"Oh yes! I often go up past there in the speedboat to the Straightaway."

"The Straightaway?"

"About half a mile past the lodge there's a straight stretch of water nearly two miles long that the speedboat fans call the Straightaway. It's the only place on the river where you don't have to make a turn every quarter of a mile. But the new Meridian oil field has almost spoiled it now."

"But you weren't up to the Straightaway that day?"

"No. I didn't go any farther than the bridge on the Hutchinson highway. I had the other boat. . . . I was in my bathing suit. I often go up there to swim where there aren't so many people around."

It seemed to me that Miss Monest was becoming uncomfortable under Steele's questioning. She got up and went to a small table at the right of the fireplace, where she selected a cigarette from a lacquer box and offered one to Steele. He took one, held a match for her, then slowly lit one himself, regarding her thoughtfully as she went back to her chair.

"I presume you have read the *Times'* imaginative account of the mysterious persons we surprised in Loundon's lodge." He changed the subject again in an almost facetious tone of voice. "I don't suppose you could suggest the names of persons who might have keys to the lodge?"

"No, I'm afraid I can't."

Steele smiled and thanked her. We were about to go, and Warren was clearing his throat preparatory to his official thanks, when a peculiar muffled scratching sound accompanied by an impatient chattering came from beyond one of the doors leading to the rear of the house. Miss Monest noticed our surprise and laughed.

"That's Boloney; he wants to come in," she said, going to the door.

She opened it, and a small monkey leaped in. She lifted him to her shoulder, where he perched restlessly, his tiny wrinkled countenance in grotesque contrast with her fresh exotic beauty.

"Boloney wanted to see the men, didn't he?" she asked, bringing him toward us.

Steele took a pace in her direction, and the diminutive beast thrust his head forward and lifted his lips in a savage snarl.

Steele chuckled. "Apparently Boloney doesn't want anybody to harm his mistress." Then he looked at its paws curiously. "Are you training him to be a boxer?"

The monkey's forepaws were encased in little leather mittens comically resembling boxing gloves. Miss Monest explained with a laugh:

"We have to keep his fingers tied when he is out of his cage. He scratches the furniture and gets into things. . . . Besides," she addressed the monkey again, "you are always pulling Choo Choo's hair and making him mad, aren't you?"

"Choo Choo?" Warren involuntarily exclaimed.

"Choo Choo is our chow dog, and he doesn't like Boloney."

"I take it your uncle likes to keep animals as well as kill them," Warren observed. "Does he have many on the place?"

Despite a slight shadow of annoyance which passed over Steele's face at this question, he watched the girl intently as she answered.

"Oh, he'd make it a regular zoo! But Boloney and Choo Choo are all we have now."

Warren had no more questions, and after an awkward silence he thanked her and we started to leave. Then the monkey began chattering excitedly, jumping about on her shoulder. From beyond the door we heard another muffled scratching sound, louder and heavier, and a deep grumbling whine, and what sounded like the clank of a heavy chain. Miss Monest glanced swiftly about, then put Boloney down and let us out. As I looked back through the half-open door and saw her dark face framed against the fireplace with its gargoylish circle of bestial heads, I could easily imagine her as a ravishing Circe in the depths of some jungle kingdom.

For several moments after we got in the car the spell of her singular personality kept us silent. Finally I spoke up: "That girl could crash Hollywood in a flannel nightgown!" For some reason this observation seemed to annoy Warren exceedingly.

"Can't you keep your mind off nightgowns and bathing suits?" he asked. "No wonder you're a Sunday magazine editor!"

Steele frowned at me with a reproving chuckle.

"Not to change the subject," he interposed, "I confess I should very much like to know what was going on in that girl's head. . . . And I am looking forward to meeting her sportsman uncle. She was concealing something, that's certain; but what, I can't even make a good guess."

For the time being, however, Steele was to be disappointed. When we reached the club we were informed that Mr. Juan Monest

had been unavoidably detained, that he expressed his sincere regret, and that he would telephone the county attorney later for
another appointment. Our interest in the Spaniard had been whet-
ted by the interview with his niece, and I am sure Steele regretted
the postponement of our meeting as much as Warren. But the
county attorney was particularly provoked at what he seemed to
consider a lack of proper respect for his office. I believe he would
have attempted to run down the irreverent Juan then and there
had not the unexpected appearance of Sheriff Burke distracted him.

The sheriff had come into the lobby while we were talking with
the clerk at the desk. He wore the humid look of a fat man in a
hurry, and when he saw us his eyes lighted up excitedly. As he
strode across the floor toward Warren his bearing was unmistak-
ably that of a man who is just on the point of delivering a message
to Garcia.

7

SHERIFF BURKE PULLED Warren out of earshot of the clerk at the desk. Then, with a triumphant glance at Steele, he announced:

"Well, I guess we've got a lead at last; and it ain't any orangutan, either. The dame that got away from you birds out at the lodge last night was Mrs. Herbert Vernon."

Our astonishment was undoubtedly an immense gratification to the sheriff. I whistled expressively, and the county attorney looked incredulous. "Mrs. Vernon!" he ejaculated. "Not Dr. Vernon's wife?"

"Mrs. Dr. Herbert Vernon!" Burke asserted, with an emphasis on every syllable.

I explained our amazement to Steele.

"Dr. Vernon is our leading surgeon, and Mrs. Vernon is among the society arbiters. He's a stiff-necked domineering devil, but she's about the most popular young matron in Wichita. I'd say she's fifteen or twenty years younger than he is. If this is true it's worth a three-column head on the first page. . . . You're sure there's no mistake, Sheriff?"

"Absolutely not!" Burke scorned the thought and proceeded to enlighten us.

"When the boys reported that they had found your car at the Emsberg Lumber Company yard I went out to see if I couldn't find somebody who might give me some dope. You see, I figured that if they hadn't left a car of their own there they would have driven the *Times'* car back to town. The Emsberg people said they closed at five o'clock and that there wasn't any car there when they quit. Two or three of the other offices in the neighborhood told me the same thing. But finally I went to the bird who runs a root-beer joint about half a block away—'The Jug' he calls it: his stand is built in the shape of a big jug—and he says Yes, he remembers a man and a woman coming out of the Emsberg yard a little after dark and getting into a blue Buick sedan which had been parked in front of a little house across from his place. He knew it was a doctor's car because it had a green doctor's insignia on the radiator, and he wondered if somebody was sick across the way. He didn't think anything more of it until I began asking him questions, and then he remembered the woman climbing in behind the wheel on the left side. His place is pretty well lit up, and he could see her, but whoever it was with her got in on the other side, and he couldn't describe him. Of course it wasn't any trouble when I got back to town to find out what doctor owns a blue Buick sedan. Dr. Vernon is the only one, and since this root-beer man's description fits Mrs. Vernon I put two and two together, and—"

"You made four out of it, didn't you?" Steele finished for him. "And a prompt piece of work, too—providing you don't try to make it add up to ten!"

"What do you mean by that, Steele?" the county attorney challenged somewhat testily. "If Mrs. Vernon and this man who was with her left the *Times'* car in the lumberyard, it's pretty good evidence that they're the ones who were in the lodge. And if they were in the lodge," he concluded grimly, "it's evidence enough to me that they had something to do with this murder."

"Exactly! Four and four already make eight!" Steele observed ironically. "The Vernon car may have been stolen or borrowed, for I gather this root-beer vendor only caught a glimpse of a woman in a dim light, which is far from identification. Second, they were not seen to leave the *Times'* car. Third, as I said last night, nobody but a fool—or an exceedingly desperate person—would remain on the scene of a murder ten hours after he had committed it, and when he must have known the officers of the law were in the vicinity." He turned to the sheriff, who had been listening with growing antagonism. "I suppose you haven't questioned the Vernons?"

"Oh no!" Burke replied with weighty sarcasm. "I wouldn't think of doing that. . . . I let the county attorney handle all our social affairs!"

Steele dropped a conciliatory hand on the sheriff's shoulder.

"Well, Burke, thanks to you we've got a line that may lead to something—if not just what I'd hoped." He deliberated a moment. "You say the Emsberg people said there was no car at their place at five? Did you ask the root-beer proprietor how long the doctor's Buick had been standing across the street?"

"Yes," Burke replied promptly, "and he said he didn't know when it was left there. But he was sure it wasn't there before five-thirty or thereabouts."

"If they left their car there they would have cut across to the lodge on the path that leads to the footbridge?"

"Yes. At the south end of the Meridian pool."

"Nearly half an hour's walk for a woman," Steele reflected. "And I presume you questioned the people who live in the house where the Buick was parked?"

"There wasn't anybody home."

"Well—" Steele abruptly changed the subject—"now that you've traced one car, have you been able to learn anything about the car that was parked at the lodge? The one with the tracks of the animal about it?"

Burke shook his head. "Three new Firestone tires and one that looks like a United States, pretty well worn. . . . I've got a man on it, but I'm afraid it's no use."

"Don't let him quit too soon. Even if it probably is a spare, that one worn tire has possibilities."

Warren had been obviously irritated by Steele's comments. It was plain that he did not propose to substitute a wild-goose chase for what he considered a fresh and important clue.

"I think the sooner we check up on Mrs. Vernon the better," he declared. "I'm going to call up now and make an appointment to see her."

Without permitting further chance for argument he strode toward the telephone booths, which stood in an alcove off the lounge room. For a moment I thought Steele would stop him, but apparently he thought better of it. In only a few minutes, however, Warren came out of the booth with disappointment on his face.

"Out of town," he reported succinctly. "Be back tomorrow night."

"And the doctor?" Steele inquired with an interest which belied his previous indifference.

"He has been in Kansas City for nearly a week—or so they say."

"And did you learn where Mrs. Vernon is?"

"I didn't ask."

Steele lit a cigarette and turned away to the large window overlooking Market Street. For several minutes he smoked in silence, gazing thoughtfully up at the hot blue August sky. Then he turned back to us.

"Sarge," he addressed me, "I wonder if one of the *Times'* society reporters couldn't give us some help. Have you got one you can trust?"

"The first thing a society reporter learns," I stated, perhaps somewhat sententiously, "is that if she can't print it she doesn't know it—except confidentially."

"Apparently you think that is an answer to my question." He shrugged his shoulders. "Anyway, if one of these feminine paragons could find out where Mrs. Vernon is I'd like to know. . . But what I particularly want is as complete a personal history—printable or unprintable—as it is possible to secure."

"You shall have something," I assured him, "or I mistake my gals."

Steele turned to Warren. "Are you willing to leave it that way for the time being, Warren? We don't want to make any inquiries that will arouse suspicion."

The county attorney hesitated, then acquiesced with unexpected affability. "Sounds like a good idea to me. . . . And in the meantime—" he looked at his watch—"we've still got time to call on Ripley. He told me he could see us after three-thirty."

When we were in the car again Steele lapsed into another period of thoughtful silence. Not until we were over a mile past the city limits did he withdraw his unseeing eyes from the speeding landscape and turn to Warren.

"What does your little black book say on the subject of this next prospect?" he asked.

Warren consulted it.

"Not much," he said. "Charles Ward Ripley, age thirty-four, unmarried; lives at Town Club. Was a friend of Loundon's in the air service. Came to Wichita three years ago from Louisiana, and with Loundon's and Garnett's help organized the Dragonfly Aircraft Company. Loundon was principal stockholder and president. Ripley is vice-president, general manager and chief designer. Planes have been successful, and the company has excellent prospects."

Steele turned to me. "Have you got anything indecent to add?"

"Nothing; except that I understand he and Garnett don't always agree on everything. I've met Ripley a couple of times. He and Loundon were boys together in Louisiana. You met him that time at Loundon's party at the lodge. He put on that trick act, burlesquing Loundon and Monest attempting to sell each other an oil lease."

"Yes. I remember him. Pretty clever. So . . . he and Garnett don't hit it off?"

"That's what our oil reporter tells me."

"I suppose we are seeing him because he would have profited by Loundon's death?" Steel asked Warren. "That's always a good idea. The trouble is we already have about as many motives as are good for us!"

"Yes," Warren replied; "and also because, with the possible exception of Garnett, Ripley knew Loundon better than anybody else. I knew Garnett wouldn't talk, but we ought to be able to learn something from Ripley."

The Dragonfly plant was five miles south of town. When we were shown into the office we found in Charles Ripley a round-faced, unprepossessing young man who appeared anxious to tell us everything he knew so he could get back to work. His chief personal characteristic was a broad Southern accent. His office was a heterogeneous collection of chairs, desks, drawing boards, airplane fabrics and motor parts. The desk from which he arose was a litter of papers, plans and blueprints. Nearly all the chairs were like-wise covered. After brushing the contents of one chair to the floor he gave it up and led us into an adjoining room. This was a neat, well-appointed office furnished with a large glass-covered flat-top desk and five or six leather-cushioned chairs.

"This was Mr. Loundon's private office," he said. "I guess we might as well use it."

Warren took what had been Loundon's chair at the desk. Bluntly, as was his wont, he commenced the interrogation.

"I understand, Mr. Ripley, that Loundon had been out here a good deal just before his death. . . . What had he been doing? . . . Is it true that he had been drinking heavily?"

In some way I sensed that Ripley resented Warren's assumption of Loundon's chair and the tactless manner of his beginning, but he answered without any trace of acerbity.

"Yes, he had; he hadn't been exactly sober for a week. He hadn't been in shape to do anything. As near as I could see he came out here as a good place to sit around and mope."

"Do you know any reason for that?"

"No; except that he'd been losing a lot of money."

"No personal reasons you know of? A love affair? Trouble with friends, or anything like that?"

Ripley frowned. "No."

"Not Miss Monest—or Garnett?"

Steele began to fidget under Warren's bluntness. Ripley's re-action was plainly antagonistic.

"Well, I don't know what you know and it wasn't my business, but I think there was a little of both."

"When was Garnett out here with Loundon last?"

"The afternoon before he was killed. . . . Loundon was pretty drunk, and Garnett was trying to get him to go to the lodge for a while to sober up. Loundon finally said he'd go the next morning—more, I thought, to get rid of Garnett than anything else. Garnett left shortly after that, but Loundon stayed around all the rest of the afternoon and drove me back to town about seven-thirty."

"I suppose he had sobered up some by that time?

Ripley shook his head with a rueful laugh. "No; he had a flask with him and got worse. I didn't want to go with him, especially when he insisted on driving the car back to town himself."

"Was that the last you saw of him?"

"No—well, yes it was too. He called me up about nine that evening, but that was the last time I saw him. He dropped me at the club and said he would be back; that he was going out to see Miss Monest a minute."

Warren nodded. "That's when he honked in front of her house. . . . You didn't see him at all the day he was killed?"

"No. I left the club about eight in the morning and got to the plant about eight-twenty. I was busy with some new designs and didn't leave here until I got word he was dead. . . . He called from a pay station a few minutes before nine that morning to say he wouldn't be down. . . . That's the last I heard from him."

Although Steele had sat with his chair tilted back against the wall, I was aware from the glitter of his eyes below their half-closed lids that he was following the interview with the keenest attention. He dropped the chair legs softly to the floor and leaned forward toward Ripley.

"You say Loundon called you about nine the night before," he repeated. "Do you mind telling what he wanted?"

There was a shade of perturbation in Ripley's hesitation. "It was pretty hard to tell at first just what he did want," he said at last. "He seemed pretty drunk. . . . But I finally understood he had just called me up to say he didn't think he would come to the plant the next day." The young man paused reluctantly again. "He said he was going to the lodge to sober up, and that Mr. Garnett and Miss Monest were going too."

"Ah!" Steele seemed to receive this piece of unexpected information with satisfaction. "They were going too?"

"That's what he said. He said he had talked to them on the phone—and promised to sober up—if they would come out."

Steele slowly and absent-mindedly hitched himself back against the wall again. His eyes took on a faraway look, and he began thrusting his unusually mobile underlip forward and backward as was his habit when perplexed. Finally he turned back to Ripley with a troubled look on his face.

"You told Mr. Warren a moment ago that Garnett was trying to get Loundon to go to the lodge the afternoon they were here together."

"Yes."

"And Loundon later told you he had asked both Garnett and Miss Monest to go?"

"Yes."

"Why should Loundon have wanted Garnett and Miss Monest there together? . . . I wish there were some way to verify those telephone calls. Neither of them mentioned any such conversation."

"I'm afraid you couldn't do that," Ripley began. Then he stopped. "Say, you might, though!" he exclaimed. "I recall the operator at the club usually put his calls through for him—especially if he had several at a time—and it might be she would remember, he was so drunk at the time!"

Steele looked at Ripley a long moment and then turned to Warren.

"There's something for your little black book," he said. "And unless I'm mistaken—" he spoke slowly—"there's a lot depends on what you learn. If Garnett and Miss Monest were asked to visit the lodge. . . ."

Steele's voice trailed off into a thoughtful silence. Warren meticulously made rapid notes in his book, as if he feared the facts would lose their importance unless they were immediately recorded. Before he had finished Steele asked:

"Do you know if Loundon carried much insurance?"

Ripley received the question with a grim smile. "Insurance!" He repeated the word with a shrug of the shoulders. "He was the target for all the insurance men in town! Just a minute, and I'll show you." He stepped to the door and spoke to a girl in the outer office. In a moment she brought Ripley a typewritten sheet, which he handed to Steele.

"Here's a list of what he was carrying. It's practically all company insurance, to protect the firms he was interested in, or associates in his oil operations." He pointed to the figures. "There's

$100,000 in favor of Garnett, to cover his loans; here's $100,000 in favor of the Dragonfly plant; this $100,000 is payable to Juan Monest, though it reads Rockbed Oil Company. . . . You can see who the other beneficiaries are. Altogether it comes to over $500,000. Some of his companies were having difficulty keeping up the premiums, and he had this list made to see what he could cancel."

"Oh!" Steele pursed his lips and read through the list again. "So he was planning to cancel some of it!" He studied the items carefully as if to fix them in his memory. In a moment he looked up. "I see only one woman on the list. Who is Lola Van Roth?"

"His divorced wife. He married her in El Dorado before the war. They never lived together after he came back from France."

"Hm-m. Any relation to the Reverend Raymond Van Roth?"

"His daughter. She's been living in Chicago, but I think she's been visiting her father for a month or two. I never have met her."

Steele referred to the list again. "I see she would receive $50,000. I don't suppose you know if she had seen him, or if he planned to discontinue her policy?"

Ripley shook his head. "I never heard him mention her name in the three years I have been in Wichita. And I don't think he had made up his mind what to do about any of the policies."

Steele handed the list back and took up his hat. Warren lingered to express his thanks again—for a politician he was a most curious combination of bluntness and courtesy—and joined us at the car. During the ride back to town Steele had not a word to say. He sat beside me in the rear seat with his hat in his lap, staring out of the window with a half-frown between his eyes, and occasionally drumming with his fingers on the glass. At first Warren attempted to discuss the case with him, but the absent-minded replies he received in answer soon discouraged him.

Only when Warren let us out at my apartment did Steele make any comment. He stood on the curb with one foot on the running board of the car, still holding his hat, and now and then making that thoughtful pass through his red hair.

"Warren," he said at last, "those telephone calls have got to be checked, and we can do it only by interviewing the telephone operator who handled them for Loundon. If you have time you might stop at the club and find out if she will be on duty tonight. If she is, give us a ring and we'll meet you there sometime after seven." He dropped his foot to the ground and put on his hat. "I think that's all. Except—" and the puzzled frown came to his face again—"except, if you have a good man, get him ready to make a quick trip to El Dorado." And he added slowly, "I'm beginning to think that before we can get anywhere we're going to have to know a lot more than we do about Loundon's past."

Warren, I was aware from past experience with his forthright mind, was still pinning his hope on connecting Mrs. Vernon and her mysterious companion with the visitors we had encountered at the lodge. What had seemed to me only a cursory interest in our interview with Ripley, I assigned to the same cause. But he had too much respect for Steele's judgment not to accede to his requests, even when he could not justify them by his own interpretation of the facts.

"I've got the very man," he agreed. "Hale Ferguson, my assistant. He used to live in El Dorado."

"He lived there, eh? A lawyer, too! Maybe he could give us some information now. Next to a newspaperman—" Steele gave me a sardonic look—"there's nobody knows so much gossip as a small-town lawyer—and ordinarily he doesn't know so much that isn't so. . . . I wonder if you'd get in touch with him and have him call me up?"

Warren consulted his watch. "It's past five, and he's probably gone home. But if he isn't playing golf I think I can have him call you within half an hour."

Having made this concession, Warren suddenly leaned toward us out of the car with one of those rare, uninhibited smiles that displayed his innate attractiveness.

"I want to tell you, Steele, how much I appreciate your interest." He paused as if he had already said more than he intended, then added hurriedly, "You both have to eat; why don't you come over to the club about seven, whether the girl is there or not, and have dinner with me?"

"Why not?" Steele accepted, after consulting me with an inquiring glance. "Then we can have the telephone girl for dessert."

8

IT TURNED OUT that the telephone operator was an appetizer instead of dessert. Warren was nearly twenty minutes late, and while we were waiting for him we learned that the girl who had operated the club switchboard up to midnight on the night of August 15 was then on duty, but would be relieved at eight. Steele waited until the county attorney arrived, then questioned her at the switchboard inside the office enclosure during intervals when she was not plugging in or jerking down connections.

Although her bright hazel eyes were not unmindful of Steele's smiling good looks and tall trim figure, her answers were brisk and businesslike. She had been employed at the club only about a month, she said. She had known Loundon; he had passed the time of day with her and had joked with her at the desk several times. She distinctly remembered the telephone calls in question. She had jotted down the names on a pad and had a clear recollection of the circumstances. She still had the pad; in fact, was still using it on the board. She thumbed back through the leaves until she found the names, then she folded it over and handed it to Steele.

When Steele had studied it a moment he pointed to the telephone number opposite Miss Monest's name.

"How does it happen you don't have Ripley's and Garnett's numbers?"

"They live here at the club."

"Oh, of course." He glanced at some of the other leaves in the pad and inspected the names again. "I see you had to look up Miss

Monest's number in the directory. I should think Loundon would have given it to you."

"Well, maybe he was too drunk. . . ." The girl stopped, and a surprised look came over her face. "Say," she demanded, "how did you know I looked it up?"

He smiled at her perplexed expression.

"If he had given you the number you would have steadied the pad with your left hand while you wrote with the other. When you have to look the numbers up—as you did just a moment ago—you hold the directory with your left hand, with your forefinger at the number, while you write on the elusive pad with your right hand. For that reason, as you will observe by glancing through these other pages, some of your numbers are neat and fluent, while others are cramped and irregular. . . . So I surmised that Loundon hadn't given you the number and that you had looked it up in the directory yourself."

The girl snatched up the pad and examined some of the entries; then she slowly looked up. "Gosh" she exclaimed admiringly, "I didn't even know that myself!"

Steele looked down at her quizzically. "You do a thousand tricks a day that you're not aware of." He picked up the pad again. "You started to say that Loundon was too drunk to give you the number. Wasn't he able to remember it?"

"I didn't mean that." She shook her head. "He didn't try to give me the number, he just gave me the names. But he was so drunk that it was all I could do to even understand them. I've seen him drunk before, but, boy! I never— Hey, hey, John! Come here a minute!"

She had broken off to halt a colored porter who was going past the desk with a pitcher of ice water.

"Come in here a minute, John." He came to us, and she said, "He was still drunk the next morning, wasn't he, John? Mr. Loundon, I mean," she explained; "he was still drunk when you took him up the ice water."

John's grinning mouth drooped suddenly, and he nodded his head in vehement affirmation.

"Yas 'm; he sho was!"

Steele appeared interested. "Wasn't he able to get out of bed?"

"Yes suh; he was out of bed, all right. But what I mean, he was in the bathroom and so drunk it was all I could do to understand him when he tol' me to put the ice water on the dresser. That made him mad, and he cussed me out and called me a lazy nigger, and said get the hell outa there. But, you understand—" and the porter wagged his head—"I didn't mind that. He was from the South, and he always was that way to all the colored folks when he was drinking."

"But he didn't offer to do anything to you?"

"No suh," John grinned; "I didn't wait to let him see me! But he wouldn't anyway; that was just his way."

"Were there any bottles on the dresser?"

"Yes suh."

"What kind?"

"Gin mostly, I think they was. Some ginger ale, too. I don't know if they was any whisky there or not."

"Nothing else? There weren't any that looked like medicine bottles?"

"No suh. I don't remember if they was any."

Steele thanked the porter and dismissed him.

When he turned back to the girl his face wore a deep frown, and his fingers played an absent-minded tattoo on the top of the mahogany-stained switchboard. Then his eyes narrowed, and in a moment he nodded to himself as if in assent to some inward conclusion.

"Now of course, Miss—ah—Miss—"

"Lathrop." The girl supplied her name with an eager smile.

"Of course, Miss Lathrop, I don't want to question your ethics, but I wonder if by accident you happened to overhear any of these conversations?"

The girl shrugged her shoulders, unoffended, but shook her head.

"No sir, I didn't."

"Do you remember if Miss Monest and Mr. Garnett both answered the telephone in person?"

Miss Lathrop hesitated, adjusted her head-set, looked at her pad as if it might help refresh her memory, then answered, "I can't be sure, but I think they both did."

"There is no question in your mind that he finally talked with them both?"

She shook her head positively. "No sir. I'm sure he talked with both of them."

"Thank you." The appreciative smile Steele gave her brought a swift response to the girl's lips and a faint touch of color to her cheeks above the rouge. "You have helped us immensely."

We left her and went upstairs to the dining room. When the waiter had taken our orders Warren turned curiously to Steele.

"What I'd like to know," he said, "is why you asked that porter if he saw any medicine bottles in Loundon's room. You weren't thinking of drugs—or poison—were you?"

Steele lifted his shoulders in a Latinlike gesture. "No, not exactly. But you never know. Before you came this evening I asked the clerk if anything of the kind had been found in Loundon's room. There hadn't; but I thought possibly the porter might have noticed something which Loundon could have disposed of later." He dipped a lump of sugar in his ice water and put it in his mouth. "Everyone who talked with Loundon has stated that he was intoxicated almost to incoherence. Now no doubt it was the gin; yet it's uncommon for a man on even such an intensive spree as Loundon's to be so far gone at seven-thirty in the morning. But here're our cocktails, such as they are in Kansas! And no healthy man ever mixes murders with his meals!"

When the table had finally been cleared, Warren reverted to the problem which was uppermost in his mind.

"Why do you suppose neither Garnett nor Miss Monest mentioned these telephone conversations with Loundon?" he demanded as soon as he had got his cigar well lighted.

"You ask some very nice questions," Steele replied, selecting a cigarette and tapping it absently on the case. "You are like the would-be ballade maker who ended his second line with the word 'silver'—there aren't any rhymes to answer you with." He chuckled.

"And by way of ending a sentence with a preposition; did you ever hear of the boy who used five prepositions to end a sentence with?"

There was a hint of annoyance behind Warren's polite smile. But he had learned that Steele would talk in his own good time and no other, and he summoned his patience to listen.

"This little boy was ill," Steele went on, "and his father had brought home a book which his mother read aloud to him. The story, however, didn't please him, and when his father came home in the evening the boy complained. 'Say, Dad,' he demanded, 'why did you bring me home that book to be read to out of from for?'"

I laughed, and even Warren smiled.

Steele lit his cigarette. "Now this case ends with a lot of prepositions. When you stop to analyze them they don't make sense. But—" and he blew out a cloud of smoke—"I think if we could say 'em all together rapidly in the right order we'd find that they also have a meaning. The trouble is, this is about the way it reads now: 'Why did you bring me that book to be read of for from to out?' . . . It's a jumble; and if Miss Monest and Garnett did as Loundon evidently requested and went to the lodge the next morning, in my opinion it just adds a couple more prepositions."

Warren looked bewildered. "You mean, you don't think we can prove it?"

"No," Steele said slowly, "I believe you can!"

The county attorney's bewilderment thickened. "You don't think they were the two who were at the lodge that evening?"

"In Dr. Vernon's Buick?" Steele countered. "I think they both mentioned alibis for that evening. . . . At least Garnett said he was at the office when he got the news of Loundon's death, and Miss Monest was at home."

"Well, what *do* you think?" Warren demanded. "You surely don't put any credence in this furry animal that Burke is so agitated about?"

"About!" Steele laughed tantalizingly. "There's another preposition to put at the end of our sentence! If 'about' equals a hairy reptile, then we grammarians are cuckoo!" He gazed thoughtfully at Warren without seeing him, until he suddenly observed that the county attorney was becoming angry. He dropped his bantering manner immediately. "Forgive me," he apologized; "what I really think is that, so far, we can be sure of nothing—and by the same token we cannot be sure anything's impossible. I might hazard a few guesses, but there you are. Tomorrow—"

Steele stopped, his eyes looking past me toward the dining-room entrance. I was about to turn to see what had caught his attention when he dropped his hand on Warren's arm.

"The Reverend Raymond Dwight Van Roth," he said; "Loundon's ex-father-in-law. Warren, do you know him well enough to inveigle him into conversation? Your able assistant, Hale Ferguson, told me some extremely interesting facts about the Van Roth family over the telephone this evening. I'm inclined to think that an interview with this corpulent parson would be decidedly illuminating."

Warren was not a man to make quick decisions, particularly if they involved unexpected personal contacts. He hesitated, eying the rotund figure in the doorway, until Steele's urgent hand on his arm persuaded him against his inclination.

"Why yes—I guess so—that is, I'm fairly well acquainted with him." He got up, paused uncertainly, and then said, "Wait a minute; I'll see if he's busy. He doesn't seem to be going to eat."

"He'll eat if you offer him something!" Steele advised as Warren left. To me he added, "Boys of the Reverend Raymond's build are always willing to take on a little extra nourishment!"

We watched the county attorney's awkwardly cordial salutation and Van Roth's unctuous handshake.

"Two hundred and sixty-five pounds on the hoof," Steele observed, "and I'll bet you two to one I can induce him to eat a piece of custard pie à la mode, disgusting as it sounds."

"A dollar," I assented. "It would be worth it."

There seemed to be some momentary objection on Van Roth's part, but in a minute or two Warren returned, piloting the minister past the intervening chairs and tables as a tugboat brings an ocean liner to dock. Steele was on his feet and shook the pudgy hand like a courtier. Van Roth lowered himself into a creaking chair, and Steele, after motioning to our waiter, resumed his seat with the smile of a delighted host.

"We have just finished," he apologized as the waiter came up, "but you really must have some of the custard pie they have this evening. I've never tasted better!" He nodded to the waiter. "A piece of custard pie for Dr. Van Roth." And ignoring the clergyman's feeble protestations, he added, "Make it à la mode!"

"Really, I shouldn't let you . . ." Van Roth began.

"Oh yes, you must!" Steele insisted. "Your wonderful talks over the radio deserve more than one custard pie!"

The minister beamed at this extremely ambiguous compliment. I had to turn my head away lest he perceive my reaction to this bland pertinacity. But Steele was incorrigible.

"I had to miss the one last Sunday. . . . But there's hardly a week that I don't tune in!"

"These vast audiences of the air—" Van Roth was as voracious of praise as a prima donna and as easily flattered to pomposity— "these vast audiences of the air are an inestimable inspiration!"

"I should think they must be," Steele agreed warmly. "But here comes your pie!"

As Van Roth adjusted his napkin over his huge paunch and picked up his fork Steele turned toward me and elevated his eyebrows. I sighed, took out my pocketbook and extracted a dollar bill. He took it from me with a fish-cold eye, which softened to benevolence as he again turned it upon our guest. He listened attentively to a dissertation on religious broadcasting until the pie and ice cream had disappeared. Then, taking up a knife and balancing it as if, I remarked grimly to myself, it were a scalpel, he suddenly changed the subject.

"Dr. Van Roth," he observed in a mild voice, "I have been helping Mr. Warren investigate the circumstances surrounding the death of Ralph Loundon. We have just learned today that your daughter Lola married him in 1917, when you were living in El Dorado. I wonder if you know anything of his past life that might assist us?"

At these words the comfortable smile which had wreathed Van Roth's face instantly faded. A swift alarm came into his eyes. He nervously moistened his full lips.

"Why—ah—really, I—" He at last forced a meaningless smile. "Yes, my daughter was married to Mr. Loundon for about a year. But it was a mistake. A serious mistake. They were divorced almost immediately. I'm sure I don't know anything that would help you."

"You knew there is a $50,000-insurance policy in favor of your daughter?"

"No!" The clergyman's surprise seemed genuine. "I did not know that!"

"You didn't!" Steele's eyes narrowed at the response. "That's very strange. . . . She is living with you now, isn't she?"

"Yes, temporarily."

"And she has said nothing about such a policy since Loundon's death?"

"No!"

Again Van Roth's denial was positive, and the tone of his voice indicated a growing reassurance.

"Hm-m-m!" Steele drew a reflective circle on the tablecloth with the knife blade. "Extraordinary! It would almost seem she didn't want you to know it, wouldn't it?" He slowly inscribed a cross within the circle, and then looked up abruptly. "I understand you left El Dorado immediately after Loundon helped you out of the difficulty you had in connection with the church finances?"

Consternation seized the minister's fat face. Twice he opened his mouth to speak but made no answer. Knowing what Steele was coming to I could not help pitying his dismay. As the color came and went in his face Steele leaned over the table and looked him squarely in the eyes. Then, emphasizing each word with the knife, he said:

"What were you and your son, Jack, doing at Loundon's lodge the morning he was killed?"

For a moment I thought Van Roth would collapse. His eyes filled with terror, and his mouth sagged open. The county attorney was hardly less astounded. He gazed speechlessly from one to the other, and then he turned on Steele sharply.

"What do you mean by that!" he exclaimed. "If that's true why didn't you tell me?"

Steele held up his hand. His eyes were still on the minister.

"Well, what have you to say?"

Van Roth shook his head.

"Nothing," he at last managed to murmur. "Nothing; except that we were not at the lodge."

"You were seen on Loundon's footbridge about eight-thirty. What were you doing there?"

"I cannot tell you." A faint note of defiance had crept into Van Roth's voice. "I assure you I don't know anything about Mr. Loundon's death." He spread out his hands appealingly. "My visit there had nothing to do with Mr. Loundon. But I can't tell you now why I was there."

Warren had listened with mounting suspicion. He brushed aside Van Roth's answer and the almost convincing sincerity of his voice.

"Well, you'll tell!" he declared. "If you won't tell now you'll explain to a jury!"

Van Roth looked despairingly at Steele, hoping against hope to be believed. Steele poured a glass of water and sipped it thoughtfully. At last he answered the clergyman's unspoken appeal.

"Mr. Warren is right, Dr. Van Roth. You were seen on the premises the morning of Loundon's death, and you cannot hope to escape suspicion. Your best explanation, if you are not guilty, is the truth, no matter how embarrassing. Of course anything you tell us that has no bearing on the crime will be held in confidence."

Steele's reassurance seemed to have more effect than the county attorney's threat. Van Roth's terrified eyes looked from one to another as if to read in their faces the answers he should make. Finally he slumped in his chair and spread his fat hands hopelessly on the table in front of him.

"We were not on the premises." There was almost a sob in his voice as he began. "We went no farther than the bridge. . . . I was looking for my daughter, Lola!"

"Your daughter!" Warren ejaculated.

"Yes, his daughter," Steele affirmed. "I knew that, too, but I wanted to see if he intended to tell us." He turned to Van Roth. "I know more than you think; now tell us exactly what took place."

Once more the minister had to swallow his consternation before he could speak.

"Well, when my son Jack found out that my daughter had spent the night in Loundon's lodge he warned me that if she— You see, if she were seen there it would create a scandal, and I, well, you understand that in my position I could not afford anything of the kind. I told him I would drive out. I didn't know he was coming too. I left my car on the Meridian highway and walked across. When I—"

"Why didn't you drive directly to the lodge?" Steele snapped.

Startled at the interruption, Van Roth stammered, "Well, you see, I didn't want—that is, I didn't know who else might be there, and I didn't want to call attention to myself."

For what seemed a full minute Steele stared at the minister without a word. Then he signed him to continue.

"When I got to the bridge—"

"When you got to the bridge you met your daughter leaving," Steele supplied. "You never really crossed the bridge. You are not implicated in the affair at all. And neither is your son, Jack. You do not know what your daughter was doing there. . . . This is what you were going to say, isn't it?"

Van Roth nodded chokingly.

"Very well. Perhaps you do know why your daughter slapped both your faces when she learned you had come to the lodge to get her!"

Steele's apparent omniscience increased Van Roth's agitation. But his answer, nevertheless, bore the ring of truth.

"Because she said she did not want us meddling in her affairs."

"Didn't you know that would be her attitude?"

"Yes; but I—you see, the scandal—"

"Yes, I see," and there was a touch of irony in Steele's voice which I could not understand. "And then what happened?"

"She refused to ride back to town with either of us. She waited for the interurban."

"How do you know she went back?"

"I drove slowly and saw her pass."

"You feared she might go back to the lodge again?"

"No. I just wanted to make sure she had left."

"You have no idea, then, why she spent the night in the lodge?"

"No." He hesitated. "That is, I think it had something to do with a play she was writing."

Steele paused, as if waiting to see whether Van Roth would volunteer any further information. When it became apparent that he would say nothing of his own accord Steele turned him over to Warren. The county attorney questioned him thoroughly on every point, but the clergyman's replies supplied no additional facts. At last Warren let him go, with a warning to keep in touch with the county attorney's office.

As he got heavily to his feet Steele said, "Dr. Van Roth, if you can get in touch with your son and daughter I wish you would have them call me immediately. I'll be here at the club until ten o'clock."

Van Roth turned, leaning on the back of the chair in which he had been sitting.

"I am expecting my daughter to call for me here. She may be downstairs now. I suppose you could talk with her when she comes. I don't know whether I can reach my son. . . . He doesn't live at home any more." There was a certain pathos in the consternation on the minister's round face. "Where do you want to see my daughter when she comes?"

"We'll come down to the lounge room," said Warren, getting up. "There will be a quiet corner there this time of the evening."

"Very well."

Van Roth preceded us out of the room. As he slowly waddled around the intervening tables all its wonted dignity had departed from his corpulent figure.

9

WHEN WE HAD found seats in the lounge room, which was unoccupied except for two men playing chess at the south end, Warren turned to Steele with an eagerness that was half reproach.

"How did you know all this about Van Roth?" he demanded. "Why hadn't you told me?"

Steele held up a mollifying hand. "I was just going to tell you when Van Roth himself appeared. Your assistant, Hale Ferguson, told me everything you heard. The Van Roth history he already knew. The incident at the bridge had just been told to him by an oil-field worker who thought it might have a bearing on the murder. Ferguson tried to reach you, but you had already left the office. Since you had told him to call me he gave me the details and asked me to tell you. A bright boy, that Ferguson; he's going somewhere, or I miss my guess."

"Did he tell you anything about Jack Van Roth?"

"Enough to indicate that he's a pretty black sheep. But he didn't have a very bright report about the parson, either. It seems he was pastor of an El Dorado church that owned land on which oil was found, and mismanaged or misappropriated funds to the extent of $20,000. This was about the time Loundon married his daughter, and his new son-in-law made good the deficit. It must have been kept pretty quiet, or he'd never be able to pose now as the radio evangelist. . . . But what do you know about his son, Jack? I'm interested in this boy. Among his other accomplishments, I understand, he is city handball champion and the town's best semipro baseball pitcher. I have a premonition he'll never permit us to interview him."

"I suspected him of handball," I put in. Steele had taken up the game again, and in spite of the hot weather had been demonstrating his old form to some of the club's best players.

"Well, I don't suppose I know as much as the newspapers," Warren retorted with a glance at me, still a little out of humor. "He's been in a number of minor scrapes, but he hasn't ever been convicted of anything serious so far as I know. I understand he's connected with the Sargo bootlegging outfit, though I don't imagine he's any more than an errand boy. However, the sheriff tells me Loundon got most of his liquor through him. Did Ferguson know anything specific?"

Steele shook his head. "Nothing more than that. But the lieutenant here tells me that the local police had young Van Roth up for questioning in an Oklahoma kidnapping case about six months ago. They let him go. Apparently they couldn't force him to talk, if he did know anything. The interesting point, however, is that he got Loundon to come down and intercede for him."

"Did Loundon do that?" Warren turned to me in astonishment.

"Yes," I told him; "I got that straight from our city-hall man, Walt Douglas. But he didn't want to do it, and he didn't have any arguments; just put it up to the chief as a personal favor. Now that wasn't like Loundon. What I'm wondering is, did Jack have something on Loundon?"

Warren frowned and looked at Steele.

"If we don't hear from him tonight maybe we'd better get the chief to get out a pick-up order for him. What do you think, Steele?"

"I doubt very much if you hear from him; in fact, I'd be willing to bet a little money on it," Steele repeated. "As soon as he learns he was seen at the lodge the morning Loundon's body was found, he'll disappear—and so would I. Even if he doesn't know anything about the murder he'll know that the police will be looking for a likely victim, and he'll realize that with his reputation he'd be a most appropriate candidate."

"Well then, I'll call up the chief right now," Warren said grimly and pushed back from the table.

"You needn't." Steele stopped him before he could get up. "I took the liberty of asking Ferguson to call the chief after I'd talked with him." He smiled at the county attorney with bland apology. "You see, I thought our only chance was to find him before he got wind that he had been seen!"

"What makes you think he believes he wasn't seen?" If Warren felt resentment at this usurpation of his authority he disguised it admirably.

"Only what this oil-field worker told Ferguson. It was fairly early—about eight-thirty. The path that cuts across from the Meridian highway to the river, below the oil field, is screened all the way by a high hedge fence so that it is impossible for the workers at the derricks to see anyone who passes. But this man happened to be down by the riverbank above Loundon's rustic bridge examining a pump intake pipe. He was crouching at the water's edge behind a tree trunk when he heard voices on the bridge. He recognized Jack because he had seen him play ball. I gather that the father is pretty generally known, and there's no question that he's recognizable. He surmised that the woman was Van Roth's daughter. When she slapped them he decided to keep out of sight. He couldn't hear much of what they said and would have thought no more about it if the story of the murder that night hadn't led him to believe they might have had something to do with it. He told Ferguson they very easily could have walked from the highway to the bridge and back along the path without being seen."

"But why should she—" Warren began, and then interrupted himself in a lowered voice. "I guess she is coming here now."

We rose as Van Roth rejoined us with his daughter. There was still more than a little nervousness in his voice as he made the introductions. When Miss Van Roth had taken the chair which Steel indicated to her, the minister hesitated uncertainly, and then glanced at his daughter. It was at once apparent that he had been ordered not to remain, for after a few confused words of excuse he left the room.

The unhurried look with which Lola Van Roth had dismissed her father implied a force of personality that was still further suggested by her easy posture and her composure as she awaited our questions. She was about thirty-five, very considerably above medium size, but with a grace of carriage and a taste in dress that contained no hint of awkwardness. Her face was heavy in repose, almost dull, with pronounced cheekbones and a large, slightly curved nose. Only her eyes, extremely deep-set and of a peculiar burning blue, gave evidence of any emotion she may have felt at the situation in which she now found herself.

There was a pause, until Steele became aware that Warren expected him to assume the initiative.

"I suppose your father told you what we want?" He began so abruptly and with so little of his usual ingratiating manner that I was surprised.

"Yes."

"I saw you as Hedda Gabler in Chicago five years ago, and I have never forgotten you!" He suddenly smiled. "What, in the name of Ibsen, are you doing out here in Kansas?"

If Steele had expected to surprise Miss Van Roth he succeeded. At once her impassive features lighted up, and I saw she possessed exceeding charm.

"Ah! Did you!" She leaned forward delightedly for an instant, and then shrugged her shoulders. "I am out here in Kansas because there is no Hedda Gabler anywhere any more. That's the real reason. The theater is dead. And the only thing I could do in the movies would be Cyrano de Bergerac—or double for Jimmy Durante!"

Steele laughed, then nodded commiseratingly. "I suppose it's just as bad as that. From Gabler to Garbo. . . ."

Miss Van Roth's answering smile lingered only an instant. She apparently did not choose to reminisce, and her face became almost stolid again as she waited for Steele to come to the point of the interview. Perceiving her attitude, Steele immediately proceeded with his questions.

"Miss Van Roth, you were seen coming from Loundon's lodge the morning he was found dead. Your meeting with your father and brother on the bridge was observed. You are Loundon's former wife, and you will receive $50,000 from an insurance policy which he carried in your name. I don't need to explain further the reasons for our questions. I hope you will understand the importance of answering them frankly."

He paused for a reply, but she waited somberly for him to continue without so much as a nod.

"You did spend the night in the lodge?"

"Yes."

"Why?"

"The Junior League women were planning a picnic at the lodge on the twenty-eighth, and they had employed me to write, direct and stage a one-act play there that evening. I had been to see Mr. Loundon about it, and he gave me a key and told me to make whatever arrangements were necessary to stage it."

"When did you see him?"

"On the morning of the fourteenth. Here in this room."

"When did you go to the lodge?"

"The evening of the fifteenth—about five o'clock."

"Why didn't you make your inspection in the daytime? Weren't you afraid people would think it strange that you should spend the night there alone?" He paused and leaned forward. "You were alone, weren't you?"

"Yes, I was alone," she answered without hesitation and with a convincing simplicity. Only in her remarkable control of the varying inflections of her vibrant voice was there any suggestion of the actress. "I don't care what people think. I had to write this playlet, and when I happened to mention to Mr. Loundon that I wanted a quiet place where I could work undisturbed, he suggested that I might as well work at the lodge where there would be nobody to interrupt me."

"You couldn't work quietly at home?"

"No." She ignored all the insinuations that might have been implied in the question.

"Did you know that Mr. Loundon expected to come to the lodge the next day?"

"No. Not till I read it in the papers the day after his death." There was a slight pause. "To tell the truth, while he did not exactly say so, I gathered from our interview that he did not expect to use the lodge."

"Why did you leave so early in the morning?"

For the first time there was an instant's hesitation. "Well, for one thing, there wasn't anything but canned food in the house. I wanted some breakfast."

A hint of a smile came to her lips at the whimsical expression on Steele's face as he accepted this matter-of-fact explanation.

"Why did your father and brother come after you?"

The smile faded. "My father and I had had an argument when I told him I was going to the lodge. He was afraid of the effect on his reputation if it became known. One night was all he could stand, I suppose."

"He didn't expect you to leave so soon, then?"

I caught a challenge in Steele's voice, and I thought there was a flicker in Miss Van Roth's steady gaze.

"I hadn't told him how long I would stay."

"Why did you slap them?"

The light in the deep-set eyes flared for a moment. "I had told him what I would do. I expect people to let my private affairs alone!"

This was all; but the intensity of her voice reflected a will and a temper that were emphasized by her calm self-control. Steele leaned back in his chair and regarded her with an expression that was half amusement and half approbation. I was aware from his manner of putting the question that he had hoped to surprise her, if only for an instant, and I now unexpectedly found myself almost enjoying his failure. He thrust his fingers through his red hair and leaned forward again.

"I understand you and Mr. Loundon remained friends after your divorce. You knew, of course, about the $50,000-insurance policy?"

Miss Van Roth must have been expecting this question, yet the reluctance with which she answered and the emotion which she could not wholly keep out of her voice were in noticeable contrast with her previous equanimity.

"Yes. He took out the policy in 1920 after I—we were divorced. We have always been good friends, though I had not seen him for several years until I came back to Wichita this spring."

This was the first information she had volunteered, and I could see that Steele had not anticipated it. But, as unexpectedly, he did not pursue the subject. Instead he changed the subject altogether.

"Miss Van Roth, do you know Mrs. Vernon, who used to be Nellie Doyle of El Dorado?"

With a quick intake of breath which she instantly throttled with her lips, Miss Van Roth looked at Steele with startled eyes. Her hands pressed hard against the arms of the chair. It was a quarter of a minute before she replied.

"Why yes, of course." She recovered quickly. "I've known her ever since we were girls." She leaned toward him, and once more the rare charm of her smile was on her face. "Why do you ask me that?"

Steele's eyes had narrowed at her reaction to the question. He paused, as if considering an unforeseen advantage which he did not know how to follow up. Warren, who had taken only a perfunctory interest in the interview up to this point, had sat up in his chair at the mention of Mrs. Vernon's name.

"Was she acquainted with Mr. Loundon in El Dorado at the time you were married?" Steele finally asked.

Miss Van Roth frowned while she paused, as if in an effort to remember, though her eyes remained fixed intently on Steele's face.

"Why yes," she answered at last, "I'm sure they met at our house a few times. But I really can't see what possible connection she could have with his—with this. . . . I don't suppose they ever saw anything of each other in Wichita."

Warren shifted restlessly in his chair, and I felt that he was on the point of demanding an explanation of Mrs. Vernon's supposititious visit to the lodge. Steele caught his eye with a warning frown.

"Have you seen Mrs. Vernon since you returned to Wichita?" Steele asked before Warren could speak.

"Only in connection with the Junior League picnic," she answered promptly, and the tone of her voice gave a vague impression of relief at the question. "She is chairman of their entertainment committee. . . . But I really can't understand what she could have had to do with all this. Perhaps if you would tell me just what you are trying to get at I could answer you more intelligibly."

But Steele only smiled noncommittally. "Well, as a matter of fact, there's nothing to tell you. I was aware that she was in charge of the Junior League entertainment," he went on, with what I felt sure was pure fabrication, "and I wondered just what arrangements she had made with Loundon. You see, any recent incident connected with the lodge assumes importance. Perhaps an undue importance, it is true, but we don't dare ignore anything that might be suggestive."

"Yes, of course." Her attitude relaxed. "I can assure you Mrs. Vernon hadn't seen Mr. Loundon. I made all arrangements with him myself."

"Oh! Well then, we may as well forget Mrs. Vernon." Steele looked Warren full in the face, then continued without giving him a chance to interject the questions that were obviously bursting to be asked. "Now, I hope you will pardon me if I must ask you one thing more. What can you—or will you—tell us about your brother Jack's relations with Mr. Loundon?"

Miss Van Roth's deliberate answer indicated that she was prepared for an inquisition regarding her brother.

"I am afraid I can't tell you anything about Jack that you don't already know. He was the baby of our family. After Mother died I brought him up—I don't suppose I shall ever look on him as a grown man; to me he will always be just a spoiled child. However, whether you believe me or not, I do not think he knows anything about Mr. Loundon's death or his affairs."

There was something in the dignity of her answer that aroused my sympathy, and I regretted the grilling I assumed she was about to receive from Steele. But, in his unaccountable way, he did not press her further.

"Just one thing more," he said. "Did you know that Mr. Loundon was planning to discontinue some of his life-insurance policies?"

Miss Van Roth's voice held only relief at having so quickly disposed of the interrogation about her brother.

"No, I didn't."

"He hadn't informed you that he was going to cancel the policy he carried with you as beneficiary?"

"I see what you mean!" Miss Van Roth shrugged her shoulders. "Well, you may believe it or not; I didn't know anything about it."

"Then you think—" Steele began, then stopped. Instead of pursuing the question further he rose and abruptly terminated the interview.

"I'll let you hear from me if there's anything else we want to know," he smiled, after thanking her. "And if you produce any plays while I am here you can count on seeing me in your audience. I'm impressed anew with your—er—artistry!"

With this not-too-enigmatic statement he held out his hand. She took it, and for the fraction of a second her deep, bright-blue eyes looked into his. But whether there was in them the subtle defiance I imagined I perceived, I immediately doubted when she turned to Warren and then to me with one of her most fascinating smiles before she left the room.

She had no sooner disappeared through the door, however, than the impatience of our unsentimental county attorney broke loose. Miss Van Roth's momentary confusion at Steele's question about Mrs. Vernon had impressed him even more than it had me. His bushy eyebrows were pulled down into an irritated scowl as he demanded to know why Steele had warned him from interruption, and why he had so carefully avoided all reference to the suspicion that Mrs. Vernon had visited the lodge on the night of the 16th. He ended by stating, with heavy sarcasm, that about all he had learned from the meeting was that Miss Van Roth was a fine actress, and that Steele was a great admirer of fine acting. He'd be damned, he said, if he could see how you could expect to learn anything about a murder by conducting polite tête-à-têtes with actresses who admitted spending the night at the very scene where the murder was committed. He'd be damned if he could. And furthermore—

"But there was only one actress," Steele interrupted him placatingly. "But what an actress!" He leaned back in his chair, lighted a cigarette, and began riffling his red hair through his fingers as he gazed absent-mindedly at the blue smoke sifting slowly up through the lamp shade.

"As a matter of fact," he at last replied, and in his voice there was now a certain drawl which always accompanied a touch of exasperation, "I made a mistake in mentioning Mrs. Vernon's name at all—but I wasn't aware of it until it was done. Of course it was apparent from the moment she answered my first question that she would recognize all the cues and have all the speeches ready. Then suddenly, and unexpectedly I got her out of the script and I instantly realized I had to go upstage and give her a chance to get back into her lines. In other words," and with the cigarette between his upraised fingers Steele gestured an emphasis on every syllable in Warren's direction, "I didn't want her to attach any importance to my mention of Mrs. Vernon. When she said Mrs. Vernon was chairman of the Junior League entertainment committee I thought I saw a chance to allay her suspicions. Maybe I succeeded; maybe. But the point is, we surprised some connection between Miss Van Roth and Mrs. Vernon that has something to do with Loundon, and we don't want her scaring Mrs. Vernon off the reservation until we've at least had a chance to talk with her.

"Now if Mrs. Vernon did visit the lodge we have a right to presume that Miss Van Roth doesn't know it, or at least doesn't know we know it. By not telling her, we, at any rate, have the benefit of the doubt. But if we had given her cause to run to Mrs. Vernon with the news as soon as she returns to town—or before—we should have gained nothing and might conceivably lose a great deal. As to the possibility that we might have learned something about Mrs. Vernon, or her brother, or anything else she wants to keep still about, you can take my word for it, if the interview wasn't enough evidence for you, that there isn't a chance; not a chance—and there won't be until you find something to make her talk with that is more compelling than anything we have on hand at the present. . . . Notwithstanding which—" Steele rose and looked down at Warren with a smile that the seriousness of his voice belied—"if we knew what she knows we'd know a darned sight more about Ralph Loundon than we do now. Further, deponent sayeth not."

"If we knew what any divorced wife knows about her husband we'd know a darned sight more than we do now." Warren got up ruefully. Steele looked through him with absent thoughtfulness for nearly half a minute. Then he took me by the arm.

"Well, I don't suppose there's much else to be done tonight. We'll be seeing you tomorrow. Good night."

10

MY APARTMENT, which Steele shared with me when he was in town, was within three blocks of the *Times* office and almost within hearing distance of the presses when on quiet nights after the streets were deserted they began rolling off the news of the world's crimes and accomplishments. I had two bedrooms, a bath, a small kitchen and a large cheerful living room overlooking a tiny lawn consisting of an umbrella-shaped catalpa tree, a patch of Bermuda grass and a bed of petunias.

The kitchen was evidence of my graduation from a night job and the dogwatch to the dignity of an editorship, for it meant that after six years of eleven-o'clock breakfasts I was again eating according to the schedule of normal human beings. Every morning breakfast was prepared by a colored maid, and now that Steele was with me we gave the meal the added dignity of a dining table and linen in the living room.

Here, at seven-thirty on the morning of August 18, just as Steele was complimenting a bachelor's ménage which could serve powdered sugar for his grapefruit, the colored maid announced, "They is a young lady wants to see you. Says her name is Miss McCoy."

"That's right; her name is Miss McCoy," I answered. "Show her in." And to Steele I explained, "Our society reporter. Maybe she has learned something about Mrs. Vernon."

Sue McCoy was typically Irish in everything but good looks. The quarter of an inch which her nose lacked to be beautiful had been unnecessarily added to the width of a mouth which otherwise would have been classic. But any girl whose features are only a quarter of an inch out of alignment and who possesses wit, energy and curly black hair, can interrupt Steele's breakfast any morning with impunity. Smilingly he dismissed the apologies she would have made at having come so early.

"Business before grapefruit," he said as he held a chair for her; "unless we could persuade you to join us."

"No thanks, I have breakfast at seven; walk to work and am on the job at eight. Only this morning I rode down in order to see if I could find out what a bachelor apartment looks like before noon." She turned from Steele to me with a smile and a bantering look in her black eyes. "No suggestive remarks, please." She looked about the room. "Not so bad. The maid must get here early. You ought to turn her loose on that desk of yours at the office sometime." She turned back to Steele. "You know, he found a typewriter and two extra hats in there the last time he cleaned it out! That's one thing he has in common with William Allen White. They say that's the reason he does it!"

"They say!" I stopped her. "Spoken like a society reporter! Please state your business, if any."

She laughed. "I think this detective business is too thrilling! You can't imagine how pleasant it is to be able to listen to all the dirty little things that ordinarily I would try to avoid."

"Oh yeah?" I jeered. "As for instance . . ."

"What maids tell you, for instance. Honestly, I hardly ever pay any attention to what servants tell me. And you'd be surprised to know what some of them would like to see in the society columns about people they've worked for! When you've been in the society-reporting business for a while you learn that at least half of what one household knows about another comes straight out of the kitchen doors."

Steele nodded appreciatively. "I was a butler for three weeks once in a house where a murder had been committed."

Miss McCoy's eyes rounded. "Did you learn who did it?"

"No." Steele shook his head. "It was the perfect crime! I only learned to wonder why a couple more hadn't been killed."

She laughed, and then her face grew earnest. "Well, really, I didn't find out much that will help you, I'm afraid; and I'm keeping you from your breakfasts."

She hitched her chair around to face Steele.

"I went to several women who used to live in El Dorado, and from one of them I learned that Mrs. Vernon, when she was Nellie Doyle, became infatuated with Mr. Loundon. That was before he married Lola Van Roth. She was just a girl at the time—only seventeen or eighteen, I think—and their affair—that's what this woman called it—lasted only a few months. She couldn't tell me what happened to break it off; she said there was some sort of scandal, but that Miss Doyle left town and it was all hushed up."

"A scandal, eh?" Steele commented. "How much do you suppose Miss Van Roth knew about it?"

"I didn't dare seem too curious, but I gathered that nobody knew much about it at the time." She chuckled. "My guess is that if this woman couldn't find out, nobody could."

Steele smiled at the tone of voice in which she delivered this characterization. "An ex-maid, I presume, from what you said a moment ago!"

She lifted both hands in swift protest. "Oh no! One of our social lights; she slid into Wichita society on oil seven or eight years ago. The maid comes in this way: I have a friend who has a maid who is a sister of Mrs. Vernon's cook. Very casually I learned that at eleven o'clock on the morning of the sixteenth—the day Mr. Loundon was killed—Jack Van Roth paid Mrs. Vernon a visit."

"Jack Van Roth!" The amused expression with which Steele had been listening left his face. "What did he want?"

Miss McCoy shook her head. "I can't tell you. He was there about half an hour. When he left, Mrs. Vernon went immediately to her room. Her maid told the cook that she could hear Mrs. Vernon sobbing for a long time and that she didn't eat any lunch." Miss McCoy paused. "Then at six-thirty, when the boys selling the extra telling about Mr. Loundon's murder came past the house, she went out and bought one. She began crying again, but in a few minutes she called up somebody on the telephone, and at six forty-five she drove away in her car."

"The blue Buick with the doctor's insignia on the radiator?"

"Yes. I understand Dr. Vernon has another car and that she uses the Buick most of the time. She came back alone sometime before nine o'clock, put some things in a bag and left for El Dorado that night."

"I don't suppose you know whether she really went to El Dorado?"

"No."

"Do you know when she returned?"

"About four yesterday afternoon."

"In her car?"

"Yes."

Steele considered this information in silence. Indeed, he stared at her so long without speaking or seeming to see her, that in a few moments Miss McCoy rose to go. But he detained her with another question.

"Was Dr. Vernon mentioned in any way? I understand he was in Kansas City."

"The maid said he was in Kansas City. Sometime yesterday morning a telegram came from Kansas City which Mrs. Vernon's maid told the cook she supposed was from Dr. Vernon."

Miss McCoy got up again. "I think that's all. And I'm afraid I wasn't able to be of much help to you."

"On the contrary—" Steele shook hands with her and gave her one of his warmest smiles—"you have helped us exceedingly."

When she had gone we went back to our breakfasts.

"A smart girl that," Steele commented. Then a moment later, with a gesture that included the apartment, he added, "It's a strange thing to me, considering your domestic tendencies, why you don't marry somebody like that and settle down for a change."

"Yes? And hire a maid or two? No thanks."

"Well, maybe you're right. Here's Dr. Vernon running off to Kansas City from a wife, a maid and a talkative cook. I suppose he was in Kansas City. We must have a talk with Mrs. Vernon."

He started to take a drink of coffee, then suddenly put down the cup. "Say! Why didn't I think of that while she was here? Miss

McCoy could arrange an appointment for us. I'm afraid Mrs. Vernon wouldn't see us if she knew what we wanted. I wonder if you can't get Miss McCoy to make an appointment for the two of us this afternoon sometime? Strictly unofficial. And we won't say anything to Warren about it. He seems to have a complex about that Buick car, and I'm afraid, too, his official title might complicate matters. To say nothing of his official dignity!"

As I nodded agreement the telephone rang. I answered, then cupped my hand over the transmitter.

"It's Warren; he wants to talk to you. Seems to have something over the fire, too."

Steele took the telephone and listened. "Well, well," he commented after a few moments. "You don't say. . . . H'm. . . . Is that so? . . . The spare tire was still on it, eh? . . . All right, we'll be over."

He hung up and returned to the table.

"He says Burke has discovered that those tire tracks at the lodge were made by Monest's car. He is going to have Monest in his office at nine, and this was our official invitation."

I had to put in an appearance at the office and left Steele to finish his breakfast alone. I arranged with Miss McCoy to make the appointment with Mrs. Vernon and at a quarter of nine was ready to leave, when word came in from the news room that Hovey No. 4 in the Meridian pool had just blown in out of control and promised to be the largest gusher ever produced in the Kansas field. From a newspaper standpoint few murders would have been bigger news. I decided to get the details.

I found Gus Holm, our oil reporter, a one-finger artist on the typewriter, pecking away madly at his machine. He took the cigarette I offered and tilted back against the wall.

"Boy! Is this a play, or is this a play! Came in like a skyrocket and darn near took away the derrick! You can hear her roar halfway to town. Mostly gas at first, but she's already beginning to thicken. By night she'll be doing twenty thousand barrels or I miss my guess!"

He threw the cigarette away and hooked his forefingers for a renewed attack on his typewriter. "And me? I've got one hundred berries in a direct offset!"

"Oh yes?" I remarked. "Then maybe you can do something about that fifty you got me to put in on that Waite wildcat."

"Ha! Fifty!" he exploded. "Why, you slimy piker! Here I'm wild-catting every paycheck for four months, and you come crying around about a measly fifty bucks! You and this guy Monest! You ought to team up!"

"Is Monest in on this?"

"Only one fourth, that's all! Just a fourth! Garnett's got a half, and Loundon would have had the other fourth. That's the oil game for you! The squarest guy that ever drilled a dry hole, and he gets bumped off two days before the biggest gusher he ever had leased. And this greaser, Monest, whining around all the time complaining that Loundon had lost him fifty thousand. And now he'll be able to swim in oil from here to the Gulf of Mexico if he wants to!"

Gus shook his head, reached into my pocket for my cigarettes, absent-mindedly lit one as he leaned over the machine to pick up the thread of his narrative, and swiftly started in again to tap out the story that within half an hour would feature an extra edition and before night would be first-page A.P. news all over the South-west. I left him with the thrill that comes all too seldom to a newspaperman and hurried to the courthouse, wondering if Monest had heard the news and if he would be present at our interview at all.

The county attorney's private office in our forty-year-old court-house was not an attractive room, and to Juan Monest, who obviously had not yet heard of his good fortune, it must have seemed a particularly uncomfortable inquisition place on this hot August morning. When I arrived he was alone in the office, sitting in a straight-backed armchair, looking gloomily out over the burned-up lawn, mopping his swarthy brow with a silk handkerchief. He was short and stout; there was a fringe of black hair about his dark bald head; and in his rather handsome face there glittered a pair of the quickest and blackest eyes I had ever seen outside a cage. I nodded and sat down, deciding to say nothing about the oil well, and was casting about for a line of conversation when Warren and Steele, followed by Burke, came in from the outer office.

Monest got up to acknowledge Warren's punctilious introductions, then nervously reseated himself in front of the county attorney's long flat-top desk.

The county attorney began the interview by asking the Spaniard if he could furnish any information regarding Loundon's death, questioning him about their business relations, and avoiding any reference to Burke's discovery of the identity of the car. When Monest's first uneasiness had worn off his answers were prompt and succinct. He disclaimed any theories respecting the murder, had no knowledge of it beyond what he had read in the papers, and stated that aside from some minor differences of opinion he had always been on the friendliest of terms with Loundon. Only when Warren asked him to explain his whereabouts on the morning of the 16th was there any perceptible hesitation.

He had had breakfast at home with his niece a little before eight o'clock, he said, after moistening his lips and shifting his chubby white-flannelled figure in the chair, then he had driven immediately to the Meridian oil field, arriving there about nine o'clock, maybe a quarter of nine. He and Garnett had gone over the log of the well they were drilling, and after watching the work awhile he had returned to town. At ten o'clock he was in the lounge room of the Town Club reading the New York *Times*. He did not learn of Loundon's death until evening, when he read about it in the paper.

Sheriff Burke noted with a disapproving frown the Latin gesture of the hands with which Monest closed his recital, and waited impatiently for Warren to demand of Monest why his car had been parked at the lodge. Leaning back in his ancient swivel chair, the county attorney regarded the Spaniard a moment from under his bushy black eyebrows.

"Mr. Monest," he said slowly, "we have just learned that your car was parked at Loundon's lodge the morning he was killed. How do you reconcile this with your statement that you went directly to town from the oil field?"

"My car!" Monest seemed honestly startled. "My car! But how could it be my car?" He turned swiftly to me and then to Steele as if in appeal from this accusation. "I told you I went only to the oil field and then directly back to town."

"Yes." Warren eyed him steadily. "That is what we can't understand. There's no mistake about the identification of the car. We have checked the tires, and the treads tally exactly, even to the spare U. S. tire which is still on the rear right wheel."

Monest mopped his face with the silk handkerchief. He opened his mouth as if to make an explanation, and then apparently thought better of it.

"No, it was not my car. You are simply mistaken. You cannot say it was my car from those tracks. How can you prove I was over there just from some car tracks?"

"That's just what we have proved." Warren began getting warm.

"But you cannot prove it," Monest rejoined. His sharp black eyes returned Warren's gaze defiantly. "I can show when I left home, and how long I was at the oil well, and when I got to the club. There is no time for me to be at the lodge."

Sheriff Burke, from the first mention of the car, had stared menacingly at Monest. Now, as the Spaniard offered this aggressive denial, his face turned from pink to red and from red to scarlet. Finally he could restrain himself no longer.

"Yes, it was your car all right—" he planted himself in front of Monest and thrust forward a belligerent jaw—"and now maybe you'll tell us what kind of wild beast you were carrying around in it, too!"

Monest shrank back in his chair from this sudden attack.

"Wild beast!" He threw up his hands in dismay. "Wild beast? I don't know what you are talking about!" He again turned appealingly to Steele. "What is it, this he is yelling to me about a wild beast?"

Steele put a hand on Burke's arm. "We'll come to that." He waited a moment for Burke to subside. Then he said:

"Mr. Monest, this isn't a third degree, and I don't question your denial. If you were where you say you were on the morning of the sixteenth you have nothing to be alarmed about—and I don't for a minute doubt your word or the fact that you can establish a satisfactory alibi if Mr. Warren should think it necessary to ask you to do so. What we are trying to learn is how your car happened to be parked at the lodge that morning. . . . Now if you were not in it, who was?"

The expression of relief that had come over Monest's face at Steele's first words faded abruptly. His eyes shifted, and when he answered all defiance was gone from his voice.

"I have told you." He shrugged his shoulders. "It is simply you are mistaken. I was in my car, and I was where I have said; I was no place else; and if Mr. Warren will come with me I will get some witnesses who can tell him."

Steele looked down at Monest; then characteristically lifted his hands and shoulders in a gesture that was almost a caricature of the Spaniard's mannerism.

"It was your car, and I know you weren't in it. The footprints of the man who drove your car are those of the man who went to the strawstack. They were not yours—but they were the right size to be Garnett's. . . . Mr. Monest, did Garnett drive your car to the lodge that morning?"

For a second Monest's black eyes met Steele's gaze without flinching, then he looked away. So long did he hesitate that I thought he had made up his mind not to answer. But finally he said:

"No; Mr. Garnett was not in my car. I drove it myself. I have—"

"That isn't true!" Steele contradicted him flatly with a touch of exasperation. "We know when you left town in your car, and we know when you returned to town—but we don't know whose car you drove back to town. Nevertheless, I am positive it was Garnett's. Wasn't it?"

But Monest would only doggedly reiterate his assertion that he had returned to town in his own car. When Steele half angrily accused him of lying he continued his insistence that Garnett had not driven the car. Even when Warren threatened to hold him in custody until he told the truth the Spaniard merely declared, with his customary Latin lift of the shoulders, that the county attorney could hold him if he wished but that he would have nothing further to say without the advice of a lawyer. Steele at last realized nothing was to be gained by further questioning, but when Warren would have made good his threat Steele considered a moment, then slowly shook his head.

"No," he advised, after a most singular and penetrating examination of the Spaniard's obstinate face, "there's nothing to be gained by holding him, and—if you will trust me—there is something to lose. . . . For the time being it is better to let him go."

At these words Monest looked from Steele to Warren, hesitated, and got up. He bowed to Warren.

"If that is all, I may go?"

Warren frowned, looked uncertainly at Steele, then reluctantly nodded. "I guess so; but I don't want you to leave town without letting me know."

Monest lifted his eyebrows in astonishment. Then he silently bowed again and turned to the door. I decided to let a little light into his gloom.

"Mr. Monest," I said, "your Hovey Number 4 came in a gusher about an hour ago. It blew in unexpectedly and caught them by surprise. Looks like the biggest well we've ever had in the state. Thought you might like to know."

The Spaniard wheeled. "What is it you say? He is come in a gusher? Ha!" He almost embraced me. Then his face fell. "Ah, that is too bad now for poor Mr. Loundon. All his difficulties would be ended. That is too bad he should die just now, is it not?" He lifted his shoulders in resignation before an inscrutable fate; then his jubilation returned. "But I must go immediately! If you want me I shall be at your service any time you say."

When we had watched him hasten through the door, Burke banged a heavy fist on the county attorney's desk and scowled at Steele.

"No, this ain't any third degree! Now if you don't want to talk, Mr. Monest, we just don't know what to do about it! The hell! You get a guy dead to rights and what do you do? You let him tell you how sorry he is that Mr. Loundon had to die!"

Warren's heavy face reflected an irritated agreement, but Steele only smiled.

"Well, what else could you do?" he inquired soothingly. "He has his alibi, and what could you prove? And really, I believe he actually was regretful about Loundon."

"Or remorseful," amended Warren.

"That oil well will smother any regrets he may have," I said. "What do you think, Steve? Do you believe he knows anything?"

"Hell!" Burke broke in. "Did you see how he looked when I asked him about that animal that was in the car? Does he know anything! And you never followed that up, either!"

Steele replied to my question without heeding the sheriff's interjection.

"I don't know just what to think," he said slowly. "He either knows something or suspects somebody. And I'm satisfied he was lying about his car. But there you are again; you can't prove anything. And in the meanwhile, we've got some dope for you, Sheriff, about Mrs. Vernon and the doctor's blue Buick. Tell the gentlemen, Sarge, about the other developments in the used-car department."

11

I LEFT STEELE in Warren's office with the understanding that we would have lunch together at the Town Club. But when I reached the club about noon Steele was nowhere in sight. I inquired for him at the desk and was informed that he was playing handball. I took the elevator to the fourth floor and climbed the little circular stairway which led to the tiny galleries looking down into the courts. At one time I had rather fancied my ability at the four-wall game, and I was curious whether Steele, at thirty-five, was still able to hold his own at this strenuous sport with the group of younger players who had long since put me out of competition.

When I entered the gallery above the court where Steele was playing I was astonished to find it nearly filled with a group of tensely interested spectators. Steele's opponent was a powerful, aggressive-looking black-haired chap in his middle twenties, whose muscular body and nervous bearing were in noticeable contrast with Steele's lean frame and more deliberate movements. As I found a seat the younger man, with a determined look on his face, took his position to serve and called the score, 10—18. This meant that Steele was within three points of the game, with the other 8 points behind.

I was extremely curious about this impromptu match which had drawn so many absorbed noontime spectators. My seat happened to be next to that of an old-time player with whom I had battled many a hard game. When I asked him who Steele's opponent was he looked at me in astonishment.

"Why, that's Jack Van Roth!"

"Jack Van Roth!"

My amazed exclamation drew a further explanation.

"City champion! Where've you been for the past two years?"

"Oh!" I recovered from my surprise. "I've been out of the game too long to know all these youngsters, Jim. So that's Jack Van Roth! Pretty good, isn't he?"

Jim shook his head. "Well, I thought so till now. But this fellow Steele has been making a monkey out of him the last two games. Jack beat him the first game 21 to 15. But in the second Steele got warmed up and took him 21 to 7. What a left hand! I'll bet he's played that slow high bounce to Jack's left corner ten times this last game. It took him just one game to find a weakness that nobody else around here ever discovered. But I never saw anybody else who could control a slow shot like that. If Jack doesn't get in he kills the return low and if he does get in Steele slowballs another high one or bangs a hard one around him. There they go again!"

Steele served from the right wall. Apparently young Van Roth anticipated another slow high ball, for he edged a trifle to the left expecting to make his return on the volley to forestall the high dead bounce out of the corner. Steele, however, let the ball fall almost to the floor before he hit it and brought a low hard serve straight back along the right wall. The ball was never more than a foot above the floor, and it cleared the service line by inches. Jack was caught flatfooted, and the score was 19 to 10.

As Steele picked up the ball he glanced up at the gallery and caught my eye; then, with a strange and almost imperceptible shake of the head, he prepared to serve. It was a swift ball, but straight down the middle. Jack took it off the back wall and brought it back at Steele's left with the speed of a bullet. Steele never touched it, and Van Roth went in to serve. Again Jack served a hard twist to the left corner, but this time Steele flubbed the return against the ceiling. His next return was a setup, which Van Roth killed in the corner. Three more serves, and the score was 15 to 19. The gallery buzzed.

Once more Steele shot me that odd glance, and this time I realized that he was throwing the game. With six straight serves Jack counted to 21, and some of his youthful friends enthusiastically dropped from the gallery into the court to congratulate him. At my right my friend Jim got up from his seat and looked down at me with a mystified shake of the head.

"Bill, if I'd had a bet up on this match I'd swear I'd been double-crossed. Hell's bells! This Steele could give Jack ten points and beat him if he were a few years younger." He slapped me on the back. "That's what it is, boy, old age; it's got you and me, and now it's just beat the sweetest player I ever hope to see on a handball court." He turned to look down again at Steele, who was standing at the door with a towel about his shoulders. "But 21 to 10! Why even I could have made those last two points!"

Jim went out, still shaking his head, and Steele, who had overheard him, grinned at me and motioned me down. I climbed over the railings and dropped into the court. I had become a little excited over the game myself, and I immediately began to upbraid him. But he stopped me shortly and drew me to one side.

"Never mind the alibis," he said. "Van Roth is going to have lunch with us, and while we're dressing I wish you'd get hold of Warren and get him to come up. Also, get a private dining room if you can."

"O.K.," I agreed. "But listen, what was the idea of throwing the game? I don't get that. This kid will broadcast it the way his father does a sermon."

Steele mopped his face, and his wet red hair with the towel.

"Just because he's that kind. You should have seen him pat me on the back when he won the first game and heard him crab when I won the second. He can't take it; and I want him in a magnanimous mood for lunch. Run on; we'll be up in twenty minutes."

I succeeded in getting both the dining room and Warren, who arrived as we were placing our orders. That is to say, Steele was ordering, while Van Roth patronized him. In all my experience I had never met a more naïve and flamboyant egotism, and, as a newspaperman in constant touch with budding authors and politicians, I had dealt with some grade A egotists in my time. He kept up a running stream of comment about handball, apparently never realizing that his game left off where Steele's began, and interspersed his asseverations with braggadocio about his prowess in other sports, with a few special remarks about baseball. Steele handed the order card to the waiter and smilingly encouraged him:

"Well, I realized in the last game that I'd been hitting a lucky streak, and I wasn't surprised when you pulled out. I used to pitch a little baseball, too, but they tell me you're even better at that than you are at handball. What's this I hear about your being asked to try out with the St Louis Cardinals?"

Jack became even more expansive.

"Yeah. One of their scouts saw me let down the Wichita league team last summer with one hit. They offered me a regular job without a tryout! Said that was the first time they had ever done that, but I guess they knew there wasn't any question about me making it. I'd have gone, too, but I sprained my arm, and the next time the scout saw me pitch I got knocked out of the box. I got three hits and a home run, though, and he said that maybe I wasn't quite ready as a pitcher, but that if they didn't already have enough .300 hitters he would have signed me up as an outfielder. I batted .412 last year and got ten home runs."

Steele commiserated blandly.

"Tough break to get that sprained arm. Did you ever play any tennis?"

Van Roth gave a serious nod. "I've been working on that. Almost beat the city champion a couple of sets last week."

So it went, with Steele's encouragement, throughout the meal, while I listened and marveled. Warren, who cared little for sports, missed the unbounded self-aggrandizement of most of Van Roth's statements, and by the time dessert came was getting fidgety. I myself had begun to wonder how Steele would direct this ebullient flow into any other channel. To my astonishment, when the waiter had left the room, Jack abruptly introduced the subject of the murder himself. He discarded nothing of his positive manner, but I thought now I could detect a shrewd, half-defiant cunning in his attitude.

"My sister told me you wanted to see me about this murder."
He accepted a cigarette from Steele, tapped it on the back of a
muscular hand and stared at Warren with his bold hazel eyes.
"But—I didn't know the county attorney would invite himself!"

Warren flushed, and Steele hastened to say that he had extended the invitation.

Van Roth laughed shortly. "Oh, that's all right—only the law
seems to have it in for me. What I've got to say I wanted to tell you
personally, because Lola said you seemed like a square shooter,
and she said I ought to see you. Besides"—he blew a cloud of smoke
into the air—"I wanted to see if you were as good a handball player
as some of the boys thought. They said you could spot me five points
a game!"

Steele smiled quietly. "I guess they were just trying to kid you
a little. I'm glad your sister suggested your coming. Probably she
thought you might be able to help us."

"Well, I can!" Jack asserted. "But so long as you've got the hon-
orable county attorney here I guess he'd better go ahead and cross-
examine me."

His tone again brought the red to Warren's face. It was not in
him to submit quietly to sarcastic condescension from a man of
Jack's reputation, and he accepted the challenge angrily.

"Look here, Jack—" he made an effort to keep his voice even—
"when you were convicted of selling Jamaica ginger in the drugstore I
got you off simply out of consideration for your father—not because
of you or any of your so-called political friends. But let me tell you
right now, if I get another chance I'll send you up for the limit."

"O.K." Van Roth was irrepressible. "I suppose that's why Tony
Sargo got you elected!"

"Sargo got me elected!" Warren almost jumped from his chair.
"Why, damn you—"

"Oh, all right!" Van Roth interrupted him. "Maybe that didn't
have anything to do with it, but you didn't look so hot when you
tried to tie that Oklahoma kidnapping on me."

"I didn't have anything to do with that, and neither did Sargo,
nor any of you other bootleggers!" Warren made an effort to remain

calm. "I didn't even know about it until after Hawthorne had you arrested."

"O.K. I believe that too! Only Sargo says different!"

"Sargo!" Warren exploded so furiously that Steele laid a restraining hand on his arm to keep him in his chair. It was apparent that Steele had not been aware of Jack's animus for the county attorney and that he now realized their meeting under the circumstances was a mistake.

"Let him go," Jack urged, still intent on baiting Warren. "He just can't take it, that's all." He laughed in the other's face. "Now what is it you wanted to ask me about, Mr. Warren? I understand you think my father killed Mr. Loundon and hauled him up on that strawstack. Or was it my sister? Or maybe me!"

Warren faced him grimly, choking down his anger.

"All three of you were at the lodge the morning Loundon was killed, and your sister spent the night there. I don't say you know anything, but the circumstances are damned suspicious. You seem to forget that if I want to I can have you held for investigation."

At this threat Jack pugnaciously leaned over the table toward Warren. Steele, perceiving that a clash impended, interposed hastily:

"Look here, Jack, suppose you two settle this some other time. You came to me of your own volition, and nobody is trying to pin anything on you."

"Yeah?" Jack replied, still eying Warren. "How about that pick-up order he got out for me last night?"

"Merely a matter of routine," Steele interposed quickly before Warren could blame him. "I suppose the sheriff got a little ahead of himself."

"Well, that isn't what I heard," Jack replied. "But anyway they didn't pick me up, so I'll let that pass." He turned away from Warren. "Now if there's anything you want to ask me, Mr. Steele, I'll answer, just so long as he'll keep still."

But Steele shook his head. "I can't do that, Jack." He spoke placatingly. "Mr. Warren is responsible, and I can't assume to act without his co-operation. However, I presume you know what your sister and father told us. If you came to me to add anything to what they said, I'll be glad to listen."

Jack shot a questioning glance at Warren, who fortunately said nothing. Jack picked up his glass of water and took a drink, hesitated again and then finally began bluntly:

"What they told you was straight, and they don't know anything about Mr. Loundon's murder. But I do, and that's why I wanted to see you. I was going to make you a proposition, and I still will if you'll guarantee to keep him off of me."

Steele frowned and looked at Warren. The county attorney maintained an angry silence. At last Steele said:

"Neither of us has any right to make a promise of that kind. However, I don't think you need have any fear if what you have to say isn't conditioned on immunity for any guilty person."

"I'm not asking immunity for anybody. If you'll have them cancel that pick-up order I'll deliver your murderer to you tonight!"

Our amazement was all that Van Roth could have hoped for. He leaned back in his chair and looked round at us impressively.

"You're not joking, Jack?" Steele asked, wondering, no doubt, if this were just another instance of imaginative extravagance.

"No, I'm not joking," Van Roth repeated seriously. "I can get him to come to Loundon's lodge tonight, and if you're there I'll see that you get him."

"You say 'him,'" Steele said, more as if sparring for time than asking information; "it is a man, then?"

Jack looked at him shrewdly. "I said 'him,' but I'm not saying whether it was a man or a woman."

At this evasion Warren suddenly pushed back his chair and got up.

"Do you seriously mean to say you know who killed Ralph Loundon and won't tell us?" he blazed.

"I won't tell you now, but I'll get him for you tonight; that's what I said."

Warren's face went white. "You'll tell us now, or I'll put you behind the bars until you do!"

Steele got up, anticipating trouble, but Jack only looked up at Warren defiantly, a sneer on his lips.

"You know damn well you can't make me tell you anything I don't want to."

"You'll talk—or stay in jail," Warren declared.

"All right—and you'll never get your man, either," Jack retorted coolly, getting to his feet. Then he suddenly backed to the door. "Now make another move and I'll knock you across that table!"

Steele was on the other side of the table, too far away to attempt to stop Jack if he should bolt. Warren hesitated, knowing that Van Roth would either attempt to make good his threat or get away before he could be stopped. After a long moment and a questioning glance at Steele, who frowned warningly, Warren decided in favor of discretion.

"All right," he said shortly.

Jack still stood with his hand on the doorknob.

"None of that jail stuff or trying to make me talk?"

"No." Warren sat down. "Not for today, anyway."

"You too, Mr. Steele?"

"Of course," Steele said reassuringly. "You don't suppose I think you'd have come here if you had anything to do with the murder, do you? Now let's hear what you propose to do. Mr. Warren has given his word, and you're perfectly free to say anything you want to."

Convinced that he had gained his point, Jack rejoined us at the table. He went so far as to address his first statement to Warren, and without even an implied insult.

"I don't blame you, Mr. Warren. I guess I've done some things that a minister's son shouldn't, but I'm not mixing up in any murders—nor any kidnappings, either. I could take you to the person who did it, but I couldn't prove it now. By night I can, and I can get him to meet me at the lodge, say at eight o'clock. Now if you'll get there early and lay low he'll walk right into your hands. Then I'll be prepared to prove I know what I'm talking about, and I'll help you convict him."

Jack's undeniable earnestness was convincing. Nevertheless Steele shook his head.

"You forget, Jack, we've got a few leads ourselves. What if we should decide to make some arrests before night?"

"Who?"

"Well, what if I should say Monest?"

"Just because he threatened to kill Loundon when they had their row out at the Dragonfly plant?" Jack shook his head. "Have you got anything on him?"

Steele accepted this news of the quarrel with an impassive face.

"Maybe. Or what if I said Garnett—or Ripley—or even Miss Monest—or Mrs. Vernon? You know you were out to see Mrs. Vernon the morning Loundon was killed and she cried for an hour after you left!"

An uneasy look of suspicion crossed Jack's face.

"You do know a few things, don't you?" he countered boldly. "Well, you haven't mentioned Dr. Vernon. Any woman who is married to a husband like him can always shed a few tears! As for my being at Mrs. Vernon's, I went to see her about the properties for the play my sister was going to put on at the lodge."

He got up. "But you're all wet, and you don't need to think I'm going to tell you anything. What do you say, will you meet me out there or not?"

Steele perceived that Van Roth was growing restive, and as Warren apparently had determined to wash his hands of Jack after his promise of temporary immunity, he took the matter into his own hands.

"Yes, we'll be in the lodge at eight o'clock. The back door will be open."

"No. The doors must be locked. I've got a key, and if they were open it would look suspicious. And don't leave anybody outside and don't have a light, and don't do anything that might scare him off. I'll come in the main door off the front porch, and as soon as we get inside you grab us both. And don't take any chances, because as soon as this bird finds out I've double-crossed him my life won't be worth a plugged nickel!"

I saw Steele frown at the word "double-crossed," and I could see he disapproved of the spirit of juvenile bravado and mystification with which Jack was surrounding the affair. But he agreed without objection, and after a few more warning suggestions Van Roth finally took his leave.

I expected a tirade from Warren, but he merely flung himself into a chair and scowled at Steele.

"'Of all the damned nonsense!' Is that what you want to say?" Steele inquired. Receiving no answer, he said, "I think you're right, and yet I don't know whether I'd have stopped him if we could!"

He lit a cigarette and paced the floor a minute. Then he halted in front of Warren. "He's a psychopath of some sort, that's sure. Half gangster, half athlete—and half spoiled minister's son. No discipline at home; no discipline in his speech; no discipline in handball; no discipline anywhere. How much is gangster? Enough for a murder? Under some circumstances, by the Lord, I believe yes . . . and yet he was right: I don't think you'd have got a thing out of him by holding him—or was he just playing for an extra day's time?"

Warren grunted. "You wonder! Well, I don't! I wish now I'd tackled him if it was the last thing I ever did. He'll skip, and that's the last we'll ever see of him."

Steele shook his head, but before he could reply the door was opened by our colored waiter.

"Mr. Steele," he said, "the sheriff's out here lookin' for you. Do you want him to come in here?"

"Yes; send him in."

When Burke appeared he was a combination of apology and exasperation. This was explained, it at once appeared, by the presence of the two boys who had discovered Loundon's body in the strawstack. They had come to his office, he said, with important information about the murder, but when he had tried to find out what it was they refused to tell him, saying they wanted to talk to Mr. Steele. Not knowing how important it might be he decided to humor them, and had brought them over.

The frightened aspects of the two boys as Burke herded them into the room indicated how graciously he had humored them. Their faces lit up, however, when they saw Steele, and when he immediately ordered the waiter to bring ice cream for them their nervousness began to disappear.

"Now, boys," Steele said, sitting down opposite them at the table, "what's on your minds?"

Joe looked at his companion, but Hen's bobbing Adam's apple obviously prevented any assistance from that quarter, so he gulped and began.

"It's about Jack Van Roth," he said. "You see—"

"Jack Van Roth!" Warren's exclamation startled the boy so that it was half a minute before he could continue.

"Yes sir! You see, it's Jack Van Roth who has been keeping that booze and stuff under the strawstack. He brings it down the river at night in a boat and unloads it. And then he takes it down the river to town a little at a time. I think he is a bootlegger. The first time we saw him we was fishin' across the river. Then we saw him do it two or three times more. Didn't we, Hen?"

"But, boys," Steele's voice reproved them, "you must have known this the other day when you found Mr. Loundon's body. Why didn't you tell us?"

Joe shot a swift look at Burke. "Well, we was scairt he would think we had did it! But then we got to thinkin' we ought to tell you, so when we couldn't find where you was we went to his office to ask him and he jumped onto us to make us tell, and when we wouldn't he brought us down here."

"When was the last time you saw Jack at the stack?"

"It was about a week before we found Mr. Loundon."

"You're sure this time that's all you know, boys?"

"Yes sir." Joe vigorously nodded his head, emphatically seconded by Hen.

"All right. Finish your ice cream and then you can go, and if you find out anything else be sure to let us know. But I don't believe I'd hang around the lodge any more."

"No sir, we won't." Hen at last found his voice. "We ain't going to take any chances on running into that there gorilla!"

Burke started.

"What do you mean, gorilla! Look here, if you boys are holding out anything on us, I'll—"

"Never mind, Burke." Steele interrupted him with a chuckle and an ironic look at me. "That just means they've been following the case in the *Times!*"

12

WE LEFT JOE AND HEN to finish their ice cream alone, and when Burke and Warren had departed, following a somewhat petulant rebuke by the latter at Steele's having permitted Jack Van Roth to "slip through our fingers," I informed Steele that Miss McCoy had arranged for us to meet Mrs. Vernon at three o'clock.

Dr. Vernon's house in Eastborough was one of the most pretentious in all Wichita. It was a rambling structure of buff brick with Tudor leanings, set back from the street in a clump of half-grown elms, and attractively landscaped with shrubbery and hedges. We were admitted to a pleasant room which had the appearance of being the handiwork of an interior decorator who maintained a side line in antique furniture.

Mrs. Vernon came in at once, obviously dreading an ordeal to which, Miss McCoy had advised me, she had very reluctantly agreed to submit herself. She was a slight trim woman in her late twenties; an ash blonde with large gray eyes, heavily lashed, and a round chin deeply cleft. Her makeup as to hair, cheeks, lips and fingernails was immaculate, but her eyes and mouth betrayed an agitation that no cosmetics could conceal.

I had never met Mrs. Vernon, and it was Steele who assumed the introductions. His easy friendly manner served at once to relax somewhat the tenseness of her attitude. He said quietly that our call was not prompted by suspicion but by the hope of further information, and he began by asking her about the arrangements for the play which was to have been staged at Loundon's lodge.

Her explanation was identical with Miss Van Roth's, and she made it clear that she had had nothing to do with the details or with securing permission from Loundon to use the lodge. In fact, she said, she had not seen Mr. Loundon for nearly three years before his death. The lodge had been Miss Van Roth's suggestion; she was writing the play and had attended to all arrangements.

That was what Miss Van Roth had said, Steele assured her. He told of having seen Miss Van Roth play Hedda Gabler in Chicago, praised her ability at considerable length, and congratulated Mrs. Vernon on the club's good fortune in having been able to secure her services.

"You are lucky, too," Steele observed in the same conversational tone, "in being able to get her brother, Jack, to handle the properties. That's always about the most difficult job in producing an amateur play."

At the mention of Jack's name Mrs. Vernon started. Her eyes widened, and her face went white under the rouge. Not seeming to notice, Steele went on casually:

"He told us this morning that he had been to see you about them. I believe he said it was the day Mr. Loundon's body was found."

Mrs. Vernon sat rigidly upright and stared at Steele as if unable to speak.

"He was here to see you, wasn't he?"

Still Mrs. Vernon remained silent. Steele regarded her with penetrating eyes.

"Mrs. Vernon, what were you doing in Mr. Loundon's lodge that night?"

Although Steele's voice was not unkind, the suddenness of his question caught Mrs. Vernon unprepared. After one long terrorized look into his face her already taut nerves gave way, and she buried her face in her hands and began to sob. After a little she got up and stood at a window, wiping her eyes with her handkerchief. She did not attempt to leave the room, however, and in a few minutes she returned to her chair.

"I suppose Jack Van Roth told you." Her voice faltered, for she was wholly unaware that Steele's question had been only the result of a shrewd inference. "My going had nothing whatever to do with Mr. Loundon's death." Suddenly her tears started afresh. "I—I—I can't tell you."

When at last she could control herself again, her voice was piteous in its appeal.

"You won't make me tell you, will you? I—I give you my word I don't know anything about Mr. Loundon's death." Steele gave her a commiserating look.

"Mrs. Vernon, there is nothing official about our visit, and I don't want to know anything that isn't connected with the murder. But you must surely realize how your admission would be regarded by the county attorney. If what you know is not incriminating, yet might in any way help us, I advise you to tell me, and I promise that anything you say will be treated as strictly confidential."

She hesitated, and then fearfully shook her head.

"Then may I ask this," Steele said: "Do you think Jack Van Roth had anything to do with the murder?"

Mrs. Vernon's answer came with swift and unexpected venom.

"I think that if he didn't do it himself he knows who did!"

"That is a strong statement, Mrs. Vernon," Steele observed, hiding his satisfaction. "Could you prove that?"

Perceiving that she had made a statement which demanded substantiation, Mrs. Vernon did not answer. Steele did not urge her, but finally, after an indecision of several moments, she looked up at him with a determined expression on her face.

"I could not tell you this, Mr. Steele, if I did not trust you." She glanced at me. "Both of you." She moved her hands nervously. "Twelve years ago, when I was only seventeen, Mr. Loundon and I—well, I was in love with him, and I had a baby. I went to Kansas City, and nobody knew anything about it. He wanted to marry me, but my father wouldn't let him see me. He paid all the bills, and after I told him I wouldn't marry him he married Lola Van Roth. She didn't know about it then, but when he was in the army she found out about it and divorced him. I didn't blame him, and I don't now; it was just one of those awful mistakes that a man like Mr. Loundon can cause."

She paused in her painful narrative, then continued resolutely:

"So far as I knew until the other day, Lola was the only person outside of my family who knew. The baby was put in a home in Kansas City. Later, when I came to Wichita, I adopted her, telling everybody she was the daughter of my sister, who had died. That is what Dr. Vernon believes. My husband is extremely—almost insanely—jealous, and it was because of my fear that he would discover the truth that I did what I did the other night."

Mrs. Vernon's terror at the thought of this possibility made it impossible for her to continue for several moments.

"The morning Mr. Loundon was killed Jack Van Roth telephoned that he wanted to see me about the properties for the play. I thought that was strange, but I said I would see him. Well, when he came he told me he knew about my daughter and told me that if I didn't pay him $3000 he would tell Dr. Vernon. How he found out about it I don't know; I'm sure Lola didn't tell him. I was frantic. He must have seen that I would do anything rather than have my husband know, so he demanded the money by the next day. I promised I would get it for him, thinking my father in El Dorado might furnish it, and so he left. I planned to go that afternoon—Dr. Vernon was in Kansas City—but just before I was ready to leave Lola came to see me."

"Lola!" Steele ejaculated.

"Yes. She wanted to know if Jack had been here, and I told her Yes, and finally told her everything. She was furious. She said Jack had already told her he knew about Vivian—that is my daughter's name—and had threatened to blackmail Mr. Loundon. He knew Mr. Loundon would pay rather than have him tell my husband. She said she told Jack she'd rather see him dead than do a thing like that. But we supposed he had seen Mr. Loundon and that he had refused to pay—or that Jack thought he could get money out of both of us, and that that was the reason he had come to me."

"What time was that, Mrs. Vernon?" Steele interrupted, and his face was black. "You say Lola saw you that same afternoon?"

"Yes. It was about three o'clock."

"Loundon's body was found about eleven. What time was it when Jack saw you in the morning?"

"A little past eleven. He had called me earlier, but I had left home a little before eight to do some shopping and didn't return until nearly ten."

"Then he could have known that Loundon was dead when he came to you. Perhaps he already knew he could get no money from him." Steele's voice was grim. "Please go on."

"Well, Lola tried to reassure me. She told me she would see Jack and promised that he wouldn't go any further. So I didn't go to El Dorado. But when the extra came out telling about the murder, Lola called me and asked me if Mr. Loundon might have had any papers or anything in his possession that might give me away. I said that he might have a letter and some pictures which I had sent him after the war. I asked her why she asked, and she told me about having stayed at the lodge the night before and said she had seen a picture of Vivian in his room. I thought that if the picture was there the letters might be too. I became almost beside myself, and then I guess I lost my head, because I called Jack up—he had given me a telephone number to call—and told him about the letters and pictures, and said that if they were found the truth would be known and he wouldn't get his money. I told him he had to go out and get them. He said he would, but that I would have to go too, to identify them. By that time I would have agreed to anything. I took the car and picked him up, and we drove out to the oil field and walked across to the lodge. And I guess it was you that almost caught us just as we found them."

"Ah! You did get them, then?"

"Yes. We had just found them when we heard you downstairs. We crept to the upstairs porch, and Jack told me he would lower me so that I could get your car started. When I dropped, something ran out from under the bushes and frightened me so that I screamed."

"Something ran out from under the bushes? What was it?"

She shuddered. "I don't know; it seemed too big for a dog, and it didn't run away, but just seemed to move off to one side. I ran to the car and managed to get it started—and I guess you know the rest."

As Mrs. Vernon finished, the tears welled into her eyes again. A more pathetic figure I had never seen, and for my part I felt like a member of an inquisition who has forced a confession from a helpless and unwilling victim. Her eyes remained fixed on Steele in an unspoken appeal for mercy, but for some minutes he looked unseeingly at her, his keen face grave and his eyes narrowed in perturbed reflection. Then he perceived her agitation and attempted to reassure her:

"Mrs. Vernon, I see no reason why anyone should know what you have told us. However, I must tell you that the county attorney will probably demand an interview with you. He already knows that Dr. Vernon's car was parked near the Meridian highway the night you visited the lodge. You and Jack were seen when you got into it and drove away. The fact that the car belonging to the *Times*, which you used in escaping from us at the lodge, was found nearby has led him to suspect you. I am afraid he knows too much for you to make a successful denial. If I can protect you I will. But what I want to know is this: If I think it advisable to take Mr. Warren into my confidence in order to save you from an interview or to restrain him otherwise if he should learn elsewhere what you have told me, what shall I do?"

A swift alarm had come to Mrs. Vernon's face when Steele mentioned the county attorney's suspicion. As he finished she was trembling violently. For several moments she was unable to answer his question, but finally she spoke in a muffled voice:

"I—I can't see him. I know he would make me tell him everything. He might come when my husband is here!" She could hold back her tears no longer. "Mr. Steele, I *have* told you the truth! I *have* told you everything! In God's name don't let him go to my husband! I—I couldn't stand that! I couldn't! I couldn't!"

Steele's calm voice spoke soothingly:

"Don't worry. I will see what I can do. But if I find it necessary to confide in him you will understand why?"

Mrs. Vernon did not speak, but at last she gave him a despairing nod.

"One thing more, Mrs. Vernon. The county attorney wanted to arrest Jack Van Roth this morning, and I'm afraid now, in the light of what you have said, that I made a mistake in not agreeing. I believe he will be arrested, and if he is I'll also do my best to keep him quiet about your daughter. I can't promise, but he will be in no position to want blackmail added to the other charges against him."

By a visible effort Mrs. Vernon regained control of her emotions.

"If my husband should find out it would ruin my life and my daughter's, too. He would never forgive me. What if it becomes known that I was at the lodge?"

"You can say you went out with Jack at Lola's request to arrange about the play. He would gain nothing by denying it. And I'm sure Miss Van Roth would substantiate anything you say."

Mrs. Vernon nodded resignedly. "Yes, I think she would."

Steele got up to go.

"By the way, Mrs. Vernon, do you happen to know anything about the $50,000-insurance policy Mr. Loundon carried in favor of Miss Van Roth?"

The surprise in Mrs. Vernon's face answered his question.

"Why no! But then, there's no reason why I should. I've understood they always remained friends." Then, as she stood, a thought seemed to startle her. "Surely there wouldn't be— That is, you don't think she—"

"No," he answered her; "at least, not until I know more than I do now. . . . One thing more. I'd like to have that telephone number Jack gave you."

"Douglas 5624." She gave it from memory. "I think it is in the name of Sargo."

"Quite likely," Steele said dryly, noting it down on a piece of paper.

He put the paper in his pocket and took her hand.

"You have helped us immeasurably, Mrs. Vernon." He looked down at her kindly. "Keep a stiff upper lip, and things may turn out better than you expect."

She tried to smile as she said good-by, but the tears filled her eyes, and she turned away before we had left the room.

"Well!" Steele ejaculated when we were in the car. "I'm glad the county attorney wasn't along! What he would say now about letting Jack go I don't want to hear!" He lit a cigarette with a rueful scowl.

"How are you going to keep from telling about Mrs. Vernon's trip to the lodge?" I asked as I started the car. "They're bound to insist on seeing her."

"For the time being, my dear Colonel, by simply keeping still," he said shortly, apparently assuming an implied criticism in my question.

"All right! All right!" I retorted; "but I didn't tell you to let him go. For once, I'll put in with Warren. If you see Jack Van Roth again I'll buy you a new hat."

"I'll make that a bet—ten dollars' worth. I told you before that the man who was in the lodge that night wouldn't have gone there if he had committed the murder." He frowned and pursed his lips, as if for the moment he doubted his own statement. "No, crazy as he is, even Jack wouldn't have done that. But the fact that he came to Mrs. Vernon indicates he knew Loundon was dead, and that ought to indicate that he knew he could prove who was the murderer or he wouldn't have taken the chance of being picked up at the lodge. As a matter of fact I'm more certain than ever that Jack will attempt to make good tonight. What I am afraid of is that the damned arrogant young fool is underestimating the chances he's taking; because I tell you, whoever killed Loundon is as dangerous as he is clever, and Jack isn't the man to fool him."

After this observation Steele lapsed into a morose silence. I had planned to return to the office, but I was too curious to learn where Steele's moody ruminations would lead him to break in on his train of thought. I drove slowly across town and into Riverside Park, at last pulling up in a secluded spot by the river just off the municipal golf course.

"You see," Steele stated, as if nearly half an hour had not elapsed since his last remark, "we can't afford to have anything happen to Jack, because he's undoubtedly the only person who could actually prove before a jury how Loundon was killed and who did it."

"You talk as if you knew," I said.

"I don't know," he replied, "but sometimes I make some very good guesses."

I had long since discovered that the quickest way to silence Steele and the shortest road to his displeasure was to seek to learn his conclusions before he was ready to volunteer them, so I held my tongue. For another five minutes he sat in silence, gazing down on the sand bars and shining shallows of the river.

"There is this to consider." He spoke at last, half to himself. "If Dr. Vernon had learned of his wife's secret without her knowing it, how far might his mad jealousy lead him?"

"But he was in Kansas City!" I exclaimed.

"But if he wasn't in Kansas City!" He made a gesture of irritation. "Or suppose he had learned of it, and she knew he had learned of it—what more clever method could she have used to mislead us than her tears and entreaties of this morning. . . . Now if he was the murderer and she knew it—"

"I don't follow you."

"All right, we'll let that pass!"

The almost childish sarcasm with which Steele thus expressed the exasperation so typical of him when he had reached an impasse in his cogitations angered me even though I knew it was unintentional and wholly impersonal.

"O.K.," I said, slapping on the starter, "God knows I'd rather be working!"

Steele let me get almost to town, then suddenly he burst out laughing. For several blocks I stared straight ahead without a glance at him. But it was one of his disagreeable gifts to be able to joke me out of any resentment I ever momentarily felt for him. At last some absurd remark forced a reluctant smile out of me. When he saw he had succeeded, Steele said:

"I'm going to see Dr. Vernon. Will you drop me off there, or will I drop you off there, or will you come along?"

"I'll come." I gave in. "But you've got to buy me a drink and apologize. I'll be damned if you professionals can treat me like an equal!"

The drugstore where we indulged in our Kansas version of the cocktail hour was on the ground floor of the building where Dr. Vernon and most of the leading Wichita physicians had their offices.

When we had been served, Steele remarked: "I understand Vernon is somewhat of a character. Tell me something."

I related what was common knowledge in Wichita:

Dr. Vernon had been a major in the army, and was the domineering god and devil of the Research Hospital in whose presence all the nurses and most of the doctors alternately worshiped and trembled. He was recognized as the most skillful and resourceful surgeon in the Southwest—a rare diagnostician, unhesitating and fearless at the operating table. He was no less energetic and aggressive in civic affairs; an ex-president of the chamber of commerce, whose force and talent for organization had built the Research Hospital and had made possible the new and elaborate system of city parks. He had a reputation for ruthlessness in his dealings with patients and with business associates as well; was respected more than loved, and feared more than respected.

"What about his Wild West collection? Someone told me he is an authority on the range-cattle era."

"That's right. His father was a cattleman; drove herds up the old Chisholm Trail in the seventies. I wrote a Sunday feature story on his father about a year ago. He was a powerful, two-fisted Texan, shrewd enough to foresee the end of the range-cattle business and invest his money in cheap wheat lands in the Arkansas Valley. He's still a hero to his son—he's been dead about ten years. Dr. Vernon knows as much as anyone in Wichita about the old cattle trade and its byproducts, the cowboy, the gambler, the prostitute and the desperado. If you can't get him to talk about anything else he'll always warm up on that subject."

"There's a tip." Steele nodded. "Let's go up."

Dr. Vernon's suite of offices consisted of a large reception room, three elaborately fitted consultation rooms for himself and two assistants, another inner office, and a long unique private office seldom seen by patients. When we had convinced the girl in the reception room that we were not afflicted, I got word to the doctor that I had a friend who wanted to see his Western relics, and we were finally admitted to his private office.

It was a large corner room, and to enter it was like stepping from a twentieth-century surgery into a nineteenth-century ranch house. Navajo rugs and Indian-tanned skins covered the floor; Remington prints, Indian bows and arrows, a couple of ancient Spanish swords and several old carbines and rifles decorated the walls. In front of the windows were glass cases containing Indian flints, beadwork, spurs and bits, pistols and revolvers, and other objects illustrative of early-day life on the plains. The only concession to modernity were a number of easy chairs and a large flat-top desk in the center of the room.

For a few minutes we were left alone, and Steele was examining a branding iron in one of the cases when Dr. Vernon entered. He was a large and muscular man of fifty-five with the appearance and carriage of forty; iron gray of hair and mustache, brusque and direct in manner. He shook hands with me, and when I introduced Steele his luminous brown eyes appraised him swiftly. If he recognized him, however, he made no mention of it. Instead he noted Steele's interest in the branding iron and withdrew it from the case.

"That's one my father used: Bar-V. I've got a larger one out at the ranch. I don't suppose you ever used one?"

Steele shook his head. "Not much. I did ride a couple of summers for my uncle in Wyoming when I was a boy, but the roundup was usually about over when I got there."

Dr. Vernon glanced at him with new interest. He pulled out a crude wrought-iron object. "Know what this is?"

Steele examined it with interest. "Looks like a bit." He twisted it about in his hands with a puzzled air. "I suppose the lower jaw goes through this ring. But I can't imagine what this perforated flange at the bottom of the ring is for."

Dr. Vernon took it. "That's what it is: an old Spanish bit, found out in western Kansas nearly forty years ago. It belongs to Saul Jones, who runs the paper out at Byrons. He's giving it to the State Historical Society at Topeka. Wouldn't let me buy it, damn him. Might have been dropped by Coronado's men when they came up through Kansas in 1541. I told him I'd take out his appendix and tonsils, cut out his hemorrhoids, fix up his prostate, and even give him a Brinkley goat-gland operation if he'd set a price on it." He turned to me chuckling. "You know Saul. He said I wasn't man enough to fool with him!"

Dr. Vernon laughed and held the bit out in front of him.

"You're the first man I ever showed this bit to who could figure out how it was used. See how that inverted V goes up against the roof of the mouth when the curb rein is used, and how the ring catches the lower jaw? Cruel! But the principle is the same as any curb bit. I'm not surprised you couldn't guess what these holes in the bottom were for. It took the secretary of the Historical Society a month to find out. They were to suspend tassels from to keep evil spirits away!"

"They were artists in cruelty—those old Spaniards—" Steele examined the bit again and then handed it back—"but they've never been beat for courage—and they carried some nice sentiments about with them too. I suppose you've seen the Coronado sword in the Historical Society Museum in Topeka?"

Dr. Vernon nodded as he returned the branding iron and bit to the case. "Yes! I've got a picture of it. It was found about the same time and in the same section as this bit."

"Then you remember the inscription on the blade:

'Ne Me Saques Sin Razon;
Ne Me Enbaines Sin Honor.'

"That means," Steele translated for my benefit, "'Unsheathe me not without cause; sheathe me not without honor.' Well," he laughed, "the day the secretary was showing the sword to me a Mexican boy happened to be standing near by, and he asked the boy if he could translate it. He took the sword and puzzled over it a minute. Then he said, 'I can't translate it, but I know what it means. It means, "Don't take me out till they jump onto you, and don't put me back until you beat hell out of 'em!"'"

"Pretty good translation at that," Dr. Vernon chuckled. Then he took out his watch. "Well, I wonder what else you'd like to see?

I'm sorry to say I've got only a few minutes more I can spare right now. How about this 'Wild Bill' Hickok revolver?" He turned to another case. "It's nothing to be so proud of, though. You know Wild Bill owned more guns than there are beds George Washington slept in!"

"He's not one of my particular heroes," Steele observed. "Tom Smith cleaned up Abilene with a lot less noise, and to my way of thinking, a lot more nerve."

"You're right!" Dr. Vernon regarded him with delighted agreement. "We'll have to continue this another time! How about lunch with me tomorrow? I can arrange to have some time to spare afterwards."

"I'd be delighted," Steele replied. "Unless I find I'm tied up. I'm working with the county in this Loundon murder case, and you never know what may bob up." He hesitated a moment. "As a matter of fact, that's partly why I came up to see you today."

Dr. Vernon's eyebrows went up, but I could detect no other indication of surprise, and there was no reluctance in his reply.

"I surmised you were interested; I remember your work in the Grayland case." He had recognized Steele, then. "But I don't know how I can be of help. However—" he glanced again at his watch—"I might take a few minutes."

"I've nothing of any consequence to ask; another time would do as well. You were Loundon's physician, and I thought possibly you might know something about his physical condition that would help explain his actions around the time he was killed."

"Oh!" Dr. Vernon's affability returned. "You refer to his drinking? I did an appendectomy for him about six months ago and warned him then that he had better cut down on his liquor. Apparently he didn't follow my advice. But he had made a nice recovery, and so far as I know was otherwise physically sound."

"Did he ever use drugs?"

Dr. Vernon shook his head. "No, I don't think so. He wasn't the type; certainly he wasn't addicted to the use of any drug. Why do you ask that?"

"No reason; except that liquor alone hardly accounts for the condition he apparently was in the last day or two he was alive."

"Well, of course, you never know. I hadn't seen him in a month. I've been out of town for a week; just drove back yesterday from Kansas City."

"You drove?" Steele displayed a polite interest. "Pretty good half-day from Kansas City here, isn't it?"

"Half day!" Dr. Vernon scouted such driving time. "It's only two hundred and forty miles. I made it in four and a half hours. Came around by way of Cassoday and El Dorado."

"Too fast for me!" Steele laughed, and held out his hand. "Well, thank you, Doctor—I'm looking forward to our lunch tomorrow."

"Good!" Dr. Vernon shook hands cordially. "Say twelve-thirty—at the club. Good-by."

When we got off the elevator Steele led the way into the drug-store again.

"I crave another drink," he explained.

He ordered and then sat drumming a long lean forefinger on the glass-topped table, scowling so absently into a case of cosmetics that he never noticed the smile with which our pert little waitress served him. I grinned hopefully, but my friendliness was always a failure in the presence of Steele's looks and curly red hair. Finally he put down his glass with this weighty observation:

"In the detective business gratuitous information is often a very valuable thing—if you know how to interpret it."

"Oh, quite!" I concurred in the dark. "Quite so, indeed!— The hell you say!"

"That is to say, my dumb young friend, that the Cottonwood Falls–Cassoday–El Dorado highway is closed, has been closed for two weeks, and will be closed for a month. I know, because I tried to drive to Wichita from Kansas City that way myself. Now, how the hell, as you so graphically express it, did Dr. Vernon make such remarkable time on a road that right now would stop an army tank?"

13

WE LEFT IMMEDIATELY for the county attorney's office. When we entered the room we found Burke and Warren in an excited conference which they at once terminated to greet us with broad smiles of self-satisfaction. The alacrity with which the sheriff jumped up to offer Steele his chair at Warren's desk indicated that some momentous disclosure was at hand and that this time credit would be due where credit was due. What this was appeared forthwith.

"Well, Mr. Steele—" Burke sat on the edge of the desk and looked down at him—"we found that Jack Van Roth was the boy at the lodge the other night, and the woman who was with him was Mrs. Vernon!"

"What! You don't say!"

Steele was properly astounded.

"Yes sir! Just what I said all along—I mean about Mrs. Vernon. Seems Jack had something on her and Loundon. Don't know what it was—it don't make any sense—but we got it straight, and it won't take long to make her talk once we get her down here."

"H'm, that *is* something!" Steele lit a cigarette and gave Burke an admiring look. "How did you find out about it?"

"One of Jack's little friends. Seems he heard Jack talking to Mrs. Vernon over the telephone just before they went to the lodge. We're laying off of Jack, like Mr. Warren says—though I guess now you can see what a damn fool idea that was—but that didn't keep us from bringing in a few of his pals. We saw right away that this boy was holding out on us; but they don't any of them like to be mixed up in murder, and he soon spilled it."

"He didn't know what Jack had on them, eh?" I recognized a tone of relief in Steele's voice. "What do you suppose he was up to, blackmail?"

"On Mrs. Vernon—my guess is Yes. And maybe that's what he started with Loundon, but it ended up in murder!"

"You still think he would have gone out to the lodge again after he had killed Loundon?"

"Mr. Steele, that bird is nuts! If it was anybody else I'd say no; but him, yes!"

Steele nodded slowly, almost convinced, it seemed to me, in spite of himself.

"Yes, maybe you're right. It's certain we can't take any chances with him tonight. Who are you going to take with you?"

"Dodge and Phelps and Bolton. With you and me and Mr. Warren and Bill here, that ought to be more than plenty."

"I wonder if I could talk with them a minute before we go? I've got an idea or two I'd like to suggest, and it might be a good thing to have them here."

Burke's glow of good nature extended even to this usurpation of his authority, which in another mood he might have resented.

"Why sure; I'll round 'em up right now."

The moment Burke had closed the door behind him Steele turned to Warren. Swiftly he related what Mrs. Vernon had told us and asked him to postpone his proposed interview at least until tomorrow, requesting as a personal favor that he also respect the promise of secrecy Steele had given her. But Warren refused point-blank. He pointed out that Burke had discovered Mrs. Vernon's complicity wholly independently of Steele and that she would certainly reveal as much to them as she had to him. I was aware that Steele had realized the truth of this assertion before he disclosed to Warren what he had learned. Whether he was merely trying to protect Mrs. Vernon or had another reason, I could not guess. To my surprise he went on to recount our interview with Dr. Vernon and called attention to the doctor's misstatement about the trip home from Kansas City.

"Suppose Dr. Vernon in some way learned what Jack knew about Mrs. Vernon's daughter," Steele said earnestly. "If he did not go to Kansas City, but instead had an interview with Loundon at the lodge, what then? I tell you, Warren, as sure as I'm sitting here, Jack Van Roth did not kill Loundon, and if you go ahead on that assumption you'll regret it."

The gravity of Steele's manner impressed Warren despite his convictions.

"Well, what do you want to do?" he demanded a little irritably. "Arrest Dr. Vernon?"

"Of course not. Do you know a good private detective in Kansas City we could get to check up the hotels? If Dr. Vernon was there it should be easy enough to find out."

Warren considered. "Fred Reed is a good man. I'll send him a wire."

"No," Steele objected, "I'd like to talk to him. What's his address?"

Grudgingly Warren agreed to the call. When Reed was on the phone he explained the situation—then let Steele talk. Steele informed the detective that he not only wanted to know when and for how long Dr. Vernon had been in Kansas City, but if he was there, any details that could be learned about his stay.

When he had finished he said, "Sounds as if he knew his business." Then he turned to Warren with a relieved smile. "Thank, old man; and now what do you say—there's no use in throwing Mrs. Vernon to the scandalmongers until we hear what Reed discovers, is there?"

The county attorney regarded Steele uncertainly under lowered brows.

"Steele, if I thought you were just stalling me off on this thing I'll be damned if I wouldn't have her down here this minute."

Steele laughed. "I'm simply trying to prevent you from making the mistake of spoiling two women's lives unless it's absolutely necessary. You know what would happen if Burke got her down here and found out the truth. The chances are Dr. Vernon doesn't know anything and hasn't done anything. If he is implicated the worst move you could make would be to let him know of your suspicions before we have something to go on. But here comes Burke."

The sheriff introduced Phelps and Bolton; Dodge was the tow-headed deputy who had discovered Loundon's car. They all knew Jack and understood what our mission was to be.

"The difficulty is, Jack isn't the man we want," Steele explained, and I had never seen him more serious. "It's the person he will have with him that we're after, and I don't need to warn you that he will probably shoot on sight the minute he suspects he's been trapped. Now it was my idea, Burke, that you and Warren and Bill and I stay inside the lodge, while Phelps and Bolton and Dodge remain hidden outside. I'd suggest that Dodge and Phelps hide in the bushes on the far end of the footbridge, and Bolton can stay on the west end of the house in the shrubbery."

"I don't get you, Mr. Steele." Burke shook his head, puzzled. "What's the idea of having them on the other side of the bridge so far away from the house?"

"Simply this," Steele's voice became grim. "Instead of Jack's trapping Loundon's murderer I believe Loundon's murderer is trying to trap Jack! I don't think Jack chose the lodge; in my opinion the man we're after made that appointment. Why? Because half the people in the town will be just across the river watching the attempt to cap the gusher, and yet only a few steps away is this secluded spot where a man could commit a murder and get back in the crowd without ever being seen. If this is a good guess, what would he do—come to the lodge and risk an ambush? I don't think so. Jack didn't say he would meet him in the lodge, he said he would bring him. Yet they wouldn't meet where they could be seen together in the crowd. For that reason my guess is that Jack is to meet him near the crowd and that somewhere between there and the lodge the murderer will attempt to wipe out the only evidence there is against him. I don't think he will ever come nearer the lodge than the bridge; therefore that's why I suggest putting two men there— and on second thought I believe all three had better be there, for he surely would never plan their meeting across the river."

It was obvious that this explanation of Jack's rendezvous had not occurred to Warren and Burke. They had assumed that Van Roth had outwitted them to gain time for a getaway, or for some other ulterior motive. The possibility that Jack himself might be the victim awoke them to the importance of the night's assignment.

Burke's face reddened with thought, then he slapped the desk with a heavy hand.

"Well then, why don't we put some more of the boys on the job to spot Jack when he shows up and tail him out of the crowd? That way we couldn't miss him."

"You might spot him, but you'd be sure to scare off the other." Steele shook his head. "If my guess is right he won't take any chances of being followed. Of course what I've said is only a guess and we can't cover all the approaches to the lodge. About all we can do is to pick out the most likely place there at the bridge and be ready at the lodge. After all, we've got to assume that Jack can do what he says he will. It may be he started out to blackmail the murderer and got cold feet. If that's the case the other isn't so likely to suspect a trap and might even decide to kill Jack in the lodge."

"You keep talking about killing!" Warren interjected. "Assuming all this imaginative guesswork is right—which I don't believe— why wouldn't he rather pay blackmail than run the risk of another murder?"

Steele stood up slowly, and I was aware that the tone of Warren's objection had nettled him. He leaned deliberately over the desk, and there was an ominous quality in his voice as he answered:

"Because whoever murdered Loundon would kill every man in this room if he thought it necessary. Now whatever you may think, that's no guess!"

Warren opened his mouth to retort, then changed his mind. His impatience at Steele's conduct of the case was understandable, but experience had taught him a respect which prevented too plain-spoken a transgression of the other's good nature. After some further discussion, Steele and I left, with the understanding that we would meet at the lodge at seven.

It was now past five, and I proposed an early dinner. But Steele, with an irritability that continued to grow as the evening progressed, said I could have dinner if I wanted to, but as for him, he was going immediately to the Meridian oil field and would pick up a sandwich on the way. As was his manner when there was prospect of action, he high-handedly assumed I would do as he asked, and when we were in the car he directed me to drive to the apartment. Here he got a revolver out of his bag and asked to see one which he was aware I kept in my bedroom. While I made up some sandwiches he carefully examined and loaded both weapons. When he had finished we ate hurriedly. Within fifteen minutes we were back in the car again.

The highway between town and the Meridian oil field had the appearance of Chicago's Michigan Avenue at a rush hour. The afternoon extras containing pictures of the gigantic gusher and describing the efforts being made to bring it under control had attracted thousands of onlookers. I perceived before I had gone a mile that if we were to get there within an hour I would have to take a byroad. These, too, were clouded with the dust of traffic, and it was almost six before I found a place to park nearly half a mile from the field.

Even at this distance the roar of the gusher, as we stepped from the car, sounded like a nearby Niagara. When we came to the highway, a quarter of a mile from the well, we found traffic officers from town keeping the double lines of automobiles on the move and saw others on the ground holding back the crowds. A rope barrier encircled the well and the hastily excavated slush ponds at a distance of several hundred feet. This, I knew, was not so much to give space for the workers as to provide against the great danger of fire, that ever-present nightmare of drillers when oil flows wild and the air is charged with escaping gas.

Oil wells were nothing new to me, although I had never witnessed such a tremendous rusty black torrent as we now beheld shooting upward into the hazy air. But to Steele, despite his wide experience in various parts of the world, it was a novel spectacle, and he reveled in the excitement with all his adventurous spirit.

As if shot from a cannon, the spouting geyser roared through the top of the 120-foot derrick, drenching the surrounding land and sending a golden, slimy mist on the south wind over the wheat fields to the north. The gas fumes were almost overpowering. The noise was deafening. Rocks and balls of mud pelted the earth. The vibration was like that of a continuous earthquake, shaking houses and rattling doors and windows as though they were hanging loose. Throbbing with the energy of a thousand subterranean turbines, the gusher spurted its purple-black cloud awesomely toward the heavens while the ever-gathering crowd looked on in wonder and the crew of workers prepared to accept the challenge nature had so unexpectedly hurled at them.

Aloft, festooned around the steel tower of the derrick, were a number of lengths of the heavy drilling pipe which only that morning had been attached to the drillers' bit several thousand feet down in the well hole. This pipe, weighing more than two thousand pounds, had flown into the air like a feather on the breeze. While men in steel helmets and dripping slickers worked beneath, a loose cable whipped around the steel rigging, threatening any minute to strike a spark that might blow them to bits.

Within the enclosure, where he was directing the work of these men, I could make out Fielding Garnett's tall figure. A few minutes later, in a car thirty or forty feet outside the barrier, I saw Monest and his niece, Dora, intently watching the battle for the flow of liquid gold that meant an unexpected fortune to them both. As I turned to point them out to Steele I saw Gus Holm, our oil editor, making his way out of the crowd. I caught Steele by the arm and hurried after Gus, knowing that he could enlighten us on the methods that would be used in this struggle against what seemed such overwhelming odds.

Holm turned around and grinned when I stopped him, then shouted for us to follow. He led us to where his car was parked in the yard of a nearby dealer in rig timbers, perhaps a quarter of a mile from the well.

"We can still see her blow from here," he said, motioning us to the rear seat, "and if she decides to put on any fireworks we won't

be so damned close. Wait a minute, till I get these plugs out of my
ears!"

He pried at his ears and in a moment withdrew two felt plugs.
Observing Steele's curious eyes on them, he explained

"They all wear 'em when these babies come in like this. If you
don't you can't hear anything for a week!"

He turned to me. "Well, what do you think? I said twenty thousand barrels this morning, and I won't take back a pint of it! Maybe
she won't do it now, but she's going into oil every hour."

"What did you mean by fireworks?" Steele inquired. "Is there
really serious danger of fire?"

For an answer Gus leaned out of the car window and pointed.

"Look over there. See those fire trucks? Those are chemical
wagons and foam tanks. And look along the ground in the street in
front of those buildings. Hose already strung. And I'll bet, if you'll
scout around a little, you'll find two or three ambulances waiting
for the explosion. No sir! This is big-time stuff, and they're not
taking any chances." He withdrew his head from the window and
faced us solemnly. "They'll be lucky if this one doesn't catch fire.
Too much gas and spraying oil mixed with that loose stuff on the
derrick! Just a few sparks, and Zowie! you'd think Vesuvius had
sprouted in Kansas!"

"How will they bring it under control?" Steele asked.

Gus shook his head. "I don't know for sure. The casing's torn
off at the ground. But I understand they've already started work
on a Christmas Tree."

"A Christmas Tree?"

"That's what they call it. It's a kind of heavy pipe arrangement
they use to try to cap these big gushers. When they get it ready
they'll haul it out and drag it into the derrick. It's equipped with a
big die nipple to fit over the mouth of the well. When they get it in
the center of the flow and chain it down they'll gradually lower it
over the end of the casing. The die will be turned by long levers.
The idea is, the teeth of the die bite new threads into the casing,
making a new connection that will shoot the oil and gas up through
the pipe of the Christmas Tree. This pipe has a series of valves.

One at a time, as they think they can hold the pressure, they will close these valves, reducing the flow, and gradually bring her under control."

Steele nodded appreciatively, and for a minute he watched the bellowing monster that had roared to freedom from its earth-bound cage.

"But these fellows who will have to do the job," Steele asked— "what chance have they got if it explodes?"

Gus shrugged his shoulders fatalistically. "If I were Bill here, now, working on the literary side, I'd call 'em the unsung heroes that put the gas in the limousines of the effete rich and provide the oil that lubricates the wheels of civilization. Or something like that. Leaving out the hooey, that's what they are. They run the risk of burning to death every time they turn a wrench. That takes guts, and they've got what it takes.

"Of course—" Gus searched his pockets for the cigarettes he seldom possessed—"they protect 'em all they can. Their hammers and mallets are made of wood or copper wherever possible. And most of the other tools are heavily taped. Some producers, I understand, have all their machinery, tools and metal equipment specially made of Ampco bronze so there won't be any sparks."

I handed him the cigarette he was still fumbling for.

"Thanks," he said. "I left mine at the office on purpose so I wouldn't be absent-mindedly lighting one out here by the well."

"Ha!" I said. "Here, take the pack! You've been bumming cigarettes off me for five years, and that's the first good alibi you ever had!"

Gus grinned, unabashed, and put the package in his pocket.

"I'll pay you back when they bring in a well on that offset I was telling you about!" He looked at his wristwatch. "Quarter of seven! Boy, I've got to beat it!"

Reluctantly we turned from the absorbing spectacle and pushed our way through the crowd to our car. By this time automobiles were parked in strings along the byroads for miles in every direction.

"Everybody and his brother is out here," Steele commented; "and most of them, I suppose, hoping for a fire. I saw Van Roth and his daughter Lola back there on the highway, and there's Ripley parking down the road ahead of us."

As I was maneuvering the car out of the jam I heard a boyish voice hail Steele and saw Joe Capello grinning at us from the side of the road.

"Hello, Joe," Steele smiled. "Why aren't you over at the well?"

"Just come from there!" Joe answered. "Been over all day. I saw her come in!" He grinned proudly. "I'm just goin' home to get somethin' to eat—I live right down there."

Steele stopped me as I would have driven on.

"You're just the boy I want to see, Joe. Come here a minute!" Joe got on the running board, and Steele asked, "Do you know Miss Monest's motorboat when you see it?"

"Which one?"

"Both of them." Steele smiled. "The small one, I think."

"Sure; that one's the *Water Bug*. The big one's the *Aphrodite*."

"Joe, if you had a chance to earn a dollar do you think you could do a job without saying anything about it to anybody, even Hen?"

"Sure!" Joe's eyes sparkled.

"All right. The first thing in the morning I want you to go down to Miss Monest's boathouse and hang around until you get a chance to examine the inside of both of those boats, particularly the *Water Bug*—and what I want you to look for is straws!"

Joe's eyes widened.

"I get you!"

"If you find any, and can gather some up without anyone seeing you, I want them."

"O.K., Mr. Steele, I won't say nothin' to anybody."

"Good. Here's a quarter for carfare. Now hang on, and we'll drop you at your house."

Because of the traffic on the highway I drove north and crossed the river two miles upstream. We left the car in a clump of trees a quarter of a mile from the lodge, reaching the building at exactly seven o'clock, to find the front door unlocked and Warren and Burke waiting inside. Warren locked the door, Burke informed us that the three deputies were at their posts, and we sat down in the huge dim room with a long hour to pass before time for the appointment which none of us felt was likely ever to be kept. The incessant sound of locusts in the trees outside made a shrill accompaniment to the ominous roar of the gusher across the river, with a cricket somewhere in the building occasionally interjecting a rasping staccato. The heat in the tightly closed room was intense, and, as the minutes slowly passed, our whispered conversations gradually gave way to a nervous and uncomfortable silence.

At eight o'clock the room was nearly dark. Burke got up, shifted his belt and holster, and moved toward the door. For fifteen minutes more we waited in tense expectancy.

Then suddenly an explosion that rattled the windows and seemed to rock the building on its foundations brought us to our feet. Instantly the room filled with a lurid glow. By its light we gazed at each other in startled apprehension. Then Steele rushed to one of the north windows and pulled aside the blind.

"It's the oil well! They've had an explosion; it's on fire!"

I ran to the window and looked out. Through the treetops a gigantic orange flame was leaping and whirling into the sky. Clouds of black smoke shot with red boiled upward. The roar had become a blast that shook the earth like continuous thunder. Suddenly Steele whirled from the window. How he could have heard anything else in the room was past my comprehension.

"Listen!" he exclaimed. "Someone's at the door!"

In a moment we all heard it. Gun in hand, Steele ran swiftly across the room and waited for the door to open. But instead, the loud, impatient pounding continued. Steele lifted the latch and flung the door open. Deputy Dodge hurried into the room.

"Jack's dead!" he announced excitedly. "He shot himself!"

"Shot himself!" Steele ejaculated. "What do you mean?"

"Come on, I'll show you. He's over by the bridge!" We followed at a run down the gravel driveway and across the rustic bridge. Thirty feet beyond the riverbank, on the little path that ran beside the osage orange hedge, we found Phelps and Bolton standing beside Jack Van Roth's dead body.

He had fallen forward and lay with the left side of his face in a pool of blood. In his right hand he still gripped a revolver. By the lurid light of the burning well we could see the dark hole in his temple where the bullet had entered, surrounded by a black smudge of powder burns.

Without waiting for explanations Steele dropped to his knees and put a finger on the wound. The blood was still moist and came off red. He moved a leg; it had not yet begun to stiffen. Then he asked me for the flashlight which I had in my pocket and carefully examined the hand which held the revolver. In a few moments he got up.

"You haven't moved him?" he asked Dodge.

"No."

"How did you happen to see him? I thought you were hiding in those bushes."

"Well, just before that explosion we thought we saw something over this way—"

"You mean, on the ground?"

"No, moving. So we were all set—and then that oil well exploded and damn near made us jump into the river. We thought we were all killed! Fred said he thought he heard a gun, but there was so much noise, with pieces of the derrick falling, etc., that we couldn't be sure. In a little bit, though, I thought I saw something on the ground here, and we came over."

"You didn't see anybody else?"

"No."

"How long did you wait?"

"Half a minute, wasn't it, Fred? Maybe a minute."

Steele grunted and turned the flashlight on the ground about the body. The path was beaten hard, and the earth was dry. It was obvious that if a second person had been with Jack there was no chance of identifying his footprints. Steele kneeled again and scrutinized the hand which clutched the revolver. Then he looked up at Warren and Burke.

"Shall we take a look at this gun?"

"Sure," Burke said. "Let's see if it's been fired."

"If he was shot with a bullet from that revolver it will certainly look like suicide," Warren agreed.

Steele made a noise that could have been either a laugh or an audible sneer.

"It was with this gun. You don't need to worry about that!"

He carefully loosened the fingers from the grip without touching the revolver. Then he picked it up by the trigger guard and minutely scrutinized the barrel under the flashlight. At last he shook his head, plainly disappointed.

"Can't see a fingerprint in this light!" He got up and turned to Warren. "Would you think it strange, if a man had killed himself, to find the barrel of his revolver apparently wiped clean?" He did not wait for an answer. "I would; but I'd like to examine it again under a better light." He shrugged his shoulders and broke the gun. The chamber was fully loaded except for one empty shell under the hammer.

"Suicide!" he exclaimed sardonically.

"Nevertheless, if you don't mind—" he took out a handkerchief and wrapped it loosely about the revolver—"I'll take another look at this later."

He handed Burke the gun and leaned over the body. "Odd that it didn't drop out of his hand when he fell. Also, very curious to see a man who has shot himself pitch forward on his face. He must have committed suicide at a fast walk! Most men prefer to take it standing still. But then, as the sheriff has said, Jack was nuts!"

Steele was going swiftly through Jack's clothing. When he straightened up he had in his hands the articles usually carried in a man's pockets, plus a square white unaddressed envelope and five revolver cartridges.

"How careless," Steele remarked, holding up one of the bullets. "Yes, Jack was certainly nuts. He shot himself with a .38 and here he was carrying around .32 ammunition for it! Or if he wasn't careless somebody was!"

Steele dropped the cartridges in his pocket and held up the envelope. "Whatever this is has a strange feel between the fingers. I wonder—"

He broke off and held before Burke's astonished gaze several tufts of long golden-brown hair!

14

THE EXPLOSION AND FIRE at Hovey No. 4's gusher will go down in oil-well history as one of the greatest disasters in the Kansas field. Three men were killed outright in the explosion, four more were severely burned, and a number of spectators suffered burns and minor injuries caused by falling mud and stone and pieces of metal.

Among the latter were Charles Ripley, who was struck on the shoulder, and Fielding Garnett. According to the *Times*:

> Garnett miraculously escaped death when one of the slush ponds ignited a few minutes after the explosion and set fire to his overalls. Fortunately, he had been called away from the immediate vicinity of the well a short time before the explosion occurred. He probably owes his life to the prompt action of a nearby tool-dresser, who beat out the flames.

One of the heroes of the disaster was Dr. Vernon. He and his wife had arrived fifteen minutes before the gusher burst into flames. He immediately established an emergency first-aid station and gave personal medical treatment to all the injured. Persons who assisted claimed that two of those whose lives were saved would have died had he not been on the ground.

The death of Jack Van Roth was minor news compared with this spectacular event. Our early-morning edition of the *Times* carried an excellent account of the explosion and fire under a four-

column head, and I got under the wire with a satisfactory support-
ing feature story. This fact served a little to neutralize the acid
observations our managing editor delivered the next morning when
he slapped down a copy of the *Herald's* first extra on my desk when
I arrived at eight o'clock. Why he was down so early I didn't inquire; I was too busy reading the thrilling account of the solution
of the Loundon murder mystery, which divided the *Herald's* front
page with the story of the fire.

I had been aware the night before that the county attorney and
the sheriff both were inclined to call Jack Van Roth's death suicide and to accept it as the solution of the case. I was not aware,
however, that Warren would go so far as to make a public announcement of this opinion. Nevertheless, despite Steele's earnest
objections, Warren had allowed himself to be interviewed by a
Herald reporter. Noting that we had played down our story, the
Herald had turned its version into an apparent scoop. It made very
good reading for the county attorney and the sheriff too, for it appeared that Jack had committed suicide at the moment when he
was on the point of being apprehended by these able and energetic
officers.

This last phrase did not appear in the news story. It was pointed
out to me by the managing editor where it stood out like a chicsale
in a fog from a ten-point boxed editorial on the first page. His heavy
forefinger lingered much longer than was necessary on the con-
cluding sentence, which read:

> And so again the *Herald* wishes to call the attention
> of its readers to the efficiency of our regular local
> officials and to remind its subscribers that the *Her-
> ald* has proved once more that it is, as always, FIRST
> WITH THE NEWS WHEN THE NEWS IS NEWS.

I had always found it difficult to conduct polite conversation
with our managing editor under such circumstances. In view of
the *Herald's* insinuating reference to "local" officers I refrained
from telling him that I had taken Steele's advice in writing my brief

story. I merely stated that I still thought Warren and Burke were gaga, without citing my authority.

"Yeah?" he said succinctly—it was his habit to be uncommonly succinct when the *Herald* used that "First with the News when the News is News" line. "But what are you going to do when the county attorney and the sheriff tell you the case is closed? Bring in Scotland Yard? If you ask me we've already had too much Sherlock Holmes in the news end of this story!"

I had a very succinct comeback on the end of my tongue, but it wasn't one that is generally used on managing editors. After all, I knew he had some confidence in me, and despite momentary misgivings I still had confidence in Steele. I said nothing, meekly, and let him wear himself out.

Nevertheless, when Steele came in the office half an hour later I explained my predicament and demanded reassurances.

"Reassurances, is it?" He breezily took a chair and picked up the *Herald* from my desk. "Well, isn't that a strange coincidence! As I was reading this very editorial, not fifteen minutes ago, I thought to myself, now who might be standing in need of some reassurances this fine morning? And pop! whose name should come into my head but yours?"

"What's one man's humor is another man's pain in the neck!" I got one succinct remark out of my system.

"Well how are these for reassurances?" He reached into his pocket and pulled out a tiny bundle of straws. "Joe brought them to the house this morning just after you left."

"What! Did he get those out of Miss Monest's boat?"

"The *Water Bug*." Steele nodded. "Apparently our diving beauty lied to us when she said she did not go farther up the river than the bridge over the Hutchinson highway the morning of the sixteenth. To my mind these point conclusively to the strawstack where Loundon's body was found." He crumpled up the *Herald* and threw it in the wastebasket. "Now anyone—even a managing editor or a county attorney—knows she didn't go there alone."

"Who, then?"

"Garnett or Monest—probably Garnett. Weren't he and Miss Monest invited by Loundon to visit the lodge that morning? Monest was back in town around ten. We have only Garnett's word for his whereabouts—and he and Miss Monest admit having been in the neighborhood of the bridge at about the same time."

"But it was Monest's car that was at the lodge."

"And what if Garnett for some reason was driving Monest's car? They could have traded at the oil well, you know. Monest, with a perfect alibi back in town, which would not permit time to have been at the lodge, would protect Garnett, who had no such alibi, by insisting that he drove his own car and that it could not have been at the lodge that morning. Now why should they have traded cars, assuming my guess is correct? A good guesser could think of lots of reasons, but the most logical one is car trouble, with one or the other not wanting to wait. Why should Monest, with four new tires, have been driving with an old spare tire?—Because he had tire trouble after he left town. Possibly one of Garnett's men at the well made the change of tires while Monest took Garnett's car and returned to town."

I considered this rather tenuous chain of suppositions. "Pretty fair guessing, but not what I could take to a managing editor nor you to a county attorney."

"No; but even Warren can't laugh off these straws." Steele returned them to his pocket.

"And furthermore, a few minutes after you left the apartment Warren called. He had just talked with Fred Reed in Kansas City. He couldn't laugh that off either."

Steele lit a cigarette with aggravating deliberation.

"Dr. Vernon was registered at the Pickwick Hotel all right, but he checked out the night of the fourteenth, not on the morning of the seventeenth. He did not drive home in a car, he took a taxi to the Union Station. He left a telegram and a dollar tip with one of the bell boys. The wire was addressed to his wife. Doubtless it was this telegram which she found on her return from El Dorado. But it was held by the bell boy so that it wouldn't reach her till the

afternoon of the seventeenth. It stated that he was driving home
from Kansas City and would be in Wichita that afternoon. But the
illuminating point is this: Reed found that Dr. Vernon had talked
with someone in Newton just before he checked out of the hotel.
He placed the call with the hotel operator. He gave her the Newton telephone number, but no name. The number is 675."

"Then you think he was in Newton?"

"That's the only clue we have—that and another which Warren
probably wouldn't recognize. When Dr. Vernon went out of his way
to say he had driven home by way of Cassoday and El Dorado, which
was impossible because the road is closed, it was an involuntary
effort to throw us off the trail. Now Newton is on the best and most
logical route from Kansas City—and the closest to Wichita of any
town on that route. Putting two and two together—"

"And making ten out of it!"

"Five at the most: Dr. Vernon had some reason for wanting to
be near Wichita from the morning of the fifteenth to the seventeenth, when he was supposed to be in Kansas City, and he didn't
want anybody in Wichita to know about it."

"So what? I can't see how this leads to anything, and Warren
certainly won't admit that it does."

Steele laughed shortly. "No? Well, he's already admitted enough
to send Hale Ferguson to Newton with the telephone number and
instructions to check up all the hotels and garages to see if he can
locate any trace of either Dr. Vernon or his car. That car was in
storage somewhere, because he drove out of Wichita in it and he
returned in it, and he didn't have it in Kansas City."

Steele pulled the *Herald* out of the wastebasket and slapped it
on my desk.

"So far as Warren is concerned, he wasn't any too sure of himself last night. But he's like a lot of other politicians: when a reporter gets hold of him he just naturally has to talk." He crumpled
up the paper and slammed it again into the wastebasket. "And you
can take my word for it, he already regrets this more than your
managing editor. . . . And he's going to regret it a damn sight
worse!"

Steele wasn't given to expletives, and even less to predictions. From the set of his jaw I understood that Warren's premature acceptance of Jack Van Roth's guilt, and his stubborn refusal to consider any arguments to the contrary, had roused Steele more than the lightness of his manner had indicated. For the first time that morning my full confidence in him returned, and I lost my misgivings about the story.

"I hope you're right," I said; "but how are you going to prove it to Warren?"

"I'm going to have a showdown with him this afternoon, as soon as Ferguson returns from Newton. In the meantime I want to see Garnett. He's laid up at the Town Club with his injured foot. Then this noon we have that luncheon engagement with Dr. Vernon." Steele pulled out his watch and studied it a moment. "I only wish Ferguson would run into something in Newton and get back with it before we talk with Vernon. It's possible he might, at that." He returned the watch to his pocket. "Well, how about it; can you get away to go with me to see Garnett?"

When we reached the club we found the hazel-eyed Miss Lathrop on duty at the desk. She told us that Garnett was busy—that Dr. Vernon was in his room redressing his burns. She informed Steele with her warmest smile that Garnett's injuries were not as serious as had been feared, and that he would be able to get up that afternoon.

"Good! I'd like to see him when the doctor leaves. We'll be in the lounge room. If you'll just call us."

When we entered the room we found Charles Ripley, his arm in a sling, trying to manipulate a newspaper with one hand. He greeted us affably, and in answer to our inquiries discounted his injury by saying he was taking a half-day from the office only because Dr. Vernon had wanted to see his arm when he came to visit Garnett.

"I never did know what hit me," he informed us. "When I saw that slush pond catch fire and saw Garnett's clothes blazing I started to run over to help him. I hadn't gone fifteen feet before something lit on me like a ton of brick. Someone helped me up,

and Dr. Vernon gave me first aid. He says it will be all right in a
couple of weeks."

He made room for us on the davenport.

"How's the murder mystery coming on?" he inquired. "I was
just trying to read the paper, but I find I'm not very good at keeping my place with only one hand. I see the *Herald* says the county
attorney claims Jack Van Roth's death settles the matter."

"Yes," Steele answered in a noncommittal voice, sitting down,
"I suppose it does."

Ripley looked at him inquiringly.

"I take it you are not altogether satisfied?"

Steele shrugged his shoulders. "Well, there are a few things I'm
still curious about, but I don't suppose the answers would make
any difference."

"What about this wild animal the papers have made so much
of? There isn't anything to that, is there?"

Steele answered the question seriously. "I don't know. I'm not
ready to say that there isn't anything to it."

Ripley's round face expressed his astonishment. "Why, I
thought that was all poppycock!"

"Very likely it is," Steele agreed. "That's one of the things I'd
give something to know more about." He regarded Ripley thoughtfully. "Say, do you know, I believe you might be able to help me
answer one of the questions that is puzzling me."

"I?" Ripley was surprised. "What is it? I'll be glad to help any
way I can."

"It's about that pay-station call you received from Loundon the
morning he was killed. The more I think about that the more I
wonder why he should have gone to the trouble to stop at a pay
station merely to tell you he wouldn't be at the office."

"Just a drunken notion, I suppose," Ripley said, but there was
an uneasy tone in his voice.

"That's what I assumed. But the idea kept recurring that perhaps he had stopped to make another more important call from
the pay station and had merely called you as an afterthought. I
remembered that he had quarreled drunkenly with the supervisor,
and I thought she might recall the circumstances. So I went to the

telephone office and got the traffic manager to help check up. I reasoned that a supervisor who had had an argument about a pay-station call at that time of the morning with a man as drunk as Loundon ought to remember it, and he agreed with me. But do you know what we found? They are willing to swear at the telephone office that no call at all was made!"

Ripley's uneasiness had turned to obvious embarrassment. His pink cheeks flushed, and he averted his eyes.

"Mr. Ripley—" Steele's voice was firm, but not unkind—"you never received any such call from Loundon, did you?"

Ripley did not answer.

"You were trying to protect somebody, weren't you? Someone who would have an alibi if it might be made to appear Loundon could not have reached the lodge before around nine-thirty. Some-one whose alibi would be no good if Loundon had gone there imme-diately after he talked with the porter at the club here. Say, in other words, if he could have arrived at the lodge and have been mur-dered as early as eight or a little past. Who was it?"

Still Ripley could not or would not answer.

"Do you realize what you have done?" Steele's voice grew se-vere. "You have destroyed the alibis of every person who had left the neighborhood of the lodge before nine-thirty. Believing your story of the telephone call, we naturally assumed that none of these persons could have had any connection with the murder because Loundon had not reached the lodge before half-past nine. Those persons are Jack Van Roth, Lola Van Roth, Dr. Van Roth, Mr. Monest and, in a sense, Mr. Garnett, although he could have been at the lodge after nine-thirty. You put a barrier in our path when time was of inestimable importance. You have given time to the murderer, and, if I am not mistaken, this delay resulted in Jack Van Roth's death."

By this time Ripley's face was white to the lips.

"I—I didn't realize!" he faltered. "You—you surely don't think I had anything to do with it?"

"Unconsciously or consciously you were certainly of assistance to the murderer—and I assure you the county attorney won't take any chances with you if you refuse to explain. Why did you do it?"

Ripley moistened his lips, then looked at Steele apprehensively. For an instant he seemed about to speak, but finally he shook his head with aggravating stubbornness.

"You were afraid of Monest's alibi!" Steele suddenly shot at him. "You knew Monest had threatened to kill Loundon in your office. Is that it?"

Ripley started at this unexpected accusation. Then he sat limply in the corner of the davenport a full minute before he could bring himself to confess.

"Yes; I was afraid Mr. Monest might be suspected."

"You mean you were afraid he might be convicted!"

"Yes, but I didn't think he had done it." He straightened up with an unexpected show of spirit. "I don't now. But I was afraid of what would happen to the business if—if anything happened to keep him from putting the money in it he had promised. You see, Mr. Garnett and I don't get along, and it was only Mr. Loundon's friendship that kept him in. So when Mr. Loundon died I knew Mr. Garnett would pull out, and that if he did only Mr. Monest's money could keep us going. I didn't know a change in an hour or so would make so much difference. And I wouldn't have done it if I had really thought Mr. Monest had anything to do with the murder."

"Whether he did it or not, the fact that he threatened Loundon's life becomes a serious matter under the circumstances."

Steele regarded Ripley gravely.

"Why did they quarrel?"

Again there was a long pause before Ripley would speak.

"Monest felt Loundon had misled him about their oil investments. He hadn't; but instead of explaining, Loundon got abusive. He had been drinking; and Monest is naturally hot-headed. One word led to another, and finally Loundon grabbed Monest by the shoulder and told him to shut up and quit crying to him about the money he had lost. Monest was already mad, and when Loundon shoved him into a chair he jumped up and took out a big pocket-knife. Then he said if Loundon touched him again he would cut his heart out."

Ripley concluded with a gesture of deprecation. "He wouldn't have done it—and when Loundon saw how furious Monest was he just laughed, and pretty soon he left. That's all there was to it."

Steele's slow nod of understanding apparently accepted Ripley's explanation at its face value.

"Was Miss Monest mentioned during their quarrel?"

"No."

"I believe you told us the other day that you have never met her. Do you suppose their antagonism had anything to do with Loundon's resentment at having been thrown over for Garnett?"

Steele's coupling of Garnett with Miss Monest brought a curious expression to Ripley's face: a look of animosity quickly tempered by caution.

"I couldn't say," he answered slowly. "I don't know how much Loundon knew of their relations."

"I see!"

The tone of Steele's voice sounded as if he saw a good deal that wasn't apparent to me. If he intended to pursue the subject further, however, he was interrupted by the appearance of Miss Lathrop, who said Dr. Vernon had left and that Garnett would see us. As we got up, Ripley, in an awkwardly confused manner, attempted to express his contrition. While Steele did not try to mitigate the consequences of his actions, and warned him that he probably would be called on by the county attorney for further questioning, he did it in a manner to allay Ripley's obvious trepidation. When we left, Ripley shook hands gratefully.

We found Garnett propped up in bed with his right leg bandaged up to the knee. His long, furrowed face seemed a trifle haggard, but he greeted us with a smile and motioned us to chairs. In answer to Steele's inquiries he informed us that his burns were not serious and said Dr. Vernon had told him he could get up as soon as he felt able.

"And that will be this afternoon," he declared. "Dan Brady will be here from Tulsa this noon with his firefighting equipment, and I'm not going to miss watching him tackle our well if I have to go out in an ambulance!" He turned to Steele. "Did you ever see an expert fight a big oil-well fire?"

Steele shook his head.

"Don't miss it! It's damn near worth the loss to watch it. Brady's the best man in the country, and this won't be one of the easiest jobs he ever tackled. He's the man who put out the fire at the Long John gusher in California a couple of years ago after it had burned for two weeks." Garnett shifted his position in professional excitement. "They're getting ready for him this morning. He ought to be able to make a start before night."

Steele's congenital fascination for competition of any sort was aroused by Garnett's description of what the afternoon's conflict, pitting the ingenuity and courage of man against the roaring geyser of burning oil, was likely to be. For nearly fifteen minutes he plied Garnett with questions, honestly absorbed by every detail; yet I knew that behind this unfeigned interest he was keenly analyzing the other's personality. In the end it was Garnett who remembered that Steele must have had a motive for our visit wholly removed from a willingness to listen to a dissertation on the technique of oil-fire fighting. He took up the copy of the *Herald's* morning extra, which was lying beside him on the bed, and gave Steele a quizzical look.

"I see you and the *Herald* don't quite jibe on this Van Roth story. Weren't you satisfied with the county attorney's conclusions?"

His shrewd surmise that Steele had influenced my article unaccountably nettled me, and I hoped Steele would grasp the opening to ask a few of the leading questions I knew were on his mind. But instead he only laughed and reached for the paper. As if he had noticed my irritation and desired to rub a little salt into the wound, he said:

"Well, if I don't agree with Warren, the *Herald's* editor certainly does. Did you read this front-page dig at the opposition?" He folded the paper to the editorial, then with seeming gusto read it aloud. Having added this insult to my injury he dropped the paper on the floor and got up.

"I'm glad to know your injuries aren't serious, Mr. Garnett, And I'm going to be on hand this evening to watch Brady tackle the fire."

As we turned to go, Steele noticed the paper he had dropped on the floor and stooped to pick it up, despite Garnett's protestations that he had read it. One piece had floated well under the bed, and Steele got on his hands and knees to retrieve it. I waited impatiently at the door while he recovered it, folded the paper together and handed it to Garnett. When we were outside, I confronted him irritably.

"A hell of a lot you got out of him! I thought you had some reason for coming up here—or did you just want to read that editorial again!"

Steele laughed gleefully. "Reason enough, General, reason enough! Though not just what I had expected. What do you think of this?"

He reached under his coat and pulled out two well-worn bedroom moccasins.

"Garnett's!" he responded to my astonished gaze. "And my eye tells me they will be a perfect fit for those impressions we took at the strawstack!"

15

AS WE LEFT THE ELEVATOR on the ground floor Miss Lathrop called to Steele from the desk:

"The county attorney's office is calling you, Mr. Steele. If you want me to, I'll connect you, and you can use the desk phone here."

"Thank you," Steele smiled, "but if you don't mind I believe I'll use one of the booths."

"Oh sure." The girl's affability was only slightly dampened. "Right over there. The number is 3-7777."

I waited at the desk until Steele had made the call and rejoined me.

"Warren wants to see us at the office," he said. "Can you leave now?"

"Certainly."

When we were in the car Steele informed me that Warren had just received a telephone call from Ferguson at Newton. He had reported that he was already on the trail of Dr. Vernon's car, and felt sure he would have something definite later in the afternoon. In the meantime, Steele said, Warren had been stewing in the juices of his injudicious interview of the night before. He was not only ready but anxious to listen to what Steele had to say.

"As a matter of fact," Steele said, "I think he's uncovered something that has shaken his confidence, but he won't say what it is. When I told him what we had learned from Ripley he insisted that we come right over. I was glad to have a good excuse to cancel my engagement with Dr. Vernon, so I called him up. I don't want to see him until we find out whether Ferguson discovers anything in Newton."

When we entered the county attorney's office it was obvious that Warren was in a disturbed state of mind. When we had seated ourselves he faced us nervously, his heavy eyebrows pulled down in a worried frown.

"What's this you were telling me about Ripley?" He turned to Steele without preliminaries. "If this is true, do you realize what it does to all these alibis Burke spent so much time verifying?"

With what to Warren must have been a most aggravating deliberation Steele made himself comfortable before answering. He pulled his chair away from the wall and tilted it back, repeating the operation until he had achieved just the precise angle he desired. Finally he lit a cigarette, took a long inhalation, and replied:

"It knocks out everyone, doesn't it?" He blew the smoke out slowly. "But, of course, if Jack Van Roth killed Loundon and then committed suicide, that doesn't make any difference."

Warren scowled at him with an irritation that was almost anger.

"I don't say that Jack didn't do it!"

"Perhaps what you say doesn't alter the facts," Steele returned coolly.

Warren flushed, opened his mouth as if to make an angry retort, then managed to hold his tongue.

"You see," Steele went on quietly, "what you told the *Herald* last night has put Bill in a jam. He trusted me, and naturally he was entitled to an even break. Now it's made to appear that he didn't know what was going on."

"Now look here, Steele, I told you—" Warren began.

"Never mind the argument," I interrupted. "You can forget me. Let's see where we stand now on this case."

Warren shot me a glance that could have been gratitude or exasperation. After a moment's silence Steele shrugged his shoulders.

"All right," he agreed; "the question is, where do we stand?"

Warren did not answer immediately. He had been nettled by Steele's criticism, and it was not in his domineering nature to confess graciously to a mistake. After a painful silence, however, he replied:

"Well, there's no use denying that what Ripley said puts an altogether different aspect on everything. Assuming that I was wrong about Jack, it throws the doors wide open."

Having conceded that much, Warren even went so far as a conciliatory smile in Steele's direction.

"Is that what you think?"

Steele nodded. It was not in him to harbor ill-will, and I knew he had no desire to force Warren to any further admissions.

"Exactly." He pulled his chair up to the county attorney's desk. "With the exception of Ripley, who went directly from the club to his office on the morning of the sixteenth, not one of the persons we have seen has an alibi that will hold water. Let's check them over to make sure we agree on that."

The result of this suggestion was a careful resurvey of the statements of all those who had previously been interviewed. As Warren pointed out, Loundon was last seen by the porter at the Town Club at 7:30 the morning of August 16. If he had left the club immediately he could have reached the lodge as early as 7:50, instead of, as had previously been supposed, sometime after nine o'clock. The effect of this new possibility on the alibis of those who were in the neighborhood of the lodge that morning was as follows:

Fielding Garnett. Waiters at the Town Club had verified the fact that Garnett ate breakfast there at 7:45. He had reached his office at 8:10. At 8:45 he left town in his car and at ten minutes past nine arrived at the Meridian oil field. Monest was already on the ground. About ten, Garnett left the oil field and drove to the Switzer farm near Maize. Beyond his own statement that he had remained there until shortly after noon, it had been impossible to verify Garnett's whereabouts exactly. The possibility of Loundon's earlier arrival at the lodge, however, made no material difference in respect to Garnett. It was impossible to determine by witnesses how much time had elapsed between his departure from the Meridian oil field and his arrival at the Switzer farm. He could easily have spent an hour at the lodge before Loundon's body was discovered at 11:30.

Dora Monest. According to Miss Monest's story she had break-fast with her uncle at home about eight o'clock. At nine o'clock, by her own admission, she was on the river in her motorboat. She said she had not gone farther upstream than the bridge over the Hutchinson highway, a mile and a half or two miles below the strawstack. She could have visited the lodge, and, as Steele ob-served, she and Garnett could have been there together between ten and eleven o'clock. There was nothing but the unsupported word of each to prove they had not been on the premises.

Dr. Raymond Van Roth. On the morning of the 16th Dr. Van Roth, Jack Van Roth and Lola Van Roth, who had been seen on Loundon's footbridge at 8:30, were back in town by 9:30. These alibis had been checked by Sheriff Burke. Only Jack's had been questioned by the sheriff, because he had doubted the veracity of the witness who gave it. Since it had developed that Loundon could have arrived at the lodge as early as 7:50, however, it became evi-dent that Dr. Van Roth might have committed the murder before he was seen on the bridge. According to Burke, Van Roth had stated that he left home about seven o'clock.

Lola Van Roth. Miss Van Roth had spent the night in the lodge. She could have been with Loundon at any time between his pos-sible arrival at 7:50 and the time when she was seen on the foot-bridge at 8:30.

Juan Monest. In his interview with Steele and the county at-torney Monest had said he reached the Meridian field at nine o'clock, or possibly 8:45. He returned to town in time to be seen in the lounge room of the Town Club at ten o'clock. Burke had checked this statement and found it substantially correct, except that he believed Monest could have been in the neighborhood of the lodge as early as 8:30. He had left home in his car immediately after having breakfast with his niece a little before eight o'clock. If Loundon had arrived at the lodge at 7:50, Monest could have been with him at the lodge or the strawstack for at least half an hour before the hour when it was certainly established that Monest was at the Meridian field.

Dr. Vernon. Dr. Vernon had taken a taxi to the Union Station in Kansas City on the night of August 14, after having written a post-dated telegram to his wife to make it appear he had remained in that city until the 17th of August, the day after Loundon's body was discovered. Until disproved, it must be assumed he could have visited the lodge on the morning of the 16th.

Mrs. Vernon. During her interview with Steele Mrs. Vernon had said that she left the house to do some shopping about eight on the morning of the 16th and did not return until ten. During this interval she could have driven to the lodge.

Charles Ripley. Ripley's statement that he left the Town Club at eight and reached his office at 8:20 had been verified by Sheriff Burke. He remained at the plant until he received word of Loundon's death in the evening.

When Steele and Warren had finished this brief recapitulation, the county attorney pushed back his chair and looked at us dubiously. He pulled out a big black pipe and proceeded to fill it, while he ran his eye gloomily over the notes he had made during the course of the discussion. Finally he lit the pipe and impatiently shoved the papers to one side.

"Well, so far as I can see," he observed, "we're a little worse off than when we started."

"Oh, it's not that bad, Warren—" Steele shook his head— "though I'll admit it still looks pretty thick." He regarded the other speculatively. "But when you realize that every one of these persons, including Ripley, was on hand last night when the oil well caught fire it doesn't simplify the matter."

"What do you mean?" Warren took the pipe out of his mouth with a puzzled air.

Steele leaned over and picked up the papers from Warren's desk.

"I mean that one of these eight persons killed Ralph Loundon; that Jack Van Roth knew which one it was; and that he was himself killed by the same person while we were waiting for him in the lodge."

Warren sat up and reached for the list.

"Surely they weren't all there," he said unbelievingly, running his eye over the names. "And even if they were, you'd have to leave out Garnett and Ripley. They were hurt when the well exploded."

"Not when the well exploded," Steele corrected; "when the slush pond caught fire afterwards." He pulled a copy of the *Times* from his pocket. "Here's what the paper says about Garnett:

"'Garnett miraculously escaped death when one of the slush ponds ignited a few minutes after the explosion and set fire to his overalls. Fortunately, he had been called away from the immediate vicinity of the well a short time before the explosion occurred.'"

Steele returned the paper to his pocket.

"He had been 'called away' before the explosion. Ripley was injured, too, but not until after the fire. He told us this morning that when he saw Garnett's clothes catch fire he started to run over to help him. He hadn't gone fifteen feet, he said, when he was hit. So you see, at the time Jack was shot either Garnett or Ripley could have been with him on the path south of the oil field, and either could have returned to the vicinity of the well by the time the slush pond caught fire. As a matter of fact it was more than five minutes after the explosion before they were injured."

Steele took the notes from Warren's hands.

"Don't worry, they were all there!" he continued, scanning the list swiftly. "The minute I saw Jack's body lying in the path I realized we had seen most of the suspects before we went to the lodge. When I learned that Dr. and Mrs. Vernon were also present the roster was complete."

He began reading off the names:

"Here they are in order as you wrote them down. Garnett we have already mentioned. Dora Monest. Bill saw Dora Monest and her uncle sitting in a car not far from the well before seven o'clock. Dr. Raymond Van Roth. Lola Van Roth. We saw both the Van Roths a few minutes after we saw the Monests. Juan Monest. We have checked him. Dr. Vernon. Mrs. Vernon. The papers state that Dr. Vernon and his wife arrived at the field fifteen minutes before the explosion. Charles Ripley. We have already checked Ripley." Steele tossed the notes on the desk.

"One hundred per cent present!" He looked into Warren's incredulous face. "And don't suppose for a minute it was an accident, either; though I don't imagine the murderer ever hoped for such a lucky break as he actually got. But when he arranged to meet Jack out at the field last night he knew everybody in town who could get there would be on hand to see the gusher. He knew he could get away to keep his rendezvous with Jack without being seen. And moreover, he wanted to do the job at night and he wanted the body to be found as near the scene of the first murder as possible. Whether he suspected a trap, there is no way of knowing. It is possible that he would have come to the lodge. My guess is that the explosion startled him and that he shot Jack on the spur of the moment. The sudden light might even have revealed the men we had hidden by the bridge, though I don't think that's likely. There's no question in my mind that he would have much preferred to leave the body in the lodge. But he didn't wait, whatever his reasons were, and now, by the contrary gods, it turns out that every single individual we have considered in connection with the case was present last night to help muddy the waters!"

Warren's face, as he listened, had revealed a growing perturbation. For a moment he sat staring at Steele, then brought his hand down violently on the desktop.

"By God, Steele, I'm afraid you're right!" He got up and began pacing the floor. "You were right last night! What a fool I made of myself by giving that story to the *Herald*." He stopped by my chair. "I'm sorry, Bill. I didn't mean to double-cross you, but I thought Jack's death settled the thing. . . . Well, if it will do you any good you've got my permission to make me eat my words in your next edition!"

The heavy silence that followed this abject apology was broken by Steele.

"Not so fast, not so fast. And not so gloomy!" He looked up at the county attorney's woebegone countenance. "It was my fault that the *Times* didn't play up the story. And do you know, in some ways I'm glad the *Herald* did!"

"You're glad!"

Steele smiled at our astonishment.

"Yes. For the time being, at least, the murderer can assume the case is closed. At any rate he can assume that so far as the county attorney's office is concerned it is closed. If I continue to do some investigating on the side it will be only an indication that the county attorney and I have had a disagreement. What I do, in other words, will be without official authority—unless I find it necessary to ask for help."

"But we can't handle it that way . . ." Warren began to object.

"Not actually," Steele agreed; "but so far as the newspapers and the public are concerned there is no reason why you should deny the story you gave to the *Herald*. Of course we will have to continue our investigation, and the persons we interview will know the case isn't closed, but they won't know it until we get to them." He pushed back his chair thoughtfully. "I can see a number of advantages—not the least of which, from your standpoint, is the fact that you won't have to admit any mistake at all. When we finally get the person we're after it can be made to appear that your acceptance of Jack's guilt was merely a subterfuge, done to gain time and to mislead the actual murderer."

The county attorney dubiously considered this opportunity to save his face. Warren was fundamentally honest and conscientious, and he never sought to avoid the consequences of his actions at the expense of the truth. On the other hand, he was politician enough to perceive that an unnecessary confession of error would create an unfavorable impression in the public mind. When he finally spoke there was an unmistakable tone of relief in his voice.

"That's mighty decent of you, Steele. But if it will help, I'm willing to take my medicine."

"Nonsense," Steele returned, looking at his watch. "What I want to know is, where do we go from here?"

Before he answered, Warren pushed a button on his desk, and when his secretary appeared in the doorway, he asked: "Do you know if Burke got hold of Miss Van Roth?"

"Yes, I think she's out in the waiting room now," the girl answered. "I'll go see."

"Wait a minute." Warren stopped her. "I'll let you know when I want to see her. Is she alone?"

"No, I think her father's with her."

"Is Burke in his office?"

"I don't think so. He told me to tell you he had a call out in the country and probably wouldn't be back till afternoon."

Warren nodded.

"All right. I'll see Miss Van Roth in a few minutes. And I want to talk with her alone before I see her father."

The girl, a tall, thin, sharp-visaged individual with a voice to match, had backed out of the room and was closing the door behind her, when suddenly we heard her begin uttering a series of shrill protests. Before we could make out enough to determine the cause, the door was pushed open and Lola Van Roth came into the room. Her large features wore a determined look, and, although she seemed momentarily surprised to see Steele and me, she turned to Warren without any appearance of embarrassment at the unceremonious method of her entrance.

"I heard you ask for me," she announced bluntly, "so I came in, although I didn't know you had visitors. But you sent for me at a very inconvenient time, and I didn't see why I should be kept waiting any longer."

16

WARREN WAS PLAINLY NETTLED by Miss Van Roth's high-handed intrusion. It was apparent that he had wanted to explain to Steele why he had sent for her before beginning the interview. He made a gesture of annoyance and doubtless would have asked her to return to the outer office, but before he could bring himself to this decision his uninvited guest seated herself in a chair beside his desk, from which she regarded him with such an air of dignity and permanence that for a moment he was plainly nonplussed. When at last he spoke he was apologetic.

"I'm sorry if I've made you any trouble; particularly as I know what a shock your brother's death must have been to you." He hesitated as if uncertain what to say. "You see—"

"His death wasn't so much a shock as your statement that he killed Mr. Loundon!"

Miss Van Roth did not raise her voice, but there was fire in her eyes as she leaned over the desk.

Taken aback, Warren began to explain:

"That is one reason why I wanted to see you. It was unfortunate that the newspaper handled what I said about your brother just the way it did. As a matter of fact—"

"I beg your pardon, Warren." It was Steele. He turned to the county attorney in apology, then looked down at Miss Van Roth gravely. "Why was it a shock, Miss Van Roth? You must have known Mr. Warren had good reason to suspect your brother even before he committed suicide."

I perceived that Steele's interruption had forestalled an admission by Warren that he had changed his mind regarding Jack Van Roth's guilt. But why he should desire to keep Miss Van Roth ignorant of this fact I could not guess.

Miss Van Roth turned from Warren to Steele. Her eyes were of a strange burning blue, so dark and yet so bright as to be an astonishment every time they were encountered. Her heavy face, with its slightly curved nose and large cheekbones, was seldom animated in conversation; but now, as she turned to reply to Steele, its stolidness was changed by a conviction that was nearly agitation.

"My brother didn't commit suicide," she declared, "any more than he killed Mr. Loundon! That story in the paper is preposterous."

Steele's eyes narrowed as he heard this confirmation of his belief.

"Why do you say that, Miss Van Roth? If your brother did not kill himself that means he was murdered."

"Of course he was murdered! I don't know who it was, but Jack was killed by the same man who killed Mr. Loundon. And he was killed because he knew who murdered Mr. Loundon!"

"How do you know that?" Steele's voice was sharp.

"Because he told me so!"

"When did he tell you?"

"Yesterday afternoon."

"Where did you see him?"

"I didn't see him. He telephoned me."

"Who did he say had killed Loundon?"

Miss Van Roth shrugged her shoulders and laughed shortly.

"If I knew do you suppose I'd have waited until today to tell you?"

"I don't know," Steele replied coolly. "You were considerably less than frank when we talked with you last. . . . Perhaps if you had told us all you knew then your brother would not have been killed."

At this brutal statement a spasm of pain crossed Miss Van Roth's face. Her large hands closed convulsively over the ends of the chair arms. She did not otherwise display her emotion, but it was several moments before she spoke.

"I don't believe that is true. You haven't any right to say that. What did I know and refuse to tell you that could have had any effect on my brother?"

Steele appeared impervious to any feeling of sympathy for her obvious, if restrained, distress. He pulled a chair from the wall, placed it across the corner of Warren's desk and sat facing her in a position where the light at his back shone full into her face.

"Why didn't you tell us what you knew about Mrs. Vernon's daughter?"

If Miss Van Roth had been unaware that Steele had learned Mrs. Vernon's secret, her ability as an actress enabled her to accept the revelation calmly.

"Why should I tell you things that might ruin her life?" she parried. "Surely you don't suppose that had anything to do with Mr. Loundon's death?"

Steele heard her evasion impatiently.

"Come, come, Miss Van Roth," he said sharply, "I was sincere in what I said the other evening about my admiration for your acting. But I meant on the stage. . . . You know very well what I am referring to. . . . If you had told us that your brother had threatened to blackmail Dr. Vernon and Mr. Loundon, and that he was already attempting to blackmail Mrs. Vernon, you know he would have been arrested. If he had been in jail last night he certainly would not have been murdered. . . . If you didn't think he was guilty in the first place why were you trying to protect him?"

Miss Van Roth's face was a confusion of emotions, which she struggled to control. Sorrow, and what might have been remorse, were followed by indignation.

"Of course I was trying to protect him! But I didn't think he was guilty. Do you suppose he would have had a fair chance if I had told you he was attempting to blackmail Mr. Loundon just before he was killed? Certainly not!" She turned to fix her angry blue eyes on Warren. "Do you think, after what you tried to do to him in that Oklahoma kidnapping, which he didn't know a thing about, that I would believe you would give him an unprejudiced hearing? How could I? You would have jumped to the conclusion that he was guilty; you would have rushed to the papers with your accusations; and you would have had him tried and convicted before he had a chance to defend himself. . . . Exactly as you have done now, when you know there is no way for him to defend himself or to clear his name."

Warren frowned and moved uncomfortably as she continued to glare at him.

"Miss Van Roth, I told your brother I didn't have anything to do with questioning him about that kidnapping. And so far as my—"

"What else could you expect?" Again Steele prevented Warren from reverting to his opinion about her brother's guilt. "Blackmail, kidnapping, murder—do you suppose the police can draw nice distinctions as to where a man will stop? If your brother didn't kill Loundon, who did?"

Miss Van Roth was startled by this direct and unexpected question.

"Well, I don't know . . ." She hesitated. "That is, I am only—I only know my brother didn't."

"You *know.* How do you *know?*"

"Of course I don't *know.* But I am positive he didn't do it." Steele leaned back in his chair and looked at her with disapproval. I was unable to understand why he assumed such an aggressive and uncompromising attitude toward her. I knew he had some reason for his harshness; but whether he believed Jack's sister had detailed knowledge of Loundon's murder, perhaps had been an eyewitness; or whether he suspected her of knowing more about Jack's death than her replies indicated, even my familiarity with his methods failed to suggest. It was probably true, as he said, that Jack would not have been killed if she had told what she knew at the first. But, supposing her innocent of complicity in Jack's evildoings, she still had done only what might be expected of any sister under the circumstances. All this, I was aware, Steele comprehended, and I soon perceived that a deadly intent underlay his interrogation and that in her answers there was an undertone of wary and fearful apprehension.

"Miss Van Roth—" Steele's voice was inexorable—"I'm afraid you don't appreciate the position you are in. Unless you give us a more satisfactory explanation of some of the things you have done—and some of the things you have left undone—the county attorney will be justified in holding you as a material witness, if not as an accessory to Loundon's murder."

Only in a narrowing of the eyes and a slight contraction of the lips was there evidence of emotion in Miss Van Roth's face. She did not reply, and in a moment Steele continued.

"Perhaps you aren't convinced," he said, when he saw she did not intend to answer. "Then I must mention some of the circumstances that demand an explanation:

"In the first place, you say you have had no dealings with Loundon since your divorce. Nevertheless, you were the beneficiary of a $50,000-insurance policy on his life. You knew he was in financial difficulties and was planning to cancel most of his insurance. You arranged to spend the night in his lodge, and the next morning he was found dead there. Your only reason for having been in the lodge is the flimsy pretext that you needed a quiet place in which to write a play!"

"And I suppose," Miss Van Roth broke in, "that I killed him and pulled him up on the strawstack by myself!"

"Second," Steele went on, ignoring her interjection; "you were the only person, excepting Mrs. Vernon's father and mother, who knew her adopted daughter was in reality Ralph Loundon's illegitimate child. Yet the morning Loundon was found dead your brother informed Mrs. Vernon that he knew her secret and threatened to tell her husband if she would not pay him $3000. You went to see Mrs. Vernon later that same day and admitted to her that Jack had also threatened to blackmail Loundon, and you said you supposed he had already approached him. You pretended to be furious, and you made the statement that you would rather see him dead.

"Third. You knew Jack and Mrs. Vernon visited the lodge on the evening of the day Loundon's body was found in the strawstack.

"Fourth. You knew Jack was bootlegging liquor from Loundon's shack. You were aware that Loundon, against his inclination, had interceded for Jack when the chief of police was questioning him about the Oklahoma kidnapping. You must have known your brother was holding some sort of club over Loundon's head, even at that time.

"Fifth. You not only kept still about all these things, but when we asked you to help us you lied to us."

Steele pushed back his chair from the desk as he watched her reaction to these statements. For half a minute or more Miss Van Roth maintained a perturbed silence, but I was surprised to note that she was not agitated, and that indeed she seemed more astonished than alarmed.

"You have discovered a great deal I did not suppose you knew," she said at last. "That will make it easier for me to answer your questions."

"Very well," Steele observed, with a trace of irony in his voice, "just start at the beginning with the questions I have asked."

"You haven't asked questions," she returned acidly. "You merely made a number of statements in such a way as to make them sound like accusations. I can explain everything I have done or said, but I am not going to be put in the position of a defendant without a formal accusation and without a lawyer."

Steele's eyebrows went up. When he answered I knew Miss Van Roth's composure and determination not to be hurried into a compromising position had not been lost upon him.

"There is no need for a lawyer—at present," he declared. "In the first place, will you explain why Mr. Loundon continued a $50,000-insurance policy in your name for so many years after your divorce?"

Miss Van Roth considered with an annoyed frown, tapping the ends of her fingers on the arm of her chair for several seconds.

"Since you know about Mrs. Vernon's daughter, I suppose there is no reason why I shouldn't tell you—if it will help relieve your mind about me." She paused, as if still resisting Steele's demands. "Mr. Loundon and I were always good friends, even after I divorced him. Mrs. Vernon thinks I divorced him because I learned about their affair. That isn't true; as a matter of fact, I knew something about it before we were married. What I didn't know was that he was incapable of—it seems rather old-fashioned to mention it in these days—that it was impossible for him to be true to anybody. That, and my ambition to go on the stage, which he didn't sympathize with, brought about our estrangement. When he enlisted I went into Y.M.C.A. work as an entertainer, and in a short while I divorced him. . . . He had always helped Mrs. Vernon—she was Nellie Doyle then—and he continued to send her money, I suppose, until she married Dr. Vernon. A few months after Mrs. Vernon finally managed to adopt her daughter I received a letter from Mr. Loundon—I was playing in a stock company in Baltimore— and he told me he had taken out this insurance policy of $50,000. . . . He had learned that Dr. Vernon was a terribly jealous husband, and he feared if the doctor ever discovered the truth about his adopted daughter he would divorce his wife and leave them both without money. So in case of his death I was to receive $50,000 to hold in trust for his daughter!"

Miss Van Roth looked calmly into Steele's incredulous face.

"Now, that doesn't make sense either, does it?" she said. "But it's the truth, and I think I could still find Mr. Loundon's letter to prove it if it became necessary."

Steele regarded her somberly, and his expression was that of a man convinced he is being hoaxed.

"Then I presume you do not think he was expecting to cancel this policy?"

"I don't know. I saw him for only a few minutes. He never mentioned any business or personal affairs. But knowing him as I did, I think this would have been one of the last to be canceled."

Steele nodded as if determined to accept this explanation without further argument. He looked at her speculatively through half-closed eyes, then abruptly continued:

"Why did you leave the lodge so early the morning Loundon was killed?"

At this sudden shift in Steele's attack Miss Van Roth started in her chair and braced herself as if fearful of what was to follow.

"What did you say?" she said, sparring for time.

"I asked, why did you leave the lodge so early the morning Loundon was killed? In case you have forgotten, you told us it was because you were hungry!"

Miss Van Roth did not look up to see the ironical smile with which Steele was regarding her.

"Yes," she said, "that is right. There wasn't anything in the lodge but canned food."

"You did not see Loundon when he came to the lodge a little before eight?"

At this question she looked up swiftly, her eyes dilated with sudden apprehension.

"Eight o'clock! But he was in town at nine!"

"No, that was a mistake. There was no telephone call at nine. Apparently he was not seen after seven-thirty. In other words, Loundon could have been at the lodge as early as ten minutes of eight. . . . Of course you didn't see him!"

At this revelation Miss Van Roth's eyes filled with an unaccountable terror. She half rose from her chair, then sank back and gazed speechlessly at Steele. Several times she opened her mouth as if to reply, but changed her mind. At last, with an expressive gesture of the hands indicative of dismay and resignation, she said:

"Yes, I saw him. That was why I left!"

17

STEELE ROSE FROM HIS CHAIR as if he had been stuck by a red-hot needle.

"You saw him!"

He gazed at her, astounded. I knew him well enough to realize he had not anticipated this admission. But I could not understand why he continued to stare at her with such astonishment and disbelief. He reached for his cigarette case without being aware of it, and automatically withdrew another cigarette and lit it. Slowly the expression on his face changed from amazement to incredulous comprehension.

"What time was that?" he demanded. "Where did you see him?"

Miss Van Roth had her answer ready, as if, having made up her mind to confess, she proposed to withhold nothing.

"It was exactly twenty minutes past eight," she declared. "He knocked on the front door and then went around to the kitchen door on the east."

"Ah!" Steele observed. "He came to the lodge!"

"Yes. Of course I knew he knew I was there, so I let him in."

"You let him in the lodge!"

"Yes. But when I saw how drunk he was I decided to get away at once. I persuaded him to lie down on one of the davenports and told him I would get breakfast. I threw my things into my bag and sneaked out the back door."

"And that was the last you saw of him?"

"Yes."

"I suppose it was when you were leaving the premises that your father and brother met you on the footbridge?"

"That's right. They drove back to town, and I went on the interurban."

"In other words, when you and your father and brother left the footbridge about eight-thirty Loundon was still alive inside the lodge?"

"Yes."

"He didn't follow you out of the lodge? He wasn't with your father and brother when they had the quarrel with you on the bridge?"

"No, of course not," she protested. "I told you the last time I saw him was when I left him on the davenport."

Steele shrugged his shoulders.

"And I believe you said he was alive when you left him on the davenport?"

Miss Van Roth looked at him angrily.

"Yes, of course he was alive."

Again Steele expressed himself with an incredulous lift of the shoulders. The tone of his voice had become more and more ironical. Under the circumstances his bearing was to me wholly inexplicable, and apparently this growing facetiousness was also distasteful to Warren. The county attorney had shared Steele's amazement at Miss Van Roth's account of Loundon's visit to the lodge and had followed the interview with excited interest, but now he could no longer restrain his impatience.

"If you will pardon my interruption, Steele," he said; "it seems to me Miss Van Roth has made a very serious admission. She should realize that what she has said may be incriminating. I don't understand why you should seek to discredit her story—particularly by innuendo."

As Steele turned to Warren his face displayed a trace of irritation, but he answered with a superpolite smile.

"No one realizes as well as Miss Van Roth how incriminating it was meant to be. Unfortunately I don't believe a word of it is true!"

"Not true!" Warren exclaimed. "But why in the world should she ever—"

"Perhaps," Steele interrupted, "you had better ask her."

Miss Van Roth returned Steele's gaze defiantly as they turned to her.

"Of course it's true," she insisted, but there was a nervousness in her manner that discounted the sincerity of her voice. Warren was obviously not convinced. He was puzzled; and when Warren became puzzled he became impatient. He turned to Steele.

"Well, if you don't believe it, why don't you believe it?" he demanded.

"Because, in the first place," Steele replied, his eyes fixed on Miss Van Roth's face, "I am satisfied that if she had actually met and talked with Loundon under such circumstances, where there would be no chance of guilt attaching to any of her family but herself, she would have said so the day his body was found. She would have known that neither her brother nor her father could be the murderer. So long as she believed their alibis for that morning were good she said nothing about having seen Loundon. But the minute she learned Loundon could have been on the premises by seven-fifty and remembered that her father, for instance, left home as early as seven o'clock to go to the lodge—and apparently didn't arrive there until after eight—she immediately recalled having seen Loundon alive as late as twenty minutes past eight!"

Miss Van Roth sat tensely in the chair while Steele spoke.

Several times she swallowed and moistened her lips with her tongue. Her hands clutched at the ends of the chair arms, and she gave the impression that every muscle in her body had gone taut. For the first time during either of the interviews she appeared fearful and ill at ease. Steele's keen eyes had never left her face, and he now said coldly:

"Why did you think it necessary to go to such lengths to protect your father?"

Miss Van Roth had perceptibly stiffened under Steele's icy stare, but now she stood up and faced him with blazing eyes.

"What do you mean by that?" she demanded. "Are you accusing my father of murdering Mr. Loundon?"

Steele gazed at her calmly, but his voice was peremptory. "You have accused him yourself in this preposterous story of having seen Loundon. Why did you do it?"

She bit her lips angrily at his insistence.

"That's all I can tell you," she replied shortly, attempting to regain control of her emotions. She turned her back on Steele and addressed Warren, who had remained seated at his desk. "If there is nothing more, I'd like to be excused."

The county attorney rose as she faced him. He had listened to Steele's reasons for discrediting Miss Van Roth's statement with astonished attention. At the mention of her father he had leaned forward in excitement. Now, as she made her request, he shook his head gravely.

"I'm afraid we cannot let you go now, Miss Van Roth. Please sit down."

As she resumed her chair, Steele looked at Warren questioningly, a mild surprise on his face. The county attorney's air was that of a man who has just received intelligence of great importance. He leaned forward and regarded Miss Van Roth under momentously lowered eyebrows.

"As a matter of fact," he said solemnly, "this brings us to my reason for wanting to see you—and your father. . . .

"Miss Van Roth, what was your father's name and where did he live before he went to El Dorado?"

The effect of this question was startling in the extreme. Miss Van Roth gasped, her face went white, and she involuntarily shrank back in her chair, her handkerchief at her mouth. She instantly attempted to recover herself, but all she could do was to stammer a repetition of the question.

"Where—where did he live?"

"Yes. . . . And since you don't want to answer, I'll tell you. He was in the Ohio State Penitentiary—under the name of Rothwell!"

Lola Van Roth's bowed head affirmed Warren's charge. But in a moment she straightened up and met his eyes resolutely.

"That isn't exactly true. We moved to El Dorado in 1910. My father was pardoned in 1890. He was in the penitentiary only two years. He has lived honestly for more than twenty years. It is unfair and unjust to bring that against him now. . . . I know he had nothing to do with Mr. Loundon's murder."

"He was convicted for murder, and he was pardoned over a strong protest."

Miss Van Roth did not reply, and as she averted her eyes I saw Steele glance at her sympathetically. He was always opposed to the practice of citing previous crimes against a suspect unless there were peculiar and compelling reasons for so doing, and I perceived he was regarding Warren's accusation of the father to the daughter on these grounds with particular disfavor. Nevertheless he held his tongue while Warren continued:

"That is the reason you are trying to protect your father with this fabricated alibi about Loundon's visit to the lodge, isn't it?"

"I am not trying to protect my father," she repeated. "He couldn't have been guilty."

She had recovered from her consternation and sat in rigid self-possession on the edge of her chair. Warren looked at her intently for several seconds, then sat up decisively and pressed the button on his desk. "We'll make up our minds about that after we talk with your father," he declared shortly.

A moment later the county attorney's sharp-featured secretary responded to the buzzer.

"Send in Mr. Van Roth," Warren said. "Miss Van Roth will wait in the reception room."

"Yes sir," she said, turning to go.

"Just a moment, please." Steele stopped her with a smile, turning to Warren. "I'd like to ask Miss Van Roth another question or two before she goes."

The secretary remained just inside the door. Steele twisted around in his chair and looked at her inquiringly. She gave her head a toss and went out with a bang.

"God!" Steele chuckled. "What an inspiration she must be. Does anybody ever get out of here with an acquittal?"

Warren did not deign to answer, and Steele swung around to Miss Van Roth.

"You told us your brother said over the telephone the afternoon before he was killed that he knew who murdered Loundon. Do you believe that?"

"Yes." Her voice and manner had every evidence of sincerity.

"Did he say anything to you about intending to turn this person over to the police?"

"No, not precisely—" she hesitated, considering—"although when I told him that was what he should do he said, 'Don't you worry about that, I've got him where I want him.' . . . That may not be exactly what he said, but I think those are about the words he used."

"'I've got him where I want him,'" Steele repeated thoughtfully. "That could have meant more blackmail—or, as you infer, it could have meant he expected to inform the authorities." After a pause, he asked, "Did he say when he expected to go to the police?"

"He couldn't have planned doing it last night—out at the lodge?"

"I don't think so," she replied slowly. "No, I'm quite sure he couldn't. He came to the car where my father and I were watching the well, just a few minutes before it caught fire, and said he wanted my father to meet a man he used to know in El Dorado. If he had had anything else on his mind he wouldn't have bothered with a thing like that."

At this apparently simple observation Steele uttered a sharp exclamation. Then, as if to cover his confusion, he pushed back his chair and walked the length of the room and back, finally stopping in front of Miss Van Roth, grasping the back of his chair tightly with his long sinewy hands. It was obvious there was more than astonishment in Steele's manner; he had plainly come face to face with some consideration that disturbed and unsettled him.

"Did your father go with him?" he finally asked, with exaggerated casualness.

"Why yes."

"Did he meet the man from El Dorado?"

"No, I think not." She looked at him curiously. "I believe Father said they couldn't find him. I really don't see what connection that has with—"

Steele broke in sharply, leaning hard on the back of the chair: "How long was your father gone?"

She sensed the tenseness in Steele's bearing even if she could not fathom the cause of it, and carefully considered her reply.

"I can't say just how long. He came back to the car just a little while after the well caught fire."

"Ah!" Steele brushed his red hair back with a gesture that was an unconscious but characteristic indication of high nervous tension. "He didn't return until afterwards!"

He studied her closely without change of expression, then turned abruptly to Warren.

"I think you're right! We'd better talk with Dr. Van Roth." Warren pressed the buzzer, and the hatchet-faced secretary appeared in the doorway.

"Ask Mr. Van Roth to come in now," he told her.

She hesitated. "Why—ah—he— I'll tell him as soon as he comes back. He stepped out of the room for a moment."

"Where did he go?" Steele unexpectedly confronted her. The face of the sharp-chinned girl wore a distinct blush. "Why—er—he asked me," she faltered, much embarrassed—"he said he was going to the toilet!"

"Have one of the boys go after him at once," Steele ordered. When she had gone he turned to Miss Van Roth. "You had better wait—in the reception room."

She was plainly puzzled, but she left the room without protest or question.

Steele whirled on Warren.

"What do you make of that? Could it have been his own father Jack was trying to double-cross?"

Warren had risen from his chair in undignified excitement.

"My God, Steele, you don't suppose the old man murdered his own son too?"

Steele was manifestly perplexed, but in answer to this question he shook his head slowly.

"It looks damned peculiar, but it doesn't fit." He stared meditatively out of the window. "And yet, it would be a strange coincidence if—"

He was interrupted by a young man who hurried into the office.

"Mr. Van Roth's gone," he announced. "He went straight down the stairs and outdoors. One of the boys in the sheriff's office saw him drive off in his car!"

Warren looked incredulous.

"Gone!" He stared blankly at Steele, then gave the clerk a hasty order: "Tell whoever's in the sheriff's office to go after him!" He followed the young man through the door, and I heard him call brusquely to his secretary, "Get the police station on the line and then come into the office."

He went to his desk, and in a moment the buzzer sounded. When he was connected he hastily explained his predicament and requested that Van Roth be picked up on sight and placed in custody, subject to the orders of the county attorney. He hung up to find his secretary facing him nervously across the desk.

"Look here, Miss Grinter," he demanded, "why did Mr. Van Roth leave in such a hurry? Did you say something to scare him off?"

Miss Grinter gripped her notebook hard, stood speechless a moment, then nodded with anxious reluctance.

"Yes sir. My tongue slipped—I don't know why I did it—but by mistake I called him Mr. Rothwell."

"You called him Rothwell!"

"Yes sir. You see I had been copying out that information, an—"

"What did he say when you called him that; how did he act?"

"Well, he seemed startled, and then when I began to apologize I guess he must have realized you had this information. It was just a little after that when he left." Despite the rigid severity of her face the young woman was on the verge of tears. "I—I—I'm terribly sorry, Mr. Warren; I don't—"

"Sorry! Oh my God!" Warren exploded.

18

THE DISAPPEARANCE from the Sedgwick County Courthouse in broad daylight of the Reverend Raymond Dwight Van Roth, well-known throughout the city and weighing two hundred and fifty pounds was, as Steele observed, comparable with the unique achievement of the man who lost a bass drum in a hotel lobby. Apparently he walked quietly out of the building to his own car and unhurriedly drove away into a total eclipse. At the most, he did not have ten minutes start of the city and county police, yet after three hours of intensive search no report or trace of him was forthcoming.

Warren, in his mortification, had immediately summoned Miss Van Roth from the outer office for another grilling. He learned nothing that was of any help in the search. She professed to believe her father would not attempt to leave the city and gave it as her opinion that he would return of his own accord. After a close questioning of more than half an hour, during which the county attorney verified from her own lips Van Roth's criminal, record, he reluctantly permitted her to go. By this time, however, Warren was so far convinced of Van Roth's guilt that if Steele had not interceded he would have held the daughter in custody. As she left she paused in the doorway to thank Steele, her face lighting up for a second with a flash of the extraordinary charm that was hers when she smiled.

When she had gone Warren explained that the "tip-off" on Van Roth's record had come in the form of an anonymous letter. From the top drawer of his desk he produced a soiled, cheap, plain white envelope, which he handed to Steele. It was addressed to "Mr. County Atorny" in a crude, uneven print, apparently done with a heavy black pencil. Steele glanced at the envelope and then took out the enclosure and hastily read it through. It said:

> Dere Sir, *I thoght you would like to know that rev van Roth is a exconvick. He was in the pen for killing his cusin, that was 30 or 40 years ago and it was did in Ohio. But his name was not van Roth it was Ramond Rothwel. Yours truly but I will not sine my name,* John Doe.

"Hm-m." Steele handed the letter back to Warren. "Who do you suppose wanted to sneak up on the doctor this way? Maybe it was one of his radio listeners! . . . When did you get it?"

"It came in this morning's mail. I wired to Ohio immediately, and here's the answer they gave me."

Steele took the telegram and read aloud:

> "Raymond Dwight Rothwell convicted December 1888 for murder June 26 of cousin Herbert Rothwell at Toledo. Pardoned October 1890 over strong protest. Governor persuaded by new evidence. No subsequent record."

"I could get photographs and fingerprints," Warren remarked as Steele returned the telegram; "but his daughter admitted it was true, and the fact that he ran out on us when he found we had learned his real name is proof enough."

Steele gave the county attorney an odd, provoked look.

"You can't try a man twice for the same murder," he observed.

Warren shoved the papers in his desk.

"A man who would kill his cousin isn't automatically exempted from suspicion, is he?"

Steele shrugged his shoulders and got up. "Well, we'll see you this afternoon. If anything exciting happens call Bill at the office."

I didn't expect Steele to talk, and he didn't disappoint me. We ate a hasty lunch in silence, and I returned to the office. For the next two hours I was busily engaged in collaborating with Gus Holm on a four-page Sunday feature story explaining and illustrating oil-well gushers and fires in general and the Hovey No. 4 in particular. About three o'clock Steele wandered in, fresh and chipper, to inform me that Ferguson had returned from Newton. He was concerned lest this should interfere with his plan to watch the attempt to extinguish the fire at the well. When Holm told him that Brady, the expert from Tulsa, would not be ready before late afternoon, Steele insisted on dragging me off at once to the county attorney's office.

Hale Ferguson, Warren's chief assistant, was a shrewd-faced, small-featured man of about twenty-five, with black eyes, a small black mustache, short-cut black pompadour hair, and a distinct air of self-confidence, which, however, was not so obtrusive as to be offensive. He made his report concisely and stopped when he had nothing further to say.

Briefly, he had learned that Dr. Vernon's car was left in a Newton garage from noon, August 12, until between eight and nine o'clock the morning of August 15. The same man who brought it in called for it; the garage man's description perfectly fitted Dr. Vernon. It was assumed he had arrived at 5:30 that morning from Kansas City by way of the Santa Fe, since the train at that hour was the only one he could have caught at the Union Station after 10:30 the night before, when it was known he had checked out of the Pickwick Hotel.

This still left the period from about nine o'clock on the morning of August 15 to the middle of the afternoon of August 17 unaccounted for. No one answering Dr. Vernon's description had been registered at any of the Newton hotels. None of the leading Newton physicians, most of whom were acquainted with Dr. Vernon, had seen him or heard of his having been in town. A check of the hospitals failed to provide any further information.

The only other clue was the Newton telephone number, 675, which Dr. Vernon had called from Kansas City. This number belonged to a Newton lawyer by the name of Allen A. Spencer. He had been in Chicago since the 8th of August. His wife had left the morning of August 15 for Colorado; so the next-door neighbors informed Ferguson. Spencer was to join her in Denver, and they were not expected back until the middle of September. He was a man of forty-five, his wife was in her early thirties; they were childless and lived alone in the home without servants. The last the neighbors had seen of Mrs. Spencer was on the evening of the 114th, when she gave a little lawn party for some of the small children of the neighborhood. Conversation with these neighbors disclosed the fact that Dr. Vernon had operated on Spencer for appendicitis the preceding winter. Since Dr. Vernon's call had been a station-to-station call, Ferguson assumed it was of a professional and not a personal nature.

Warren listened to his assistant's recital with a scowling impatience that contrasted sharply with the keen attention Steele gave to every word. It was typical of Warren's single-track mind that he was unable to free himself from the chagrin of Van Roth's unceremonious leave-taking, for he was clearly convinced that the solution of the case lay in the reapprehension of the minister. Steele, on the contrary, found something in Ferguson's account of the investigation that aroused his interest almost to the point of excitement. What it was I could not surmise, but I recognized the unmistakable symptoms of suddenly stimulated mental activity in the quick and absent-minded way in which he pulled out his cigarette cast and in the vacant stare he gave Ferguson after he got his cigarette going. Finally he turned brusquely to Warren.

"I believe we ought to talk with Dr. Vernon. Will you ask your secretary to see if she can get him on the phone?"

Warren nodded, pushed the buzzer and gave the order.

Fifteen minutes later we were sitting in the doctor's inner office waiting to begin the brief interview he had said he could grant us. When he appeared he greeted us cordially, but with the air of a man who has been unseasonably interrupted, and waited with ill-concealed impatience for us to disclose the reason for our call.

This Steele did without equivocation.

"Dr. Vernon, why did you tell me yesterday that you drove home from Kansas City on the seventeenth by way of El Dorado?"

At this unexpected frontal attack Dr. Vernon's lips closed under his iron-gray mustache, and his gray eyes narrowed.

"What do you mean by that?" He glanced at Warren and me and then back to Steele. "Is this some sort of inquisition?"

"Not at all," Steele replied calmly. He smiled with cool assurance into the doctor's face. "But we have found it necessary to come to you for some information."

Dr. Vernon walked to his desk, jerked out the chair, and for a few seconds sat in it glaring at Steele's immobile countenance. At last he said:

"Well, what do you want to know?"

Steele shrugged his shoulders slightly at the doctor's still truculent voice.

"Where were you from August twelfth to August seventeenth?"

"You know where I was. I was in Kansas City."

Steele frowned at this insistence on what we all knew was a lie.

"That isn't so. You left Kansas City the night of August fourteenth."

At this second flat contradiction Dr. Vernon jumped up from his chair, his face red with fury. He was a powerful man, and as passion laid hold of his domineering face one could easily understand the ascendancy he held over his associates and subordinates. He banged his hand down hard on the desk and leaned across toward Steele with his teeth half bared.

"It's none of your damned business where I was!" He turned viciously to include Warren and me. "None of you! Do you understand? . . . I suppose you think I know something about this Loundon case. Well, I don't! I had no connection with Loundon in any way; I had no interest in him except as a patient; and I know nothing about what happened to him. Now if that's what you came here to find out, that's your answer!"

Warren's face turned red at the doctor's bold and insolent attitude, but Steele received his tirade with perplexed surprise.

"Look here, Doctor," he began mildly, "we have reason to think you might be in a position to know a good deal about Loundon. Now if—"

"What reason?" Dr. Vernon snapped.

Steele hesitated, giving him a penetrating but unhurried look out of his deep-set blue eyes. Finally he shook his head.

"I'm not at liberty to give you our reasons."

Steele apparently had determined not to disclose Mrs. Vernon's connection with the case. I assumed from this he supposed there was still the possibility that Dr. Vernon knew nothing of his wife's former intimacy with Loundon and that he had no knowledge of her visit to Loundon's lodge in company with Jack Van Roth. I was aware from his attitude that Dr. Vernon's evasions and belligerent disavowals had aroused his liveliest suspicion, for of course it was natural to suppose Vernon had knowledge of his wife's complicity either from her or from Jack Van Roth, if not from some outside source. Yet rather than run the risk of doing Mrs. Vernon a lasting injustice he chose to pass up a weapon which certainly would have brought Dr. Vernon to terms immediately—always provided he was not guilty or criminally implicated. There was the possibility that Vernon had guilty knowledge of the crime but did not know of his wife's past connection with Loundon or of her visit to the lodge; and it was also assumable that she had no cognizance of his possible guilt. These were the considerations that prompted Steele's reply; and I knew he must have been prepared for the very virtuous fury it precipitated.

"Not at liberty!" Dr. Vernon banged the desk again. "But you think you're at liberty to intrude here and make charges and call names without excuse or apology. Well, by God, you can't do it! I'll ask you to leave! I'm very busy, and I haven't time to waste on insults! . . . Good-by."

"Just a minute, Doctor." Steele's manner was unruffled, but there was a vague menacing inflection in his voice that Vernon seemed to recognize, for he turned from the door through which, in his anger, he was about to dismiss us. "Our reasons for coming to you may be unfounded, but they are good reasons. They are sufficient to make us suspicious of your attitude and your attempt to mislead us. Unless you can account for your whereabouts at the time Loundon was killed we shall have to try to find out for ourselves where you were. And before you make any further denials I may as well tell you that we know you were in Newton the morning of August fifteenth, that you left your car there on August twelfth, and that presumably you were in the vicinity of the strawstack until the afternoon of the seventeenth, when you returned to Wichita. We know about your attempt to mislead your wife by sending her a telegram dated the seventeenth which you actually wrote on the fourteenth." Steele paused, took two or three slow steps in the doctor's direction, then added, in a tone that held an indefinable threat, "And what is more, we have further information that may lead to disclosures you would not care to make public!"

Dr. Vernon stared at Steele with a face from which every expression save angry dismay had fled. He opened his mouth as if to make a retort—and changed his mind. He crossed to his desk, then turned resolutely. When he spoke it was with a touch of sarcasm.

"I assume from what you say about the telegram that you have already been harassing my wife and that you have told her all your suspicions?"

"I talked briefly with your wife," Steele denied, "but she knows nothing of what I have told you. We learned about the telegram from a Kansas City detective."

As he spoke Steele eyed Dr. Vernon with curious intensity. Behind the surface antagonism of the two men I detected a subtle and mysterious byplay I could not comprehend. It was as if they waged a desperate conflict on a ground of mutual understanding not apparent to the rest of us. At last Dr. Vernon shifted his eyes and shook his head.

"I've said all I'm going to say. I don't know anything about Loundon or his death."

"You will not explain where you were the day he was killed?"

Dr. Vernon lifted his iron-gray head and looked steadily into Steele's eyes for a moment, then turned away. "I've said all I'm going to."

"Very well." Steele shrugged his shoulders. "We may as well go." He picked up his hat, then, noticing that Warren still hesitated as if considering whether to continue the interview, he took him by the arm. "But I promise you, Doctor, that we will be back, and it may be under circumstances you will greatly regret."

With this parting warning we filed out. When we had got in the car Warren turned to Steele with a half-aggrieved curiosity.

"Why the devil didn't you tell him we know about his wife's mix-up with Loundon and Van Roth? Laying money aside, he had more good reasons for wanting Loundon and Jack out of the way than anybody else."

Steele rested his straw hat on his knee while he wiped his forehead with his handkerchief. As he answered there was a gleam of amusement in his eyes.

"Do I understand you now choose Vernon instead of Van Roth?"

Warren took the question seriously. He considered.

"I don't know just what I believe," he replied slowly. "Van Roth has a criminal record, and no matter what you think, that weighs against him in my mind. But Vernon's motives spring from revenge and jealousy both, to say nothing of fear."

"Right. And if he was threatened with blackmail you could also add a mercenary motive."

Warren shot Steele a quick look.

"I don't know. There isn't a man in the city with a higher standing. But just the same I wouldn't put it past him to commit murder if he got mad enough."

"Or if he thought it necessary to his happiness."

Again Warren gave Steele a startled and inquiring look. Steele hesitated, then added, "The question now is, how are we going to check up on him?"

Warren pulled out his big pipe and loaded it thoughtfully.

"Steele," he said in a speculative voice, "I can't bring myself to believe either Vernon or Van Roth killed Loundon. They're too old. It would have been physically impossible for anybody but a strong and active man to drag Loundon up that stack. And why should Loundon have gone up there alone, or have gone up with anyone else?"

Steele gave him a surprised look.

"Surely you're not still permitting that little circumstance of the strawstack to interfere with your suspicions!" He chuckled. "I naturally supposed you had put that out of your head." He gave Warren a quizzical glance, but when he perceived the other was in earnest, he went on seriously, "Anyone having a key to the room under the stack could have put up the rope ladder. Or, to make it simpler, suppose Loundon was already on the stack and the rope ladder was in place. Anybody, even a woman, could have killed him, put away the ladder and departed without a trace. A further flight of fancy would make it possible to assume Loundon was killed at his car or in his lodge and was moved by boat to the stack and pulled up the side. Two persons could have managed it easily. Or, as the newspapers will remind you, one person and a trained ape!" Steele shook his head reflectively. "No; weird as it seems, it may be made credible applied to anyone we've had up for consideration, even if it wouldn't make sense." He paused. "And when you ask, why should Loundon have gone up on the stack of his own free will, there is always a woman. And so far as that goes, *I'm willing to bet even money there was a woman on that straw-stack the morning of the sixteenth!*"

Warren and I gazed at Steele in astonishment. This sort of statement was so contrary to his customary secretiveness that I suspected him of joking, but his face wore every evidence of honest sobriety.

"Look here, Steele, are you holding something back on me?" Warren demanded. "You act as if you knew who killed Loundon and Van Roth!"

Steele regarded Warren half a minute with a curious hesitancy before he answered.

"I think I do," he said simply; "and I am not holding out on you."

"Then who, in God's name, is it?"

"I can't tell you, because I may be wrong. . . . And even if I'm right I can't prove it!" He put on his hat and paused to light a cigarette. "In the meantime, let's get out of the sun; we can't solve any problems sitting here in this car. . . . Suppose you drop me at the *Times* office with Bill."

Reluctantly Warren started the car. Dr. Vernon's refusal to explain the discrepancy in his statement that he had been in Kansas

City at the time of Loundon's death had shaken Warren's assumption that Van Roth's leave-taking was a tacit confession of guilt. Obviously he wanted to question Steele further, but from experience he knew this would result in nothing but evasions. When he stopped the car to let us out, however, his face bore such a look of discouragement that Steele gave him a word of hope.

"Cheer up," he said, "and keep the boys on Van Roth's trail. That shouldn't be any harder than tracking an elephant across a wheat field. . . . You know, if Van Roth didn't have a hand in this affair he may know who the guilty party is. In any case, I'm expecting something to happen before tomorrow night. . . . No! I can't say what I mean; it's just a hunch. Well, we'll be seeing you."

19

Steele followed me into the lobby of the *Times* Building, but when I would have taken the elevator to the news rooms, he stopped me. Glancing into the street to make sure Warren had gone, he said:

"How would you like to take a ride into the country?"

"I'm your man! When do we start?"

"Right now. My car is in the garage at the apartment." He pulled out his watch. "It's four-thirty. We should be able to make it in half an hour."

We walked to the garage, and fifteen minutes later were speeding west on the paved highway known locally as the Cannonball. Ten miles from town we turned north on a graveled road, and Steele reduced his speed to a conversational fifty miles an hour.

"We're going to Dr. Vernon's ranch," he informed me. "Do you know the exact spot?"

"Straight ahead. I'll give you the turns. It's on the bank of the Arkansas."

"I've a hunch he drove straight over here from Newton the morning he returned from Kansas City. How far would you say this ranch is from Loundon's lodge?"

"Well, let's see. Fifteen or eighteen miles. It's almost due west of the lodge, perhaps a little south."

"Would the highway south of Loundon's place—the Hutchinson highway—have taken us across to Vernon's ranch?"

"Correct. In fact we would have had a little more pavement that way; but I believe the stretch of road north of Vernon's place to

211

the Hutchinson highway isn't so good. This is the usual route from Wichita."

Steele drove thoughtfully for a couple of miles.

"Sarge, this escapade of the doctor's has some damned peculiar angles. Is it conceivable that a man of his shrewdness and medical experience has been deceived all these years by his wife? Is it possible he doesn't know his adopted daughter is his wife's own child? Supposing he knows, isn't it still more improbable that a man of his temperament would have kept his knowledge a secret from his wife?"

"Sounds unreasonable. I take it you're implying he is aware of his wife's secret and she knows it—in other words that there is no secret."

"It's a thought, just a thought. But if you assume that much you also assume that the hesitatings and pleadings and terror of our interview with her were staged for our benefit."

"You mean, to keep suspicion away from the doctor?"

"Right. And it entitles us to one more assumption—that instead of its having been Jack Van Roth who accompanied her to the lodge the night she stole our car it might have been her husband. After all, we have only her word it was Jack. And if that assumption is correct what more logical than an attempt to implicate someone else?"

This was a line of reasoning that had not occurred to me. I ran over in my mind the details of our visit with Mrs. Vernon.

"I doubt if that's the answer," I decided in a few moments. "If it is, she's the cleverest actress off the stage. What do you believe?"

"Me? I don't believe anything. . . . I'm just thinking aloud. But just bear this in mind: imagination often leads to truths reason would never dream of."

With this philosophical observation Steele lapsed into a silence that lasted until I pointed out the Vernon ranch buildings silhouetted against the dark fringe of trees bordering the river a couple of miles to the northeast. A few minutes later we came to the sandy lane leading to the house, three quarters of a mile distant. Steele stopped the car, and we got out. While I slipped the ring off the gateposts and dragged the crude barbed-wire gate-end across the lane, Steele walked along the shallow ruts, carefully scrutinizing the sand. In a few minutes he got in the car, drove through and waited for me to close the gate.

"No sign of anyone in or out for a day or two," he observed as we proceeded. "Last tire tracks were those of a big car. Maybe Vernon's."

Dr. Vernon's ranch was not a show place. It was merely a sentimental preservation of the homestead his father had established on the prairie in the days when buffalo and antelope dotted the flat limitless grassy acres, before the great herds of Texas longhorns wended their way north to the encroaching railroads, before lines of barbed-wire fixed the circumscribed checkerboards of civilization. The father had himself left it years before he died, to make his home in a modern and much more pretentious farmhouse nearer town. Dr. Vernon had kept the buildings in repair, but no improvements had been made and nothing had been added. They lay bare and gray and weathered under the beating August sun, crouching low in the vast landscape as if to escape the constant tug of winds that swept unhindered across the rolling plains. There was no other house in sight—there were only the illimitable lonely prairie and the straggling river trees, desolate as the palms of an oasis in a desert.

The ranch house was a single-story, five-room cottage with a small unroofed porch at the front door and a wider lean-to porch at the rear. Back of the house were a barn, two smaller outhouses, a well pump and a large high-fenced corral. The ground within the corral had long been untouched by hoofs; grass grew untrodden before the wide doors of the barn; the sandy yard, patched with straggling buffalo grass, seemed unmarked by any sign of human or animal life. On the worn floor of the back porch a tiny dune of fine sand lay sparkling in the sunlight where it had drifted against the bottom of the screen door.

Steele gave a perfunctory try at both doors. As he expected, they were locked. He gave the windows an appraising look, but turned away, after a moment, with the remark:

"Before we do any housebreaking perhaps I'd better take a look in the yard. . . . Let's see. . . . Maybe the wind hasn't obliterated everything yet."

He began at the back porch and proceeded to a minute examination of the paths leading to the pump and the outhouses. Presently he dropped to his knees on the ground near the pump platform, where the earth held a trace of moisture. As I approached he looked up with a delighted smile.

"As a guesser, Sergeant, my boy—" he beamed with gratification—"I will have to go to the head of the class!" He pointed. "Look there. A woman's footprint! I knew it; I knew it! But I couldn't be sure." He crawled along the path toward the house. "Here she is two or three more times, but the sand has almost covered her up. And here—" he carefully scraped the sand out of a longer and wider depression—"is the doctor's footprint. You can also see where they stepped out of the car, but the rest of the tracks there are gone."

He got to his feet and brushed the sand from his trousers.

"Well, now to get inside!"

The blinds in all the windows were down, and a hasty push and shake proved all the sashes locked.

"Let's try that one off the back porch," Steele suggested when we had made the rounds. "It's loose, and we may be able to pry the lock around."

He got a screwdriver from the car and found he could insert the blade between the ill-fitting window sashes. In a few minutes the lock had been turned and we were inside.

The heat in the low rooms, with only the roof shielding them from the afternoon August sun, was stifling. We threw open the doors and raised two or three windows. The glaring light disclosed an interior that could have been moved back into the seventies with only three anachronisms: some gasoline pressure lamps, a telephone and a gasoline camp stove in the kitchen. The rest was pure Western pioneer, even to the coarse, faded carpets and the triangular whatnot in the corner of the "sitting room," with its hand-painted pictorial china and its glass-enclosed bouquet of bright wax flowers.

What Steele hoped to discover in this desolate old-fashioned farm home I could not imagine, but he set about his search swiftly and methodically. He first went to the largest bedroom, where he remained eight or ten minutes; then he made a careful examination of the remaining rooms, ending in the kitchen. He scrutinized the back porch and made a survey of the outbuildings. When he had finished he brought into the dining room a newspaper-wrapped package, which he triumphantly opened out on the table.

"Wastebaskets are the repositories of the mistakes of mankind," he announced in a professorial tone greatly exaggerated, as he began piecing together a handful of bits of paper. "Here, for example, is Dr. Vernon's receipt for his room at the Pickwick Hotel, stamped and dated August fourteenth." He slipped the pieces into an envelope and began on another similar jigsaw puzzle. "Here is his Pullman berth receipt, and here is a cash-register receipt from the Gem Drugstore of Newton, dated August fifteenth. Hm-m. Most people don't even pick 'em up; must be the clerk stuck it in the package.

"Here," he continued in his role of classroom-demonstrator, "are the Wichita *Morning Times* of August fifteenth and the Newton *Kansan-Republican*, dated August fourteenth. These items were all brought into the house by Dr. Vernon. You will notice that with the exception of the newspapers they are all torn across at least once. Now to you, my dear Lieutenant, that very likely indicates a desire to destroy them as evidence. But such is not the case. It is merely indicative of the habit many persons have of tearing or mutilating anything thrown into a wastebasket to confirm the fact that the object is of no further value. I assure you that if Dr. Vernon had supposed these mementos would ever meet our eyes he would have taken them into the yard and burned them thoroughly."

Steele paused and rubbed his hands as if to heighten the suspense of his nonexistent audience.

"And here now, my friends, as I am sure you will agree, is a scrap of paper Dr. Vernon most assuredly would have destroyed had he known of it. Unfortunately for him it was left in the bottom of the bedroom wastebasket, where it became hidden by this wrapping paper. I am positive, in fact, that the lady responsible for its presence there was not even aware she had brought it into the house. In other words, it is a statement which accompanied some article of wearing apparel—could it have been, young gentlemen, a nightgown?—which she charged to her account and carried away with her from the store. It says, in the very illegible scrawl of the typical clerk, something that appears to be 'N Gounn . . . $4.50.' The name of the store is the New York Dry Goods Company, Newton. The name of the woman is Mrs. Allen A. Spencer!"

Steele paused dramatically, bowed respectfully in all directions and folded up the slip. He picked up a handful of other objects.

"These small accessories, while interesting, are not illuminating. Three so-called 'bobby pins' for milady's hair, four very blonde hairs further examination might prove were once scorched into a permanent wave, several empty cigarette packages and numerous butts, two milk-bottle tops from the Jersey Dairy of Newton, etc., etc., etc."

Steele threw these into the wastebasket, but put the other articles carefully into his pocket. He took off his coat, fitted it over the back of a chair, and sat on the table to mop his forehead and glistening red hair while he regarded my wondering approval with satisfaction.

"A hunch that worked, my boy," he declared. "There is one point more to be noted: It must be observed that nothing we have found bears a date later than August fifteenth. The newspaper of that date is a morning paper. From this it seems logical to assume that Dr. Vernon and Mrs. Spencer came directly here sometime the morning of the fifteenth of August. That, of course, may be an incorrect assumption. How long they stayed here is a question. One or both, I think, until the morning of the seventeenth. Coffee grounds and other garbage indicate a stay of at least two days."

I considered these deductions thoughtfully. As Steele presented the facts it seemed very logical.

"You think the woman, if it was Mrs. Spencer, stayed here all that time?" I asked. "You remember Ferguson reported that her neighbors said she left for Colorado on the fifteenth."

"True. A nice question." Steele nodded agreement. "My explanation is that she made her arrangements to go to Colorado, met

Dr. Vernon in some inconspicuous place and came to the ranch with him. She then went on to Colorado. Now where would she have taken the train? Newton or Wichita? Of course not. Neither would want to be seen in either town. My guess is, Hutchinson—and it is possible he took her there as early as the night of the fifteenth or sometime on the sixteenth. But why, in that case, should he have stayed here alone until the seventeenth?"

Steele indulged in a rhetorical pause.

"Very possibly because—"

Suddenly, as Steele spoke, a terrific screeching clamor sounded from the sitting room. My heart turned a somersault, and Steele whirled violently off the table. Twice more it ripped the hot silence of the room. Then Steele leaned back against the table and began to laugh.

"That's what a guilty conscience will do!" He wiped his face nervously. "A damned party-line telephone equipped with some kind of fire gong so it can be heard from the barn! Whew!"

I got my breath back slowly and then went cautiously and suspiciously to peer through the window toward the road. There was nothing to be seen but the heat waves shimmering above the sand. Relieved, but still unnerved, I turned back to Steele.

"Let's get out of here," I said. "I haven't been so scared since the Argonne. Baby! If that's what it takes to be a crook I'll stick to the typewriter."

"We might as well close up before somebody else wants to talk over that fire alarm," Steele agreed, beginning to pull down the windows. "But what I started to say is that Vernon might have felt he had to wait until the seventeenth in order not to beat his post-dated telegram home. . . . Or it may be this was merely his head-quarters for something more sinister than a liaison."

I turned around from the window I was latching.

"But how could this be connected with Loundon?" I demanded. "It looks to me as if he and Mrs. Spencer simply took advantage of her husband's trip to Chicago for a little extramarital excitement."

Steele shook his head. "Oh now, Major," he said, "is this your idea of a love nest? This ugly, comfortless, stifling oven? You don't do the doctor justice. I can't believe this is what he would choose for a sentimental dovecote for an August holiday. This has the appearance of a hide-out. Take my word for it, there was some motive beyond mere infatuation. Now if Vernon were in the twenties . . ."

Steele's voice trailed away into silence. For some time he stood looking thoughtfully through the open door across the hot, level landscape. At the end he shook his head as if once more to deny the supposition, then turned energetically to tidy up the rooms and close the house. A few minutes later I had let him through the gate and was getting into the car seat beside him. He gave a last look at the squat, lonely gray house quivering in the heat of the late afternoon sun.

"This the August rendezvous for a Don Juan of fifty-five?" Emphatically he shook his head. "I can't believe it, Colonel; I simply can't believe it."

20

INSTEAD OF RETURNING to Wichita as we had come Steele drove by way of the Hutchinson highway to the Meridian oil field in the hope of being in time to witness Dan Brady's attempt to extinguish the fire at the gusher. It was a little past seven-thirty when we crossed the bridge over the river south of Loundon's estate. As we cleared the trees lining the banks we could see the flame-shot clouds of black smoke billowing and spiraling into the sky. Soon the roar drowned out the noise of the car, and by the time we found parking space a quarter of a mile from the well and secured a point of vantage near the rope barriers, our ears could register nothing but the continuous pounding thunder of the spouting flames.

We soon perceived that we had arrived at the crucial moment. Groups of men who had been working in the heat from the pillar of flame, protected by helmets and moving under a constant deluge of water played upon them by fire hoses, had finished their task of snaking out with grappling hooks and cables the metal equipment at the mouth of the well. This was necessary to prevent the white-hot metal from reigniting the oil and gas when the fire was extinguished. In the meantime Dan Brady, clad in an asbestos suit and helmet, made his preparations, while several thousand spectators gathered at a respectful distance on the prairie near by.

My work with Gus Holm on our Sunday feature story had acquainted me in a general way with Brady's system of fighting fires of this nature. Briefly, he would attempt to blow out the flames with a charge of nitroglycerin precisely as one blows out a candle.

219

His first task was to get the charge into position over the well hole. This he did by stretching an asbestos rope across the flame, tying it to a cable attached to a derrick on one side and a truck on the other. The truck was then slowly driven away from the well until the rope was stretched tight six or eight feet above the top of the torn casing.

Brady then mixed a twenty-quart bomb of nitroglycerin. This cartridge was made by wrapping the charge in asbestos, then packing it into a steel oil drum, also asbestos wrapped. A fuse was placed in the cartridge, and this was connected to the two or three hundred feet of asbestos-wrapped cable running to the spot where the electric detonating switch stood, which would flash the spark into the torpedo when it was in readiness in the center of the flames.

When Brady had wrapped the last asbestos covering around the bomb he signaled to the crowd that he was about to start the fireworks. He suspended the nitro cartridge over the line with a loop of the asbestos rope, tightened up the belt of his asbestos suit, and began pushing the explosive along the rope into the fire. The protected wires connecting the detonator to the switch trailed along behind him. As he slowly edged toward that roaring inferno into a heat so intense as to be almost unbelievable, the faces of the staring spectators grew tense in the lurid glow. The taut rope began to sway; as he gradually approached the center it almost sagged to touch the casing. For a breathless moment or two the loop caught and refused to move. Doggedly the lone figure in the ghostlike costume worked his sensitive burden into the center of the volcano. He placed the charge within two inches of the casing head and beat a precipitous retreat. Out of range, he signaled for the detonator to be exploded.

A blast that would have shaken a mountain rocked the prairie. The flame and smoke disappeared, but the roar of the well, only a little diminished, continued. Suddenly, with a terrific blast, the gusher flared into flame again. It had been reignited by a piece of white-hot metal.

By now the August twilight had faded into darkness, and the great candle flared blue and red and orange against the black sky. By its weird light Brady philosophically and methodically set about constructing another torpedo. As he worked, every available stream of water was played into the flames in an effort to reduce the temperature of the metal it had been impossible to pull away. This time Brady mixed a "shot" of thirty quarts of the "soup" as casually as a cook would stir up the ingredients of a cake.

A new asbestos rope was tightened over the flames. Again Brady waded into the fiery furnace, and the crowd cheered—a noiseless, eerie applause unheard against the roar of the fire. Once more he worked his tortuous way toward the center of the twisted remains of the derrick. At last he succeeded in placing the charge, and retreated. Again the terrific charge shook the earth, instantly followed by the roar of oil and gas in a different key, as if some Mephistophelian conductor had suddenly begun directing the modulations of a Purgatorial orchestra. Brady, at what he supposed was a safe distance, was thrown for fifteen feet, but struggled up immediately, uninjured.

The gigantic torch was snuffed out. A sudden curious darkness enveloped the plains. Stars, not apparent at first to our eyes, which were accustomed to the incandescence, began to reappear one by one in the vast black expanse of the sky that stretched to the encircling horizons of the prairie. Brady's truck and the nearby cars began switching on their lights. For a few expectant moments the motionless figure of the firefighter stood outlined against the swishing curtain of falling oil. Then he turned away, satisfied that the danger of reignition was past, and slowly propelled his heavy boots across the enclosure to his truck, where one of his helpers began to assist him out of his asbestos accouterments.

The drama over, Steele and I made our way through the excited crowd. When we finally succeeded in dodging across the highway and were nearing the place on the side road where we were parked, Steele suddenly grabbed my arm.

"Look!" he shouted. "Van Roth!"

I looked up and saw a dingy green coupé disappearing into the darkness ahead of us. We ran to our car and tore down the dusty road in an effort to overtake him. But there was too much traffic. Steele gave up the attempt, and we turned back toward town.

"What the devil do you suppose he was doing out here in this crowd?" I asked, when Steele had slowed down.

Steele received my question with a frown, but did not answer. For several minutes he drove in silence, a troubled expression on his face.

"I can't make up my mind about that old boy," he said at last. "What I think is, he is flirting with death and doesn't know it."

I had long ago ceased trying to pump Steele, but after considering this ambiguous statement a moment, I could not repress my curiosity.

"What do you mean?" I asked. "Are you implying that Warren can convict him, or that he knows too much about the murderer for his own good?"

"Warren might convict him, and he may know too much," was Steele's lucid answer. "We'll be able to tell more tomorrow."

"That will be fine." I thanked him with all the irony at my command. "And not to change the subject, do you realize we haven't had anything to eat? There's a White Castle stand in the north end, just as you get into town."

"Right. Now you mention it, I'm starving. And I think I'd better telephone the sheriff's office about Van Roth."

When we had seated ourselves at the polished counter of the tiny all-night stand and had ordered hamburgers "with lettuce, pickles and onions both," as Wimpy puts it, Steele dialed the sheriff's office from the desk-set telephone the waiter shoved in front of him. For half a minute he waited, in the odor of frying beef, without response.

"Try the county jail," I suggested; "there's always someone there. Burke has probably gone home."

A moment later the sheriff's own voice burst from the receiver. Steele made a grimace and moved the instrument a couple of inches away from his ear. It was like a loud speaker without any volume control.

"This is Steele, Sheriff. I just saw Van Roth on the road near the Meridian oil field. He was driving an old green Chevrolet coupé. The last we saw of him he was going east."

"The devil you say!" Burke ejaculated to the world. There was silence for a second, then the diaphragm blasted, "Never mind about him, Mr. Steele. Come on down to the office! I got something to show you!" Every word bristled with exclamation points. "We got the guy who committed those murders!"

"What!" Steele was properly amazed. "Who?"

"Monest!" Burke announced through his electrical megaphone. "I got the goods on him this afternoon."

"Has he confessed?"

"No, he hasn't confessed yet. But you come on down here, and I'll tell you about it."

"All right. We'll be at your office in twenty minutes." Steele hung up slowly and turned to me with a perplexed face.

"I wonder what's up now." He watched the waiter put the sandwiches together, then, with a half-smile, said, "I knew Burke wasn't satisfied about Monest. He acted like a suspicious bulldog with a stranger about. No Spaniard was going to put anything over on him!"

The sheriff's office was almost a counterpart of the county attorney's, except that it was dingier, dirtier and even more depressing. In the middle of the room, under unshaded electric lights, Burke's flat-top desk squatted with shiny authority, weighted down, as we entered, by its master's feet. These were promptly removed when we came through the door. Burke came forward through the smoky atmosphere with a smile on his face; while the two deputies, Dodge and Bolton, also dropped their feet to the floor and with shy uncouthness acknowledged our greetings and shoved chairs forward for us.

When we were seated, Burke pulled out the right-hand drawer of his desk and withdrew a small revolver. This he handed impressively to Steele.

"Let's see if you can guess where that come from," he invited, with a wink at the deputies.

Steele took the revolver and examined it curiously. It was a pearl-handled .32 with a nickel shield inlaid in one side of the grip. Scratched on this shield were the initials *J. V. R.* Steele bent over this inscription for a moment, ran the tip of his finger across it, then looked up.

"You haven't got a glass handy, have you?" he asked. Burke nodded and rummaged through the top drawer of his desk, finally producing a cheap magnifying glass. Steele switched on a desk lamp at his elbow and carefully scrutinized the shield. In a few seconds he switched off the light and handed the revolver and glass back to the sheriff.

"I suppose those are Jack Van Roth's initials," he observed. "Where did you get it?"

"Out of Monest's car." Burke's voice had the finality of a judge pronouncing sentence.

"Hm-m!" Steele's eyebrows went up. "Wonder how long Jack had it. I don't believe those initials have been there a week. The edges of the scratches are still rough. Fine shavings still curling up from the surface. . . . You don't suppose they could have been put there after he was killed, do you, Sheriff?"

Burke picked up the gun, ran his finger over the shield and squinted his eyes thoughtfully as he pondered this unconsidered possibility.

"I don't know; besides, what difference would it make?" He shook his head. "It sure must have been Jack's. Those shells were in it when we got it—and they're the same make and the same age as these—" he took a box from the drawer—"and these are the ones you took out of Jack's pocket the night he was killed."

Steele glanced at the cartridges casually.

"I don't doubt it's Jack's," he stated. "What I'd like to know is why it was still in Monest's car—and how it got there." He pulled the revolver toward him again and gazed at it thoughtfully while he absent-mindedly took out his cigarette case, slowly extracted a cigarette and finally lit it. "Suppose you tell us how you found it," he said, leaning back in his chair; "you must have had some reason for searching his car."

The sheriff was obviously waiting for this opportunity.

"You bet I did," he agreed promptly. "I didn't like the looks of that bird from the first, and when he wouldn't tell how his car happened to be at the lodge the day Loundon was killed I made up my mind I was going to go over it with a fine-toothed comb the first chance I got. So this evening, when I got back from the country, me and Dodge here drove around past his place, and we spotted his car parked out in front. Well, without saying aye, yes or no to anybody I just climbed in and took a look."

Burke paused, and lowered his big voice importantly.

"Well sir, Mr. Steele, what do you think was the first thing I saw?" The sheriff reached his hand in the desk drawer again and took out a large envelope, which he placed beside the revolver in front of Steele. "I found these sticking to the cushions in the rear seat!"

Steele opened the envelope and withdrew several bunches of long, golden-brown hair.

"Well, I guess you can imagine what I did then," Burke went on when he had given us time to comprehend the importance of this disclosure. "I began turning the insides of that car upside down—and down behind the front-seat cushion I found the gun!"

Steele said nothing, although I knew from the expression of his eyes and the way he pursed his lips as he smoked that he was puzzled. The sheriff went on with his narrative:

"Well, right about then I heard a yelp from Dodge, and I looked up and saw this here Monest galloping down the sidewalk from the house with a big rifle in his hands."

"A rifle!"

Burke laughed explosively. "I'll say it was a rifle! There she sits over in the corner! Got a bore big enough to stop an elephant! About fifteen feet from the car he stops and covers us with it.

"'What you doin' een my car!' he shouts. 'Come out of there before I keel you bot'!'"

Burke's crude imitation of the Spaniard's excited accent and intonation brought an appreciative laugh from the tallow-haired Dodge. Even Steele smiled.

Burke grinned widely and went on: "That gun looked like a cannon, and he handled it like he knew what it was for, so naturally I piled out. Then Monest saw who I was.

"'What you want een my car?' he says, lowering the gun. 'You go away from here, Meester Sheriff, and leaf my car alone.'"

Again the impersonation found a delighted audience in Burke's deputy. Plainly Dodge was just discovering that the chief was a real card. With a pleased glance of acknowledgment the sheriff continued:

"Well, when he lowered the gun I walked up to him, and before he knew what was going on I grabbed it out of his hand. Then Dodge came up, and we marched him to our car and brought him down here to the office. He wouldn't talk, so I put him in a cell to think it over, and we went back to his house. I rang the bell and knocked at all the doors, but nobody answered. Finally we walked in, and when we couldn't find anybody I decided to give the place the once-over."

"What did you find?" Steele asked in an interested voice as the sheriff paused for breath. "Did you locate the animal?"

"No, I didn't find it, but I found where they keep it. It's out back, in that big circular brownstone barn that's been made over into a garage. They got a regular den—dirt floor, a big chain and a pile of hay in the corner where it sleeps." Again the sheriff emphasized his story with a lowered voice. "And Mr. Steele, the floor was covered with the same funny kind of tracks that we found around the car out at Loundon's lodge!"

Steele received this startling information with an unmoved face, although his long fingers played a nervous tattoo on the desktop for several moments before he spoke.

"Where do you think it is?" he inquired.

"What I think, Mr. Steele, is that they've made away with it," Burke replied earnestly.

Steele considered a moment, then shook his head. "It's probably with Miss Monest in her car!"

"In Miss Monest's car!" Burke turned to his deputy in astonishment. "By God, Dodge, we never thought of that!"

"Where is she?" Steele asked. "Would her uncle tell you?"

"Would he tell us! He told us plenty, but nothing we wanted to hear. Can that Spaniard cuss! Mr. Steele, I believe there's more dirty words in Spanish than there is in English!" He hesitated with a reminiscent grin. "Though he's picked up plenty of American words too!"

Steele laughed. "I take it he protested when you put him in jail."

"Did he protest! Did you ever see a wildcat on the end of a chain? I thought those black eyes would pop out of his head. That bird would have bumped me and Dodge off like a cat lickin' milk!" The sheriff got up from his desk with a relieved shake of the head, and walked to the corner of the room and took up Monest's rifle. "He's our man, all right, Mr. Steele. We're just lucky he didn't drill a hole in us with this. If he had we'd 'a' looked like a couple of overstuffed doughnuts!"

Steele glanced at the heavy rifle but was not interested in examining it.

"What does Warren think?" he asked.

Burke laid the rifle across his desk. "He don't know what to think. He still wants Van Roth—I telephoned the police after you called and told 'em to keep a special lookout for him—but he don't try to deny that I got the goods on Monest."

Steele regarded Burke contemplatively for several moments; then, after lighting another cigarette, he got up and walked the length of the room and back. He paused at the desk a second, picked up several bits of the fur in his fingers, thoughtfully let them drop, one at a time, shrugged his shoulders, and crossed the room again to one of the windows, where for some minutes he smoked silently, gazing unseeingly down onto the dimly lighted courthouse lawn. When he turned I caught a curious sardonic look on his face which, however, was instantly replaced by an expression of sober gravity as he returned to the desk.

"Coupled with Monest's threat to kill Loundon, it does look bad," he admitted. "But let me give you one tip, Sheriff. If you can locate Dora Monest, by all means do it. That gun you found in their car applies to her as much as it does to him. . . . And in my opinion we will never get a confession or a conviction until she returns to town!"

21

THE MORNING OF AUGUST 20, when Steven Steele brought the case to an unexpected and dramatic close, was also the culmination of one of the hottest sieges of weather southern Kansas has ever endured. Following our visit with Sheriff Burke the night before, I went to the office and remained there until nearly one o'clock catching up on my neglected work. Even at that hour the temperature was above ninety degrees, and as I walked home I could see lawns and porches, in the sweltering gloom, dotted with little patches of white where restless sleepers sought deliverance from unbearable interiors.

When I reached the apartment I found Steele, clad in pale-green pajamas, sleeping peacefully on a mattress and sheet under the catalpa tree in the middle of our little Bermuda-grass lawn. Beside him was another makeshift bed which he had thoughtfully dragged down for me. I went into our ovenlike rooms, undressed, and donned my pajamas. Thus attired, I stood for several minutes under the cool spray of the shower bath before I joined him, dripping, to fall asleep and dream of asbestos suits and breathless struggles against gargantuan oil-well fires.

Sometime in the dawn, when a tiny cool breeze had begun to stir the broad leaves above us, we awoke and sleepily carried our beds indoors. Despite the heat I went back to sleep. When I awoke again the sun was pouring its atmospheric lava into the room and Steele was nowhere in sight. I looked at my watch and saw it was past eight o'clock. As I got up to dress I found a note pinned to my trousers. It read:

Van Roth and Lola picked up at Union Station at six
this morning. Have gone with Warren to have a look
in their house. Will be at his office around nine.
Great God, why do people live in such a climate?

Yours for nudism,
Steve

I dressed, got a hasty breakfast, and after a look-in at the office
reached the courthouse just as Steele and Warren drove up.

The county attorney, hot and irritable, was already showing the
stress of a restless night and the gathering complications which
confronted him. His seersucker suit was damp and wrinkled, and
his bushy eyebrows seemed to drip perspiration. Steele, on the
contrary, was immaculate in a fresh white suit, and as he gave me
the details of their early morning sortie his gleaming panama was
pushed back from his forehead, revealing the crisp auburn curls
no intensity of heat, apparently, could wilt.

He had not yet seen the Van Roths, but according to the report
of the patrolman who had picked them up they were having breakfast in the Harvey House at the Union Station when he strolled in
for a cup of coffee. Their story of a supperless and sleepless night
and an early-morning decision to fortify themselves with a good
breakfast before going to the county attorney's office where, so Lola
said, her father, at her insistence, had planned to give himself up,
was of course discredited by the officer. While they had no bags,
he naturally assumed they were planning a getaway by train, and
he scorned their explanation that no hotels or other good eating
places were open at that time of the morning. They offered no resistance, and he allowed them to finish their breakfasts before calling a car to take them to the courthouse.

"This officer said the only thing that tended to prove their
story," Steele chuckled, "was the fact that Van Roth stowed away
one dollar and seventy-five cents worth of toast, eggs and
griddlecakes. 'A guy who could do that on a morning like this,' he
said, 'sure didn't have any supper, and maybe not much to worry
about!'"

"There may be something in that," I remarked; "I couldn't get past my third spoonful myself. What did you find at their house?"

"Nothing." Steele shrugged his shoulders.

We had followed Warren into his office, and as Steele stood across the desk from that harassed official his bantering manner left him abruptly.

"What about Monest?" he asked. "Has he said anything about his niece yet?"

"No."

"Then let's have a talk with him. Do you want to bring him here, or shall we go to the jail?"

"I suppose it will be quicker to go over."

The jail was in the courthouse square. In a few minutes we were standing in a corridor of the brick, steel-barred structure, looking through the bars at the disconsolate figure of the somewhat chastened, but still angry, Monest. When he recognized the county attorney he loosed such an impetuous stream of indignation that it was several minutes before his wrathful Spanish had dwindled to understandable English. He ended by turning to Steele with an appeal for justice and a lawyer. Steele told him soothingly that he should have both, and finally reconciled him to talk without imprecations. At first, when Steele broached the subject of his niece, Monest refused point-blank to say where she had gone, but at last admitted she was visiting friends in Arkansas City. Apparently this was all the information Steele desired at the moment, for after a few more perfunctory reassurances we returned to Warren's office.

Here Steele immediately put in a call for Miss Monest at Arkansas City. When she was on the phone he informed her briefly of her uncle's predicament and urged her, in his behalf, to return at once. I thought his statement that this request came from Monest was a little more than the truth warranted, but the smile with which he hung up the receiver indicated that his ruse, if ruse it was, had been successful.

"She says she'll be here by ten-thirty." He looked at his watch. "If she does, I'll say she drives as well as she dives!"

"I suppose you want to wait until she gets here before we question Monest," Warren said. "How about having Van Roth and his daughter in now?"

Steele considered, then shook his head. "There are two or three other things I'd like to do first." He pulled the telephone to him again. "We'll need Ripley here when we talk to Monest. He heard Monest threaten Loundon at the plant, and I want to see if he'll tell the same story when we get them face to face. You remember he admitted he was trying to protect Monest when he concocted that pay-station call. He may try to squirm out of his story when he learns how serious Monest's threat becomes in the light of Burke's discovery of the gun. Then I want a little private conversation with Dr. Vernon. I think a hint or two will persuade him to pay us a visit. Also, we will want his wife handy, just in case." Steele reached for the telephone book. "And last but not least, I have some pertinent observations I'd like to make to Mr. Garnett." He began paging through the directory and jotting down numbers on the cover. "All in all," he remarked as he began to dial, "it looks like a busy and perhaps an exciting morning!"

Despite the levity of his words there was an undercurrent of anticipatory tenseness in Steele's bearing. He dialed his calls swiftly; and, although at each connection he adapted his request subtly to the other's personality, his voice held a crisp authority that did not brook refusals. Only Garnett and Dr. Vernon, apparently, offered serious objections. To the former Steele suavely intimated that Miss Monest would be present and in possible need of certain help that only he could give her. In the case of Dr. Vernon it was only necessary for Steele to say that he had visited the ranch, to receive a prompt, if somewhat vicious-sounding, promise of an immediate interview.

When he had finished, Steele ran his eye over his notations on the directory cover, then pushed back his chair and looked up at Warren.

"I don't want either Dr. Vernon or his wife to know the other is here. She'll be here at ten, and he will come at a quarter after. Have you a room she can stay in until I want her?"

"Yes," Warren nodded; "but how do you know they won't call each other up or come at the same time?"

"Ha! They won't call each other up!" Steele laughed shortly. "And she'll be on time, never fear, and he won't come a minute before he has to!" He glanced at his notes on the directory. "Here's a tentative schedule, if it's agreeable to you:

"First, the Van Roths. We'll have them in here. By the time we are through with them Dr. Vernon and his wife should be here. After we have had it out with the doctor we can bring in Monest. Ripley will be here about ten-thirty, and I want them together. Garnett promised to come at ten forty-five, and Miss Monest should be in then from Arkansas City."

Steele got up and glanced quickly about the big bare room. He went to the windows and raised the blinds, throwing a hot bright light across Warren's desk. Then he rearranged the chairs so that their occupants, in facing the county attorney, would be compelled to look across the desk into this unshaded glare. Finally he placed one chair near Warren's, gave another brief survey of the room, and announced:

"I'll sit here near the inquisitorial seat. All right; if you're ready, the stage is set."

To Steele, with his love of the theatrical, that is what it was: a drama. But to the matter-of-fact Warren it was a serious legal matter, and I could see he did not relish Steele's lightness of manner. Nevertheless he knew there was a reason in the other's calculating mind for this seeming artificiality, and after a momentary hesitation he pressed the buzzer. When his angular secretary responded he instructed her to send in Van Roth and his daughter.

As the corpulent figure of the clergyman came through the door I was shocked to see the change two days had made in him. He had lost at least twenty pounds in weight, and his once fat and rosy face was seamed and worn. Even his ponderous dignity had become furtive, and the bold eyes appeared abashed. The death of his son, I knew, was largely responsible for this alteration; yet I felt that his demeanor reflected as much apprehension as sorrow. His daughter, on the contrary, revealed nothing of her emotions. Her heavy face was impassive, and as she took the chair Steele indicated she moved with a self-possession that bespoke her long experience on the stage. When Warren began his interrogation she sat erect, her strange intense blue eyes fixed on him warily.

"Mr. Van Roth—" the county attorney turned first to the minister—"when you left yesterday after hearing we had learned of your past record you confirmed my suspicion that you either had a hand in the death of Ralph Loundon or have some knowledge that will implicate you." Warren regarded him with judicial severity. "I must therefore warn you that anything you say in the presence of these witnesses may be used against you. Do you wish to make a statement?"

Van Roth, who had sunk listlessly into his chair, looked up with a start.

"I have nothing to say," he replied slowly, "except that I do not know anything about it."

"Why did you attempt to leave town this morning after you had been expressly requested to keep in touch with this office?"

"I told you before that I was not leaving town."

Warren shrugged his heavy shoulders. "Very well, we will pass that. Do you deny that you served a term in the penitentiary for murder?"

Van Roth lifted his head with unexpected spirit.

"No. But I was pardoned and cleared of the charge."

"You mean you were not guilty?"

"I was justified. You would have found that out if you had taken the trouble to go to the records."

Warren frowned at this criticism; he continued in a harsh voice:

"Did you or did you not see Ralph Loundon on August sixteenth—the morning he was killed?"

"I did not."

"You left home that morning before seven o'clock. We now know Loundon reached the lodge a little before eight—your daughter admits seeing him. I have reason to believe that she lied to protect you—that you, alone or in company with your son Jack, saw Loundon and killed him either at his car or the strawstack, and then went to the lodge to bring your daughter away. If that is not the case, then suspicion falls wholly on your daughter, since she admits being with him there alone. Your son knew the truth. He committed suicide to escape the consequences. Whether you were party to his attempt to blackmail Loundon, which presumably led to the murder, I cannot say. We are prepared to prove that you misappropriated the funds of your church in El Dorado and that you financed your son's drugstore in Wichita, where he was arrested for the illegal sale of Jamaica ginger. Your son was a professional bootlegger. There is the further circumstance that your daughter was the beneficiary of a $50,000-policy on Ralph Loundon's life."

The county attorney paused grimly.

"Is there any reason why I should not make formal charges against you?"

Van Roth's lackluster eyes dropped to his fat, creased hands in his lap. His whole bearing indicated hopeless dejection; yet in a moment, when he spoke, there was still defiance in his voice.

"I did not see Mr. Loundon, and I do not know anything about his death. I think my son did know, but I am sure he had nothing to do with it. You can put me in jail, but you cannot prove anything."

Warren regarded the minister with heavy suspicion, waiting to make sure he would make no further statement. The silence was broken by Steele as he pulled his chair to the desk.

"Mr. Van Roth, on the night of the fire, just before your son was killed, he came to your car and asked you to go with him to meet an old friend." Steele's voice was quietly ominous. "Did you find this friend?"

Van Roth shifted uneasily, and the chair creaked. "No. We could not find him in the crowd."

"Did you go back to your car?"

"No," the minister answered after a pause; "I found a good place to see from, and Jack went back to bring Lola where I was."

At this simple statement Steele pushed his chair back sharply.

"He went back to see Lola! Was this the last time you saw him?"

"Yes."

Steele turned from the father to the daughter, and his face was dark. His deep-blue eyes narrowed.

"Miss Van Roth, did Jack come back to the car?"

"No," she answered evenly; "I never saw him again."

Steele examined her face a long moment in silence. Apparently satisfied with what he saw there, he changed the subject.

"Miss Van Roth, do you still claim you saw Loundon at the lodge the morning of the sixteenth before you met your father and brother on the footbridge?"

A tiny blush appeared around Miss Van Roth's prominent cheekbones. There was an instant's hesitation, then she replied steadily:

"Yes. I let him in the lodge a little after eight."

Steele shook his head regretfully. "That is a very foolish statement, considering what serious consequences it might have. On the stage, I suppose, it would be a noble gesture."

He sighed and moved to face Warren. Before he could speak the buzzer on the desk sounded. The county attorney answered the telephone, then turned to Steele.

"Dr. Vernon is here and so is his wife. They haven't seen each other. Shall we ask him to wait or see him now?"

Steele turned to give Van Roth and his daughter an appraising look, shrugged his shoulders, then slowly got to his feet.

"We may as well see him now." He went round the desk as the Van Roths rose. "We will want you again in about half an hour."

Two assistants accompanied Van Roth and his daughter out of the room, just to make sure, as Warren remarked when they had gone, that the clergyman did not absentmindedly take another departure. The county attorney was obviously convinced of the father's guilt. When he said as much to Steele, however, he received a disconcerting reply.

"The whole family is extremely neurotic, of course, which doesn't mean anything. Unless something else turns up you can't possibly make a case against either of them."

"But, Steele—"

Warren was about to dispute the matter when Dr. Vernon was shown in. As he crossed the room anger projected from him like quills from a porcupine. His iron-gray mustache and eyebrows bristled, and his long chin was thrust forward.

"What did you mean, you had been to my ranch?" He stopped in front of Steele. "If you were inside you broke in, and I'll be damned—"

"Now, now, Doctor," Steele interrupted; "let's not take it so fast!"

He sat down coolly on the edge of the desk and waited for Dr. Vernon to subside. But the doctor was not easily restrained, and he immediately launched into another scathing denunciation. Finally, however, his fury ran out and he paused long enough to demand an explanation. For an answer, Steele quietly reached into his coat pocket, withdrew an envelope and spread its contents out on the desk.

"I warned you yesterday when you refused to say where you were when Loundon was killed that I would see you again—and that you might regret it. Do you recognize these articles?"

Dr. Vernon took one look at the contents of the envelope. His face turned from red to white, and beads of perspiration stood out on his forehead. He glanced apprehensively at me and then at Warren.

"Do they know about these—these objects?" he faltered, all truculence gone.

Steele nodded in my direction. "He was with me. Mr. Warren knows nothing more than he has just heard."

Dr. Vernon sank into a chair. For half a minute the room was silent. Then he looked up at Steele.

"I admit I was at the ranch. I went there immediately after I returned to Newton from Kansas City. But what I said yesterday was the truth. I do not know anything about Loundon's murder, and I did not go near his lodge. That is all I can tell you."

Steele slowly replaced the bits of paper in the envelope, paused a moment, then said with quiet emphasis:

"That won't do, Doctor. I would not tell you yesterday our reasons for demanding an explanation for your pretended absence from Wichita. I was trying to protect your wife."

"My wife!" Dr. Vernon rose from his chair in consternation. "What does my wife have to do with it?"

"The morning Loundon was found dead your wife received a visit from Jack Van Roth," Steele informed him quietly. "That evening she and some man broke into the lodge and rifled Loundon's bedroom. She says that man was Jack. Without going into further details those are two reasons why the county attorney thinks you know something about the case if you did not actually have a hand in the murder."

"My wife!" Dr. Vernon's face was ashen. "What, in God's name, was my wife doing at Loundon's lodge?" He sank into the chair again and looked at us blankly. Then gradually a curious expression, as of dawning comprehension, came into his face. He jumped up from the chair and began pacing the floor in agitation.

"Look here!" He wheeled suddenly on Steele. "How much has my wife told you?"

Steele apparently understood this ambiguous question, but his answer was no less oblique.

"How much do you know about your wife?"

Dr. Vernon stared at him.

"Do you mean our—that is, her daughter?"

Steele nodded enigmatically. "She has told me everything, I think." He looked questioningly at the other. "She thinks you do not know, and she is afraid of you." He hesitated, then added, "Does that explain anything?"

"It explains everything!" Vernon picked up his hat excitedly and put it on his head. "Good God! To think I drove her to do that!" He started for the door. "I've got to see her at once. I'll explain everything to you later."

But Warren intercepted him at the door.

"No, I think you'll explain now," he declared. "I don't know what this secret information may be that Mr. Steele discovered at your ranch, but you're not going out of here without an explanation."

Dr. Vernon drew back, glared at Warren uncertainly, then started again for the door. Before Warren could make a move to stop him, however, Steele had come between them.

"Mr. Warren is right, Doctor," he said. "As for your wife, she is here now." He looked into the doctor's perturbed face, and there was the semblance of a sardonic smile in the corners of his mouth. "Perhaps you would like to have her come in while you make your explanation!"

This suggestion only increased the doctor's perturbation.

"You say she is here! . . . No, I don't want to say anything about the ranch to her! . . . But surely you aren't holding her—that is, you don't think she had anything to do with Loundon's death?"

Warren had noted the doctor's confusion with growing suspicion. He walked to his desk with a determined air and pressed the buzzer.

"We'll have her in here now, and maybe she will talk," he said grimly.

"No, no! Wait a minute!" Dr. Vernon interjected. "I'll tell you what you want to know. Just give me a little time to think."

The county attorney's secretary appeared in the door and waited expectantly for Warren's orders. As he hesitated, she said:

"There's a Mr. Ripley waiting. Do you want to see him?" Before Warren could speak Steele answered:

"Yes, we'll talk with him in just a minute," and to Warren he said, "I'd suggest we see Ripley and Monest now. When we're through we can talk with Dr. Vernon again." He gave the doctor another slyly sarcastic glance. "Perhaps by that time he will know just what he wants to say!"

22

WHEN SHERIFF BURKE brought Juan Monest into the county attorney's office he had the bearing of a Roman general entering the imperial city with his captives at his heels. His florid countenance radiated triumph. The dark-skinned Spaniard, however, like his haughty forbears, was mastered but not subjugated. He started when he saw Ripley, but otherwise he evinced no emotion, except that, as his bright black eyes roved ceaselessly about the room, they now and then rested venomously on the sheriff's complacent face.

On the desk in front of Warren were the .32 revolver and the envelope of hair Burke had found in Monest's car. The county attorney fingered these a moment before beginning his interrogation but did not at once refer to them. Instead, he said:

"Mr. Monest, when you insisted we were wrong in identifying as yours the car tracks at Loundon's lodge we did not push the matter because we supposed your alibi made it impossible for you to have been there. We now know Mr. Ripley lied about the telephone call he said he received at nine o'clock that morning from Mr. Loundon. He lied to protect you; because he feared you had committed the murder. He had good reason to think you had killed Loundon. In his office and in his presence only a day or two before, you quarreled with Loundon and pulled a knife out of your pocket and threatened to kill him."

Warren cleared his throat judicially and was about to proceed. But Ripley, who had been shifting nervously in his chair, interposed.

"That isn't exactly right, Mr. Warren," he objected. "I told Mr. Steele I didn't think he would have done anything, and I still don't."

Warren's bushy eyebrows came down in a frown.

"Do you deny he threatened him with the knife?" he demanded.

"No-o—" Ripley squirmed uncomfortably—"but I don't—"

"Very well—" Warren cut him short—"and if you have any further objections, wait until I have finished."

He swung around again to the Spaniard.

"When you threatened to kill Loundon you charged he had misled you in a business deal. In addition to this, your company, the Rockbed Oil Company, in which you hold over forty per cent of the stock, is the beneficiary of an insurance policy on Loundon's life to the amount of $100,000. Presumably you were aware that he was planning to cancel this policy. As a matter of fact—"

"I did not know about it!" Monest suddenly interjected hotly. "That was—what you say?—company insurance. Just a matter of forms. All his companies have these!"

"As a matter of fact—" Warren ignored the interruption—"he had decided to cancel this policy just a few days before he was murdered. And in addition to all this, there was the further motive in the animosity Loundon felt toward you because your niece had jilted him!"

At this Monest started up again, but with a Latin shrug of the hands and shoulders he settled back in his chair without speaking.

"In view of these facts, therefore," Warren continued in his precise legal manner, "when we realized you had been in the vicinity of the lodge at the same time Loundon was, and that it was your own car which had been at the lodge, our suspicions were aroused again."

He paused, as if to turn the page of a brief, then took up the revolver. Burke, who had already removed his coat, pulled out a large handkerchief, wiped his face and leaned forward in tense anticipation. Monest, facing the strong light from the windows, squinted as he fixed his eyes on the gun.

"Last night, when Sheriff Burke searched your car and found this revolver—" Warren's voice grew sterner—"you rushed out of the house and threatened to kill him. This is the revolver Jack Van Roth had in his pocket when he was murdered. The murderer placed the revolver with which he shot Jack in his hand to make it appear like suicide. Why did you threaten to shoot the sheriff to keep him from finding this gun?"

"That gun!" Monest flung out his hands desperately. "That gun—I have never seen it before. I did not know it was in my car. How could I? I run out to the sheriff with my rifle because I thought he was a car robber. I did not know what he wanted. When I saw him I put the gun down. Then he take hold of me and put me in jail."

"You deny you ever saw this revolver before?"

"Of a certainty! I have never seen it before!" He spread his hands in a quick gesture. "If I had done that, would I be such a fool? Would I put it back in my own car for you to find?"

At this denial Burke rose suddenly, slapped his moist handkerchief on the desk and grabbed up the envelope of hair. Jerking out the brownish tufts, he wrathfully stuck them under the Spaniard's nose.

"And I suppose you didn't ever see these before neither!" he exclaimed. "These came out of your car too! And a lot more like 'em was up in the tree by the strawstack, and in that place underneath, and where your car was parked by the lodge, and in Jack Van Roth's pocket—and that den out at your house was covered with them! I suppose you never saw them before! And I suppose you don't know what kind of a wild animal they come off of!"

Monest had shrunk farther back in his chair with each accusation. But now he suddenly leaped to his feet in a fury that made his dark face almost go pale.

"Wild animals!" he shouted. "Twice you have been accusing me with wild animals!" He looked about wildly, as if for a weapon; then his eyes encountered Steele. "Tell me! You have some sense. What does this—this swine mean with this wild animals?"

Steele came forward and put a hand on Burke's shoulder.

"Let me have them a moment, Sheriff," he said. Then he added, in Burke's ear, "You've got him so scared he doesn't know what he's doing."

"Well, he better be scared," Burke growled. Reluctantly he handed the hairs to Steele, then circled around to one side like a pugnacious dog.

"Sit down, Mr. Monest." Steele spoke soothingly in a quiet voice. When the Spaniard complied, he said, "I wish you would examine these hairs and tell us how they got in your car."

Monest stared up at Steele, hesitated, then, with his dark forehead wrinkled, slowly reached out his hand. In a moment he looked up and in a puzzled voice said:

"Why these—these came out of my dog! He has shed these into the car!"

"A dog!" Burke roared. "A dog that climbs trees! Why you dirty, lying, Spanish—"

"Just a minute, Sheriff!" Steele stopped him sharply. "Let me handle this."

He turned to Monest, who had risen swiftly from his chair to confront the sheriff again.

"You say these were shed by your dog. Where is that dog now?"

"That is all! That is all I will say!" Monest declared, trembling. "I demand you give me a lawyer. I will say nothing more without a lawyer. I have a right! You cannot do this to me without a lawyer! That is the very last word I will say to you!"

Despite every effort Steele made to calm Monest's anger and agitation that was all the response he would make. Whether his apparent terror was an indication of guilt I could not certainly make up my mind. Clearly his refusal to consider further questions was regarded with the utmost suspicion by the county attorney, and, it seemed to me, even Steele looked upon his stubborn protestations with skepticism. But there was nothing more to be gained against his obstinacy, and finally Steele turned away.

"We'll let him stay where he is," he said, looking at his watch. "It's time his niece was here, and he may decide to talk when we begin questioning her. After all, she was with him in the car the night Jack was killed." He turned to Warren. "Let's see if she and Garnett have come."

The county attorney rang for his secretary, and she informed us that Miss Monest had just arrived and that Garnett had been waiting for some minutes.

"Have them come in," Steele instructed her, "and also bring in the Van Roths and Dr. Vernon and his wife."

Warren stared at him in astonishment.

"You don't mean you want them all in here together?" he exclaimed.

"That's right," Steele confirmed. "We haven't got anywhere so far. Maybe there'll be some strength in numbers!" He considered a moment. "On second thought, however, I believe we'll have them all but Miss Monest. We'll send out for her when we want her."

The county attorney hesitated uncertainly. Without questioning Warren's compliance Steele crossed to a window, lit a cigarette, and for several seconds stood gazing down on the parched grass of the courthouse lawn. Then he turned and surveyed the room thoughtfully through a cloud of smoke. His red hair seemed to sparkle in the late morning sunlight, and I knew from the lithe alertness of his bearing and the gleam in his blue eyes that he was at a high nervous tension despite the superficial calmness of his demeanor. Warren stood at his desk a moment longer, regarding him with a mystified frown; then he pushed the buzzer and gave Steele's instructions to his secretary.

Dr. Vernon was shown into the room first, followed immediately by Lola Van Roth and her father. Steele apparently had decided where each was to sit, for he placed Dr. Vernon in the rear, next to Ripley, three or four feet back of Juan Monest. At their right, next to the wall, he seated Van Roth and his daughter. In front of them, also next to the wall, he pulled out a chair for Mrs. Vernon. She started when she saw her husband and turned with a frightened glance toward Steele, then with a pale face crossed to the chair he held for her. Fielding Garnett, limping a little, appeared last and was seated next to Monest in front of the desk. At the left of Monest was a vacant chair, which I presumed was reserved for Miss Monest.

As I surveyed the faces of these seven persons and thought of Miss Monest, the eighth, and reviewed swiftly their actions, their possible motives and the complicated train of circumstances that involved them, I attempted to decide in my own mind which was guilty of the murder of Loundon and Jack Van Roth. But the more I remembered and considered, the more confused I became. If at that moment I had been told that within fifteen tense minutes Steele would bring the case to a dramatic close with an accusation and a confession I should have scorned the suggestion as a palpable impossibility.

This swift last scene began when Steele, without preliminary, came to the desk and confronted Fielding Garnett.

As the two faced each other—Garnett hard and assured, his dark, long countenance impassive, almost contemptuous, and Steele, vividly quiet, with a feline suppleness of mind and body—I settled back in my chair with that deep-breathed ringside sensation one feels when the gong sounds for the main bout.

"Mr. Garnett," Steele began, "why did you tell us you were not at Loundon's lodge the morning of the sixteenth?"

That was a hard left hook for a beginning, I thought, as I watched Garnett pull himself together swiftly as if he had actually been struck an unexpected blow.

"You think I was?" he parried.

"We know it," said Steele. "You drove Monest's car."

Garnett shot a swift glance at Monest. "Well, I was." He displayed no concern at having been caught off balance. "I drove over to see if Loundon was there. When I found he wasn't I came away."

"You didn't go down to the hiding place under the strawstack where he kept his private stock of liquor?"

That jab was too sudden to be blocked. Garnett knew he had been hit, and he watched Steele cautiously without replying.

Steele saw, his opening and swung hard without feinting.

"Mr. Garnett, you led us to believe you had not been near the lodge. You not only went there, but you were there from ten o'clock until nearly eleven. You left the Meridian field about ten and did not get to the Switzer farm near Maize until sometime after eleven."

He paused, looking straight into Garnett's eyes. But the other's gaze never wavered.

"And you were underneath the strawstack where Loundon's dead body was found."

"That isn't so! I didn't go near the stack."

"I can prove that you were," Steele said dispassionately.

He took a newspaper-wrapped package from the top of a letter-file case at the back of Warren's chair and unrolled it on the desk. From it he took two worn bedroom moccasins and four long pieces of paper cut in the outlines of a man's foot. He held up two of these pieces of paper.

"Mr. Garnett, these are exact copies of the left footprint and the right footprint made by the barefoot man who was underneath the stack. That man is slightly flatfooted, much more so in the right than in the left foot. He walks with his left foot turned in. The weight falls on the outside edge of the ball of the left foot, and the little toe on that foot is buckled up over the toe next to it. He has exceptionally large feet, and they are remarkable in one other respect. The big toes are separated from the others to such a degree as to make them unique."

Steele put down the papers and held up the moccasins.

"These are your moccasins. They are identical in size with the prints. Examine the worn places on the soles. In the right moccasin the leather is noticeably worn the whole length of the foot. If it had been used by a normal foot the leather would be practically new under the arch, or at most there would be a thin worn streak along the outer edge. Now your left-foot moccasin is markedly different, yet it corresponds precisely with the left footprint. It shows much greater wear along the outside edge, particularly underneath the ball of the foot. There is considerably less wear under the arch. The imprints beneath the toes show that the little toe is bent up and does not touch the ground. But what is most conclusive, the big toes have made distinct and widely separated worn places on the bottoms of both moccasins."

Steele paused and picked up the two remaining slips of paper.

"These are the outlines of the shoes the man wore underneath the stack before and after he was barefoot. The footprints of the man who drove Monest's car to the lodge were made by the same shoes. I believe they were special arch-support shoes. Now no one, so far as we know, who might have been underneath the strawstack wears similar shoes. Yet—" and Steele walked around the desk and pointed down at Garnett's feet—"if I am not mistaken, the shoes you now have on will exactly match these prints. . . . If you are not convinced—"

"All right!" Garnett suddenly interrupted, pulling his feet under his chair. "I'll admit it. . . . Loundon said if he wasn't at the lodge he might be at the stack. I went there, but I couldn't find him."

Despite this forced admission Garnett maintained his poise. I marveled at his ability to absorb punishment. But Steele, like a pugilist who knows his antagonist is weakening, followed him up.

"Mr. Garnett," he shot at him, "you were also on top of that strawstack!"

"That's a lie," Garnett replied. "How do you know that?"

"Because you also left your footprint on the bank beneath the tree you climbed to get on top of the stack!"

For some unaccountable reason this statement seemed an immeasurable relief to Garnett.

"Yes, I climbed up there." Garnett pulled a cigarette from his pocket. "I'll admit that." He even smiled a grim smile as he lit the cigarette. "But whether you believe it or not, I did not see Loundon, and I do not know who killed him." He inhaled deeply and slowly blew out a thin stream of smoke as he met Steele's gaze. "Now you can question me all you want to; that's all I can tell you."

This sudden second wind astounded me. By all the rules the man should have been down and out. Figuratively speaking, I stood up in my seat, expecting Steele to administer the knockout. But he did not; instead he glanced uncertainly at Warren and hesitated. I had both fists clenched and was mentally yelling for blood. Warren apparently was equally excited. When he saw that Steele would not or could not continue, he unexpectedly jumped from his seat into the arena and went into action.

"Do you mean to sit there and tell us," he shouted, "that you admit all this and still expect us to believe you did not kill Ralph Loundon?"

Garnett could not repress a slight tremor at this bald accusation, but he answered firmly.

"That is what I tell you," he repeated. "I did not do it; I can't help what you believe!"

The county attorney was drawing breath for another explosion when Steele took his arm, drew him aside and began talking to him in a low voice. At first Warren shook his head in vigorous remonstrance. In a few moments, however, he reluctantly turned away and instructed the sheriff to bring in Miss Monest.

When she entered the room Dora Monest made a strikingly beautiful figure in the yellow sport costume she had characteristically selected for her visit to the county attorney's office. As she sat in the chair Steele held for her the room appeared to center on her colorful, vibrant personality. If she felt surprise at finding the others present she did not permit it to disturb her self-possession. She looked calmly from Steele to Warren, awaiting their questions.

Steele stood by the desk facing her.

"Miss Monest, I believe you told us you did not go up the river as far as Loundon's lodge on the morning of the sixteenth."

Her face betrayed a sudden apprehension. She glanced at Garnett, then answered evenly:

"No; only to the bridge."

"You did not see Loundon or Mr. Garnett that morning?"

"No."

"Did Loundon telephone you the night before he was killed?"

Again Steele's question startled her.

"Yes," she replied, after a noticeable pause.

"Did you say you would meet him at his lodge the next morning?"

"No," she answered decidedly.

"Why? You don't deny he asked you?"

"He asked me . . . I guess . . . . He was so intoxicated I could hardly understand what he wanted. . . . He wasn't himself."

Steele nodded. In an absent-minded manner, as if considering his next question, he slowly withdrew a large envelope from his coat pocket. She regarded him nervously. In the most casual voice he asked:

"I suppose you know Mr. Garnett did go?"

She could not restrain a gasp, and turned quickly with a questioning look at Garnett. He made no sign, and she turned back, as Steele continued:

"And I know you were there too, Miss Monest!"

Her dark cheeks paled, and her fingers closed tightly over the bag she held in her lap.

"I know," he said, "because the bottom of your boat was covered with these straws from the stack where Loundon's dead body was found!" With terror-widened eyes she watched him shake a handful of straws from the envelope. "Weren't you?"

"Yes." Her answer was almost inaudible.

"And you and Mr. Garnett were up on that stack together—in your bathing suits! You got there by using the rope ladder from underneath the stack. And Mr. Garnett first got on the stack by climbing the tree and releasing the ring and the rope, down which he slid to the top of the stack!"

Steele saw the admission in her face. The room was tense.

"Where he got in your boat, I don't know." Steele's eyes fixed themselves on her face, and I sensed, though his voice was level, that he was approaching a vital point. "He admits he drove your uncle's car to the lodge."

Miss Monest turned sharply halfway toward Garnett and her uncle, her lips parted; then she checked herself and faced Steele again without comment. He waited until he was certain she intended to say nothing.

"But he had his bathing suit with him, and he changed in the room underneath the strawstack, and he changed back again there when you were ready to leave."

Steele looked down at her, and his voice grew sharp. "Miss Monest, what were you and Garnett doing on that strawstack?"

Garnett jumped to his feet before she could answer.

"Look here," he demanded, "there's no use putting her through this. . . . Ask me whatever you—"

"You sit down!" Sheriff Burke broke in. "You're to keep out of this!"

But Garnett did not sit down. He brushed the sheriff back into his chair with a sideward sweep of his right arm and confronted Steele and Warren.

"The only reason I lied before was to protect her. . . . Ask me your questions now, and I'll answer them. But there's no need of—"

Before he could finish, Burke was up again, with his revolver in his hand. His face was aflame with anger. He stepped in front of Garnett menacingly. But Steele caught him by the arm.

"Let him alone, Sheriff," he requested soothingly. "We'll let him talk."

Burke was not easily persuaded to overlook this affront to his dignity. He returned to his chair growling, his revolver in his hand.

Steele turned back to Garnett, who began slowly:

"I know this looks bad. . . . But here is the truth. Loundon called both of us the night before he was killed. He said he was going to sober up. He wanted us to take our bathing suits to the lodge and be with him. That probably sounds stranger to you than it did to me—though it did sound strange to me, and I thought it was damn peculiar that he would want Miss Monest and me at the same time—but he was drunk, and to humor him I said I would come. I tossed my bathing suit in the car, and after leaving the new well I drove over. . . .

"Well, as I was going over the bridge below his place I saw Miss Monest in her boat in the river below. I told her I had my suit and asked her to bring her boat up to the lodge. When I got to the lodge Loundon wasn't in sight, and the buildings were locked. When Miss Monest came up I told her he hadn't come and suggested a swim. There was no place for me to change—she had on her suit—so we went to the strawstack. That may also seem strange, but it isn't, because for two or three years we used to swim there a great deal. I had a key to the room underneath and changed there. Then I climbed the tree and got the ring down, and we used it to dive from. As you guessed, we used the rope ladder to climb back up on. We were there—most of the time in the water—an hour or an hour and a quarter. Then I changed, and Miss Monest took me back to the lodge landing in her boat. . . . That's all."

Garnett's earnestness gave his recital an almost convincing authenticity. But he could not have expected to be believed, and there was a certain hopelessness in his eyes as he looked from one to the other when he had concluded.

Warren jumped up, ready to tear his story to shreds, seeing in this circumstantial admission an easy conviction. But Steele spoke first.

"You didn't see Miss Monest again after you left her at the lodge?" he asked.

Steele faced Miss Monest.

"Miss Monest—" his voice was quiet—"did you stop at the stack again after you left Mr. Garnett at the lodge?"

"No."

"Did you see Ralph Loundon at the stack as you went back down the river?"

"No."

"You deny that you saw Mr. Loundon at all that morning, either at the stack or at the lodge?"

"Yes."

Steele hesitated and was about to ask another question, but the county attorney's righteous indignation interposed. He confronted Garnett, ignoring Miss Monest for the moment in a wrathful accusation.

"Do you seriously expect us to believe that story, Mr. Garnett? To believe Ralph Loundon's dead body lay on that stack and you did not know it? Or to believe he was killed and hidden there in the short time that elapsed between the time you left and the time he was found dead?" He pointed his finger demolishingly. "Of course you don't expect us to believe it! Nobody could believe it!" He stepped a pace closer. "I'll tell you, Mr. Garnett, what happened! . . . What you two were doing on that strawstack, I do not know. If the man whose lifeless body was found there were here, he could tell us! You say you had gone there to swim! But you were discovered there by Ralph Loundon, your friend—the man who loved this woman you stole away from him—*and you killed him!* . . . Yes—"

he shook his finger dramatically—"one of you—or both of you together—murdered Ralph Loundon, covered him up in the straw—
and ran away!"

Garnett's face had gone white.

"That's a lie!" he swore; "a damned lie! And I'll make you eat
what you've said if it takes every cent I've got!"

As Garnett spoke there was a sudden stir back of him and another voice shouted:

"It's not a lie!"

We turned to see Ripley advancing toward Garnett. "It's not a
lie!" he repeated. "It's the truth!"

Ripley's face was flushed. As Miss Monest heard his voice and
saw him confront them, her eyes widened in fear.

"And I know it's the truth," he said, pointing down at Miss
Monest, "because Mr. Loundon told me not two days before he died
that this woman had repeatedly threatened to kill him if he tried
to interfere in her affair with Garnett!"

Dora Monest's fright changed to an almost convulsive terror
as she gazed at him. For what seemed minutes she stared; then
she jumped to her feet in horrified recognition.

"It's not so! No! No! No!"

Suddenly she spied Sheriff Burke's revolver in his hand, and
before he could prevent she had snatched it up and leveled it at
Ripley. Steele leaped forward and took the revolver from her hand.

"Hold her," he said, and turned to Burke. "Sheriff, let me have
your handcuffs!"

Steele spread the handcuffs as Ripley helped twist Miss
Monest's hands toward him. Then he leaned over and snapped
them—not on the girt, but on Ripley's outstretched wrists.

He gave the man a push in Burke's direction.

"There's your murderer!" he said.

Dora Monest suddenly swayed. Steele put an arm about her and
supported her to a seat. All the color had gone from her face, and
as she slumped down in the chair she seemed scarcely to breathe.
Steele wet his handkerchief at the ice-water bottle in the corner of

the room and dabbed it on her face while her uncle fanned her anxiously with his coat. In a few moments the color began returning to her cheeks. Then she opened her eyes.

When she had fully recovered Steele said:

"Miss Monest, tell us where you have heard this man's voice before."

Her eyes widened again momentarily when she looked at Ripley. But she answered promptly in a positive voice:

"It was he who called over the telephone—not Mr. Loundon—the day before he was killed. Oh, I knew there was something about his voice that wasn't natural, but I just thought it was because he was so terribly drunk."

"You mean the day he was killed," Steele said; "for Mr. Loundon was already dead when Ripley tried to deceive you." He wheeled suddenly on Ripley.

"Wasn't he?" he demanded. "You killed him in your airplane that evening. You dropped him in the strawstack and then cold-bloodedly tried to fix the blame on Garnett and Miss Monest—didn't you?"

Ripley could not face him. But at last, in a muffled voice, he confessed:

"Yes."

Steele's tense figure relaxed. He turned to Burke. "Take him out, Sheriff."

23

WHEN THE DOOR had closed behind Ripley, Steele sank into a chair beside Warren's desk with a sigh. He reached into his pocket for his cigarette case. "You realize now, I suppose, that all this—" with a wave of the hand he indicated the chairs, the moccasins, the revolver, the tufts of hair—"was nothing but a trap—a trick—but, by George, it worked!"

Steele lit his cigarette, blew out the first deep inhalation, then faced his impromptu cast with a contrite smile.

"I'm awfully sorry I had to submit you to this ordeal—I owe you all an apology—but I saw no other way to lead Ripley to believe his plan had succeeded." He turned to Miss Monest and Garnett. "If he had doubted in the slightest that we were going to throw you in prison he would have kept still, and I question whether we could ever have made a case against him. But when he saw what he thought was a chance to add his report of your supposed threat on Loundon's life to the beautiful circumstantial evidence he had luckily been able to establish, he couldn't resist attempting to forge the link that seemingly would weld the whole chain."

Steele paused to take another puff at his cigarette, then threw it away.

"I knew from the first one of you was his intended victim, and I hoped, by working our accusation of you up to a convincing and dramatic climax, to induce him to take a cue somewhere in the proceedings. I felt sure that if he would speak up without restraint Miss Monest would recognize his voice. Our first talk with her convinced me that his voice had puzzled her. But even if she hadn't recognized him—"

"But Steele, wait a minute," Warren interrupted, sinking into his seat with a dazed expression on his face; "I don't follow you. How did she recognize his voice—how did they happen to go to the lodge—why didn't they find the body— how did he happen—"

"It didn't happen," Steele broke in with a smile. "That was the devilishly ingenious part about it. Ripley was responsible for their going to the lodge; it was part of his scheme. . . . But here's the story as nearly as I can put it together:

"Loundon and Ripley, as you know, were the principal stockholders in the Dragonfly company, with Garnett and Monest also interested. When Loundon's financial troubles grew serious Ripley became panic-stricken. Realizing he could look for no assistance from Garnett, he planned to kill Loundon for the $100,000 insurance to safeguard his own and the company's future. The afternoon of the fifteenth, when Loundon came to the plant drunk, Ripley waited until all the employees had gone, took Loundon up in a plane, hit him over the head with a wrench and tried to drop the body in the river as near the lodge as possible. The only gap in the trees there is a narrow place at the strawstack. He swooped low and accidentally dropped the body through the edge of the elm tree and into the stack. That accounts for the bruises, the broken bones, the straws thrust into the skin of the face, and the fact that branches of the tree were broken above the stack. . . .

"Now comes a shrewd point. If he had been seen returning to the factory alone—in other words, if anyone had chanced to see him go up with Loundon—he was prepared to say Loundon had drunkenly fallen or jumped, counting on the effect of the fall to cover the wound. But he depended on finding no one at the factory when he got back, and presumably he wasn't disappointed. He ran the plane into the hangar, perhaps put on an old coat of Loundon's, took Loundon's car and drove to town. He then went to Riverside, honked drunkenly outside Miss Monest's window to make it appear that Loundon was still alive and drove to the club.

"That is why—" Steele turned to Miss Monest—"I questioned you so closely on that point. When I learned Loundon had himself honked that way before with another person in the car, I knew Ripley must have been with him on some previous occasion. And when you said he leaned over the empty seat to wave I realized you had not seen his face."

Miss Monest's black eyes widened, and she leaned forward intently as Steele continued:

"Now, if the body had fallen into the river, as Ripley undoubtedly planned, he probably would have been satisfied with thus making it seem that Loundon was alive and with preparing an alibi for himself. But the knowledge that the body had not fallen into the river doubtless preyed on his mind. It was then that he must have conceived the idea of telephoning to you and Garnett, in the person of Loundon. He not only wanted to establish a more complete alibi for himself; he wanted to implicate one or both of you by getting you to go to the lodge and, in the case of Garnett, by trying to send him to the strawstack."

"I don't understand yet how he put over those telephone calls," Warren interposed. "They came through the switchboard at the club."

"Of course," Steele nodded; "he did that purposely. . . . You see, Ripley apparently has considerable ability as an impersonator—you will recall—" he turned to me—"telling how he burlesqued both Loundon and Garnett at one of Loundon's parties—and he knew he could simulate and exaggerate Loundon's drunken voice. The fact that they both came from Louisiana and had broad Southern accents may have suggested the idea, and of course he had no fear of recognition by Miss Monest because they had never met. . . . So Ripley went to Loundon's room, let himself in with Loundon's key and placed the calls with the operator."

Steele turned to me again.

"You remember the club telephone operator seemed surprised when I proved she had looked up Miss Monest's number in the directory herself. That was an illuminating point, because I knew Loundon would certainly have remembered her number and would not have asked the operator to place the call. But Ripley had a double purpose. He wanted to place these calls on record, and he wanted to test his impersonation with a girl who was familiar with Loundon's voice. When she unhesitatingly accepted his voice as Loundon's he felt safe to go ahead. . . . While he was about it he put in a call for himself, which of course was never completed. . . .

"That night he ran Loundon's car out, smashed the glass and planted the wrench with some of Loundon's hair still on it. Then in the morning he let himself into Loundon's room again, disarranged the bed, rang for ice water, went in the bathroom and, when the colored porter appeared, called to him in a drunken voice to put the pitcher on the bureau. In doing this he not only risked recognition of his voice by the porter, but he had to assume Loundon's body had not yet been found and that it would not be found for at least half an hour. While these were risks, they were not particularly hazardous ones, and he doubtless justified them by supposing he was clearing himself from any possible connection with the murder. When he had accomplished this he called attention to himself at the club, and within twenty minutes he was at the Dragonfly plant, where he remained continuously until, late in the afternoon, he received the news which he must have been apprehensively awaiting all day. . . . The other telephone call which he fabricated—the one from the toll station at nine o'clock—was an afterthought, concocted the next day to protect Mr. Monest, who, because of his early arrival at the Meridian field near the lodge and because of his hot-headed threat on Loundon's life at the factory, seemed to be in line for serious suspicion. He may also have known that the tire tracks at the lodge had been made by Monest's car."

"But, Mr. Steele," Garnett interposed in a perplexed voice, "if Loundon's body was on the stack why didn't Miss Monest and I see it? We were there nearly an hour. . . . That straw was packed tight. The body couldn't have been buried, falling from a speeding plane."

"That was the most baffling circumstance I encountered," Steele admitted, "and I confess it had me puzzled. If the body had not been covered I think I should have trusted to my first conclusion—

that it had fallen or been thrown through the broken branches of the trees."

He turned to Burke, who had just re-entered the room.

"But the boys who found the body told the sheriff they saw the feet from the ground. They said, however, that the rest of the body was completely buried. I realized this was a vital point—it meant that if the body was covered some guilty person had been on the stack—but the boys insisted they had merely put the straw back over the body as it was when they found it. Certainly they buried the body. I later decided that in their fright and excitement they either became confused or felt they must stick to their first statement. They could see only the feet from the ground, and that gave them their first impression that the body was buried. . . . Of course I should have seen the truth at once, but I permitted the knowledge that someone else had been on the stack—as evidenced by the footprint in the mud which proved not to be Loundon's—to lead me astray."

Steele made a self-deprecatory gesture of the hands and leaned back in his chair.

"So far as your not seeing the covered body, Mr. Garnett—that isn't strange. The stack is nearly fifty feet long. You remained continually on the end overlooking the water, while the body lay on the sloping edge at the west end, buried out of your sight. . . . You see—" he leaned forward—"Ripley obviously flew from east to west across the river. He came across at an angle through the gap in the trees, throttled down almost to landing speed, and tumbled the body out a second too late to hit the river. The momentum carried it through the top of the elm over the water, through the lower branch over the stack, and down to the straw almost underneath the ring. It hit with tremendous force, and bounced and rolled to the far edge. . . .

"If you had found the body, as Ripley hoped, that would have been difficult enough to explain, what with the telephone calls and the car with the wrench a few hundred feet down the river. . . . Of course he couldn't foresee the action of the boys and the fact that you wouldn't find the body. And he couldn't foresee—" here Steele hesitated as if to make a careful choice of words—"he couldn't fore-see that you would fear Miss Monest had returned to the stack after you left and had met Loundon, or that Miss Monest would have the same doubt and fear concerning you, or that you both, therefore, would deny ever having gone near the lodge or the straw-stack."

We were all silent a moment when he had finished.

"But how did you guess the answer?" Warren demanded. "And why did you lead us on these wild-goose chases?"

"I didn't guess," Steele stated. "Frankly, I first suspected Garnett or Miss Monest. That was the simplest answer—and ninety-nine times out of a hundred the simple answer is the correct one. I surmised they had gone to the lodge as a result of the telephone calls, and I felt they were both lying when they explained their actions that morning." He smiled at them apologetically. "But it became increasingly illogical to believe they could be such fools as the appearances indicated. Therefore I set about fitting new theories to the facts. I eliminated getting the body on the stack from the liquor room or up the rope ladder. That would have been too difficult and too purposeless. It was too bizarre to suppose Loundon fell or was thrown from the tree, either before or after he was killed. Yet there were the broken branches. That was where the airplane occurred to me; and I kept returning to it even though the boys insisted the body had been buried. . . . Now it had been proved that Loundon couldn't possibly have been in the airplane that morning, so I went back to the preceding afternoon. It was then that those shadowy telephone conversations positively rang for attention."

"Do you mean you suspected Ripley when we interviewed him at the plant?" Warren asked.

"No—" Steele shook his head—"not for sure until we talked with the telephone girl at the club that evening. . . . And then everybody else in town seemed clamoring for suspicion!"

Steele lit another cigarette.

"By that time we surmised it was Mrs. Vernon we had surprised at the lodge the night before; and Ferguson had told me the Van

Roths had been seen on the footbridge that morning. And shortly afterward Miss Van Roth admitted she had spent the night at the lodge. That confirmed my belief that Loundon did not ask Miss Monest and Garnett to come there and that he never had any idea of going there himself. . . . Then the next day Jack Van Roth made his amazing offer to bring the murderer to the lodge. I knew then for the first time that there had been a witness to the murder—if not an accomplice—and I began to realize that if Ripley was guilty we could hardly expect a conviction without Jack's help."

At this mention of her brother's offer Lola Van Roth looked at Steele with an expression of surprised relief. "Did he offer to do that?" she asked.

"Yes, Miss Van Roth," Steele replied gently, "he did. And I must apologize for the harshness of my manner to you yesterday. I knew you were protecting your father from Mr. Warren's accusations, but I thought Jack might have told you or your father who the murderer was. I believed you might be withholding that knowledge in the fear that telling us would bring further suspicion on your father."

Steele leaned over and ground out his cigarette in the ashtray on Warren's desk. Then he stood up.

"That's about all," he said. "There's no reason why we should keep any of you longer."

"But, Mr. Steele," Sheriff Burke began as they started to go, "I don't see . . ."

Steele, however, did not hear the sheriff's question. Dr. Vernon had him by the arm and was drawing him aside. For several minutes, while Mrs. Vernon waited anxiously in the doorway, the doctor spoke earnestly in a low voice. Then, with an understanding smile and a friendly pat on Steele's back, he crossed to his wife, slipped his hand under her arm and left us alone.

"What were you about to say, Sheriff?" Steele asked.

"Well, for one thing, I don't understand yet how Jack got wise to Ripley."

"I can't say positively," Steele replied, "but I think he must have been near the strawstack when Ripley dropped the body—although he might have been at the Dragonfly plant when Ripley took Loundon up in the plane. . . . But he signed his own death warrant by telling Ripley what he knew—probably in another attempt at blackmail. My guess is that Ripley agreed to give him the money at the oil field that night. Jack possibly expected to get the money, turn Ripley over to us and make a getaway. That's the only way I can account for his proposed rendezvous at the lodge."

"But if Ripley wanted to throw suspicion on Garnett," Warren said, "why did he put the gun in Monest's car after he killed Jack?"

"He meant that for Miss Monest. He thought his nine-o'clock telephone call had definitely cleared Monest from suspicion. And I'll also hazard the guess that he scratched the initials on first, to make doubly sure it would be identified as Jack's revolver."

Warren sat at his desk and loaded his pipe contemplatively. Then he looked across at Steele with a warm but somewhat reproachful smile.

"Well, you pulled me out of the fire all right! . . . But I'll be damned if I think I'll ever forgive you for egging me on to those wild accusations of Garnett and Miss Monest."

"I'm sorry," Steele apologized with a contrite grin, "but I'm not sure what we'd have done without your fireworks. If you hadn't been so thoroughly convincing in your onslaught Ripley would never have spoken up."

Burke considered this a moment, then burst out:

"Yeah, that may be true all right, but I've got a bone to pick with you," he declared. "What the hell reason can you give for sending the sheriff's force all over the country hunting gorillas?"

Steele laughed.

"I'm sorry, Sheriff, but I warned you. I knew that was out when I saw Miss Monest's monkey wearing the paw pads and convinced myself that Garnett had driven Monest's car that morning." He moved toward the window. "Maybe I can show you that gorilla now—it was in Miss Monest's car when she drove up a while ago. . . . Here! Come here, Sheriff! You're just in time to see them take it away."

Burke hurried to the window.

"That green car belongs to Miss Monest—" Steele pointed—"and that chow dog you see sticking its head up in the window is your beast. And I'm sure if you were down there you'd find he's equipped with leather pads that make strange tracks and keep him from scratching furniture—and cars!"

"And trees, too, when he climbs 'em, I suppose!" the sheriff exploded.

"No." Steele shook his head with a smile. "But you must remember Garnett drove Monest's car to the lodge. We know Garnett took his bathing suit with him, and we know the dog went with the car. Now chows shed heavily in hot weather and they also shed on bathing suits when they lie on them, and as a result bathing suits shed on trees—if you happen to climb trees while you're out swimming!"

Thus the case was brought to a conclusion. Ripley did not attempt to deny his confession, and before Steele left town he had the satisfaction of knowing that Jack Van Roth, as he surmised, had been on the river in a boat when Ripley dropped the body, and that Jack had later tried to blackmail the murderer. His other deductions also were in the main correct. Apparently he was mistaken, however, in supposing that Ripley had scratched Jack's initials on the revolver; at least Ripley consistently denied it.

As a result of the revelations concerning his past, the Reverend Van Roth was forced to resign his radio pastorship, and he and his daughter soon left town. Steele's high opinion of Lola Van Roth's ability as an actress has since been justified, for under another name she has achieved recognition as one of the most accomplished character women in motion pictures. . . . Fielding Garnett and Dora Monest were married the following spring, and still make their home in Wichita. . . . Juan Monest, enriched beyond his fondest dreams—thanks to Hovey No. 4—removed to Havana soon after his niece's marriage. . . . Dr. Vernon, while as autocratic as ever in his practice, is by way of achieving a reputation as the town's most devoted husband and stepfather. This is the report I receive, at any rate, from our ubiquitous society reporter, Miss Sue McCoy. But the whispered explanation Steele received from the doctor about his mysterious tryst at the ranch must still remain a secret. When I at last obtained Steele's consent to publish this account of the case he expressly stipulated that the episode must forever remain "off the record."

Coachwhip Publications

CoachwhipBooks.com

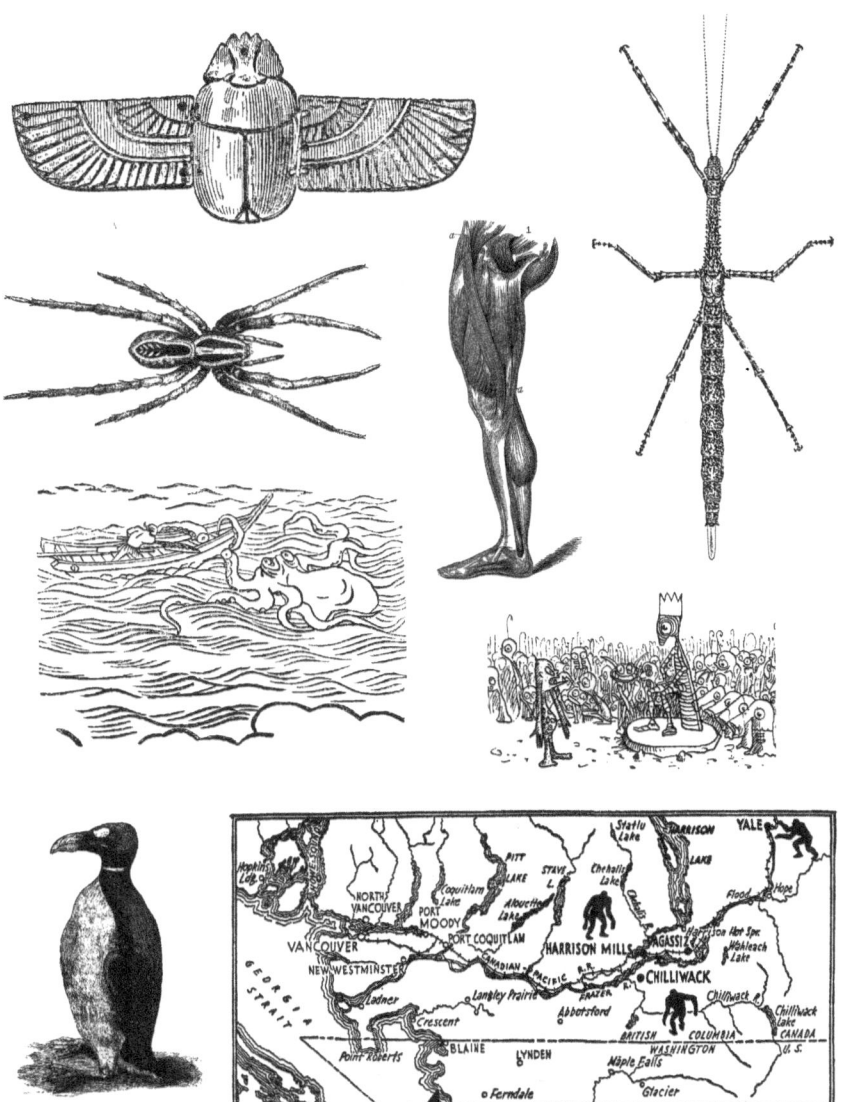

THE CAT SCREAMS

A HUGH RENNERT MYSTERY

TODD DOWNING

The Cat Screams
ISBN 1-61646-148-9

Vultures in the Sky
ISBN 1-61646-149-7

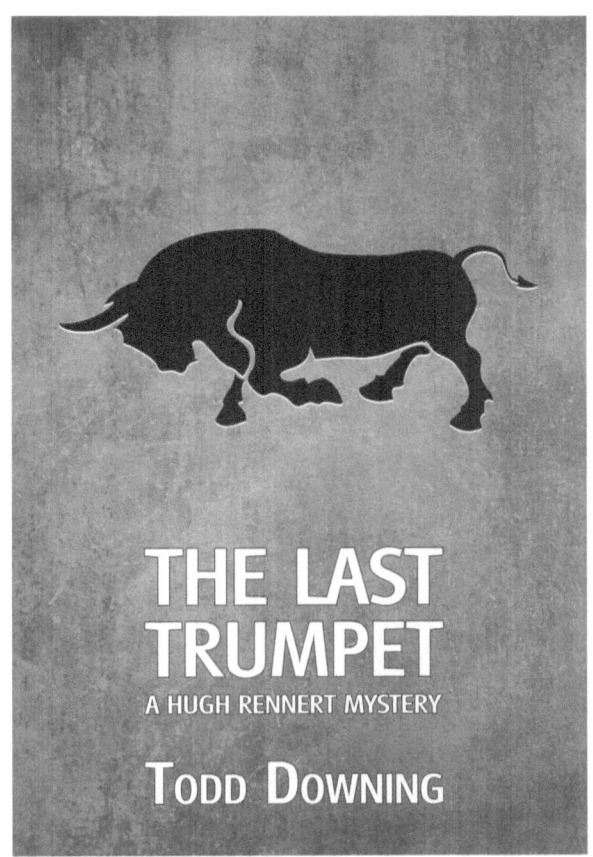

The Last Trumpet
ISBN 1-61646-152-7

www.ingramcontent.com/pod-product-compliance
Lightning Source LLC
Chambersburg PA
CBHW031926060726
47496CB00007BA/2146